GEMJA

THE MESSAGE

1

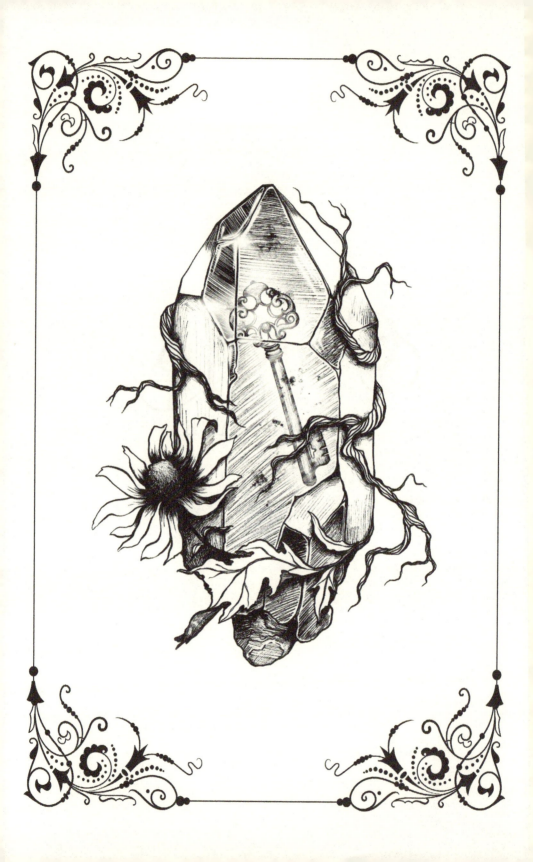

THE MESSAGE

K.M. MESSINA

ILLUSTRATED BY NATALIIA PAVLIUK

Lunalore Books
Rocky Point, New York

Gemja – The Message
Copyright © 2023 by K.M. Messina
Illustrated by Nataliia Pavliuk
Cover artwork by RAVVEN
Cover design/book design: K.M. Messina
Typesetting by Formatting Experts
"Surrender" Lyrics by Steven Leonard Messina

All rights reserved. No part of this book may be reproduced in any form or by any electronic or mechanical means including information and storage retrieval systems—except in the case of brief quotations embodied in critical articles or reviews—without permission in writing from its author, K.M. Messina, or its publisher, Lunalore Books.

The characters and events portrayed in this book are fictitious or are used fictitiously. Any similarity to real persons, alive or dead, is purely coincidental and not intended by the author.

All brand names and product names used in the book are trademarks, registered trademarks, or trade names of their respective holders. Lunalore Books is not associated with any product or vendor in this book.

Published by Lunalore Books
P.O. Box 1611
Rocky Point, NY 11778
info@lunalorebooks.com

Library of Congress Control Number: 2022924055

ISBN 978-0-578-83956-1 (Paperback, digital cover art)

ISBN 978-1-7367231-4-2 (Paperback, hand-drawn cover art)

ISBN 978-1-7367231-2-8 (Hardcover. digital cover art)

The universe gives messages
to those who look for them.

FOR SWEET LITTLE GURU AND LUNA

PROLOGUE

It starts when I lose the last of my waking consciousness at night. I get the sudden, strange sensation of falling, and then I feel myself dropping into another place, a realm where the laws of physics break down and anything is possible.

The dimension I visit is an unearthly place of eternal night and endless stillness, where the trees grow crystals of every size and shape, sparkling brilliantly under the pale purple light of two full moons. I find myself in the same spot each time—the channel, a clearing through the jeweled forest where the trees arch overhead to form a long corridor. It is at the end of this channel where she appears, a hazy apparition of a young, shrouded girl who holds her head down, eyes closed. I stand paralyzed as she approaches slowly to deliver her message: You are the one.

Once I asked for her name, and she replied in a ghostly murmur, Nitika. It is the only other word she has said to me besides that haunting message…a message that still jolts me from sleep, my body trembling in a cold sweat, leaving me with an overwhelming sense of fear.

THE NEW ARRIVAL

The atmosphere on planet Wandelsta screamed Halloween. It was barely noon and the tangerine sky was already cluttered with sooty clouds that hung like tightly packed marshmallows, all scorched and bubbly, getting ready to burst. Such a twisted and dangerous sky would send most people running for cover. But I'm not most people. I head outdoors when the weather gets rough. The more energy nature brings my way, the better.

Which is as it should be, for someone who wants to be a witch.

I gazed skyward at the bulbous canopy and watched as writhing, ghostly forms surfaced, then vanished, living and dying at the whim of the currents in the air. It was an eerie reminder of my own dark cloud. Nitika had haunted my sleep for the past two years, and she showed no sign of disappearing.

I shivered despite the warm breeze that swept my bangs sideways. Meranda Blaine, my witchcraft mentor back on Earth, had taught me that dreams contained messages. If the dream was recurrent, your subconscious was trying to tell you something. And if it was frightening, there was an urgent need for you to take notice.

I didn't know what my Nitika dream meant, but it was both

recurrent and frightening, and ever since I'd moved to Wandelsta, it had become more real. At times, I felt a presence in my waking life, as if Nitika had somehow slipped out of my mind and was hiding in the shadowy crevices of my room. The only people I'd told of her existence were Meranda and my best friend Sarah, who was as interested as I was in all things Wicca. But my witchy friends were back on Earth, and the dream had followed me here.

A second warm gust fluttered the pages of my sketchbook, pulling my attention back to the drawing in my lap. I smudged a soft charcoal stick against the paper and blended the line with my fingertip. Before we came to Wandelsta, my mother had suggested I keep a journal of our experiences on the planet, complete with detailed illustrations. It was her way of ensuring I had something to occupy my time. She got so carried away by the idea that she lined up a publishing house for the project before we left Earth—not much of a challenge given that we were among the first humans to step foot on another planet. Now I couldn't slack off even if I felt like it. I welcomed the artistic challenge, but the sky here posed problems I hadn't anticipated. It was hard to capture the essence of Wandelsta's clouds, which were as beautiful as they were ominous.

I could relate to their duality.

I was a logical, straight-A science geek, yet I believed in magic and ghosts. I would take the time to stop and help a turtle safely cross the road, but then I'd rush home to join my brother in watching a UFC fighting match where guys in a cage pounded each other to a pulp for sport.

My grandmother used to boast that she and I were alike in that way—we both possessed a perfect blend of yin-yang energies that allowed us to see every side to a story. I wasn't sure what to make of that, given that Grams had been admitted to a long-term care facility for catatonic schizophrenia two years ago. I did know one thing for sure: I wasn't like other seventeen-year-old girls.

Grams always said that being different was a good thing. "If you had a choice," she told me when I was younger, "to be an ordinary white daisy in an endless field of ordinary white daisies, or to be the lone red one that captures the eye of all who pass by the field, I can't see any good reason why you'd choose to be white."

She was wrong. I wanted to be the white daisy, always had. And that's saying a lot because I loathed the color white.

But though I'd like to fit in with the crowd, I've been told that I come across as a mysterious loner—the pretty, too-smart, quiet girl with the long dark hair and dark eyes and a monochromatic wardrobe. I'm not sure why my love for alone time or the color black would make people think I'm brooding or depressed or harboring some deep dark secret. Well, to be fair, I do have secrets. Everyone does. But that's not why I wear black. I like it because it has the magical power to hide bodily imperfection—even a crooked spine.

"How's the journal coming, Resa?"

The whiny voice startled me and my hand jerked, causing the charcoal stick to snap. "Willie," I grumbled under my breath as I examined the large, dark streak that had destroyed my rendition of the spooky marshmallow sky. Heaving a sigh, I leaned over from my perch on the sand dune where I was sitting. Sure enough, there he was, fellow dune-dweller Willie Petrone, a twelve-year-old misfit boy who lived several bunkers down from me back on the base. Despite my constant efforts to change dunes daily, Willie always found me and interrupted my drawing sessions.

"Following me again?" I said, trying to mask my frustration. Luckily for Willie, I was blessed with saint-like patience, otherwise I would have already hurled myself off this dune and gone all UFC on him for making me ruin my picture.

"No-o," the stocky boy stammered, sounding defensive. His pink crewneck ran two sizes too small; his pastel checked shorts, two sizes too big. To my dismay, he started to trudge up my dune, his unkempt black curls flopping wildly about.

I've always had a soft spot for "fringe" people—people like Willie who didn't quite follow societal norms—Gram's red daisies, if you will. It was how I'd ended up acquiring my unwanted permanent shadow.

THE NEW ARRIVAL

"I wasn't following you," he corrected, "I was following him." He dragged his forearm across his nose and the sun shone off the newly formed, slick smear on his skin. I wasn't a fan of bodily excretions and Willie was the king of them. Then, to my utter dismay, he plopped down next to me, so uncomfortably close that I spotted what looked like a chunk of petrified tuna stuck to his shirt.

"You always think I'm following you," he said. "I was following him." He folded his legs Indian style to mimic mine, and a spurt of crimson sand shot me in the face.

"Willie!" I said with disdain, casting him a disapproving look. I wiped the gritty debris off my face, being careful not to scratch my eyes. He seemed completely oblivious to the fact that he was causing me discomfort. I shook my head. "Following who?" I finally asked.

"The new kid."

Willie was a notorious liar and often fabricated stories to gain attention, so I was shocked when I turned in the direction of Willie's pointing finger and saw the silhouette of someone sitting atop a distant dune behind me. The person was facing west, toward the incinerator spires that lined the horizon.

"My parents didn't mention a new arrival," I said. "Who is he?"

"I don't know," Willie said, shrugging. "But he brushed me off quick."

"You spoke to him?" I turned my head to avoid staring at a mucous bubble that was creeping out of his left nostril.

"Yeah, but all he wanted was my water. Then he acted like he didn't want to know me or something."

"But you gave him the water?"

"Uh-huh."

"And he still blew you off?"

He had difficulty responding because he was in the middle of a gurgling snort.

"And you wonder why people treat you this way," I said flatly. I couldn't blame the new arrival for shunning him. Besides his obvious hygienic challenges, Willie was immature for his age, so most people kept their distance.

"What do you mean? What did I do wrong? I gave him the water, didn't I? That was nice."

I sighed and handed him a tissue from my backpack, but he just mindlessly wadded it in his hands. I felt the disappointment radiating off him as he stared at the new arrival.

"Listen. If I were you, I wouldn't waste my time on him. Why would you want to hang out with someone like that, anyway?"

"Uh, I dunno," Willie said, shrugging. "I thought your bro might like him. He has that freaky look like Dakota. Even freakier."

"Freaky-cool? Or freaky-scary?"

"Freaky cool *and* scary. His eyes are whack. Like purple or something."

"Are you sure he's human?"

"He looked human except for those eyes. And his hair was all spiked, like Dakota's. But not tiny spikes. Long spikes." He gestured with his hands above his head to show spikes that were at least two feet tall.

"That long?" I said, one eyebrow raised.

"Maybe longer." He lifted his hands higher. "Really weird hair."

"Weird hair, huh?" I said, smiling. Like Mr. Caveman Mophead here had a right to cast stones about such things. "Want my advice? Stay away from him if he's so weird. And don't go following him. It's not right to follow people. It's creepy stalker behavior."

Willie thrust his nose into my sketchbook. "So, what's up with the streak?" he said. "It looks horrible. You'll never get it published like that. Do you think that looks good?" Despite my resistance, he pulled the book from my hands, and that solidified meat thing on his shirt grazed my arm. I recoiled in horror.

"Willie, come on, please?" I urged. "Personal space? Remember what we said about that?" I grabbed my book back. I was rapidly approaching my W.T.T.—Willie-tolerance-threshold.

"Why did you put in that awful streak?" he persisted. "It looks bad. Everyone's gonna see it when we get back to Earth."

I rubbed my temple. A headache was brewing like it did every time Willie was around me for more than a few minutes. It didn't help that his words rang uncomfortably true.

THE NEW ARRIVAL

"I'm trying not to think about that, thank you very much," I said, my body tightening. I closed my book and drew it toward my chest, resting my chin on its edge.

Five years ago, an alien culture had presented itself on Earth, changing everything humans knew and thought they knew about the universe. Besides Earth, there were twenty-five other known planets in the cosmos that harbored sentient life, and alien technology had made interstellar travel among these civilizations simple and quick. My father was the first Earthling to have made contact with an alien, and that chance meeting was what had ultimately landed us 4.4 light years away on the planet Wandelsta, as part of a universal sociologic experiment dubbed "Worlds Meeting Worlds." We were one of a small handful of Earth families that had been chosen to experience life on a foreign planet for six months. We were almost three months in.

"Well, you better think about it," Willie said. "When we get back, we'll be famous. They'll want us to be on all the talk shows, I bet."

"I certainly hope that's not the case." The thought of appearing on TV sickened me. A public speaker I was not. In fact, I had a hard time speaking in front of a gathering of more than two or three people. I always feigned illness on days when I had to present something in class. I was pretty bad at vocalizing for myself in the best of situations. When I was six years old, a woman snatched my grandmother's purse from our shopping cart while Gram's back was turned. After grabbing the bag, she walked toward the exit, rummaging through Gram's things as if they were hers. I had seen the whole thing and wanted to scream, "There's the woman! Get her!" but I just stood there, paralyzed. Things haven't gotten too much better since, I'm sorry to say.

"My journal will do the talking for me," I said.

"But you'll have to do publicity for the journal," he said. "Maybe we can go on Lady Mia's show when we get back." His eyes widened. "Wow, could you imagine us being interviewed by Lady Mia?"

W.T.T. met and surpassed. I entered ignore mode to stave off a full-blown panic attack.

He continued to ramble about our potential celebrity talk-show tour. It was amazing how successfully I could tune something or someone out when I put my mind to it.

A sharp prickle on my face reminded me that I wasn't alone. Willie had launched himself to his feet, blasting me with sand again in the process. Only this time, I didn't get mad at him.

I, too, had felt the air begin to thicken.

"The weather's changing," he said, as if I hadn't noticed. "We have to get back."

I gathered some loose chalk sticks embedded in the sand and cast my eyes skyward. The spooky charred lumps I had been sketching had morphed into an overcast, steely watercolor wash.

The air on Wandelsta was dynamic. It started in the morning as a hazy but breathable mixture of gases that slowly changed in thickness and transparency as the pollution increased throughout the day. By late afternoon, the air became downright dangerous, holding so much pollution that it morphed into *toxia*, a thick substance you could mold into shapes that kept their forms for several seconds before dissipating.

"It's time to go, Resa," Willie said, sounding tense.

"You head down," I instructed him. "I'll be there in a minute."

I needed some time to admire my favorite stage in the atmosphere's transition. The eerie stillness in the air reminded me of being at home in Maine right before a snowfall. I always loved to wander about in the sullen fog that preceded a winter storm. I would pretend I was lost in a cloud until the air released the pent-up snow that made everything instantly quiet and peaceful. For a moment I could almost imagine that I was back there, but Willie's perpetual nagging and the stench of rotting eggs in the air reminded me that this was anywhere but Earth. We were on Wandelsta, or as my brother Dakota called it, *Wandelstinka*. And instead of snow, we would be getting toxia—the noxious soup of gases and particulate matter that could burn flesh or asphyxiate anyone who wasn't wearing an oxygen mask and a protective suit. I was outside wearing nothing more than flimsy yoga pants and a lightweight tank, bare-skinned and vulnerable.

"Come on, Resa," Willie whined urgently. "We have to go. I mean it. We're never gonna make it back in time."

"All right, already. You don't always have to wait for me, you know." I gave in, though—not because I was worried, but because I couldn't stand the sound of his moaning.

I stuffed my art supplies into my backpack and slung the bag over my shoulders. After tightening the laces on my tan, knee-high combat boots, I headed down the gentle slope of the dune, Willie in tow. Then it hit me. What about the new kid? He must have been briefed about the toxia before coming to Wandelsta, but did he realize that since he'd wandered so deep into the dune field, he had to start heading back now, before the warning system was activated?

"You go ahead," I said. "I'll be down in a sec. I have to warn the new kid." I started back up the dune.

"What for?" Willie asked, pouting. "He'll know what to do. Everyone does. We have to go."

"Did he have a mask on when you saw him earlier?"

"I dunno."

"Then I have to warn him. I'm not going to live with the guilt of this kid dying out here." As I turned to race to the top of the dune, I heard Willie murmuring under his breath, probably jealous that I was giving someone else my attention. Patches of murky fog had settled on the peaks.

"Hello?" I called out loudly in the direction of the guy's dune. "Hello, can you hear me?" There was no reply. "The air is changing. You need to get back to the bunkers now. Hello out there. Can you hear me?" Again, silence. I tried to catch a glimpse of the newcomer through the breaks in the drifting fog, but the air had become too dense.

"I can grab a little, Resa!" Willie cried, bouncing on his toes. "Resa, I can grab a little! I'm not kidding. We have to go now."

It was always about this time when I started to wish I'd worn a rubber suit and breathing mask. Not because I was afraid—I'd been out here enough times to know exactly how long I needed to make it back before developing any symptoms of breathing in toxic air—but because toxia was irresistible to play with: a 3D, interactive modeling clay of sorts.

I started down the dune and caught up with Willie, who was trying to clench the air between his fists.

"It's starting to clump up," he warned, sounding panicked. "We have to go. My skin is starting to tingle."

I dismissed him with a wave of my hand and took the lead. "Your skin isn't tingling. Relax. You shouldn't come out here anymore if you're always going to freak out over toxia."

He caught up with me. "No, really, Resa. I'm serious. My skin is burning." He was shaking his arms like that was somehow going to prevent it from happening. "I feel it. It's tingling. Honest. I'm not lying."

"The air's not thick enough for it to burn your skin yet," I said with certainty. "We have at least an hour. You're fine, let's go."

I scampered to the base of the dune with Willie at my heels and headed back to the bunker, hoping that the new arrival had the sense to do the same.

THE WASTELAND

I wondered how long it would take before television programming back on Earth included extreme battles for survival on extrasolar planets. The trek through the waste-decomposition field could have easily been the final challenge on some godawful reality show, and with Willie as a partner, the task could break the nerves of even the strongest-willed competitors.

The crimson dune field was riddled with trash, making it a dangerous obstacle course in the thickening fog. Wandelsta was an interplanetary garbage dump, and as such, spaceships came here daily, dropping off tons of waste from their homelands for disposal. Most of the trash was burned in the incinerator complexes, while the rest was left to decompose beneath the sand in the fields.

The dunes had become my stomping ground, and in my three months of living on the planet, I'd become a guru of its topography. I was adept at deciphering the contours of the sand to determine where items were buried shallowly enough to pose a threat. This had in part been accomplished by my trusted poking stick—a knobby wooden staff I'd found a few weeks back, which I used to probe the sand for buried objects. It slowed down my progress a bit, but that was better than stumbling upon a jagged piece of rusted scrap metal waiting to give me tetanus or some comparable Wandelstan disease.

Willie had the luxury of following behind me, so he was oblivious to the potential dangers that lurked underfoot. Once he had accepted that his flesh wasn't yet melting off his bones, he bounced about like a jumping bean, babbling about some old, discarded snowboard that he'd found this morning and how he was going to use it to surf the dunes. I "yessed" him to death, focusing on how I would get him back to the bunker if he maimed himself on some buried object. Luckily, the atmospheric alert system finally kicked in, redirecting his focus.

"Toxia alert. Toxia alert." An automated loudspeaker issued its warning. "Atmospheric pollution levels will become toxic in approximately sixty minutes. All unprotected life forms must begin to seek shelter. All unprotected life forms must begin to seek shelter."

Tiny red lights atop pole-mounted toxia sensors began to flash like beacons through the fog. We followed the trail of twenty-foot wooden poles right up to and through the twenty-foot wire fence that surrounded the bunker complex.

"So, maybe you'll watch me dune-surf tomorrow?" Willie asked as he turned left down a dirt road that separated what looked like two identical rows of cabin-sized aircraft hangers.

"Not tomorrow. I have to redo my atmosphere picture. You didn't like that streak, remember? You should go home now. You don't want to burn."

Willie made some weird animal whimper and tore off into the fog. He lived in the nineteenth of twenty bunkers. I was in Bunker 1. The oversized tin can I called home had no visible doors or windows, only a huge identification number spray-painted in blood red on the front. I went around back, punched in the access code on the outdoor panel, and entered the detoxification chamber through an air-sealed portal, which automatically locked behind me. Only one person was allowed into the chamber at a time.

The detox chamber, which was used to sterilize people and things from outdoor contaminants, was the worst room ever. For starters, it was insane-asylum white. I despised white, which was the color of padded rooms. Why not paint the room a reassuring sage green? Or maybe a dusty lilac-gray?

Nope. The designer had opted for hundreds of tiny, stark-white tiles to line all the floors and walls, making the room feel like a sterile prison.

Even worse than the color was the placement of the shower—smack in the middle of the room with no frosted privacy door or curtain, just an open-air, two-foot elevated platform with a bare silver nozzle and a chain hanging from the ceiling.

The perimeter of the room was equally uninviting. It had an industrial-warehouse feel, cluttered with strange, mechanical-looking things, including a UV sterilizing machine and specialized vats for washing clothes. Rows of large red cylindrical tubes that held several weeks' worth of fresh air and water stood in the corner like soldiers. Dangling overhead were exposed ceiling wires and a maze of noisy, crooked pipes.

I unclasped my rope bracelets and jute choker-necklace and threw them into the UV machine, along with my backpack, clothes, and boots. I gave them all a healthy zap of sterilizing UV radiation before stepping onto the cold concrete shower floor.

Even though the room was private, I felt totally exposed, standing naked in the middle of the room on an elevated platform. I took a deep breath and pulled the chain, which released a cold glob of disinfecting soap from one nozzle and a strong, short blast of barely warm water from another. I lathered violently, knowing the next blast of water would come thirty seconds later to wash away the grime.

Showers here just weren't the same. In fact, they were mildly tortuous. Back on Earth, shower-time had been all about leisure. It was a time to daydream. A time to map out my next art project or rehearse a chant for a new spell. Not so on Wandelsta. Clean water was in short supply here and showers lasted one minute and thirty-two seconds, automated to the millisecond. Their sole purpose was to wash away toxins.

After the final blast of water, I buzzed myself into the adjoining dressing room and pulled open the thick metal door that separated the detox chamber from the main living quarters of the bunker. I entered a changing room and dried off, using a biodegradable towel that made sandpaper seem soft. It didn't help that there wasn't enough room for me to turn around without knocking into the wire racks that lined the walls. I'd earned many bruises in my futile attempts to dry off, and today was no exception.

After peeling all the bits of shredded towel off my still-damp skin, I rummaged through some metal crates that were neatly stacked on the wire-shelving units. I found my comfy gray sweats and favorite tee—a jet-black beauty with three-quarter-length sleeves, a deep V-neck, and silver scrollwork—and got dressed. The shirt was tailored perfectly, fitted enough to show off my waist, yet loose enough that no one would notice the 45-degree S-curve in my spine that made my right shoulder blade protrude slightly more than my left one. When I was first diagnosed with scoliosis, my doctor suggested corrective surgery, but my mom decided against it because I wasn't in pain and the curve posed no immediate health problems. She didn't think the risk of a major surgery was justifiable for cosmetic reasons. Needless to say, I had become an expert at finding styles to camouflage my back. Most people would never even know that my spine wasn't straight, but it was a rare day when I didn't think about it.

I stood in front of an unframed mirror that was barely large enough to see my whole face and began the arduous task of trying to detangle the tumbleweed knots that resulted from having long, baby-fine hair and essentially waterless showers. The procedure was more tedious than surgery since I had to pull one strand of hair at a time from the knot, breaking dozens in the process. It took nearly an hour before my hair was smooth.

That was about when I overheard Dakota blow a gasket at my mother in the kitchen.

"I'm done with this 'Worlds Meeting Worlds' scam. This is nuts. Who in their right mind would volunteer to come to a garbage planet? Really? This is insane."

"Watch the tone you take with me, Dakota."

"Or what?"

This was getting good. I slipped into a pair of comfy tan slipper-boots, grabbed a sour-apple lollipop from my purse, and went to the kitchen to watch and perhaps contribute to the show.

THE STONES

I'd be lying if I said that my twin brother was a tolerant person. He always had difficulty accepting people who were different from himself, and his attitude toward diversity deteriorated rapidly when the Colored Lights first appeared over our hometown of Bar Harbor, Maine five years ago in May. I can still remember the look of disgust on Dakota's face when my father, the chief of police at the time, called home after investigating several reports of seven rainbow-colored orbs hovering above Cadillac Mountain in Acadia National Park.

"It's finally happened," he told my mother, who relayed the news to us. "They've made contact. I just spoke to an alien."

Dad was an instant celebrity, having been the first person to meet someone from another world. The alien was Mr. Hanz Cuticulor, a greenish-skinned, photosynthetic man from Yrd, an arid planet 4.4 light years away, circling the star Alpha Centauri.

Mr. Cuticulor spoke perfect English, along with French, Chinese, and seven other languages. He and his people had studied the various cultures on Earth for decades before making contact in Maine. To facilitate communication between our species, they brought a couple of ingenious devices with them. One was an earpiece called a modulator, which would translate any spoken word into any language spoken on Earth. The other was a thin contact lens that converted any known written symbols the wearer saw into the language of their choice. Not a big fan of touching my eyes, I preferred to use the handheld version of the decoder, a pocket-sized rectangular device that displayed English words on a screen when it was passed over foreign text. Even though the Yrdians were far more advanced than us, Mr. Cuticulor had taken a particular liking to my father. Dad was one of a small group of Earthlings the Yrdians asked to join their Interplanetary Peace League, IPPL for short, an organization dedicated to spreading universal peace. My father accepted the invitation with honor, and our lives have been anything but ordinary since. Throughout it all, Dakota had made no effort to hide his displeasure about the complete uprooting of his life.

I entered the kitchen nook and took my front-row seat atop an aluminum stool at the eating counter. My mother was standing by the portable stove wearing a white sweat outfit spattered with brown splotches—gravy, maybe? She shared my grandma's Native-American tresses, jet black and thick as rope. Today her gorgeous hair was knotted into a sagging bun sprouting dozens of tendrils. She could have been a model, with her olive skin, thin nose, and dark tarantula-lashed eyes, but she had chosen to be a chef. She had taken a break to come to Wandelsta.

"Whatcha got cooking there, Ma?" I teased. "Your famed grilled wild Alaskan salmon with garlic-whipped potatoes and truffle reduction?"

She was an uptight mess, and my question only caused her more distress. "This is nothing but a complete disaster," she replied, pulling a pot off the heat without telling me what was in it.

Typically, we ate like royalty. Growing up, I craved spices and exotic dishes that most kids my age didn't even know existed. What I wouldn't give for her creamy peanut butter pie with decadent chocolate ganache right about now. Ridiculously awesome.

The only downside of eating gourmet my whole life was that it made the food on Wandelsta painfully unbearable. Except for the spiral-shaped guanadane fruit from planet Yrd, which tasted almost like pineapple if you could get through its tough, spiny red skin, the food here was unappetizing, to say the least. Fresh food was in short supply, with a small shipment of exotic otherworldly edibles arriving once a month. Most of our rations were canned meats packed in oil or freeze-dried foods with the consistency of soft Styrofoam. Thankfully, I'd smuggled a one-pounder bag of Dum Dum lollipops from Earth in my backpack, though my stash was running low. I'd also brought half a suitcase of peanut butter, since it was non-perishable and downright delicious. I was surviving on spoonfuls right out of the jar. Mom, on the other hand, was struggling with the whole food situation. She kept trying to prepare worthy meals, but the limited ingredients, improper air pressure, and sad stove were just not working in her favor. Today her attention was on Dakota, though, not whatever was simmering in her pot.

"Whether you like it or not, we have a new role in the world. No, a new role in the universe," she preached, pointing a wooden spoon at my brother, dangerously close to his face. "You need to change your attitude before we go home. We're making history. Do you understand me, Dakota? History. Our faces. Our story. Everybody, and I mean everybody, is going to want to hear it. This is a once-in-a-lifetime opportunity that's been afforded our family. Be gracious about it."

Dakota stood there in his typical Dakota gear. Black-and-white-checked, low-slung shorts. Matching Converse sneakers. Faded retro rock T-shirt. Belt chains. Nose stud. Attitude.

"So that's what you're calling this now? An opportunity?" Dakota scowled. He stretched his neck up and plastered a serious look on his face, morphing into the character of an Yrdian. He stiffened his arms and legs to resemble the aliens' long, tree-like limbs.

"Oh, let's see," he said in a somewhat English-sounding accent similar to how the aliens spoke. "Which schlep of a dumb family is gullible enough to fall for our scam? Oh, I know. The Stones! Yes, yes. The Stone family. Come to Wandelsta free of charge. Breathe in the toxic air. Coexist with the vagrant mole people. Work for free at our factories. Come. Come. What a wonderful opportunity, indeed."

I struggled to keep a straight face. My brother had always been great at impressions.

My mother softened her tone. "Dakota, I understand these last five years have been a whirlwind, but it's been that way for all of us. I'm sorry, but this isn't just about you. Our entire planet has to cope with the reality that we're not alone in the universe and that there are other species who are more technologically advanced than we are. We're lucky they met your father first. Now we're on the inside track of the new planetary order. They invited us to this place so we can understand more about the IPPL and their program for maintaining universal peace."

"Yeah, okay. 'Invited,' " he said, his fingers making quotation marks in the air. "More like Dad is practically running the waste management facility—with no pay, mind you—while our physical and mental health deteriorate on this toxic world. Oh, how lucky we are. I can't believe you're falling for all their 'we need to work together to bring peace and harmony and unite the universe' garbage. And you don't think it's slightly odd that only people from Earth were sent to Wandelsta? I don't see any of the other twenty-five sentient species in the cosmos working here…besides the Slopees, and they have no choice since they're from here. Humans are completely being used. We're on track to becoming modern-day slaves in the name of spreading peace."

My mother pulled an excessive number of wipes from a plastic flip-top container and started to mop down the drips on the counter. "Don't be ridiculous," she said, her voice hardening. "Wandelsta was just the closest habitable planet to Earth—that's why we're here. Every official in the IPPL has to perform one charitable act per year, including your father. He volunteered for this duty in good faith."

"Wow, they've already brainwashed you. Unbelievable. Have you even stopped for a minute to question why they chose Dad to become a member of this Interplanetary Peace League in the first place? He wasn't the president or a world leader on Earth. He just happened to be the chief of police of the town where they made first contact. I'm telling you…the president wouldn't be volunteering on this hellhole.

These IPPL people are just looking for free labor and they're passing it off as altruism. Wake up, Mom."

"Can I say something?" I asked, raising my finger.

"What?" Dakota seemed annoyed.

"A lot of people thought it was odd that they had asked Dad," I interjected. "I thought it was odd at first, too. But Dad is an awesome human being, and his personality and good nature overrode his status. That's what I like about the aliens—they value important stuff more than 'titles.' You always said that many of our political leaders are self-serving, wear-a-fake-smile charlatans. I have faith in the Yrdians. I think they have the right idea."

"The right idea? The supposed goal of the IPPL is to unite all species, which is totally impossible. Oh, but of course Little Miss Hippie Witch is into all that peace-and-love crap." Dakota made his voice higher to mock me. His talent with impressions was admittedly less amusing when he used it against me. "Oh, let's all get along. Peace, love, rainbows, and unicorns make the world go round." Then he returned to his normal tone. "Let me tell you: that big, happy love-fest is impossible. People on Earth can't even get along. You want peace? Everyone should mind their own business and stay with their own kind. That'll give us peace. The aliens should stay away from us, and we should stay away from them. Things were better that way."

"That's enough, Dakota," my mother warned with unconvincing bravado.

"Actually, global crime has decreased since the Colored Lights," I said. "It's brought people together."

Dakota huffed. "Yeah, against the aliens."

My mother had the same incredulous look she always had when fighting with my brother. "So you think that joining an organization whose aim is to spread universal peace is a waste of time?"

"That's exactly what I think," he said smugly. "I actually think it's a cover for something else. We run around and do their dirty work while they plan to overtake our planet."

"If they wanted our planet, it would be easy enough for them to take it," said my mother. "Anyway, why would the Yrdians have helped us if that's what they wanted? They shared their technology for interstellar travel. They're trying to help us eradicate cancer."

"They want us to owe them. Who knows what they'll ask for in return? Our souls?"

My mother looked at me and shrugged. "Maybe you can talk some sense into him. At least one of my kids has their head on straight."

I nearly gagged on my lollipop. Sound the bell for Round Two.

Mom stirred something in the small pot on the portable stove, completely ignoring Dakota, who looked about ready to combust.

"Are you serious?" he cried. "Honestly? Are you serious right now? The girl sits in her room and performs spells!" He turned to me. "No offense, Rees."

I shrugged. "None taken."

"She thinks she's a witch, and she's the one who has her head on straight?"

"Clarification," I corrected. "I am a witch."

"What you are is nuts. And I'm talking Grams-level nuts. You need to be evaluated."

My mother cringed. "Dakota!"

"I'm just saying, your daughter thinks she's a witch. Grams heard voices in her head. Uh, am I the only one who sees a pattern here?"

"I wish I could turn you into a toad," I said dryly.

"All your father and I are asking is that you be more open-minded, that's all," my mother redirected. "The Yrdians have given us no reason to distrust them. And your father works with them, so you absolutely cannot vocalize your feelings about them when we go back home. It's bad publicity, Dakota." She looked at me. "And Resa, it's probably a good idea to keep the whole witch thing down when we get back, too. The press would have a field day with that."

Dakota threw his hands into the air. "You're all nuts," he proclaimed, speaking to himself. "Every last one of you! Dad for volunteering to work on this hellhole of a planet in the first place. We never see the man anymore. You," he emphasized, pointing at my mother, "for following him here like an obedient dog, and you"—he held his finger out at me for some ten seconds before coming up with a brilliant enough diss—"for thinking you can actually manipulate nature for your own benefit!"

"Oh, but I can, thank you very much."

His face was about as red as the spray paint he'd plastered on the tips of his short, spiky black hair.

"And apparently I must be good at it, because my life appears to be going a little better than yours at the moment. In fact, my life has always gone better than yours, hasn't it?" I smiled and then bit into my candy.

Dakota practically growled as he stormed into the corridor and out of sight. The obnoxious sound of his clanging belt chains was followed by the heavy clap of his bedroom door slamming shut. My mother looked about ready to cry.

"Why do you let him talk to you that way?" I asked. "He needs to face consequences for his behavior or he's never going to change."

"Resa, please. He's just having a hard time adjusting here. I wish his guitar hadn't broken on the shuttle ride here. He's going stir crazy, and he misses his friends. You know how much he likes Luna. He regrets that he didn't ask her out before leaving. He's angry and frustrated."

"It's been months. He needs to get over it. I miss my friends too, but you don't hear me whining about it all the time. It's not like I've gone on any dates lately, either."

The truth was, I didn't blame Dakota for being aggravated. I missed normalcy and pre-Colored-Lights life, too, and I suspected things would only get worse once we got back home. Dad had done a great job of shielding us from the media prior to this trip, but upon our return, we'd be obliged to speak out about our life on another world. Mom had a right to be concerned about Dakota's anti-alien philosophy.

I had mixed feelings about going home. The thought of being bombarded by reporters and having my face plastered all over the news was sickening, but I yearned for the comforts of home, especially the company of my best friend Sarah Payne. I'm convinced that I either knew Sarah in a past life or that we were twins separated at birth, because there's just no way it was a coincidence that two teenage girls who practiced witchcraft, detested high-school-girl drama, and used a higher condiment-to-food ratio when eating just happened to live in the same small town of Bar Harbor, Maine.

My mother started her famous, "Why can't Dakota be more like you?" speech, so I tuned her out, giving an occasional uh-huh to pretend I was listening.

"So, maybe you could talk some sense into your brother?" my mother pressed. "I can't get through to him. He just won't listen to me."

I didn't blame Dakota for that. It was hard to have a meaningful conversation with my mother about anything deeper than food or the weather because she was such a worrywart. One time when I was in the seventh grade, I made the mistake of telling her that I thought Devon Berkshire was cute. Let's just say, I was tortured by the pregnancy speech for months thereafter. Since then, I've never tipped her off on anything too personal.

"I've tried to talk to him. Many times," I admitted. "He doesn't care what I think."

"He looks up to you, Resa. Don't let his tough act fool you. Could you try to talk to him just one more time?"

My mother had no clue how little Dakota and I actually had in common. In fact, she would die if she ever found out that her son was a stoner. I'm not sure how much of the stuff he actually smoked, but I caught him raiding the food-ration bin last week, smelling all musty and herbal, his eyes bloodshot. I had no idea where he had even gotten the stuff, but I hadn't blown his cover. Still, pain or not, he was my brother, and I had been keeping a secret eye on him ever since.

"I could try to give him a piece of celestite," I offered.

"I wish you'd talk to him instead," my mother insisted.

"Celestite offers clarity. He needs clarity."

Rocks and crystals of all shapes and sizes and colors were my thing. When I was four, I adopted my first pet rock. "Herman" was a big hunk of pink-and-black-speckled granite that I found broken off from the cliffs behind our home in Maine. Herman now belongs to a larger rock and mineral family that I've gathered over the years. On my twelfth birthday, Grams gave me a book that explained how every mineral carries a different energy suitable for different purposes. A chunk of baby-blue celestite was exactly what Dakota needed. Too bad he'd never accept it. I chewed off the final gooey nub of my lollipop and threw the stick in the trash.

A stinging pulse of energy radiated across my brow and I gasped out loud.

My mother walked toward me. "Still getting those headaches?" She placed the back of her hand on my forehead as if checking for a fever.

I pushed her arm away. "I'm not sick, Ma," I said quickly. "I've just been getting a lot of them here." Luckily Mom had been so preoccupied with helping Dad at the waste management facility that she hadn't realized just how often I'd been having them. She was paranoid enough without any encouragement.

"That's because you keep going outside without a mask. You did it again today, didn't you? Resa, how many times—"

"Ma, not now, please?" A second pulse shot across the top of my head. Her words amplified themselves and small white spots fluttered at the edge of my vision. This was quickly entering migraine territory. "It's because I haven't been sleeping well."

"Or because you've been breathing too much toxia. Who knows what that stuff might be doing to you? You have to wear a mask outside, Resa."

"You know I can't draw with a mask on. And I always come in when the alert system first sounds. It's not the toxia. I just need more sleep, that's all."

"Do you want me to call the medic? Have them look at you to be sure?"

"Ma, please? I promise you, I'm fine. I'm just tired."

"Well, go lie down and get some sleep, then."

She continued to rant about the possible underlying conditions that could be causing my headaches as she rummaged through a crate of medications beneath the sink. The sounds of the clinking pills in the bottles might as well have been landslides in my brain. As soon as

THE STONES

I heard her utter the word tumor I slipped away into my room, popped two Advil, and curled into a ball on my cot.

I tried to relax my mind with meditation. Ease the tension, I told myself. Relax. Let the pain dissolve. Close your eyes. Just whatever you do…try not to fall asleep.

Because if I did, I knew she would be waiting for me.

NITIKA

The forest sparkled with flashes of color as the light from two lavender moons struck hundreds of crystal points that bobbed from willowy tree branches. I could barely breathe as a ghostly teenaged girl emerged from the jeweled woods, her head tilted downward, her eyes closed. She approached me slowly and whispered, "You are the one."

* * *

"You are the one."

    The ghostly phrase continued to cycle through my mind as I lay in bed somewhere in the hazy suspended mist that separates the dream state from reality. I bolted upright, fearful of falling deeper into sleep… fearful of getting lost in my dream. The same dream I've had night after night for longer than I care to remember. The same dream that always leaves me feeling like I'm not alone. Like someone is hovering over me…

    "What's your problem?"

    It took me a minute to place my surroundings before I realized Dakota was the one who had spoken the words.

"What did you say?" I said, squinting against the blinding overhead light. "Shut that off." I still had all the lingering symptoms of a migraine hangover—the queasy stomach, the biting sensitivity to light, and the unnaturally heavy body.

"I asked what your problem was. Or should I say, problems. You have many."

"With you being the biggest," I quipped. Of course, it wasn't true. The migraines, the dreams...these things were pressing, but my brother didn't need to know that.

"You look like death," Dakota said, rummaging through my personal stuff. The racket of his clanging belt chains felt like a hammer hit to the head.

"Thank you," I grumbled. "I feel like it. Uh, did I invite you in here, or did you just take it upon yourself to invade my space? What are you doing?"

"Looking for a lollipop." He continued to dig through the contents of my metal crates.

"There's this thing called asking first..." I didn't have the strength to fight him, so I leaned over the side of the cot and grabbed my colorful patchwork fabric backpack, which lay open on the floor. My skin felt tight from a slick residue of medicinal soap that I hadn't been able to fully wash off in the decontamination room. I scoured the bottom of the bag and found my least-favorite flavor—root beer—and held it out for him.

"Here," I said, shielding my eyes from the light. "Dakota, here. Take it, shut the light, and get out."

I threw the candy at him, rolled onto my side, and pulled the blanket over my head, hoping that would be the end of it. But a few moments passed, and I could still hear him rustling through my stuff. "Get out, Dakota," I yelled.

There was a momentary silence. Then the sound of flipping pages. "What the hell is this?"

My heart sank. When I threw the covers off my head and turned to look at him, Dakota was holding open my sketchbook, staring at

You are the one.

a picture I'd drawn of a sullen, brown-haired girl cloaked in a salmon-colored shroud. Her eyes were downcast. The words "You are the one" were etched beneath her head.

It was the ghostly girl from my dream.

"Give that to me!" My queasiness turned into full-blown nausea. I'd always done such a good job of hiding these sketches. How could I have left them out?

I launched myself at him, which proved to be a huge mistake when I nearly passed out from the head rush. Even worse, I'd shown my hand. Now he knew that this was really important to me, and since he was a foot taller than me, he easily dangled the sketchbook over my head and out of my reach.

"Dakota, come on. I don't feel well. Give it to me."

He continued to rifle through the pages. "What's with the million sketches of this girl?"

I felt completely ambushed. How could I explain away thirty identical pictures back-to-back in the same book? I bit my lip, trying to form a believable lie.

"Who is this girl?"

"Dakota, just give me the book, please. If you have any human bone in your body, you'll see I'm not feeling well and you'll leave me alone." He was bending the pages in his eagerness to see all of the drawings. "You're ruining it, Dakota! Give it back!"

"First tell me who she is."

"Dakota, please!" I was begging now, and it was pathetic.

"Tell me." He was relentless.

"Her name is Nitika. Now give the book to me."

He pursed his lips. "What kind of name is that? Is she your gay lover or something?"

"Yes, she's my gay lover, Dakota. Now give it to me." He still refused.

My mother must have overheard the ruckus because she cracked the door open and popped her head inside. "What's going on in here?" she said. "Professor Mangleton just arrived for tutoring. Get it together."

"Resa's gay," Dakota stated matter-of-factly. He held up the portrait of Nitika for her to see.

"I'm not gay, Ma. Not that there's anything wrong with that. Your son is just a complete moron and I want my sketchbook back."

Mom took one glance at Dakota's Cheshire-cat smile and snatched my book from him.

"That's enough," she said to Dakota as she handed it to me. "Professor Mangleton is waiting."

"You mean, Professor Molemanton?"

"Dakota, please, he can probably hear you. Don't be rude."

"How is calling him what he is rude? He's part man. Part mole." Then he pointed at me with both index fingers. "Gay Girl's going solo with the molo today. I have no use for learning about interplanetary politics, thank you. Let me know when John gets here to tutor me on things I can actually use in my life."

"Yeah, like you'll ever use calculus," I said. "So what am I supposed to tell the professor?"

"You'll think of something," he said. I swatted his hand to prevent him from squeezing my cheek. "Love ya, sis."

I rolled my eyes as Dakota snickered and left the room. I was physically exhausted from the migraine and trying to get my drawings back from my brother. School was the last thing on my mind, but the professor was waiting. Luckily, it was only a session with Professor Mangleton about IPPL politics, which wouldn't affect my school grade back home. I was seeing John, my tutor for Earthly subjects, later in the day.

"I know you don't feel well, honey, but the professor came a long way to see you two," my mom said in a soft voice. "Do you think you can pull it together?"

Like I had a choice. Sometimes being the good sibling and daughter had its drawbacks. I slipped in my earpiece translator and reluctantly joined Professor Mangleton at a small, square folding table in the corner of what you could call the living room, while my mother resumed her cooking at the portable stove. A burnt-sugar smell hung in the air, which wasn't doing any favors for my already-upset stomach.

"Good afternoon, Resa," said the professor. He was always cheerful, which was one of the things I liked best about him.

"Afternoon, Professor," I said, sounding lackluster. My eyes shifted to his outfit and it was hard not to smile. Dressed in an outdated red-plaid blazer, a gaudy yellow necktie, and khaki pants with a makeshift hole for his tail, he looked like a stuffed animal. The members of his species only wore clothes in the presence of alien species, and piecing together a wardrobe from the discarded trash in the dune fields was not an easy task for them.

"You're looking dapper, as usual," I complimented.

"Thank you, dear girl," he said, blushing slightly. With wobbly hands, he lifted a beanie cap off his head and placed it on the table. Wiry strands of white hair coated his thick, scaly skin.

The professor belonged to the Slopee race, Wandelsta's indigenous people, who resided in cavernous tunnels deep underground, away from the toxicity on the surface of the planet. Their subterranean existence had favored the evolution of rodent-like qualities such as beady black eyes and a long, whip-like tail. Both their feet and hands sprouted cupped claws for digging. Slopees walked clumsily on two legs in the presence of otherworldly guests, though they preferred to leap around naked on all fours when underground. The professor was out of his element up here on the surface. He had to wear thick, dark glasses to protect his eyes from the light of day and our artificial lamps.

"Where's Dakota, my dear? He's not joining us today?"

"I'm afraid not. He wasn't feeling well and didn't have the strength for two tutoring sessions today."

"Oh, that's too bad. But I do understand. Mine would be the one to miss, as he mustn't fall behind in his Earthy studies. You can fill him in on our session, no? Now, let's see," he muttered as he tapped his dense claws against the table. "Ah, yes. Today we must discuss the origins of the unrest between the Siafu and the Ploompies of planet Glucosa. Quite a relevant topic in light of the Siafu's looming threat against that peaceful culture."

I did my best to feign interest in what he was saying, but I kept nodding off. A couple of times I gasped out loud as I jolted from near-slumber. On top of that, I couldn't stop thinking about what had just happened with Dakota. How could I have let him find my pictures of Nitika? Maybe it was a sign that I needed to tell someone about her. Keeping her secret was costing me much-needed sleep and possibly causing my headaches, too.

The history lesson lasted for an hour before Professor Mangleton brought it to a close. As I gathered my papers, the professor told me about a weekend reading lecture that he thought I'd like.

"Madame Molina is recounting the legend of Gemja this Saturday. She thought you might take an interest since it involves minerals and gems."

"That was nice of her," I said. "What's it about?"

"The legend of Gemja recounts the origin of our universe and explains its dependence on glowing crystals with unique powers. All right up your alley, my dear. It will be this Saturday, down in the hole, if you are interested."

It was nice that both he and Madame Molina had thought of me, but I needed a day to work on my journal. "Thanks, Professor. I'll see how I feel." Then I remembered the new arrival. "Oh, by the way. Have you started teaching the new kid? Who is he and where is he from?"

"Is there a new arrival I should know about?" He glanced at my mother, who was still puttering in the kitchen. She shook her head no. "Why do you ask, dear girl?"

"Willie Petrone said he saw a boy out in the dune field," I replied. My eyes shifted to the door as Dakota entered the room. I stood up and gathered my books.

"Well, hello there. Feeling any better?" the professor asked as Dakota slid into my seat, nearly knocking me over in the process.

"I'm good," Dakota said. After dropping his math and science textbooks on the table, he turned to look at my mother. "John's not here yet?"

"He's running late," my mother said.

"Willie is certain that he saw a new teenage boy in the fields," I emphasized. "Yet no one else has heard of him. Isn't that odd?"

"Since when do you believe sniveling Willie?" Dakota said.

"Since I saw the person myself," I said, shooting him an evil glare.

"Maybe you're seeing things. Maybe he doesn't exist."

"Sometimes I wish you didn't exist."

Then I gathered my sketchbook, art case, and poking stick and headed out to my dune for a little peace.

THE ENCOUNTER

The weakness and nausea that always accompanied my migraines were still with me the next morning, and my mom, worried as ever, insisted that I might need an MRI. As much as my body needed rest, it needed distance from my mother's neuroses even more. I also didn't want to stay cooped up inside, easy prey for my brother's taunts. I toyed with the idea of telling him the truth about Nitika on the off chance he'd stop bugging me. I came close a few times, but the last thing I needed was for him to run to my mom with the news that I was hearing voices. She'd be worried sick that I was crazy like Grams. And if I ended up in some white-walled institution, I probably would go crazy.

I waited until Mom was immersed in another cooking debacle before I quietly slipped outside. I headed to my dune, curious to see if the new arrival would be out in the fields. I breathed a sigh of relief when I saw him across the way, sitting in the same statuesque pose as yesterday, facing the horizon. So he was real…and okay. I wondered if he'd heard my warning the previous afternoon.

I sat watching him for a while, finding it odd that he never moved. I made a game of seeing just how long it would take before he changed positions. I gave him fifteen minutes. As I waited, I put the final touches on my re-creation of the Halloween-sky picture.

Before I knew it, an hour had passed, and the new arrival still hadn't flinched. My fifteen-minute mark had been a gross under-calculation. I was debating with myself whether someone could sleep sitting upright when Willie found me, struggling to drag a surfboard up my dune.

"Isn't she a beaut?" he said, heaving the board. He plopped down beside me with his new toy, shooting sand all over my picture and me...yet again.

The weathered board was faded black with the peeling remnants of two canary-yellow stripes running its length. There were so many nicks and scratches on its surface that it looked like it had been in a catfight.

"It's kinda ruddy," I said. "Does it go down a slope easy?"

"No," he said, looking deflated.

"What if you sanded it a little?" I suggested.

"Yeah, I gotta do something. It doesn't work good. I'll show you."

He perched the board at the edge of the dune and sat atop it with crossed legs. The board resisted his animated wiggling and attempts to push off with his hands.

I took pity. "Hold on," I said. I shoved the board with my foot, but it barely slid a couple of inches. "Try smoothing out the dune a little."

"Okay," he said, bright-eyed. He leaped up and started to vigorously kick the sand out from around the board.

He leveled the ground and resumed his position atop the board with a look of excited anticipation. I pushed again. Nothing happened.

"Sorry, Willie," I said, brushing some sand off my hands. "I'm too exhausted to be of any help." It was true; I had used the last of my energy on that push. I glanced over at the new arrival to see if "Mission Dune-Surf" had grabbed his attention, but he was oblivious to us.

"Here, take this." Willie pulled a mangled granola bar from his pocket and handed it to me. It felt hot and melted through the wrapper, but I was hungry enough not to care.

"Thanks," I said and took a bite. The chocolate chips were a delicious, gooey mess. I scarfed the bar down in three bites. "That was good. I needed that."

Willie pulled his head erect as I crumpled the chocolaty wrapper and wedged it into the sand.

"I still feel like I'm littering when I do that," I said, covering it with sediment. "Hey. Guess what? We hit the hundred-day mark."

"What's that?"

"I've been counting down the days since we got here. We only have a hundred days left."

"That's a lot."

"At least we crossed the halfway mark." My eyes shifted to the new arrival again. "Statue Man over there seems a little strange, doesn't he? He just sits there."

"I told you he was weird," Willie said. "He asked me for water again."

"Didn't I tell you to stay away from him?" I asked.

Willie dropped his head to avoid eye contact with me. "Yeah, well, he asked me if I had anything for him to eat, too."

"Did you?"

"Yeah, I gave him one of my granola bars and a bottle of water."

I huffed. "He's not your friend, Willie. He's using you. Just stay away from him."

He shoved his hands deep into his pockets and rolled back on his heels. "Yeah, well, he asked about you today, too."

"He did?" I said, shocked. "What did he say? When did you speak to him?"

"Earlier. He wanted to know what you were doing out here."

"What did you tell him?"

"The truth. You're creating a journal about being one of the first humans to spend time on another planet." He started to kick the sand on the side of the dune to even out any lumps.

I was annoyed. "I hope he doesn't steal my idea now."

"He didn't have art stuff with him."

I turned to a clean page in my sketchbook and started to trace a rough outline of the statuesque stranger perched on his distant dune.

"I don't like this, Willie. I really think you should stay away from him. You're wrong about his age, too. No one has heard of a new teenage arrival. Who knows what that guy is up to, sitting in the dune field all day? He could be dangerous."

"He's a teenager, honest," Willie said. "I saw him up close."

"You don't have to lie about it. It's okay. Just stay away from the guy."

Willie catapulted to his feet, pummeling me—yet again—with sand. "I'm not lying, Resa!" he said, all whining, half defensive. "He looks your age or just a little older. He's not a man. Honest. And he asked about you."

I didn't have the strength to argue with him. If I wanted answers, I'd have to go and meet this person for myself.

* * *

The following morning, I hiked into the waste decomposition field and headed to my dune to draw the incinerators along the horizon. The miasma from the factory spires looked particularly interesting today, reminding me of the thick tubeworms that live deep beneath the ocean by thermal vents.

The morning was hotter than usual, and the atmospheric haze was thinner. The heated air above the ground shimmered and rippled in the distance, like spirits writhing above the dark-crimson sand. I had skipped my usual black attire, opting instead for a beige midriff, khaki cargos, my mid-calf combat boots, and a big, floppy cotton sun hat so my hair wouldn't fry.

In the clearer-than-normal air, the dune fields literally twinkled as sunlight reflected off the garnet and mica mineral grains in the sand. If this beautiful display had been back on Earth, it would easily attract as many tourists as a national park. The glittery sparkles reminded me of the crystals dangling from the treetops in my dream. These days, most things reminded me of the dream in some way.

Across the way, the unknown dune dweller was in his mannequin pose, same as always. I didn't like that he was using Willie, and I wanted to see for myself if Willie had told the truth about his age. I also wanted to find out his story and why no one else had heard of him.

I slathered a creamy coconut-scented sunscreen on all my exposed skin, applied a double layer to my face, and went to pay him a visit.

Approaching strangers in the dunes was not a typical occurrence for me, and I had no clue what I would say when I made it to the top of his favorite perch. Since I'm not good at sparking conversation in the best of times, this was way out of my league. Midway up the slope, my left arm started to tingle with anxious excitement.

I reached the peak, and there he was in front of me, in his usual pose, facing west. This time he was only twenty feet away, though, so I could see details.

He had a slim, athletic build and was barefoot. He wore black, loose-fitting linen pants and a matching long-sleeve button-down that fluttered open, exposing a golden set of rippled abs. I liked him already. A "wears black in the summertime" kind of guy. Just my style.

Willie had lied about the hair spikes. This guy's shoulder-length raven locks were pulled back in a sleek ponytail. A small earring dangled from his left ear. It looked like two small twigs secured by a thin rope into a cross-like shape. I wondered if he was Catholic, but then I realized he might not be from Earth. The moist skin above his thick, dark eyebrows glistened in the sunlight. He sat motionless, staring at the horizon, his arms loosely corralling his bent knees.

I immediately wished I could disappear. I hadn't dressed for this—I didn't have on any makeup, not even a swipe of lip gloss. Willie could have mentioned that the guy was gorgeous.

This was horrible. He had to have heard me traipsing up the dune, so I had to do or say something. The longer I stood there, the more awkward this would become.

"Hello," I said, cringing internally at my voice, which came out sounding way too young and cutesy. I approached him but he didn't turn toward me. "Mind if I join you on your dune?"

I accidently kicked some sand on his pant leg as I sat down about a foot to his right. "Sorry," I said, wiping the sand off his leg. I suddenly felt like his Willie. Kicking sand on him. Invading his space. Touching him. Ugh! This was all wrong. Still, I forced myself to smile. "I'm Resa.

THE ENCOUNTER

Resa Stone. Sorry to have invaded your personal space, but I had to see if you really existed. Willie's been talking about you, but he has a reputation for telling stories."

He didn't budge. Flinch. Turn his head. Nothing. He just sat there and allowed the awkward silence to stretch out between us, intensifying with each passing second.

"Oookay, then," I finally said, drawing out the word. "This was fun. I guess I'll be going back to my dune now." I pushed off the ground to help myself stand. But just as I was about to walk away, he finally spoke.

"Welcome to my dune, Resa Stone." He said it slowly, in a hushed voice that was so calm, it was almost hypnotic. He didn't turn his head to look at me.

"Thanks," I replied, and pulled off my ridiculous sun hat to fluff up my hair. "I know how possessive I can be about my own dune, so I wasn't sure how you'd feel about having company." I was trying to be lighthearted to ease the tension, but it wasn't working.

"So. Do I exist?" he said in a sexy perfume-ad type of voice.

The question caught me off guard. "Uh, yes? I believe you do." A huge, awkward smile stretched itself across my face. I didn't know what to make of this guy.

"How do you know?"

What an odd question to ask, I thought. My mind instantly reverted to bio class and I blurted out every characteristic of a living being. "Well, you metabolize, you excrete, you react, you move…" I paused, sensing an opportunity for a joke. "Well, wait. Let me rethink this. Maybe you don't exist, because I actually haven't seen you budge from that exact position."

I waited for a laugh or a smile, but he didn't react at all. Okay. Trying to be cute and funny wasn't working for me.

"Try again without an answer from a textbook," he said. "How do you know we exist?"

"How about, I can see you." It bothered me that he still hadn't looked at me directly.

"You can see things that don't exist." He had a cool, calm confidence that made him seem much older than his looks would suggest. My mind raced for an answer that would prove him wrong, but it didn't come up with anything worth repeating.

"Such as?"

"A hologram."

I gave him a look, not that he was in a position to know. "The last I checked, we're pretty solid." If I popped him in the nose, he'd see just how solid my fist was. I thought about moving in front of him to force him to look at me.

"You're certain of that?" he challenged.

I sat down next to him again, this time being careful not to get sand on him. I extended my index finger and slowly jabbed it into his bicep.

"Uh-huh. Solid," I affirmed.

Extremely solid. He was ripped.

"Solidity is an illusion," he replied, rolling some grains of sands between his fingertips. "You quoted a textbook before. Isn't it true that atoms are mostly empty space? That if the nucleus of an atom were the size of a sand grain, the first electron would be all the way over that dune?"

"Maybe not that far. But yes, atoms are mostly empty." Where was he taking this?

"And do you agree that we are composed of thousands of atoms?" He studied the grains of sand on his fingertips.

I nodded. "More, definitely."

"Then aren't we mostly empty space ourselves?"

I'd never thought of it that way. I stumbled for a reply.

"And if that's true, then our solid bodies are an illusion."

I just sat there processing his words. This was quite possibly the most difficult conversation I had ever had. He was forcing me to think in new ways. "Okay, then. We exist because we can think."

"Do trees think?"

"How do you know they don't?"

A faint smile grazed his lips. I gave a victorious, playful harrumph, which only seemed to make him more determined to prove his point, whatever it was.

THE ENCOUNTER

"Do you think in your dreams?" he asked.

My skin prickled at the mention of dreams. "I most certainly do," I replied.

"Then how do you know that we are not in a dream right now?"

The prickles intensified. "I can't prove that we aren't, I guess."

He leaned back upon his elbows, still gazing into the field. "Are there limits in your dreams, Resa Stone?"

My heart erupted when he said my name, so much so that I missed the question. "I'm sorry, what?"

"In your dreams? Are there limits?" He had said it impatiently.

I thought of the lavender moons and the crystal trees. "No. Anything is possible."

"Exactly." He nodded slowly. "So we are limitless."

The s's slid off his tongue like a snake's hiss, hitting me with unexpected power. His words sent a surge of energy through my body that stole my breath away. It wasn't your typical adrenaline rush. It was unnatural. It was as if a blue-hot electric current had jumped through the air from his body to mine.

I hadn't realized that I had reached for my heart until I felt his warm hand cover mine, a sinfully bold move for him, being that he barely knew me. I glanced up at him and every tense fiber of my being fell limp. He was looking at me now, dead-on, and I could finally see his eyes.

Violet eyes.

Creamy lavender and lilac swirls tinged with a subtle glimmer of gold. The power of his gaze on mine was uncomfortable. Excruciating. Exhilarating. I couldn't look away.

"Why do you come to the dunes?" he said, still holding his hand firmly atop mine.

"I don't know. I'm drawn to them." My words were feather light. My heart pounded so fiercely I feared he might hear it. Feel it through my hand. Feared he might catch on to my complete and inexplicable fascination with him. What was that energy I had felt? Had he felt that same intense rush? "I know it doesn't make sense, especially in such a foreign place," I said. "But when I'm out in nature, I feel as if nothing can harm me."

"Not even me?"

The question was vexing. Dangerous. "No."

I was paralyzed, drowning in the violet sea of his stare, my heart thundering beneath our joined hands. Slowly he stood, taking my hand with his. He lowered his head and gently kissed the back of my wrist. Never had anyone been so forward with me.

Then he looked up at me and winked.

I melted.

He slipped away silently, disappearing into the misty fog that had rolled in from the west unnoticed. The moist, cool shadow of his kiss lingered on my skin.

I couldn't move.

Perhaps I should have said yes.

SPELLBOUND

I was the girl studying to be a witch, but the new arrival was the one who had cast the spell on me. Hours had passed since my encounter with him earlier in the day, and I couldn't stop dwelling on the magical energy that had danced in the air between us. It had been tangible. Undeniable. Just the thought of it sent tingles through my veins. I couldn't explain it, and I couldn't stop thinking about it. I had to know if he had felt it, too. I would visit him again the next day, I decided, only this time I would look presentable, which meant I needed to lose the dark circles under my eyes. Only real sleep would do the trick.

I turned in early, around 8:00 p.m., feeling a bit nervous as I slipped beneath the sheets of my cot. What if Nitika really did come out of my dream this time? It seemed more possible after the conversation the new arrival and I'd had about dreams. Still, I needed sleep, didn't I?

The cot was mildly more comfortable than concrete, and I tossed about for a couple of hours, dozing on and off, willing myself not to dream. The last time I remembered gazing at the clock was at 11:11 p.m.

I awoke two hours later, my T-shirt damp and stuck to my skin.

Something wasn't right.

I was shivering with cold. Almost feverish. White smoke was huffing from my mouth with every breath and my skin was studded with goose bumps. I flipped on the light, which relieved my anxiety a little…until I saw it. I wasn't alone.

Something was in the room with me.

Chills ravaged my body as I imagined Nitika standing at the foot of my cot, a cloak pulled over her body. I launched myself out of my bed and into Dakota's room next door.

"Dakota, get up!" I said, standing at the edge of his cot, my arms folded defensively across my chest. "Dakota, please!" I nudged his lifeless body several times with my foot, but he was a comatose lump. It had always been next to impossible to wake up my brother.

I flipped on the light and nudged him hard. He twitched and tossed for a few seconds before realizing I was there. "What the hell are you doing?" He glanced at his clock through squinted eyes. "It's the middle of the night. Go back to bed."

He shut the light, but I turned it back on. Just having him alert eased my tension somewhat.

"I think Nitika's in my room."

"Like I give a damn about your lesbian lover right now! Go to bed." He threw the covers over his head.

"No, Dakota. She's a ghost, and I really think she's in my room. I need you to come in there with me."

He didn't respond.

"Did you hear me? I think she's haunting me. She comes to me in my dreams and gives me these messages, only I have no idea what she's talking about. I can't sleep. My headaches are out of control." I knew I'd probably regret sharing the truth with him, but I could no longer keep it to myself. "And tonight? Tonight I think she followed me out of my dream and into my room. Are you listening? Say something already."

Silence.

"Dakota?"

He uttered something, but the covers over his head muted the words. I ripped the blankets off him just in time to hear him calling for our mother.

"Keep your voice down. Say anything to her and I'll tell her you smoke pot."

"Wow. You really are insane," he replied as he deflected the pillow that I had hurled at him.

"Give me a break. I've smelled it on you before."

"What? When?" He was sitting up now, better positioning himself should I throw something else at him.

"I'm not doing this with you now, Dakota."

"Then leave," he insisted, motioning toward the door. "I didn't ask you to come in here in the first place."

"Can you just come into my room with me for a minute? I don't want to go in there by myself. It feels like there's a presence hovering over me even in here."

He grimaced. "Well, get it away from me. I don't want your freaking spirits to start haunting me. Keep your voodoo-witch crap in your own room."

"Fine, come with me, then, if you don't want it in your room," I whispered harshly. "And stop talking so loud."

I hadn't expected him to actually follow me to my room, but I was thrilled when he walked through the door ahead of me.

"So? Where is this spirit of yours?"

I followed him in with trepidation and stood still for a moment when I reached the middle of the room. "I don't feel it anymore."

"How convenient." He huffed angrily and marched toward the door. "You are such a freak."

I grasped his arm as he tried to shoot past me. "No. Dakota, come on. Stay in here for a minute." I pulled him back into the room.

"Why? What is wrong with you? There's nothing in here. You seriously need your brain examined."

"Please. I have to try and get rid of her. I just don't want to be in here alone right now." I motioned for him to sit on the bed. Instead, he pulled himself atop my metal dresser, his back against the wall, his knees bent in toward his chest. His stare was burning a crater into the side of my head.

"Your issues have issues...you know that, right? I mean it. You're losing it. No. You've already lost it."

"Whatever," I said, lighting a mini beeswax candle and placing it in a small silver pentacle-shaped holder next to him on my dresser. Then I pulled out a box with my magical trinkets and started to prepare a small altar on the floor. "This won't take long," I said as I spread open a square cloth of purple silk on the floor. It was decorated with a large pentagram—a circle-enclosed five-pointed star. "I can't handle this anymore. I need to get rid of her so I can sleep." I arranged a small tapered candle in each of the four cardinal directions on the mat.

"Get rid of who? There's no one here but us."

"Hand me that water bottle," I ordered, pointing to the half-full bottle next to him on the dresser. He did as asked, and I poured a small amount of liquid into a tiny clay bowl, which I set down in one of the tips of the star. In the remaining tips, I placed a chunky black-and-white agate crystal, an urn filled with spices and herbs, a feather, and a stick of burning incense. "Hold this," I said, handing Dakota my box of supplies.

He slipped off the dresser. "You realize I think you're nuts, right? That I'm only entertaining your psycho witch-babble because I don't want you to blow this whole pot-smoking thing out of proportion? I tried it once."

"Then you tried it one time too many. That stuff is terrible for you. It alters your mind, Dakota." I started lighting the candles.

"You're talking about altered minds? Please. It's not like you don't inhale toxia every day, which is probably a billion times worse. Not to mention, you think ghosts are coming out of your dreams. That's how it happened with Grams, you know. She started hearing voices...first in her dreams, then in everyday life. She went completely catatonic not long after that. You need to get your brain checked out. I'm not trying to be mean. I'm just saying." He fiddled through my box. "Horehound?" he huffed. "What the hell is this stuff?"

"There's nothing wrong with me," I snarled, grabbing the small herb-filled muslin pouch from Dakota's hand. "Stop touching things,"

I said. "It's for protection. Everything in the circle is here for protection. Now back up before you knock something over."

The candles atop my makeshift altar flickered as Dakota retreated from the purple silk cloth square that I had spread out on the floor. "What am I doing here?" Dakota sounded irate as he watched me secure a single white feather tied with natural jute around my neck. It was a necklace that Grams had made for me using an owl's feather she'd found in Acadia National Park back home in Maine. It had an air of magic about it, and wearing it made me feel empowered.

"You don't have to do anything. I just don't want to be alone. You're my witness," I explained, pulling my hair into a ponytail. I twisted my necklace so that the feather lay in the exact center of my chest.

"For what?"

"In case anything goes wrong. There's a waning crescent moon outside."

"And that's supposed to mean something to me?"

"It's a good night for a banishment spell. But I've never done anything this big on my own, and I'm a little tense, okay? I just want someone else in here with me." Dakota took a big step forward, as though he'd spontaneously decided to leave the room...and this whole sorry situation. His baggy black sweats came close to taking down a candle and he jumped back, nearly ruining the altar.

"A banishment spell?" he thundered. "What the hell is that?"

"Please keep your voice down," I ordered in a harsh whisper. "They'll hear you. I learned about it in Meranda's classes. I just never did one before." I flipped through a small leather journal and reread my handwritten notes on setting up an altar. I'd placed the correct candles in the correct points of the pentacle: yellow in the east represented wind, red in the south represented fire, blue in the west represented water, and green in the north represented earth. I had matches. Paper. Pen. I was ready. It was time. I took a deep breath and stroked the feather on my necklace, hoping to awaken its energy and intelligence. Grams believed that animals were spiritual messengers with innate powers. The owl was a symbol of ancient wisdom, intuition, and the supernatural.

I picked up my crystal-tipped tree-branch wand and stood. "Nothing will go wrong so long as you don't set yourself on fire or destroy my altar," I said to Dakota. "Are you up for this, or what? I can't have any negative energy around."

"Well, this has hardly put me in a positive mood. Let's just assume for a minute that you actually are sane, and that everything you've said is true. What happens if something does go wrong? I don't know anything about this stuff. What am I going to tell everyone? Oh, Ma, by the way…some wormhole thing opened up in Resa's room and an evil caped dude with a sickle transported her to the underworld. Yeah, that'll go over well. They'll think I killed you."

"Will you knock it off? I'm not getting sucked in anywhere. Stop it. You're stressing me out. I need calm, focused energy to do this successfully."

"You're not the one who's going to end up with a murder rap." He shook his head. "You know what? I'm out of here. This is your deal, not mine. I'm out of here." He made another lunge for the door.

"Fine. Leave," I said. "Thanks for nothing."

I found it interesting that he continued to complain without leaving. He just kind of stood there by the door. Whatever his reasons for staying, I didn't care. I felt safer having him around, even though I knew it was a false sense of security.

"You don't have to do anything," I said. "Just hold this." I gave him a piece of jet. "Sit in the corner and don't make a sound. And whatever you do, don't break my protective bubble."

"What the hell is that?"

"Is it possible for you not to curse in every sentence? It's an energy field that I'm going to build with my mind."

Dakota settled into the corner behind me like I'd asked, but he had frustrated me so much that I was in no frame of mind to start the spell. I popped a meditation music CD into the portable radio on my dresser and took a deep breath, letting the sounds of the Tibetan singing bowl put me at ease. I turned to face the altar.

"Now don't say anything," I said, my eyes closed. "I'm going to talk out loud, but you can't make fun of me or do anything distracting."

Dakota didn't respond. I turned to look at him, and he made the bulging-eyed "why are you looking at me, you just told me not to talk" face.

"Don't get up or leave the corner, either," I demanded. "And whatever you do, don't move the purple fabric on the floor. If you get too close and break the circle, you may let loose every demon, fairy, and God knows what else."

His expression was priceless.

My Wiccan mentor back on Earth had always taught me that before any ritual, a witch should summon some external power for protection and assistance. Meranda preferred to work with goddesses; Sarah, fairies. I always chose nature. For me, there was nothing more powerful than Earth, Wind, Fire, and Water. Being that the atmosphere on Wandelsta was such a dynamic presence, I decided the power of the wind would be the primary force to help me with this ritual.

I clutched my wand with both hands and held it up at a forty-five-degree angle in front of me. Facing north, I started to walk very slowly clockwise. As I walked, I imagined a protective shield of purple light forming a dome over me. I stopped in the east and focused my stare on the burning yellow candle.

"I invite the power of the wind to join me on this night and protect me through this rite." The elemental spirits of air are called Sylphs, fairy-like creatures that dance in the air, and I tried to feel their magical presence. After a few minutes of quiet contemplation, I finally felt a light tingle on my neck. A chill ran the length of my spine. They had arrived.

"Hail and welcome."

I continued to pace the circle and stopped in the south, focusing my eyes on the burning red candle.

"I invite the power of fire to join me on this night and protect me through this rite." I envisioned Salamander flames flicking in the firelight. Again, it took minutes of quiet meditation before a warm flutter on my cheek made me gasp. The spirits of fire were in the circle.

"Hail and welcome."

I walked on and stopped in the west. "I invite the power of water to join me on this night and protect me through this rite." I envisioned the tiny mermaid-like Undines undulating through crystal-blue, serene water. A cool, rippling chill tumbled down my spine almost instantly. "Hail and welcome."

I completed the circle by stopping in the north. "I invite the power of the Earth to join me on this night and protect me through this rite." I envisioned small gnomes swinging merrily through the twisted root system of a grand oak tree. My toes started to tingle.

"Hail and welcome."

All the elementals were in the room.

I pushed the wand higher in the air as I turned to face the altar. "I evoke Zephyrus, God of Gentle Wind to protect me on this night and help me with this rite. Hail and welcome. Carry away all negative dreams so that my sleep may be restful and good."

Suddenly a cool breeze swept over the altar, causing the candle flames to flicker. Goose bumps raced across my skin. I slowly twisted my head to see if Dakota had witnessed the breeze. I didn't need to ask. His mouth was frozen into an 'O.'

With trembling hands, I lowered the wand and placed it on the altar as I sat cross-legged, facing north. I picked up a small piece of paper, upon which I wrote, "Negative Dreams." I held the paper with both hands above the altar and chanted:

O powerful winds of the Wandelstan air,
Hear my words. Answer my prayers.
Breathe over me a breath so warm,
Guard my dreams, protect me from harm.
Blow away my bad dreams so deep,
So that I may have a restful sleep.

I lit a match and held it to the corner of the paper, watching as the words Negative Dreams curled and blackened before bursting into a single, yellow-orange flame. When the heat grew too strong,

I placed the burning paper in the small black cauldron on the altar and meditated while watching the rising smoke. I visualized Nitika drifting away within the swirling dusty ribbons, until there was nothing left but a mound of powdery gray ash.

It was over. I had sent Nitika away.

And I felt as light and airy as the wind itself.

I stood and deconstructed the imaginary circle in my mind, stopping again before each direction, this time thanking the elementals and bidding each a "hail and farewell."

"Zephyrus. God of Gentle Wind," I said. "Hail and farewell."

A cold burst of wind rushed across the altar, snuffing out each of the candles. Every nerve in my body fired simultaneously. I felt electrified. I sat silent in the dark, overcome by an extraordinary sense of empowerment and self-confidence. For the first time, I felt in control of my life, my destiny.

"Dakota?" I said quietly. My voice sounded funny to me. Dakota didn't respond. "Dakota, are you okay?" My eyes hadn't adjusted to the dark. "Are you okay?" I asked again as I jumped up and turned on the light. I was relieved to see that he was still sitting in the corner.

"What the hell was that?" he said. His features were twisted with some emotion. Fear, maybe? "Did you see that wind?"

"I did."

"Did you see the wind?" he repeated, as if I hadn't answered him the first time. "The wind that nearly blew out the candles when you invited the God of Wind into the circle? Are you kidding me? And it blew out the candles when you bid it farewell? Are you kidding me? Are you freaking kidding me?"

He kept asking derivations of the same question as I led him into the kitchen, where I opened us up a bag of popcorn and jazzed it up with a sprinkle of cinnamon, cumin, and chili powder from Mom's stash of spices she'd brought from home. Wind food was light and airy, so popcorn was the perfect choice.

I made us eat on the floor to better connect with the Earth's energy, and Dakota couldn't plop himself down fast enough. Eating, or the "sharing of cakes," as my Wiccan mentor calls it, was the ritualistic closing of any spell, and we both sat there reliving what had happened with the wind like giddy schoolchildren, mindlessly munching away on our snack until the sun came up.

Suddenly my brother, who had always treated my interest in Wicca like it might be a slightly contagious disease, wanted to know everything that I knew. Everything about the dream. Everything I'd learned from Meranda. I probably could have turned him into a little witch if I'd chosen to press the issue.

I had never felt closer to my brother.

THE GIFT

I've always been a believer in things. Superstitions. Wishes made on birthday candles and blown dandelion seeds. A magical man traveling the world in a sleigh, showering everyone with gifts on a single winter's night.

When I was a child, I used to wander around the edges of the woods near our home in Maine, searching in the tree hollows for the colorful sparkle of fairies. No idea had ever been too crazy for me. And now, on this new planet, the idea of energy crossing the bridge from dream into reality didn't seem very far-fetched either. I was positive that someone or something had come out of my dream. And I was equally positive that I had banished whatever it was with my ritual. There was no denying the wind that had swept through my room. Not even my brother could pretend it hadn't happened.

I felt like a flower that had bloomed with vibrant new petals. I had conjured the God of Wind on my first solo ritual attempt. Grams would have been so proud. She was the one who had first introduced me to the Craft. I was only nine when I accidentally stumbled upon the back room in her house that was filled with candles, trinkets, gems, and funny-smelling air. I knew there was something special about that room from the way Grandpa whisked me away and locked it to prevent me from going back inside.

Grams and I often took walks into town, and one of our regular stops was Meranda's store. "For the room?" I would ask her on these visits, and she would nod as she placed beautiful crystals and pouches of earthy-looking materials on the counter. She and Meranda would have whispered conversations that made no sense to me at the time, but it always seemed as though they were planning something. I could tell they were good friends.

I asked Grams endless questions about the room, and she told me fanciful stories about how anything was possible in that part of the house if only you believed in it. She promised to explain everything when I was older, but she got sick before then and took her secrets with her to Windamere Hospital.

Years later, when I was sixteen, Sarah and I were walking through town one day when we saw a sign for a spell-writing class in the bay window of Meranda's shop. You had to be eighteen to register, but Meranda made an exception for us on account of Grams. "Your grandmother and I had hoped you'd take an interest in Wicca," Meranda told me privately during the first class. "We wanted you to learn the way of the Craft. We knew you had a gift."

I hadn't understood her comment at the time, but spellwork fascinated me, and I loved the idea that witches played an active role in what happened in their lives. A spell was a prayer said with intent, and earthy objects like wood and stones held the energy to give life to your most far-fetched wishes. Meranda couldn't help but shower me with these magical trinkets to aid my progress. It was empowering. It was energizing.

And last night I finally tapped into that power.

I felt worthy of the title of Witch.

* * *

Later in the afternoon, I walked to my dune, enjoying how effervescent I felt, as if my feet weren't touching the ground. My mind was filled with the confidence that I could do anything. That I was powerful. That I was higher than this world.

To my great disappointment, the new arrival wasn't on his dune when I arrived. I waited an hour and worked on my sketches, but he never showed. Perhaps it was for the best. My eyes were still droopy, and I was incredibly tired from having stayed up talking with Dakota all night. I packed up and headed home for bed. Tomorrow I would arrive earlier so I wouldn't miss him.

* * *

I awoke the following morning after a good night of sleep feeling rested and peaceful and buoyant. I hadn't experienced one single flash of a jeweled forest, a shrouded girl, or a strange message. The spell had worked. Nitika was actually gone.

Only someone else had taken her place.

He had been in my dreams.

I bounced out of bed, humming a remake of an old tune, "Walking on Sunshine," as I slipped into my favorite black T-shirt and yoga pants. I ate a light breakfast of dried apple pieces with natural peanut butter, all the while daydreaming about my encounter with the new arrival. I couldn't stop thinking of that wink and that kiss.

That kiss…

I still felt his lips' moist, warm imprint on my hand.

After eating, I returned to my room, intent on achieving the impossible—making my hair look decent. Given the water restrictions, my only option was to camouflage it. I wrapped a sheer silver scarf around my head, tying it at the nape of my neck so that the ends hung down my back. I applied eyeliner and shimmery lip gloss, keeping my makeup light because I didn't want him to think I was trying to impress him.

Even though that's exactly what I was trying to do.

I gave the mirror a final glance and smiled at my reflection, impressed by the cool retro-rocker-hippie vibe that I'd achieved.

The hike through the fields seemed effortless today. My whole body hummed with nervous energy. No guy had ever shaken me up like this before. I hadn't even asked for his name. I hadn't asked him anything, I had been so caught up in that voice, those questions, those…eyes.

To my great disappointment, he wasn't on his dune. I waited with my sketchbook open in my lap, but I couldn't summon the energy to sketch even one line.

My heart grew heavy as the hours passed with no sign of him. When the afternoon fog rolled in, I headed back to the bunker, trying to rationalize why he hadn't shown up, why he would be there tomorrow.

But the same scene replayed itself the next day.

And the next.

And the next.

Four days passed with no sign of him and I started to worry that he'd met with an accident; perhaps he'd stayed out too long in the toxia. I questioned my parents about his identity, but they hadn't heard anything about a new arrival. But then I saw Willie, who claimed to have recently seen—and fed—the new arrival. That was when I started to question whether the connection between us, that strange electric energy, might have been one-sided. I felt foolish. I had been lying in wait for days to see a nameless guy who apparently wanted nothing to do with me.

Still, I kept going back to the field. And, despite myself, I kept looking for him. The whole thing made me angry with myself, but I couldn't help it.

After more time had passed without any sightings of the mysterious guy in black, I stayed inside and away from the dunes for a while, which wasn't so bad since Nitika was no longer keeping me up at night and Dakota was no longer tormenting me.

Still…I couldn't shake him off me.

THE PLOOMPIE

Strangely, I awoke on day ninety-one with a slight migraine, something I hadn't experienced since ridding myself of Nitika. I didn't want to admit it, but perhaps my mother was right about the air here taking a toll on me. Even so, I needed to finish my journal, which had taken a back seat since the new arrival moved to Wandelsta. The only illustration I hadn't yet attempted to draw was the waste-management facility, which was too far a walk for me, feeling the way that I did.

Dad had already left for work by the time I awoke, so I asked the field supervisor, Fred Cooper, for a lift to the facility in his Sand Rover. With its rectangular sea-green body, white roll bars, and deep-rutted tangerine tires, the thing looked like a kid's toy from back home—an intentional design choice made by the Slopee engineers, who wanted us to feel at home. Fred quickly agreed because he loved to gab and never passed up the opportunity for a captive audience.

The building was on the opposite side of the dune field where I had been keeping my vigil for the new arrival. I couldn't decide if that was a good or bad thing. I desperately wanted to see him again, but I was embarrassed by the idea that he might be purposefully avoiding me.

"Thanks for the lift, Coop," I said, waving to the rotund little bald man, who was wearing a neon-yellow, airtight body suit with the words MICROBIAL UNIT written in big, orange block letters across the chest.

"There's a bacterial dump scheduled for 'bout a half hour or so," Fred said, pointing to three other yellow-clad men who were unloading vacuum-sealed canisters from a large white truck in the distance. "You'll want to stay away from the east section; that's where we'll be letting out the critters to help decompose the trash in that sector. Don't want you to get infected. I'll be back for you by lunchtime." He hesitated and looked at me quizzically. "You're looking a little pale, kiddo. You sure you're up for drawing today?"

"Migraine hangover," I said. "I'm a little weak, but I'll be fine. I feel better out here than in that bunker. And you saved me a good hour of walking by giving me a ride."

"Hangover?" His face twisted like a pretzel and he pounded both palms against the steering wheel. "Well, blow me over like a feather. Which ship brought in alcohol? You're too young to be drinking, missy. Your mother will have your head. And mine, too!"

I laughed at the absurdity of the thought. "No, Coop. It's not what you think."

"You'll never see the light of day out of that tin can when she gets ahold of you. And your father's going to blow his lid when he finds out." He let out a low whistle and gestured for me to get back aboard the Rover.

"Coop, I said I had a migraine hangover. Not an alcohol hangover. I just feel weak. I always get this way after a bad headache."

"A migraine hangover?" There was a look on his face like he was trying to solve a complicated algebra problem. "I don't know what it is with you kids nowadays. Migraine hangover. Never heard of such a thing."

He was a nice guy, but he was draining what little energy I had left, so it was time to go. "Thanks again for the ride, Coop," I said with a tight smile, grabbing my backpack off the front seat. Then I waved and headed for Sump Field, hoping he'd take the hint.

He didn't try to stop me. He just nodded and rolled up his window before driving toward the group of yellow-clothed men.

I walked a quarter of a mile toward Sump Field—the landing base for incoming waste shuttles from other planets. It was the facility Dad was supervising while we were stationed on Wandelsta. I stopped a good fifty feet from the loading dock, far away enough that I wouldn't get in anyone's way yet close enough to get enough detail for my drawings.

I glanced back to make sure Coop couldn't see me and then stepped out of the large, bulky gray protection suit that he'd forced me to wear as a prerequisite for getting a ride. He was busy working with the other guys, who had erected a temporary fence of chicken wire to cordon off the section of land that would be treated with the bacteria. I sketched them for about half an hour until the dim headlights of an incoming space shuttle caught my eye.

I closed my book and pulled a pair of binoculars from my backpack, watching the workers inside the glass-enclosed air tower prepare for the landing. My father emerged from the tower and waited for touchdown on the tarmac. As the silver vessel neared the ground, I noticed that the word GLUCOSA was written in maroon script on the side. My modulator contact lens had done a decent job translating the actual name of the planet into something that would make sense to humans. Just last week I'd learned about the history of the small planet, which was at the edge of the Alpha Centauri star system, and it was indeed a sugar-based planet. It reminded me of real-life Candy Land.

"It's not made of lollipops or licorice," Professor Mangleton had told me dreamily, "but in some places the ground consists of a transparent, gelatinous substance that gives you the feeling of walking on gumdrops. The gel melts on warm days, forming syrupy lakes of caramel. Surrounding the lakes are forests of sugar-crystal structures that resemble towering rock-candy trees. A favorite Glucosan treat is a sugar cube freshly snapped from one of the branches."

I suddenly had an urge for salty-sweet peanut brittle. My stomach rumbled hungrily as the shuttle finished docking, and the side panel slowly lifted open. A retractable metal ladder descended, and down climbed an

THE PLOOMPIE

older male Ploompie that looked surprisingly like a person compared to the other aliens I'd seen. It had two arms, two legs, and humanlike facial features. It was four feet tall, pale in color, and hairless.

"Whoa," I whispered out loud. The Ploompie seemed more like an actor in costume than a real living creature. And the translated species name didn't make sense. I suspect the modulator had meant to call them the "Plumpies."

The creature was quite rotund. Shouldn't the beings on a sugar planet have evolved digestive systems that could easily metabolize carbs? Apparently not. It glistened as it moved, and I had the impression that thousands of sugar crystals were clinging to its skin.

The creature extended a hand to my father and they shook for an awfully long time. Was that Ploompie etiquette? Uncomfortably drawn-out handshakes? Then I burst into laughter when I realized what was happening. The Ploompie's hand was so sticky that my father couldn't break away!

I watched their interaction for some time and made a few sketches of the scene. My father's cool composure with the alien impressed me. I was proud that he was one of Earth's representatives in this new world order. Like I'd told Dakota, it spoke well of the Yrdians that they'd chosen to work with Dad.

I missed him. He was away too much now. But I understood why.

A loud gurgle in the pit of my stomach reminded me that I had to meet Coop around lunchtime if I wanted a ride home. I suited up, found him, and hopped into the Sand Rover. I bopped and jerked in place as the machine began to tread over the dunes.

"So those headaches of yours have been bad lately, missy? Your mom says you've been getting them here a lot lately."

I gave Coop a look, wondering if he'd called her about the hangover.

"Aw, she's just worried about you. Says you've been in the toxia without protection too much. It's well documented that overexposure to toxia can cause headaches, you know."

I grabbed the handrail as Coop ripped the Rover to the right to miss a buried object. "I haven't been sleeping. That's what's causing my headaches."

"Lack of sleep. Also a well-documented sign of toxia overexposure."

I smiled. He was trying to be helpful, but he didn't have all of the facts. He didn't know about the dream.

The dream.

It hadn't fully dawned on me what life would be like without it. Would I ever again hear Nitika's ghostly message about my being the one? The thought of not having her in my life anymore felt strange.

Had I done the right thing? That message had become such a big part of my existence. With Nitika gone, I might never learn its significance.

That's assuming there was any significance.

I had been trying to figure out what the dream meant for the past two years, but today my mind was like a blank slate. I hoped that sending Nitika away had been the right decision.

"Hello? Where'd you just drift off to?" Coop said. "Did you fall asleep?"

"Sorry. No." I wondered how long I'd zoned out on him.

"I think your mom might be right, you know. The toxia could be wreaking havoc on your system. You seem a bit out of it."

"We won't be here too much longer, Coop," I said, forcing myself to sound chipper. "Ninety-one more days."

"Toxia can do a lot of damage in that time," he said. "You need to be smarter, you hear? Now go get some sleep and try to stay indoors."

Coop dropped me off at the bunker and I decided to take his advice. I had to forget about the new arrival. Maybe, I thought, I should just hunker down and get through the rest of my time here without looking for any trouble.

Because one thing was for sure: whoever the new arrival was, he was trouble.

THE WOLF

Over the next week, I perfected my pictures of the waste-management facility and sketched a final drawing of my favorite dune field beneath the dynamic Wandelstan sky. Willie left me alone for the most part, not because he was thoughtful about my need to complete my journal, but because his surfboard required really steep slopes to overcome the friction, and I made certain to plop myself on the shortest and stubbiest dunes.

By day eighty-three, I'd finished my last sketch and I couldn't help but admire the realism of my illustrations. Dakota especially liked my rendition of the bunker complex, the way I'd portrayed the tall wire fence and crooked, pole-mounted toxia sensors that encircled the metal homes, giving a prison-yard feel to our living quarters. My mother said she liked the images of the dune fields best. She couldn't wait to show it to the publishing house when we returned home, and I couldn't wait to see the journal professionally bound and standing on bookstore shelves.

Unfortunately, the days seemed to drag on endlessly now that I didn't have a task to do, and the new arrival returned to my thoughts with a vengeance. I still wanted to talk to him, but I couldn't bring myself to look for him if there was a chance that he might not want to see me. I thought about sending a note through Willie, but it seemed a juvenile and desperate attempt. I had to stop thinking about him.

I had to let it go.

* * *

Things changed on day seventy-six when my mom received a call from Dad at the base and immediately called Dakota and me into the kitchen after talking with him. The tension in her face accentuated the small lines around her eyes, which immediately told me that something was wrong.

"The Ploompies are under attack," she said darkly. "The Siafu have invaded."

I didn't know how to respond. The Ploompies still didn't seem real to me—even after seeing my dad greet the visitor a couple of weeks ago—so I had no emotional reaction to her news.

"That's terrible," I finally said. "Professor Mangleton told me about the tension between the two cultures. He said that the insectoid Siafu have threatened to overtake Glucosa for years because they want to control the planet's sugar resources. He told me it was only a matter of time before they invaded. How bad is it?"

"The Ploompies are docile pacifists," my mother said solemnly. "They have no army. It's not good."

"And from what I've heard, when the Siafu attack, they come in droves and keep coming until they've decimated the landscape, taking every last resource for themselves." I thought of the beautiful candy world melting under the toxic venom of the Siafu.

"Those bugs need to get their as—"

My mother raised her hand to stop Dakota. "That's what the IPPL is for," she said. "They won't allow the Siafu to occupy Glucosa. Too many planets rely on their sugar resources. The IPPL is organizing an army as we speak. Your father's been asked to leave tomorrow for the Capital on planet Oganwando. They want him at the IPPL headquarters to observe the planning of the defensive. They want to train him for a higher role in the organization, it seems."

Her words didn't fully register.

"Dad's being sent to another planet?" Dakota clarified. The phone rang and my mother reached for it. He looked at me with hopeful eyes. "Well, we're not staying here if he leaves. No way. We better not be staying here."

"That's right," my mother confirmed before answering the phone. "You can start packing. We're going home."

My heart dropped. I listened as she spoke in what seemed to be slow motion about dates and shuttle numbers. Dakota let out a howl and fist-pumped the air.

"We're outta here!" he cried, slamming into me with his shoulder in some sort of full-body high-five. "Goodbye Wandelstinka! Kiss this dump goodbye!"

My mother hushed him. "I can't hear, Dakota. Keep it down." He continued to hoot and holler even after she resumed her conversation.

I just stood there, blindsided. There was only one thought in my mind: the new arrival.

Mom hung up the phone, seemingly unaware that I'd been giving her a zombie-eyed stare-down for the last two minutes. "When are we leaving?" I asked, feeling panicked. Desperate.

"Your father's flight will be here tomorrow. A craft is on its way from planet Yrd to return us to Earth. It should be here by Friday."

That was less than a week away.

"I gotta go."

"Where?" My mother's voice was stern. "You shouldn't be outside, Resa. Not now. It's too late in the day. You need to pack."

"I need to finish my journal." I grabbed my backpack and bolted to the dunes. No one even commented on the fact that I had already finished.

* * *

I was too late. By the time I had reached my dune I saw him in the distance, a black, shadowy figure getting smaller as he headed deeper into the heart of the waste decomposition field, in the opposite direction from the bunker complex. It didn't make sense, given the fact that the fog was already starting to gather. It seemed like a suicide mission. My heart dropped to my toes. Was that his intent? Was that why he had been escaping to the dunes…to plan his own death?

"Wait!" I called out, horrified by the thought. He walked on, unaffected by my voice. Was he too far to hear me, or was he just ignoring me? If my suicide hunch was correct, I had to try and help him.

A light foggy mist slithered across the dunes, stealing him from my sight. Against my better judgment, I ran into the fog, tracing his footsteps. The tightly packed sand in this part of the dune field made it easier to navigate, so I abandoned my poking stick to make better time, assuming that if I stayed in his tracks, I'd be safe from buried debris.

My skin tingled as I followed the endless, straight path of footprints through the thickening fog. The trail had taken me beyond the border of the alert system, farther than I had ever been in these fields. With each step away from safety, my heart pounded faster and my pace quickened. My behavior was completely illogical. I was risking my life with no guarantee that I would reach the stranger in time to save him. Still, I couldn't stop. I had to try.

The alert system sounded behind me in the distance, warning me to take shelter. I prayed that the signal would force him back in my direction.

Suddenly something to the right of the trail of footprints caught my eye. A soft amber glow through the white mist. There were no lights this deep in the dune field, so the sight startled me. What could it be? With time dwindling away and no sign of him, I ignored the strange sight and forged ahead.

Only the light wouldn't let me.

It got brighter and something drew me to it—a strange, magnetic force that I couldn't resist. Without intending to, I veered off the path of footprints and headed for the light.

My skin ignited like fire in the desert brush as I approached the strange amber glow. A surge of prickly pins and needles sizzled through my entire body, from head to toe. Something wasn't right. The dune field began to spin. I fell to my knees in a panic. My throat was closing! I gasped for air and tried to yell for help, but no sound emerged. What was that light doing to my body? Was it radioactive? Were gamma rays coursing through my DNA, slowly killing me from the inside out?

And then something pulled me forward.

It was as if an invisible hand was dragging me to the light.

"Fulfill your destiny. You are the one."

"Nitika?" I was certain that it was her voice even though it was barely audible.

"Fulfill your destiny. Retrieve it."

I couldn't breathe. I would soon die from asphyxiation. I had about eight minutes before brain damage would set in. At any moment now I would fall asleep. Maybe Nitika was an angel, waiting to help me cross over into the next life.

"Retrieve your destiny."

Her image flickered in the air above me, and then a glaring white light panned across my face. After it passed, I couldn't see anything but haze. Sand clawed my body as that nameless force continued to drag me toward the intensifying amber light. I shuffled my hands forward blindly, desperate to find the source of the light, and then I finally felt it. It was cool and small enough to hold in one palm. I rubbed my fingers across the surface of the object, marveling at how smooth and silky it was.

A white light flashed again, followed by a heavy crack of thunder. Cold rain hit my face, accompanied by a second flash. The precipitation intensified, the stinging, icy bullets pelting me from above.

And then…I was knocked backward by a majestic black wolf with searing lavender eyes. I felt its warm breath against my neck and heard its growl in my ear. Suddenly it said my name. What! I knew I had to be hallucinating. And then I realized it wasn't a wolf at all.

It was him. Straddling me, crouching over me on all fours, his face inches from mine, paralyzing me with those…those eyes. Piercing. Powerful. Glowing a subtle violet that was visible even in the chaos of the storm.

"Don't resist," he growled. "Surrender to me." His words engulfed me as the rain came down in torrents, making everything around me a watery blur. Water streamed down my face and neck and flowed under my shirt, chilling every nerve ending.

I felt his warm lips touch mine and my chest inflated, filling with his sweet breath. I expanded in an instant, growing lighter, as weightless as a kite. Someone had let go of the string and I was drifting away, climbing higher. Frictionless. Easy. Was I dying? Was I on my way to Heaven?

"Resa, can you hear me?"

I gasped for air as my body plummeted back to land. My eyes jerked open.

Coop was lifting me into a Sand Rover, and the next thing I knew, he was slipping an oxygen mask over my face.

"I have a toxia overexposure out here," I heard him say into a walkie-talkie.

Then everything went black.

THE FIND

"Resa? Can you hear me?"

I squinted in the bright-white light. A hand was stroking my head, and something hard was digging into the side of my face. This was a migraine hangover on ten.

"She's back," a male voice announced.

There was a flurry of footsteps, and then my mother's face came into focus. I could tell she'd been crying. Dakota was there, too, looking even more somber than usual. A handful of white-coated people scurried about the room.

I was in the medical bunker. And it felt like Mount Everest was resting on my chest.

I struggled to sit up and remove the hard plastic oxygen mask from my face, which is when I realized I was wearing a light-blue, barely-there gown with matching socks. Where were my clothes? More importantly, who had undressed me?

"No, no, no, no," said a young nurse. She placed the mask correctly on my face. "Wear it a few minutes longer, until you're fully back."

"Resa, it's Doctor Snow," said a middle-aged, sandy-haired man sitting on a stool to my left. He grabbed my wrist and took my pulse.

"Resa, is the purple-eyed wolf still in the room? Resa, can you hear me?" I could hear him, but I didn't have the strength to speak.

"Resa, can you nod or shake your head to let me know if the purple-eyed wolf is still in the room?"

I was confused.

"Resa, you told us before that there was a purple-eyed wolf in the room. Do you still see him?"

I shook my head no.

The doctor turned to the nurse. "The Provolax is working. The hallucinations have stopped."

Hallucinations?

The doctor looked at my mother hopefully. "She's coming out of it. When she's ready, she can remove the mask." Then he looked at me and patted my hand. "You're a lucky girl. You had someone looking over you out there in the wasteland."

The medical staff left, leaving me alone with Dakota and my mother and…Coop? Coop. Suddenly it all came back to me. I had spent too long in the toxia and hallucinated that the new arrival was a violet-eyed wolf.

I yanked the mask off my face and winced as the rubber straps pinched my ears.

"Careful there," Coop said, helping me take it off.

"Did you rescue a guy out there with me, Coop?" My lip split and I tasted metallic blood.

"Here, honey," my mother said urgently. She held out a small tube of pale-yellow cream. The waxy balm smelled like cherries, but it had a medicinal aftertaste.

Coop pulled his chair closer to me. I'd never seen him out of his protective suit, and he looked completely different in jeans and a T-shirt. "No. It was just you out there," he said. "We checked the footprints like you said, but we only saw yours and mine. You must have been having some real bad toxia hallucinations." The round-faced man smiled and patted my hand.

I didn't remember telling him about the footprints. "Are you sure,

Coop? I saw someone out there. I'm positive of it." I tried hard not to move my mouth too much when I spoke. My throat felt like it was lined with sandpaper.

"I patrolled the whole area. Twice. Nope. It was just you and me out there. Well, I'll let you get some rest now." He stood and pulled his chair to the side of the room, out of the path of the young male nurse who had just entered the room to check my IV. "All that matters is you're okay."

"Thank you, Coop," my mother said, embracing him.

"If you hadn't let me know she was out there…" He shook his head, then left. The male nurse followed him out shortly thereafter.

My family looked like a wreck. "Do you want some hot tea with honey for your throat?" my mother asked, pushing a strand of hair off my cheek.

I didn't want a drink, but I nodded anyway so Dakota and I could have a moment alone. She left to get the tea and my eyes shifted to my brother, who was sitting in the corner staring blankly.

"Are you okay?" I asked. My voice was hoarse and it hurt to speak. Dakota nodded and smiled but said nothing. "Nitika is still here."

His smile faded.

"I heard her out there. Maybe that's a good thing. The banishment spell was for negative thoughts and energies. Maybe she's actually a good spirit. Maybe I just didn't word the spell right."

Dakota looked at me strangely. "Or maybe she doesn't exist, Rees."

He had said it gently, but the words stung like ice.

"What are you saying?"

"I'm saying, what if she was a toxia illusion all along?"

My head went into a tailspin. Never. It was too real. The dream was real. Nitika was real. He was real.

"Come on, Rees. You went out into the toxia just about every day without protection. You must have inhaled liters of the stuff. Think about all those headaches. You just claimed to have been attacked in the dune field by a wolf with glowing violet eyes. Toxia does warped things to your mind."

"Oh, and I guess the cold wind I conjured in my warm, windowless room was just my imagination, too? You were there. You felt it. You're telling me that was a toxia illusion? Give me a break already."

Dakota exhaled deeply. "I know. I know I did," he said, shaking his head. "I mean, I think I did. I don't know anything anymore. I mean…Rees. You almost died out there. I'm just trying to make sense of everything."

This was not happening. I waved my index finger at him. "Please don't pull this on me now. My world is too upside down for you not to make sense to me, either. Your Mr. Caring act is freaking me out. You know what you felt in that room. Yes—we're dealing with something inexplicable here. But it's real."

He looked at me, clearly unsure of how to respond.

"I mean it. Drop the suspicious, over-caring brother act. I need your help with this stuff. Not your skepticism. You felt the wind."

"Rees…" His voice was still too serious.

"I mean it, Dakota. Do you want me to go insane for real? Trust me. Nitika visited me in those fields, and I need to figure out what she wants. I need your help, please. At least admit that you felt the wind."

After a very long pause, he dropped his head. "I felt the wind."

I exhaled heavily. "Thank you, and I can prove that I'm not making this up. There's someone who can corroborate my story. I need you to ask Willie to find out what bunker the new arrival lives in. Willie will know what I'm talking about. Get his name, too."

"Who's the new arrival?"

I shook my head, not wanting to explain the whole thing. For simplicity's sake, I said, "It's the wolf. Trust me. Just get Willie to help you."

"The purple-eyed wolf is your witness?" Dakota snickered. "Really, Rees. You're not helping your own sanity plea here."

"Come on, Dakota," I said in a whiny voice that annoyed even me.

"Okay," he said, backing away from me with palms facing outward. "I'm off to find your wolf. Who's crazy now? I'm off to find a purple-eyed wolf."

"He's not really a wolf, Dakota. I freely admit that part was a hallucination. It's a guy. Just go find him for me, okay?"

Dakota left to look for Willie, giving me a few moments alone with my thoughts. He was worried about me. My brother never worried about anyone but himself, so that fact alone was alarming.

I fell backwards onto my pillow, completely exasperated. The stark white medic walls started to close in all around me. Was everyone right? Was my mind just playing tricks on me? I had to accept the possibility. Hallucinations were a documented side effect of prolonged exposure to toxia.

But it had all felt so real…

The sight of my backpack leaning awkwardly against the wall in the corner of the room filled me with unexpected joy. It was good to see something so familiar, ordinary, and comforting in this cold room. I had the sudden urge to look at all of my pictures. I wanted to see the details in the drawings. Details that couldn't possibly have come just from my imagination.

I managed to drag myself off the cot to get it, though it felt like I was using every muscle in my body. And it took twice as much effort to pull it back up into the bed with me.

My arm tingled as I unzipped the bag, and I noticed several small burn marks on my hand from the caustic toxia. To my horror, the unsightly red patches weren't just on my hands. They ran the entire length of my arms up to my shoulders. I had forgotten about the paper-thin tank top I'd been wearing when I was caught outside. I would have to be vigilant in applying the burn ointment or they would scar. Then again, one scar might be cool. I'd always have a story to tell.

I already had a story to tell.

When I pulled out my sketchbook, I noticed a light emanating from the bottom of the bag.

I froze.

There, in the corner of the bag, lay a smooth, oblong crystal, radiating a pale amber glow. It was the object that had called to me out in the fields.

And it did indeed exist.

THE MOLE HOLE

It was a gem. A jewel of sorts. A translucent, pale-amber crystal about two inches at its widest with pointed ends. It reminded me of a quartz crystal but with the unusual property of luminescence. The thing constantly glowed.

Over the next twenty-four hours, I had to keep the gem hidden as the doctors continued to monitor my progress. They put me on some kind of sleep medication and I always worried that the gem would be gone when I came to, despite my feeble attempt to conceal it in a massive wad of tissue that I wedged deep into an interior pocket of my backpack. Mom was almost always by the side of my bed, so I didn't dare look at the glowing gem for fear she'd take it, thinking it was dangerous or radioactive.

Surprisingly, Dakota hadn't once visited me, which I found odd given his newfound concern for my health. Had he found the new arrival? Or was he avoiding me because he thought I was nuts? I was dying to show him the stone, not only because it seemed to defy every law of nature, but because it was proof that something had happened to me in the fields. I desperately wanted my brother to believe that Nitika was real and that all my mental capabilities were intact. I'm not sure why it was so important, but it was.

I was released after forty-eight hours with the typical residual signs of toxia overexposure: body aches and raw, itchy red sores on my arms and neck. A positive side effect was the rasp in my hoarse voice. I prayed that the new arrival had survived the toxia. I had so much to ask him, so much to tell. More than ever, I needed to know that he was really out there in the fields.

Coop gave Mom and me a lift back to the bunker. When we got there, Dakota was in his room packing boxes. His hair spikes were doused in yellow paint to match the tight, long-sleeved shirt he was wearing over his checked shorts. I liked the yellow better than his standard red hair dye. It was uplifting, like the sun—like my current mood. I slid off my backpack, on the verge of combusting. I was so eager to show him the stone.

"Nice of you to visit me," I said, bothered by his no-show.

"Like I had the time. Thanks to you, I was running all over the place with disgusting Willie, trying to find your hallucination-induced wolf."

"Did you find him?"

"Of course not. We went to every bunker looking for the guy. He doesn't exist." His eyes zeroed in on my toxia marks. "Nice arms. I hear the plague look is in nowadays."

"Thanks."

"Oh, come on. Lighten up. How do you feel for real?"

"About ready to explode." I tugged on the zipper of my backpack, but it was stuck. "I have proof."

"Of what?" He eyed me suspiciously as I struggled to unzip the bag.

"Everything. Nitika. The dream. My sanity. The wolf. The whole deal. I can prove it all." I held the material taut and the zipper slid open, accidentally catching the dolman sleeve of my black gypsy-style shirt.

"Nice move."

I huffed. "I love this shirt!" The sheer fabric was so delicate that it would surely be ruined.

"Give it to me," Dakota said, reaching for the bag. I jerked away from him and my sleeve ripped, leaving a small swatch stuck between the zipper's teeth.

"What's wrong with you?" he said. "Did they really let you out of the medic, or did you escape?"

"Ha. Ha. Not funny." I yanked open my bag. "Wait till you see this. Shut the light."

"What for?"

"Just shut it already."

Dakota hit the light. "And we're sitting in the dark, why?"

"You thought the wind was cool," I said, "but this is so above and beyond that. Are you ready?"

"Ready for what? The white-coated people who are going to barge in here and take you away?"

"Now, that was funny," I said. "You're gonna freak."

"You are a freak."

I pulled out the stone and the room lit up with a spooky amber glow that reflected off the tin walls of the bunker. Dakota's jaw dropped so fast, it nearly cracked against the floor. His facial expression was Christmas-morning delight tinged with horror.

"Nitika led me to this on the night Coop found me in the fields," I said as I handed it to him. He didn't budge, so I pushed it toward him. "Take it. Look at it. I'm not crazy. She wanted me to have this for some reason."

He took it from my palm, his hand shaking slightly. Its luminosity dimmed to a mild peach glow when the gem was in his possession.

"Oh my God," I exclaimed. "Did you see that?"

"Holy—" He pulled the stone away from his body and looked at it cautiously. "What was that? You saw that, right?"

"It dimmed when you took it."

"How is that freaking possible?" Dakota tossed it back to me as if it was hot, and its glow intensified in my hands. "What the—?"

"It's responding to us." As a test, I handed it back to Dakota, with the same result—the stone's luminosity decreased in his possession.

My brother's face went as white as a sheet.

"Uh huh. Explain this," I challenged him, my voice heavy with the unvoiced words every sibling hates to hear: I told you so. "Tell me how this is possible. Tell me how an inanimate object like this could react to human touch."

He stood silent with his eyes fixed on the gem.

"Exactly. There's no logical explanation, at least not on our world." Energy was mounting exponentially inside me. "I told you I wasn't having a toxia hallucination. Everything I told you is true, and this stone proves it."

"It can't be real," he said and then flipped on the light. He squinted as he rotated the gem in the artificial glow. "There's got to be a battery in this thing." He was running his fingers over the flat mineral surface, looking for a hidden compartment.

"It's perfectly smooth and see-through, Dakota. There's no place for a battery. It's real, just like everything I told you. And what's more, it reacts to us. You saw it with your own eyes."

It reacts. The same way, every time.

"I'm telling you. Nitika led me to that stone. It wasn't a coincidence that I found it. I'm supposed to have this crystal. And it's not normal. I know gems pretty well, and I can tell you that much."

Dakota uttered an emphatic, "What is it?"

"My destiny, apparently. Nitika told me to retrieve my destiny right before I found this stone. I guess I'm supposed to do something with it."

"Do you know what kind of stone it is?"

"I have no idea," I said, "and believe me, I've investigated it." While in the medic, I'd asked my mom to bring me my book on crystals. Nearly a thousand pages long, it was set in fine print with small color photographs and advanced mineralogical information about every crystal known. I had scanned every entry in the guide in search of a stone like this one. There was no mention of a self-luminescent stone.

"What do you remember before blacking out?" Dakota asked, stroking the stone as he spoke.

"Nitika told me to retrieve my destiny and I found the stone. Then I had this crazy vision of the new arrival."

"The wolf guy?" he clarified. "Did he see the stone?"

"I would think so. I was following him. He must have seen the glow before I did." Dakota was now rubbing the crystal rigorously between his palms. "Stop that."

"Why?"

"I don't know. I don't want you to aggravate it. Give it to me." Overhead, I heard the first pings of rain ricocheting off the tin roof. Dakota was still examining the gem. "Give it."

The rain's intensity increased, and my thoughts swept back to how the new arrival had shielded me from the storm. Dakota reluctantly handed me the stone and it instantly glowed brighter. He made a face.

"It's not my fault if it likes me better," I said proudly.

He helped himself to a lollipop from my backpack. "That better not be sour apple," I said. He held up a blueberry one and I gave an approving nod.

"So now what?" Dakota asked.

"I'm not sure," I said, swaddling the gem in more tissues. "Here, hold it for a minute." He took the stone from me as I rummaged in my backpack for my pencil tin. After I dumped out the contents, I took the stone and placed it inside. "That should protect it a little."

"What about Mole-man-ton?" Dakota unwrapped his pop and crumpled the wrapper into a ball.

"What about him?"

"Didn't he say something to you about glowing stones? Wandelsta might have different minerals than Earth. Ones that glow." He tried to shoot the wrapper into the trash bin from clear across the room and missed the target.

I hadn't even thought of such a simple explanation. I didn't want it to be that simple. "Where are they, then? We would have seen them unless they're buried underground somewhere. I've been down the Slopee holes before, and I've never seen any down there." Thunder exploded overhead and rattled the bunker. We both jumped and I nearly dropped the pencil tin.

"Careful with it!" Dakota barked, as if the stone were his property.

"Okay, I know. I'm sorry. I'm just a little shaky. It's not every day you get ahold of a glowing stone that responds to your touch." I carefully returned the pencil case to my backpack. "Yes, there was a lecture that involved glowing gems. Gemja, Professor Mangleton called it. Madame Molina was going to deliver it. But that was a while ago."

"So, the professor likes you. Get him to arrange a retelling."

It was worth a shot. I had my mother contact Professor Mangleton, who was all too eager to call Madame Molina on our behalf. And Madame quickly agreed to retell the Legend of Gemja for us the following morning.

* * *

It was another sleepless night for me, not because I feared a recurrence of the Nitika dream—I felt more comfortable about it now that I knew she didn't intend me harm—but because I couldn't stop staring at the impossible gem and wondering about my connection to it. Morning couldn't come fast enough, but when it did, Dakota surprised me by refusing to go to "Moleville," stating communicable rodent-human diseases as the reason. I thought an impossible glowing stone might have helped him overlook his distaste for alien species, but my brother wasn't so simple. It took me playing the "I almost died" card and a few idle threats about exposing his pot use before he grudgingly agreed to accompany me down the hole.

Mom had left to help Dad at the facility, so she couldn't give me grief about going outside in my condition. I was still incredibly weak from my toxia exposure and wasn't up for hiking in the hot sun, so I put on a peppy face and managed to convince Coop to drive us several miles into the waste fields. He dropped us off in the center of a barren, flat plain that was void of all surface structures except a red manhole cover embedded in the ground.

"I still don't think this is a smart idea, Resa," Coop said. "You just got out of the medic. You should be in bed resting. Is this trip so critical that you'll risk a relapse for it? It's a long climb down there. Let me just take you back, okay?"

"I'm fine, Coop, really," I lied. "We have to say goodbye to the

Slopees before we leave here." Adrenaline was masking any aches in my body. I was desperate for intel on the origins of the stone.

"Well, we could just ask them to come to the surface for you."

"Coop, please?" I was getting frustrated now. "I'm fine, really. I want to see the underground tunnels one more time before we leave."

"Well, alright. I know you. Once you get your mind set on something, there's no changing it. I'll be back here in an hour or so to pick you kids up. You wait for me. Don't go walking back on your own." Then he glanced at Dakota. "Look after her, okay?"

"Will do," Dakota replied, giving him a casual salute. I returned Coop's wave as the supervisor drove off in a cloud of dust.

I stopped in front of the cover in the ground and bent down. "Now listen," I said, fumbling through my backpack. "I like the Slopees, so be nice. Just remember why we're here, okay?"

I handed Dakota a black wristband-flashlight and then bent down and grasped the wheel on the manhole cover. I gave it a tug, but it barely moved. I wished I could blame my weakness on my recent illness, but I just had zero muscle tone in my arms.

"What are you doing? For someone so smart, you're pretty damn dumb sometimes. Get out of the way." Dakota pulled the cover, and it sprang open with a deafening squeak. He beamed his light inside and gave a disgusted huff. "Are you insane?"

The hole was about forty inches in diameter and dropped straight down into darkness. Tiny red steps were embedded in its walls, spiraling downward and out of sight. I crouched to make my descent.

"Rees. There's no way we're doing this. This is nuts. Like, actually nuts. You just got out of the medic." Dakota stood and turned to leave, probably assuming that I would follow. I ignored him and stepped into the hole.

"It's really not as bad as it looks," I said as I slipped on a breathing mask and began my descent. "Don't flake on me, please. You came all the way here. Besides, I'm going no matter what, and I shouldn't be alone." I could hear him muttering to himself behind me. "Come on, Dakota. Put on your mask and get down here."

THE MOLE HOLE

When I looked up, his face hovered above the opening.

"Come on, Dakota. We have a glowing stone that defies all logic and we have absolutely no other leads. Let's at least ask them if glowing gems are part of Wandelsta's geology. Please just get in the hole. And wipe off your shoes. I don't want sand falling on my head."

Dakota eventually succumbed to my wishes, and I felt mildly responsible when he started to freak out midway down the tunnel when the shaft bent and the last traces of surface light vanished. I had deliberately omitted the fact that this climb would have to be made by only the light of the wrist flashlight. The hole was not meant to accommodate human bodies wearing bulky breathing masks, so it was uncomfortably tight, and even though I'd made this trip before, it was hard not to feel claustrophobic.

Dakota couldn't help but imagine all the worst-case scenarios, which he felt compelled to express out loud. Wandelstaquakes. Broken limbs. Being buried alive. Mutant worms in the hole. I had never once worried about any of these things. A quake could prove fatal, but it would be uncommonly bad luck for one to happen right when we were climbing underground.

"Think about something else," I encouraged. "What about Luna? Are you getting excited to see her again?"

"You have no idea," he said, sounding brighter.

"Oh, I have an idea, all right." Luna Blair was a super-cute skateboarder girl with long blonde braids dyed blue at the tips. She was Dakota's best friend and, as Mom and Dad and I all knew, the secret object of his affection. She could skate circles around him, which is probably why he never had the guts to ask her out. She was the one person who could get Dakota to do things he might not otherwise do. He had it really bad for her.

My feet finally touched level ground, and I stumbled backward as I let go of the handles on the wall. It took a moment to stabilize myself in the darkness. I waited motionless for several moments, hoping that my eyes would get accustomed to the lack of light, but it never happened. The light on my wristband only illuminated a couple of feet in front of my body, so I fumbled for a real flashlight in my bag and switched it on.

"Where the hell did you take me?" Dakota said. I heard him stumble as he stepped off the last stair. "I can't see a damn thing."

We were in the central cavern of a series of underground tunnels. The cavern was narrow and cool, and its walls consisted of fine, dark-brown, compacted sediment. Everything was damp, and what little air was present felt moist against my body. Every so often, a tiny drop of water dripped from the low-lying ceiling and spattered off my mask. I swiveled my flashlight around to get my bearings.

Eight circular passageways lined with mismatched wooden and metal doors led away from the cavern in different directions. Each door had a makeshift doorknocker and a unique identification number.

I waved Dakota, who had pulled out a flashlight of his own, toward the leftmost passage. "This way. The Molinas live behind door eleven." As I walked, my feet shuffled through a layer of loose papers on the ground.

"You better hope this is worth it, dragging me through these damn rodent holes," Dakota barked as he ducked to avoid hitting his head on the top of the tunnel. He looked about ready to yak. "If I hear one more word about pot from you—"

"Fine. We're even—although you want to know about this stone as much as I do. Okay, we're here. Be nice."

I stopped outside door eleven and rapped on it several times. There was no answer.

"Excellent, they're not home," Dakota whispered. "Let's get out of here. I'm done with this."

Just then the door flew open.

Madame Molina greeted us with a smile.

THE LEGEND

The Slopee matriarch was a hefty beast, standing four feet tall and weighing about two hundred pounds. Her round body was stuffed into a calico print apron. Judging from the look on Dakota's face, he hadn't expected her to be so rotund.

"Hello there, Resa! So good of you to come," she said jubilantly, waving us in. Her spiky brown hair was graying, and her white whiskers were long and looked brittle. "Well, who do we have here? You must be Dakota."

"Uh, yes," Dakota replied, staring with what I suspect was disgust at Madam's long, callused hand, which she'd extended toward him. He held his breath as he shook her hand.

"No. We should be thanking you for doing this for us," I said, giving Dakota a gentle push toward the open doorway. The Slopees' eyes were designed to see in complete darkness, so it was pitch black. I directed the beam of my flashlight toward a patchwork quilt that had been spread open on the floor where I usually sat during Madam Molina's storytelling sessions. "Here," I said to Dakota, navigating him around a rickety wooden table to the quilt. "Sit down here."

"Well, you know how much I enjoy telling tales," the elder Slopee

THE LEGEND

replied, sliding her rump with difficulty into a rocking chair near the quilt. "And the legend of Gemja is my all-time favorite. It's the oldest and most revered of all the myths about the origin of the universe."

"We can't wait," I answered, even though Dakota's expression clearly indicated otherwise. He was tentative about sitting, so I pulled him down next to me.

"Very well, let's not wait any longer," she said, sucking in a deep breath. "I need to take you on a journey, back to the beginning of time. The universe was a far different place then. There weren't twenty-six planets that contained intelligent life, like there are today. There was only one, a gigantic superplanet. It was called Gemja and it was a magnificent place, too beautiful for words to describe. Some said it sparkled with every color of the rainbow when the light from its six suns glistened off its crystalline surface. Although it shone brighter than the light of a trillion stars, it didn't hurt to look at. It was truly a sight to behold.

"Gemja was ruled by a kind-hearted being called Kryolite. No one is exactly sure what Kryolite was. Some say it was pure energy. Others say it was a fantastic diamond-like structure. Kryolite possessed magical powers and was thought to be the most powerful force in the universe.

"It was said that all of the species that exist in the universes today lived peacefully and harmoniously together on Gemja. There was no war or hate. No hunger or pain—"

"Tell that to the Glucosans," Dakota interrupted, much to my embarrassment.

Madam Molina smiled and exposed a mouthful of rotten teeth. "That's today, child. This was billions of years ago, when they had the Garden."

"Garden?"

"Yes, the Garden. Located in the middle of Gemja was a huge, magical crystal garden. It was a place where thousands of crystals grew, each possessing a unique power. There were crystals for relieving pain, for making creatures happy, even crystals for making food."

"I could use one of those right about now." Dakota was just being rude for the sake of it.

"My apologies," Madam Molina said. She reached for a plate of dark baseball-sized objects. "Would you care for a mud ball?"

We both shook our heads adamantly, and Dakota grimaced as she bit into one and crumbs of dirt fell into her lap.

"There was a crystal for anything you could possibly imagine," she continued. "Any species that resided on Gemja had access to these crystals and could use as many of them as often as they liked, as long as the crystals remained within the confines of the Garden. The species shared the Garden, and they all coexisted happily for billions of years.

"But then…Matchewa found Gemja." Her tone suddenly hardened.

"Who's that?" I asked half-heartedly.

"Not who…what. Matchewa is evil in its purest form."

"What did it look like?" Dakota asked, a hint of incredulity in his voice.

"Many have seen it manifest as a murky fog that can take form," Madam Molina explained. "But it can appear as both nothing and everything. It is believed that in the beginning of time, all that existed was energy—half positive, half negative. Kryolite and all that it represented was the positive half of the equation. Matchewa was the negative. A perfect balance of good and evil.

"Energy, of course, can change form. Positive can become negative; negative, positive. Matchewa wanted to upset the balance of good and evil. It created followers from itself, the Miseries, to try and destroy Gemja. Disguised as humans, the Miseries enticed the species of Gemja to steal stones from the Garden and keep them in their mansions. 'Why should you walk to the Garden each day, when you could have the stones for yourself in your homes?' the Miseries tempted. Several species turned greedy and did just what the Miseries had enticed them to do. When the other species on Gemja heard of these crimes, they became angry, and they stole crystals from the Garden, too. This ultimately led to warring among the species.

"Matchewa had succeeded. Hate, anger, fear, and jealously were all negative energies. Matchewa grew stronger as the species of Gemja gave in to these emotions. Kryolite had no choice but to destroy the planet."

"Why would he destroy such a beautiful place?" I found it hard to believe that such a peaceful being would resort to such violence.

THE LEGEND

"Kryolite was disheartened," Madam Molina continued. "It couldn't understand how the system had fallen apart when all species had equal access to all possible riches. It gathered representatives from all the species to express its concern and to offer advice, but they weren't interested. They didn't want to share anymore. They didn't even want to live together. Matchewa had won.

"Kryolite destroyed Gemja to separate the species from one another before its entire population fell victim to Matchewa's evil ways. With one wave of Kryolite's hand, the planet shattered into twenty-six smaller planets, shooting crystal fragments, rock debris, and stars outward in all directions at the speed of light. To this day, the planets and stars are still spinning away from one another in the wake of Gemja's explosion. Though there is interplanetary travel, the species have become isolated from one another, confined to their own planets, destined to live apart."

"Well, that's an interesting twist on the origins of the universe," I whispered.

Dakota played along. "A pissed-off diamond dude spawns the Big Bang."

My mind shifted to the amber crystal I'd found. "So, the crystals from the Garden," I said to Madame Molina. "What happened to them? They were destroyed?"

"Well, not exactly. Kryolite realized that it didn't want to be alone. It wished for a return to the glory days of Gemja. After several solitary years, it developed a plan. It dispersed its magic crystals randomly throughout the universe—one beautiful, glowing crystal per planet, each with a unique power. If all the stones were ever simultaneously activated by representatives of their harboring planets and the resulting energy passed through a keystone—a physical object to channel and concentrate the energy—a doorway would open in the fabric of space to Gemja, a place where the species could once again reunite and live in peace as one."

Madam Molina paused and looked deeply into my eyes. I found myself totally absorbed by the old Slopee's words. Had she said glowing crystals? Could I actually have found one of them? "Who told you all this?"

"The words come from an ancient text of unknown origin," Madam Molina replied. "Slopees can't read—our eyes are not designed for that. To this day, I have no known proof to support these myths. All I have are the words that have been passed down."

"No proof until today!" I blurted.

Madam Molina's eyes widened. "What did you say, my child?"

Dakota motioned viciously for me to stop, but I unzipped my backpack and pulled out the stone.

"The Citrine!" she hissed, eyes wide. "The Citrine!"

"The citrine?" Dakota said, forcefully pulling the stone from my hands. Madam Molina shielded her eyes from the glow. "You know what this is?"

"Why, yes. The myth says that Wandelsta's magic stone is a glorious orange gem called a citrine. That's what's in your hands right now. I'm certain of it!"

"Do you know how to activate it?" I said, excitement surging through my body. "Do you know what its special power is?"

"No," Madam Molina replied. "But seeing this gem validates everything that I've heard. It tells me Gemja must exist. Gemja must really exist!"

FALLING

We were obsessed.

Neither of us could shake the idea that the Citrine was indeed a remnant of the ancient superplanet Gemja and might possess great power.

I had another obsession: the mysterious violet-eyed guy who spent far more time in my thoughts than any nameless stranger should.

In two days, we were to return to Earth. I had to see him again before we went home. I had to know if he had really saved me that day. I had to know if the energy I had felt between us was real. I had to know that he was okay.

"Any luck last night trying to activate it?" Dakota said, poking his head through my bedroom door as I finished tracing some black liner across my upper eyelids.

"No, and I tried everything that wouldn't damage it."

"Like?"

"Shaking it. Tapping it with my crystals. Sprinkling salt on it. Putting it in water. Passing a magnet around it."

"What about smoke?"

"Ooo. No. I didn't do smoke. I'll get matches."

He slipped his hand into his pocket and pulled out a book of matches. "Here."

I gave him a disapproving look.

"You know, we're assuming that we *can* activate it," I said as I lit a match and held the crystal above the flame. "I was thinking about the legend. Madame Molina said that for Gemja to reunite, the energies of all stones must first be concentrated by using a keystone. I imagine that to be a device of sorts. Something that you put the crystals in, or on? Maybe all the stones need to be together for their energies to be unlocked. Maybe they don't work in isolation." I blew out the match, disappointed that nothing happened.

"God, can you believe this conversation we're having?"

"I know. It's crazy." I couldn't stop staring at the unbelievable gem. "And I don't know if you caught this part of the legend. She said that Miseries disguised themselves as humans. Humans. Us. That's been bothering me."

"We're not evil, Rees."

"I know. I don't know why, but it just bothered me."

"Listen, I know you trust the moles. But if they believe the legend is true, once word gets out that you found the Citrine…they're gonna come for it."

I hadn't thought of that. "Madame Molina would never do that to me."

"Maybe she wouldn't, but others will. If they actually believe we have a power stone from their planet? Please. They'll raid the bunker for it."

"Should we tell Dad, then?"

"Sure, if you want him to take it. It's Wandelsta's property. He's not gonna let you keep it. And I don't think Mom will respond too kindly if you tell them a ghost led you to the stone. She'll have you in therapy faster than—"

"No, I know. Trust me, I don't want to tell them. Nitika wanted me to have this, and I need to figure out why. They can't know." I handed the gem to Dakota. "You're in charge. Do whatever you need to do to keep it safe until we leave. Honestly, if anyone comes here looking for it, we'll just deny it. It's not like Dad would ever believe them if they said we found a magic stone."

"That's true."

I felt uncomfortably vulnerable. I hated that Dakota had planted the idea in my head that I could lose the gem. I had to get out. I slathered on sunscreen, grabbed my bag, and headed to the door.

"So, where you off to? Wolf hunting?"

I smiled. "You know it."

* * *

I saw him in the distance as I approached his dune. He was sitting in his usual statuesque pose, looking west. My stomach was a ball of knots, but I felt confident, too. I looked good this time—hip black cargos and a long-sleeve black tunic to cover my toxia marks, with knee-high combats and my magical white-feather necklace. I wasn't going to act cutesy or funny this time, either. That wasn't him. He was a deep, intellectual type. Plus, I had almost died following him into the fog. I deserved some answers.

"Why do you stare out into nothing all day?" I said as I took my place beside him. He looked exactly as he had before, barefoot, clad in black, with a tight ponytail. In fact, he was wearing the same outfit. I deliberately avoided looking at him. Instead, I stared in the direction of his gaze, toward the incinerators. "What do you see out there?"

"The point is to see nothing," he said coolly.

Once again, this had all the makings of a circular conversation. He cast a spell on me the last time with all his cryptic messages; I wouldn't let him drag me in again.

"Where were you going the other day when I followed you into the fog?"

"You followed me into the fog?"

"You don't remember?"

"No."

"You kissed me."

"I don't remember that either."

We sat there in silence for a long moment. Was he lying? There was no way it had been in my head. I had proof. I had the Citrine.

"Did you see the glowing stone out there?" I looked at him, hoping to get some insight by studying his expression, but his face was blank, his eyes still fixed on some distant point. He seemed detached.

"The mind is a very powerful thing," he said in his intoxicating, monotone way. "Perhaps you created this illusion you remember. You wanted to kiss me. So your mind made it happen. Anything is possible in a dream state. And, as we've already established, our existence here is just a dream."

"No. You established that. And I wanted to kiss you, eh?" I was getting feisty. A warm gust sent my hair aloft and his unbuttoned shirt rippled in the wind, blowing open to reveal a black mark on the left of his abdomen.

"What is that?" I asked, pointing to it.

He nonchalantly draped his shirt to cover it.

I boldly moved his shirt so I could have a closer look. It was a tattoo that reminded me of a barred-spiral galaxy with random scattered dots between the arms.

"What is it?"

"I was born with it." He closed his shirt again and I resumed my original seated position.

"Come on. There's no way that's a birthmark. Clearly it's a tattoo." I was positive, but when he didn't respond, a terrible thought hit me. Maybe he had abusive parents. Who would subject a child to the pain of a tattoo? Maybe that's why he came to the dunes—to escape a bad situation at home. It could also explain why no one except for me and Willie had seen him. I suddenly felt sorry for him.

"You know, I never got your name the other day," I said. I waited, but he didn't offer it. "You don't pick up on verbal clues very well, do you? What's your name?" Again, he said nothing, which seemed downright rude. "Why won't you tell me your name? What are you hiding?"

"I'm not hiding anything. I'm training my mind."

"For what?"

"To be limitless."

"What does that even mean?" I sifted the warm crimson sand through my hands. "Are you trying to be cryptic? I don't understand you."

"Then you have a weak mind."

I was taken aback. "No I don't." I poured handfuls of sand between my palms.

"Could you sit in one position all day, staring out at nothing? Blocking all other thoughts?"

"Who would want to?"

"I didn't ask if you wanted to. I asked if you could. You can barely sit still now."

I stopped playing with the sand. "I've never tried, but I'm sure I could. I just don't see the point."

Silence descended between us again, but my mind was racing.

I have a weak mind just because I can't sit for hours on end? No. I have more important things to do. But then again, isn't that what I try to do when I work a spell? Control my mind? My thoughts?

He was doing it again. I was getting confused. He was pulling me into his strange way of seeing the world.

"When you control your mind, you become limitless," he said. "Endless possibilities unfold before you. I'm training my mind to overcome my body. So that I can do anything."

"I don't need to sit in a dune field to do that," I said, giving an unintended little snort. "I can just sit in front of my altar."

He snorted back and swiveled to look at me. "You're a witch?"

"Yes. What's with the tone?"

"You don't look like a witch."

"Oh, I'm sorry. I didn't realize this was a formal affair. I left my hat and broom at home today."

"Don't forget the cape," he added lightly. I smiled at his joke, which seemed less than typical for him. For the first time in his presence, I felt myself loosening up.

"No, really. Why did you say it like that?" I probed.

"You seem too grounded and logical to be a witch. Are you a full-blown Wiccan?"

I hadn't expected him to know anything about the nature-based religion. "Funny you should ask," I said. "I'm not exactly sure what I am. A green witch, I suppose. I'm attracted to all things earthy. But I guess you can say I made up my own religion in a way."

"Is that legal?" He outright laughed. "What do you call it?"

"It doesn't have a name. I just take parts of different philosophies that I like and meld them. I guess you can call me an eclectic witch. I don't know. I just try to treat people well." The conversation was flowing naturally now, and it felt good. "I have to say, I like you much better this way."

"What way?" He brushed some sand off his hands.

"Like a normal person. Your Mr. Cryptic Philosopher-Man act was starting to hurt my brain."

"What makes you think it was an act?" he said, leaning backward and propping himself on his elbows. "It's good to think."

"I agree. But it shouldn't hurt."

He smiled, and his whole body seemed to soften. "So, tell me more about this made-up religion of yours. How do you celebrate?"

I remembered the cross thing that was in his ear the first time we talked. "Well, my family is Catholic, so we do the whole the Christmas thing, but Grams—my grandmother—was really into nature. She was the one who first introduced me to Wicca."

"She was the only Wiccan in your family?"

"As far as I know. But don't get me wrong. She loved Christmastime. She was a giver, a do-gooder. But she was also part Indian, and she kept the tradition of celebrating the changing seasons. We always burned a candle or did something special in nature on the equinoxes and solstices. I remember this one thing she told me that really stuck with me. She said that her church was the Earth. And I got that. I don't agree with the whole women-can't-be-priests thing and I never ever felt entirely comfortable in an organized church. But in nature, there's an energy I feel. A connectedness. There's no place that I feel safer or more at ease. But Grams went a bit too far with Wicca. I overheard my parents talking one night about how when she was younger, she participated in some naked group dances around bonfires and stuff. I just took the pieces that I liked."

"Naked grandma dances?" He furrowed his thick brows. "Not something I'd like to see." He smiled. "You, on the other hand…"

My face suddenly felt as red as the sand. "Well, that's not exactly the part of the religion that spoke to me, but I do like the idea of nature harboring power. Of us harboring power. Spells are just prayers said with intent…and the belief that we can play a role in making them come true."

"Have you ever made something happen?" he asked.

I hesitated. Should I tell him about the God of Wind, or would he just think I was crazy?

"Your mind needs to be strong enough to change reality," he said.

"Well, then I guess mine must be." I became instantly defensive. That was it. I was going to tell him.

"Show me, then."

"How?"

"Stand."

I followed his lead and stood. Although he was only a foot taller than me, he seemed gigantic, staring down at me with those impossible purple eyes. I was insanely curious about what he intended to show me. He took me by surprise when he grabbed my wrists and drew me closer to him. I didn't resist.

"Do you still want to kiss me?" he asked. My heart tumbled as his fingers slipped between mine.

"I already have. It's too bad you don't remember," I sassed him, impressed by my quick-witted response. He raised my arms up at my sides and pressed his chest to mine. My pulse skyrocketed.

"Remind me." In an instant, his warm, moist lips covered mine, once again filling me with his sweet and suffocating breath. Every nerve ending tingled with an electric quiver.

"Fall back," he breathed in a whisper against my neck, his mouth barely grazing my skin. Chills ran down my spine as I felt his sweet lips once again connect with mine. "Let yourself fall."

It was too late. I'd already fallen for him.

He held me close in his warm grip. A grip that grew firmer and more forceful. The hairs on my neck tensed. Something was wrong. I turned my head away from his and gasped. He had led me dangerously close to the edge of the dune. A sheer drop lay behind me.

He stretched my arms out to the sides again. "Fall back," he said. "If your mind is strong enough, no harm will come to you. Do you believe?" I felt him forcing me toward the edge.

Reality struck hard.

I tore myself from his grasp and bolted—a full-fledged, must-get-away-from-this psycho sprint. I didn't care what I looked like, either. Maybe I was wrong about his intentions, maybe not; I wasn't going to wait around for him to push me off the dune.

I practically slid down the entire face of the dune on my butt and then ran at full speed toward the bunkers, looking back every few minutes to make sure he wasn't in pursuit. When I was a good half-mile away, I stopped to catch my breath. I leaned over, my hands on my knees, my lungs on fire. I could still see him atop the dune, facing me with his arms outstretched, his head flung backward.

Then in one fell swoop, he leaned back, stiff as a board, and free-fell off the steep side of the dune, disappearing from sight.

THE MANUAL

I had stupidly left my backpack with all of my drawings at Madam Molina's. Abandoning my bag down there was not an option but walking through the fields with that psycho on the loose didn't seem like a good idea either. I told Dakota what had happened and asked him to take me to the hole. He agreed and suggested that we swing by the scene of the crime first to see if we could find any sign of the new arrival. My brother was eager to prove that the guy was just a fabrication resulting from toxia inhalation.

"We checked every bunker for that guy," Dakota said. "No one heard of a kid with purple eyes on the base. He doesn't exist, Rees."

Sure enough, there was no body at the base of the dune. In fact, there was only one set of tracks going up that dune, and one coming down—mine.

My thoughts spiraled at tornado speed. He was real. He was, I knew it. But why was there no proof? Willie had seen him, thank God. Or had he just been lying the whole time? Maybe he was pretending when he talked about the new arrival, and he thought I was pretending back? I had to get it together.

I knew one thing for sure: the stone was real. Nitika led me to it, and she wasn't a toxia fabrication. The stone was proof that I was sane.

Dakota waited outside the door of Madam Molina's den while I went inside to get my backpack and say my goodbyes. My mind was still circling around the new arrival's impossible plummet from the dune. I was also worried that Madam Molina might ask for the stone back. Luckily, she didn't. Instead, she held my hand and whispered, "Your secret is safe with me. The Citrine wanted you to find it. It is now up to you to find out why."

When I finally left the Slopees' home, I found Dakota crouched over the ground with a flashlight and his text decoder, scanning the brittle magazines and the weathered remains of old newspaper pages, many from planets that were completely unknown to us. Although I was eager to return to the surface to do some more investigating about the new arrival, Dakota insisted on shuffling through the debris and looking for interesting headlines that he could take back to Earth.

> The Acetics Invade Soohanian
> Liquid Water Reaches $100 a liter in Alganon
> Plebloid Queen Passes One-Car-Per-Family Rule

"Come on, Dakota," I said impatiently. "I want to check out the dune again." I turned to leave without him but stopped when I heard him gasp. "Seriously, Dakota. Enough with the headlines. Let's go."

"Oh my God." He was passing his decoder over the cover of a tattered booklet. "Oh my God."

"Come on, Dakota. Just take it and let's go. You can read all that when we get back to the bunkers."

"Oh my God." His tone had turned serious.

"What is it?" I grew impatient as he recycled the same exclamation.

"You need to look at this." He handed me the booklet and his decoder, and I gasped when I read the title:

> Instructions for the Reunification of Gemja:
> The Words of the Almighty Kryolite

I lost my breath. The manual was 150 pages thick, with a baby-blue card-stock cover and soft binding. In the upper right-hand corner was written: IPPL AGENDA ITEM 15: Validity of Gemja Manual.

The hairs on my neck prickled. "The IPPL knows about Gemja?"

Dakota looked perplexed. "Right? That's what it seems like, right?" He closed his eyes and blew out a slow, deep breath. "This can't be happening right now. You don't just learn about a legend and then happen to stumble upon a text of it while wandering underground through rodent holes on a foreign planet."

"You think that's what this is? A recording of the original legend?" I scraped off what looked like a piece of solidified, wilted lettuce from the cover. I reread the title out loud, just to be sure I had seen it correctly. "It's definitely the property of the IPPL. What was the IPPL doing investigating a fairy tale?" A surge of adrenaline made my hands tremble as I carefully pulled back the front cover. The print was small and blurry, illegible in places. "It's too dark down here. Let's take it up."

Once we reached the surface, we found a spot on the nearest dune and carefully opened the delicate, weathered pages. The binding cracked and many of the pages were stuck together, so our progress was slow. The first thirty pages looked like they'd been photocopied from a smaller book. Beyond that were additional sections, other translations of the original text.

"It seems like an informational text," I said. "This whole passage is about a planet called Gargon. It gives information on the star system where it's located, the planetary conditions, even what the indigenous species are like."

"Is it accurate?" Dakota asked. "Is Earth in there?"

"Let me see." I scanned the pages with my decoder and stopped when I saw a picture of our planet. "Yes! Here we are."

"What does it say? Did they get us right?"

"Atmospheric conditions 78% nitrogen, 21% oxygen. Eighty percent of the surface is covered in dihydrogen monoxide."

"Dihydrogen monoxide? Well, that's wrong."

I gave him a withering glance. "No, that's water." I read on. "Diversity of plant and animal life. Prominent species, homo sapiens. Primitive culture."

"Primitive, my ass."

"They probably mean in a technological way, and if that's the case, they're right. I mean, the Yrdians found us. We didn't find them. This description is really general, but it's accurate."

"What else does it say?"

"It's hard to make out the rest." I flipped to a readable section on a planet called Corrodis and read silently. "This book is a goldmine. Do you think this is copyright-protected by the IPPL? I'd love to use some of this information in my journal."

Dakota shook his head. "How should I know about alien copyright laws? Shouldn't you be more concerned that we found it in the first place? You don't just find something like this."

"Nitika intervention?" I pondered. "I don't know. I didn't feel like she was down here with us. But then again, it's not like me to leave my bag anywhere." I skimmed through the pages again. "I wonder if Dad has seen this? Probably not, or he would have told us, no? Unless they have an updated version. I don't know how—" I lost my words. "Oh my God."

"What?"

"Oh my God."

"What?" He tried to pull the book away.

"Native power crystal," I stuttered, pointing to the words. "There's a native power crystal listed for this planet!" I drew my hand to my mouth in disbelief. "Corrodis. Power crystal: octavian opal, with the gift of inducing an electric current."

Dakota took the book and flipped to another planet. "Planet Doimis. This says its power crystal is rhonami rutilite."

"I love rutilite!"

"Power: levitation?"

"Oh my God! These crystals do have powers!"

Dakota shook his head. "How is this possible?" He continued reading. "Uh, Rees..." he paused for a painfully long time. "This manual tells us how to find them. Well, not directly. But it gives some kind of clue—"

"What? It does?" I pulled the book back from him. Color drained from my face. "What about the Citrine?"

We scanned wildly, looking for the information, but part of the section on Wandelsta was water damaged, blurry, and illegible.

I felt like a closed soda bottle that had been shaken. I skimmed the entire book again. "There's a power crystal listed for all the planets in this book…at least as far as I can tell from the un-ruined bits."

"The Citrine has a power," Dakota stated with conviction.

"Oh my God. Do you think so?" My heart beat faster at the very thought of it.

He pointed to the manual I was holding. "It wasn't a coincidence that we found that."

When I couldn't hold it in a moment longer, I let out the longest, most high-pitched squeal a human could make. "We have a power stone!" I jumped to my feet, raking my fingers through my hair. "We have a power stone!"

I held my head in my hands and sank back to the ground, falling into a sloppy cross-legged squat. "Okay, Resa. Get a grip," I said out loud. "Get a grip." I stared hard at Dakota. "You know what this means, right? The legend is real. Gemja exists."

Dakota made a face. "I still don't know about the diamond dude."

"But you do know about the stone. Do you think it's from Gemja?"

"It's definitely possible," Dakota said, his eyes brightening with excitement. "What if it generates money?"

"Money? Forget money. I want to fly."

"Or walk through walls."

"Or see into the future."

"There's no limit to what this thing could do," Dakota said.

My heart stopped. No limits. We are limitless.

"We have to ask Dad about this," I said. "The IPPL knows something about Gemja. We have to ask."

Dakota shook his head. "Yeah, if you want to lose it. He's so brainwashed, he'll just give it over to them."

Dakota was right. Dad would confiscate it and we'd never learn its power. Still, Dad would have been able to offer us some valuable insight.

I rifled through the pages again. "The aids to discovery they provide in here are more like riddles, or poems, or codes."

I turned to the next legible section, marked, "The Keystone, The Kreyliss, and The Krowe: The Ceremony of Unification," and silently read about the procedure, mumbling the final passage out loud:

"Having come in peace, with good intentions, a group composed of one chosen representative from each species shall form a perfect circle exactly twenty-six feet in radius from the keystone, where all shall simultaneously activate their stones. The energies produced will be drawn into the keystone, wherein these energies shall be concentrated—so much so that space itself will tear, exposing a safe passageway to Gemja…"

I flipped to the inside front cover and squinted as I struggled to read the faint, smudged words through the decoder's screen. The passage was written in frilly calligraphic letters. I gasped. "Listen. This is a description of Gemja."

Hidden in a dark, unknown corner of space spins a mystical glass planet, sparkling more brilliantly than the glow of a thousand bursting stars. As it rotates, rays from its six golden suns bounce off its crystalline surface, creating giant rainbows that dance around the planet. They encircle the orb, twisting and turning, cloaking it in a cloud of pulsating color.

Below the swirling rainbow sky, the land is covered in glistening gems and riches, all twinkling brightly in bold shades of gold, crimson, and violet. There are towering amethyst cliffs and shimmering trees of beaded blue sapphires. Warm rivers of molten gold flow over the crushed emerald sand. This enchanted land is a place that holds endless possibilities.

In the center of the planet, high atop a mountain of red ruby, sits my majestic ice-crystal castle. I am Kryolite, the keeper of planet Gemja, protector of peace and tranquility. I watch over this place to ensure that it remains a harmonious sanctuary free from pain, sadness, and evil. I allow only good and happy thoughts to exist here, making

Gemja a rare jewel in the universe. It's a place where all species can live together in peace and harmony for eternity.

The remaining paragraphs were too blurry to read. I looked up at Dakota with wonder.

"It's awfully childlike," Dakota said. "It doesn't seem like this could be real."

"Why does childlike have to mean fake? What's more innocent and pure than childish thoughts? Gemja is supposed to be the purest of places, so it would be childlike."

"All the jewel stuff reminds me of those drawings you made of your dream."

I froze. Was my jeweled forest on Gemja? Had Nitika been trying to tell me something about this place?

I closed the book and clutched it to my chest, gazing off in wonder at the incinerators along the horizon, mesmerized by the thick charcoal-colored plumes of pollution that danced above the spires. Creepy shadows spilled over the dunes as the sooty clouds drifted overhead.

Questions flooded my brain. Could such a magical and beautiful place truly exist? Was the Citrine a key to getting us there? Was I the chosen representative for the human species?

I was lost in a daydream of possibilities.

THE HOMECOMING

MATCHEWA

Ace	Ham	Hem
Wet	Met	Mat
Tame	Mate	Team
Came	Awe	Cat
Hat	Chat	What
Watch	Match	Chew
Them	Wheat	Cheat

I continued to stare at the word Matchewa, rearranging the letters in my head to make as many smaller words as possible. I had a self-imposed rule that two-letter words and proper names didn't count. I kept analyzing until I found five more hidden words—hate, ate, meat, heat, and act—and added them to my list. I did a recount—twenty-six.

Twenty-six.

I remembered a passage from the legend: "A group composed of one chosen representative from each species shall form a perfect circle exactly twenty-six feet in radius from the keystone…"

Was the number twenty-six a sign?

I jotted the word KRYOLITE in my sketchbook and began the word-creation process again.

This was how I kept myself distracted on the seemingly endless three-day ride home. Still, I didn't mind the trip. Leaving Wandelsta behind—and the threat posed by the new arrival—was a huge relief. But a new weight of responsibility pressed down on me. In my possession was a stone linked to an ancient legend that, if true, could have profound impact on all of humanity. I wouldn't be able to relax until I had the chance to tell Sarah and Meranda the news. But how do you even start a conversation like that?

After dissecting several more words, I closed my sketchbook and mulled over every crazy thing that had happened to me in the past several weeks, trying to make sense of it all. The headaches. Nitika. My encounters with the new arrival. The stone. The manual. There had to be some connection.

I took several catnaps, willing myself before each one to dream about Nitika so I could ask her for guidance, but she never appeared, which frustrated me to no end. For years, I had unsuccessfully tried to ditch her, and now, when I wanted and needed her, she wouldn't show. I was desperate for answers. I glanced at my mother, who was sitting by the control board, talking quietly with the captain about the Siafun invasion. Dakota was amusing himself by floating in the low-gravity environment. His attempts to lure me into an aerial backflip competition had been futile. Instead, I unzipped my bag to look at the Citrine. I rubbed it between my fingers, wondering what powers might lie dormant inside it.

"Whoa. What was that?" the captain said, glancing back at me. I flinched and quickly zipped the bag, fearing he'd caught a glimpse of the Citrine. The last thing I needed was for my mother to ask me questions about it. "Have you kids ever seen anything like that?"

"Like what?" I asked, trying to sound nonchalant.

"Like a storm in space."

I was confused until I saw the white streaks of lightning outside through the window. "No, I don't think I have," I replied, relieved that my secret was safe.

"I've heard they were possible, but I've never seen one till now. They're very rare. No need to be frightened. We're just witnessing something quite unusual here."

I wasn't too impressed with the storm. I closed my eyes and rested my head back. "Unusual" had taken on new meanings for me after my time on the planet with red sand. Unusual was living in a place with toxic air. Unusual was a world made of sugar. Unusual was talking to ghosts. Unusual was possessing a magical crystal…

My conscious thoughts faded, and I slipped into a much-needed, well-deserved slumber.

* * *

The shuttle touched down in Florida at the Kennedy Space Station, where we were immediately whisked away to a private plane that brought us to Bangor, Maine. We arrived near midnight, and we were warned that a wall of paparazzi awaited us at the Arrivals gate. I'd been so preoccupied with the Citrine and the new arrival that I had forgotten about how others would react to the news of our homecoming.

What a gross oversight on my part. I looked horrible. No makeup. Ratty hair. I dragged my lip-gloss wand across my lips and then slipped into a hoodie sweatshirt from one of my bags as we disembarked the plane. I hung my head as we turned the corridor and were greeted by an eruption of cheers and an endless series of white flashes.

"This way," said a black-haired man holding a walkie-talkie. He redirected us down a private hallway, away from the reporters. The man seemed to have appeared from out of nowhere, but he was wearing an airport security ID tag, and we were happy to escape the reporters. "How does it feel to be famous?" he said, looking back at us with a smile.

"I don't feel famous," I said.

"Trust me, Resa. People will know who you are. Did you draw much on Wandelsta?" He unlocked a large metal door and pulled it open, revealing a metal staircase.

I was shocked that he knew anything personal about me.

"They interviewed your teachers. And your grandfather. Anyone in town who knew you," he explained in response to my stunned expression. "For the past two weeks, we've seen nothing but information on your family in the news. Your mother is a professional chef. You're an artist."

My interest was piqued. "What did they say about Dakota?" I shot my brother a sideways glance. He and my mom looked as stunned as I felt.

The man smiled. "Ah, yes, Dakota. Well, let's just say, there are several girls who will want posters of Dakota."

"Why?" Dakota's face blushed almost as red as the spikes in his hair.

"Seriously?" I echoed. This was so not what I had expected.

"He's quite the heartthrob," the man explained. My mom looked like she wanted to laugh. "They aired pictures of Dakota from a high school talent show. Teenage girls are swooning for the guitar player with the spiky red hair."

"You gotta be kidding me," I said in disbelief. Dakota's face had stretched into a Cheshire cat smile. He was loving this.

We descended two flights of stairs and found ourselves in another insanely long corridor that had a lingering musty smell. There were no windows, just dull, motion-activated lights.

"Where are we going?" my mother asked tentatively. It felt like we had been walking forever.

"Call it our secret passage," the man said proudly. "The only other people who have used it are political leaders and famous entertainers who wanted some privacy. I can't tell you where you'll be let out, but a car and driver will be waiting to take you to the island." He pulled his walkie-talkie to his mouth. "All clear?"

"Wow. Who knew we had underground tunnels like this, too," I muttered to Dakota, thinking about the Slopee hole.

I hadn't fully registered the fact that we were finally back home until the man unlatched a heavy door and the chilly October Maine air kissed my face. I'd forgotten what time of year it was since Wandelsta was always warm, like a hot summer. The fresh autumn air filled me with new life. The waning crescent moon was barely visible through the web of tree branches overhead. A black sedan, which practically blended in with the night, was parked on a nearby gravel road.

"Good luck to you, Stone family," the security man said. "Get a good night's sleep. You deserve it." He closed the door behind himself.

"My name is Mac." I hadn't noticed the man leaning against the car until he spoke. "Let's get you home."

* * *

It was about an hour's drive from Bangor to Bar Harbor. There was no traffic on the road, and we must have successfully ducked the reporters, since no one appeared to be tailing us. I felt mildly guilty about having abandoned them back at the airport after they'd waited so long to see us. As we neared the entry point to Mount Desert Island, flashing red lights and a line of police cars came into view.

"What's going on?" I asked. "More reporters?"

"Oh no," Mac said. "They wanted to take extra security measures to keep you safe. There was a public vote on it. The people of the island agreed to a checkpoint. Only locals are allowed on the island until further notice. No tourists. No outside reporters. It's also a measure that will help protect the exchange family when they get here."

"Exchange family from where?" asked Dakota.

"A Yrdian family. The first extraterrestrial family will be staying on our island. It's hard to believe, right? They're arriving the day after Halloween. I'm sure they'll be happy to have you back home, since you just went through a similar experience."

We pulled up to the checkpoint and received a warm, receptive greeting from the cops. The police barricade comforted me. Hopefully, it meant we could resume a somewhat normal life free of annoying press people.

THE HOMECOMING

As we headed home, I couldn't get enough of the familiar sights. I pointed out the window at a fawn and her mother nibbling the grasses at the edge of the road as if I were on safari. The driver stopped the car for a better look and the animals raised their heads, chewing in a circular motion, tufts of grass dangling out the sides of their mouths. When they lowered their heads and continued to graze, we slowly pulled away.

The familiarity of the winding, tree-lined roads brought with it a comfort factor that was hard to describe.

"Ooh, can we take a detour through town?" I asked the driver at the last minute. After my mother gave him an indulgent nod, he made the turn. It was dark and quiet, except for the pub house, where a couple of sauced patrons were chatting loudly out front. We passed Grandpa's ice-cream shop, "Sheer Deliciosity," and my stomach gave a little pang when I thought about his frozen yogurt with peanut butter sauce. First thing tomorrow, I would walk into town to get one before heading over to Meranda's shop.

Several miles from town, our quaint, seafoam-blue, salt-box colonial was tucked away in the woods at the end of a long, tree-lined gravel driveway that wound gently uphill. With its weathered mauve shutters and crooked river-rock fireplace, our house looked like it had been transported straight out of a fairytale. I was surprised to see the outdoor floodlights shining through the limbs of the trees as we drove up the hill. When we made it to the top, I was even more surprised to discover that the interior lights were on, and three big, fat, happy pumpkins sat on the stoop. Grandpa's blue sedan was parked in the driveway.

"Get me outta this car," Dakota crowed as he pushed open the door and leapt out. He grabbed his bags despite the driver's offer to carry them.

I was so tired that I welcomed the man's help. The car door seemed unnaturally heavy as I pushed it open and stepped out into the salty night air. My skin literally tingled with excitement when I heard the gentle sloshing of water against the granite coast that was our backyard.

There was no better place in the entire universe than right here.

I had never been happier to be home.

"Welcome back!" I heard my grandfather cry out. I turned and saw my Gramps in the open doorway, wearing his classic red woolen vest over a long-sleeved tan shirt. He gave Dakota a hug and then patted my brother's back as he raced into the house.

"Dad, you didn't have to come," my mother said, hugging my grandfather. "But I'm so glad you did."

"Gramps!" I called out. I slammed the car door a bit harder than I'd intended and then dashed up the stone steps to the front door to greet him. I nearly knocked him over with my ginormous bear hug. I'm barely 5'2" and he's only slightly taller. Only slightly heavier, too.

"Alrighty, alrighty," he said, laughing and trying to regain his footing. He pushed what little gray hair he had left across his brow. "Come in. Get out from the cold." He pulled his wallet from the pocket of his trousers, tipped the driver, and closed the door behind us.

Dakota was nowhere in sight, but he'd already managed to clutter the foyer with his bags. The interior of the house was warm and cozy, thanks to the fire Gramps has started in the fireplace. I smelled the aroma of spicy cinnamon. Then I saw them. Hot sticky buns cooling on the counter. Three cell phones were lined up next to them.

"Yep, I reactivated all your phones," said Gramps when he caught me staring at them.

"You're the greatest," I said, hugging him again.

"And I just took the buns out of the oven. Get them while they're hot."

Dakota reappeared as if by magic at the mention of hot buns. "Nice," he said emphatically and somehow stuffed an entire bun in his mouth without smearing the icing all over his face. He grabbed two more buns and then started back upstairs.

"Take your bags with you," my mother ordered. "And easy on the sweets. Your stomach may not be able to handle such rich food anymore."

As much as I wanted one of the treats, I wanted a shower more.

"Do you mind if I go up?" I asked my grandfather. I felt guilty to be abandoning him after all he'd done to make our homecoming pleasant.

THE HOMECOMING

"No, no," he said and pushed his hand through the air at me. "You go. Get some rest. I'll see you tomorrow. Glad you're home, kiddo."

I lugged my bags up the stairs, smiling to myself when I heard Dakota singing and strumming his acoustic guitar in his room. He didn't sound at all rusty.

I'd forgotten how I'd left my room. There was little space to walk amidst the easels, workstations, drop cloths, and assorted paint bottles and brushes that were lined up everywhere. And most of the surface was covered by my crystal collection. They were on the bookshelves. Atop my nightstand. Occupying the cubbies of a collector's wooden wall-frame display that hung on the wall next to my leaning mirror.

The creamy mauve walls were barely visible beneath the brightly colored paintings and pictures that covered them. One picture in particular drew my attention. Leaning against my wall was a large oil painting of a beautiful yet haunting jeweled forest. The one from my dream. Little had I known at the time that I might be painting Gemja.

I rummaged through my drawers in search of a sweater and was excited to find a cute gray merino wool minidress that I'd forgotten about. I grabbed clean undies, a bra, a T-shirt, and baggy flannel pajama pants and headed to the bathroom to take the longest and hottest shower of my life. Ah, to be clean. Really clean. My nose tingled at the forgotten smell of real lavender soap and the comfort of hot, misty steam.

I adjusted the water temperature to barely tolerable heat and allowed it to work its magic on my muscles. The water took with it all the leftover aches of toxia overexposure, and the residual soap scum on my skin melted away for the first time in months. I must have stayed in there for at least an hour before drying off with a terry-cloth towel that was so soft, it felt like a cloud. My hair was even softer after I blew it dry. I felt like a model in a shampoo commercial. I slipped into my sleep clothes and went to pay Dakota a visit.

"Practicing for your new 'guitar idol' role in the world?" I teased, peeking my head into his room. He was sitting Indian style on his bed, holding a beautiful black acoustic with gold hummingbirds painted on the body.

"Ah. You look human again," Dakota said as he picked up a piece of loose-leaf paper from the bed. "I forgot I was in the middle of a song before we left."

"What's it called?"

"'Surrender.'"

"Let's hear it," I encouraged. I was sure it would be good. As harsh as my brother's speaking voice sounded at times, his singing voice was a warm, comfy blanket that you wanted to draw around you. He had a gift when it came to writing songs and playing the guitar.

Dakota was a fan of minor keys, which always seemed to have a certain contemplative sadness to them. This new song was a love song. I couldn't help but think it had to be for Luna. It always amazed me how my brother could write songs about things with which he had little experience.

Strangely, the new arrival crossed my mind for the first time that night. That energy I had felt arc between us had been so tangible. Even though I would never see him again, even though our few encounters were shrouded in mystery and possibly danger, he was still on my mind.

Maybe I would feel differently after a full night's sleep in a soft, cozy bed with clean air.

It was good to be home.

THE REUNION

"Pieces?"

I rolled over and gazed through sleepy eyes at my friend Sarah, who stood in the doorway to my room in her dark movie-star sunglasses, a huge smile on her face. Her chocolate mane of golden-highlighted hair reached down to her waist. "Welcome home, Reesie Pieces," she said, in a pitch that seemed awfully high for so early in the morning. "Your mom let me in."

"Sarahsitis?" I said. Our preteen pet names for each other had stuck. Sarah earned hers while suffering from a bad case of tonsillitis. The origin of mine was obvious. "What time is it?" I felt like I'd been hit by a truck.

"Oh, let's see…four in the afternoon?" She spread open the drapes. Sure enough, the sun was already on its way down.

"It's four already?"

"I could have just let you sleep the day away, but I was dying to see you."

"I'm glad you came. I have so much to tell you, you won't even believe it." I forced myself to sit upright, but I wasn't ready to get out of my comfortable bed yet.

"Well, I'll believe just about anything these days. Did you know that your brother has a fan base of twelve-year-old girls in town?"

"So, that's true?"

"Please. The news played a tape of his High School Idol competition, then interviewed a couple of preteens who thought he was, and I quote, 'dreamy.' Don't get me wrong; your brother is a great musician. But that news report would have had you thinking he's the next rock god."

Sarah leaned in and gave me the biggest hug.

"Still going crunchy, I see?" I said playfully, gently tugging her hair between my fingers. It was stiff as a board, just as I remembered it. Sarah's hair was a daily project. She spent at least an hour blowing out her curly hair, then plastering it with gel and spray until it had the perfect amount of kink. To the eyes it was magazine worthy. To the touch, it felt like strands of hardened glue.

"You know it. You wouldn't want to see this," she circled her finger around her head, "without some serious work." She looked me up and down. "Look how tan you are. And so skinny, you little B." Sarah was my height but with a muscular snow-boarder bod. She always complained about a nonexistent extra five pounds around her waist, but it never stopped her from eating, particularly fettucine alfredo—her favorite meal.

"You girls up for pizza tonight?" I heard my mother call from the base of the stairs.

"Yes!" I cried. At the moment, pizza sounded like manna of the gods. "Pepperoni, and lots of basil!" I glanced at my reflection in a standing mirror on my dresser. I looked tired. I pulled my fingers through my hair to detangle a knot.

"I'm going to run out and do some shopping. I'll pick up a pie on the way home."

"Two," I insisted, pulling my hair into a loose ponytail. I wanted cold pizza for breakfast the next morning. And the next. And the next.

"Two pies it is. Tell Dakota I'm getting dinner." I heard the front door open. "Have fun catching up, girls."

"Catching up" was an understatement. After my mother left, I told

Sarah everything, ending my story with a triumphant unveiling of the stone. She was a list person and before long we were swimming in flowcharts and timelines and Venn diagrams and outlines, both of what we could explain and what we couldn't.

"Your headaches stopped immediately after your last vision from Nitika in the dune fields," Sarah pointed out. "They had nothing to do with toxia. I bet they were a side effect of communicating with the spirits."

"You have no idea how good it is to hear you say that," I said. "I started questioning my own sanity after a while."

"Please," Sarah said. "Nitika led you to the power crystal. We just have to figure out why. And I don't like that the purple-eyed dude tried to off you. I wonder if it's somehow connected. Do you think he was after the stone?"

I shrugged. "I don't think so. He was ahead of me in the fields. He would have seen it before I did. He could have taken it if he wanted it."

"I don't know. Why no prints in the sand? What if he's a demon or something?"

"He didn't seem demonesque."

"No. He just tried to kill you and then miraculously fell off a dune backwards and vanished. We need to tell Meranda all of this. Maybe she can make some sense of it. Maybe she's heard of a purple-eyed demon."

"What's with all the demon stuff? It's freaking me out. Since when do you believe in demons walking around, anyways?"

"Uh, since green, photosynthetic Yrdians came to Earth and revealed there are at least twenty-five other civilizations out there in the cosmos. Why are demons so hard to believe in? You conjured up the God of Wind, for crying out loud. I'd like to see what Meranda knows, just in case."

"I am so glad to be home," I said, pulling out that cool merino sweater-dress I'd found yesterday. "Just let me put this on, and then we'll head over there."

She held up a hand to stop me. "Uh, no. You're not going anywhere, lady. You stay here and rest. Meranda has a Halloween candle-making class tonight, so she won't have a lot of time. I'll just give her a quick synopsis and leave her the manual to look over later."

"We have to make a copy of it first," I said. "And the stone stays here."

"Of course. You can show her the Citrine later, when you're feeling up for it." Her attention was diverted when Dakota walked down the hallway. "Hey, what's up, Kote?"

"What's up, Payne in my neck?" Dakota replied, stopping in my doorway. He had on a tight black thermal with baggy, to-the-knee shorts. "Miss me?"

"Endlessly," Sarah said.

Dakota pointed at himself with both hands. "Enjoy me while you can, ladies. Apparently, I'm the big new thing in town. I saw myself on the news last night."

Sarah rolled her eyes. "Please. You have three underage fans at Olsen Elementary School."

"Ah, Payne. Jealousy will get you nowhere." Dakota winked at her and left.

"Your brother is so incredibly hot. Too bad he's such a self-righteous jerk."

I laughed. "He's actually getting better. We bonded on Wandelsta, if you can believe it."

"Um, yeah, no. I don't believe it. That toxia poisoning must have stuck with you after all," she said, grabbing the Gemja manual off my bed. "Okay. You go take a shower. I'll make a copy of this in your dad's office and shoot it over to Meranda's. I'll be back for pizza. Don't eat it all."

* * *

Sarah returned an hour later, just as Mom pulled up with two large pepperoni pies, a dozen extra-garlicky knots, and a huge Caesar salad. The next half hour was heaven…or should I say, Gemja? Dakota took his four slices to the living room, while Sarah and my mother stayed with me at the dining room table, all of us gorging ourselves on the feast. Sarah and I, both being condiment queens, used half a bottle of grated Romano and excessive cracked black pepper on our pizza. And just when we thought we couldn't eat any more, Mom headed back into the kitchen to remove the cookies she had made from the oven.

"So, how did it go with Meranda?" I asked, peeling off a piece of pepperoni that was stuck to the empty pizza box and popping it into my mouth.

"She was speechless when I told her you found a glowing power stone that was linked to an ancient legend—a legend of which I just happened to have a written copy that she could study."

I smiled as I took the pizza box to the trash.

"She said she would call you as soon as she had a chance to look it over."

My attention was diverted by Dakota's urgent plea for all of us to join him in the living room. "Quick! We're on the news."

Even I was excited to see what they might have to say. We all ran in just as a reporter from Channel 5 News began her segment, positioned in front of the police-guarded checkpoint to the island.

"And just last night, one of the first families to ever set foot on a new world has returned home to Mount Desert Island. As you can see by the police barricade behind me, the island has been secured to allow the family privacy and the time they need to rest and recuperate. Only one member of the family has not yet returned home. Robert Stone, a member of the Interplanetary Peace League, was asked to travel with the organization to Oganwando, which is referred to by the organization as the capital of the universe, to help organize a defensive attack on the Siafu, an aggressive species who recently attacked a docile, peace-loving world called Glucosa. At this time, we do not have any further information about the nature of the defense or the other species involved. Our thoughts and prayers go out to Robert Stone, the IPPL, and the Glucosans."

I suddenly felt guilty. I had been so busy enjoying the comforts of home that I'd forgotten why we had returned early in the first place.

"Your father wouldn't want us to be somber," my mother said, breaking the heavy silence that had descended upon us after the news report. "It's not going to help if we sit around and worry. This is out of our control. And your dad is completely fine. He's not going into battle. He's helping monitor the situation from a completely safe and neutral planet."

I suspected that she was trying to convince herself, too. Dakota switched the channel to watch a rerun of an old UFC match and invited me to join him.

"Honestly, I don't know how you two watch that stuff," Sarah said, grimacing. "It's so violent."

The doorbell rang, causing us all to flinch.

"Reporters?" I asked, my stomach dropping. I hadn't rehearsed for potential questions they might ask and wasn't ready to confront them.

"Shouldn't be," my mother replied, walking to the door. "Your father called the local newsroom and asked them to give us some time to get readjusted. I told them that you're finalizing a journal about our stay on Wandelsta. They're reserving December 22nd to speak with you in their studio about your experiences, so you'll have time to prepare." She snuck a peek through the curtains and sighed in relief. "It's only Eddie," she said and opened the door.

Dakota's face brightened at the mention of his best friend.

"Hey hey, Mrs. S.," Eddie said as my mother opened the door. He walked in as if he owned the place. "Are those your famous maple-almond chocolate-chunk cookies I smell?"

"Of course," she said. She winked and pointed to the cookies. "They're on the counter if you want one. Is that your car out there?"

"Yeah, Uncle Bob took a clunker and fixed it up for me at his shop."

A sporty salsa-red coupe was parked out in the driveway. The rear end of the car was jacked up higher than the front, and the gold-rimmed tires looked disproportionately big for its body. A thin black lightning bolt had been airbrushed along the car's entire side panel. Eddie could never do anything in moderation. I thought he was obnoxious…always had.

"Stone!" Eddie said with a grin, giving Dakota a hard man-hug. "Nice to have you back. So, how does it feel to be famous, bro? What happened to you? You look like the walking dead."

I barely recognized Eddie. His voice had deepened, and he'd shot up several inches. He looked like a linebacker. His new hairstyle could only be described as a mullet. Then he spotted me and started to croon *Witchy Woman*.

"Hello, Eddie," I said without any emotion. Sarah intercepted for me and gave him a hug hello.

"So, Stone," Eddie said to Dakota. "You up for going out now? Luna would love to see you, bro."

Dakota's eyes lit up.

Sarah made a face. I kinked my neck to get a better look at her. "What?" I mouthed.

She leaned in. "Wait until you see Luna. Let's just say, we need to go with them."

"Why?" We never went out with my brother and his friends. "What happened to you wanting me to stay in and rest? Don't we have stuff to talk about?"

"I take it back. You're fine. Let's go." I smiled as she locked arms with me and announced to the guys that we'd be joining them.

It felt like I had never left her. It was nice to have my best friend back.

THE SKUNK

I felt completely unsafe with Eddie behind the wheel, since he found it necessary to impress us by gunning the engine wherever the road opened up. He unfairly cursed the slow-lane drivers and had no conception of the "three-car-lengths-in-front-of-you-at-all-times" rule. We nearly rear-ended five cars that didn't accelerate when the stoplight turned yellow. Thankfully no pedestrians were waiting to cross the street, or we really would have had problems.

I took my first breath when Eddie skidded to a halt in the parking lot of a gaudy establishment with a hot-pink neon sign: The Feast Beast Diner—All You Can Eat.

"What happened to Joe's?" I asked. It wasn't the same Joe's Diner that once had been here. Eddie explained that his friend's father had recently bought Joe's and opened the place.

"It's better than Joe's," Eddie said as he opened the car door. "And since Dave's dad owns the place, we can get whatever we want. And if anyone bothers us, they'll get thrown out."

I had trouble adjusting to the chaotic scene inside. There were flashing lights, scantily dressed waitresses, and huge cardboard cutouts of gorilla-like beasts holding trays of food. It was a far cry from the quaint, homey atmosphere of Joe's Diner. This was the first big change I'd noticed since getting back, and I didn't like it.

"There they are," Eddie said, pointing. He whistled across the restaurant to three kids who were sitting in a green booth, laughing and drinking. "Hey guys, look who I brought."

"Dakota!" I instantly recognized Luna's voice.

The slender girl raced toward Dakota and threw her arms around him—only she wasn't the blonde skater girl I remembered.

She had turned goth.

Her skin was milky white, offset by her midnight-black nails, lips, and razor-cut bob. She wore a cropped maroon leather biker jacket with matching high-heeled boots under a black taffeta skirt with a jagged, uneven hem. A low-cut black corset exposed a Celtic cross necklace on her chest.

Sarah nudged my waist. "Isn't Halloween next week?" she said under her breath.

"Stop it," I said and swatted at her finger, which she kept jabbing into my side. "She'll hear you." Luna's get up was definitely macabre, but I actually liked her jacket.

"What?" Sarah said innocently. "I just wanted to make sure I had the date right, that's all."

"Dakota! How are you?" Luna said with a big smile that seemed at odds with her new style. Her delicately colored blue eyes were lost inside thick rings of greasy black liner.

"I'm good," he said, flinching when she brushed a soft hand against his cheek. He looked like a deer caught in the headlights of an oncoming big rig. "So, what's up with all this?" he said. He motioned to her outfit.

"So what's up with your skeleton bod? I kinda like it. Hey, Rees. Sarah."

Sarah nodded and smiled but didn't say anything.

"Hey, Luna," I said. It was hard not to stare at her chest, which was busting out of her top. "Wow. You look so…so different."

"Good different? Or bad different?"

I was tempted to say trashy. "I love that jacket."

"Come this way," she said, pulling Dakota by the hand. "There's some people I'd like you to meet." Luna led us to a far corner and introduced us to the two new faces at the table. "This is Dave B.," she said, pointing to a dark-haired, leather-vested guy, "and this is Johnny G." Johnny had a tight blonde crew cut and a muscular build.

Both guys nodded in greeting. They looked even older than Eddie did.

"So, tell me everything," Luna said to us as she slid into the booth next to the new guys. "What was it like, being on a different planet? I can barely stand being around humans sometimes. I can't imagine how you must have felt being surrounded by aliens." She pulled out a small mirror and applied another coat of black lipstick to her already-dark lips.

Eddie slid into the booth across from her. "Well, that'll be the norm around here, if people don't start waking up," he said, motioning for us to sit. "First, one comes. Then another. And before you know it, we don't have a planet left."

Sarah rolled her eyes. "A little melodramatic. No?"

"I take it you don't approve of them coming here?" I said, not liking Eddie's tone.

Luna huffed, snapping her compact shut. "And you do? It's going to be a circus here, when then arrive. The town is overcrowded as it is."

"It'll actually be less crowded with the island being sealed," Sarah replied.

"You don't get it, Payne, do you?" Eddie said, practically jumping down her throat. "These things just beamed down from out of nowhere, and now we're obligated to introduce them to our world? I'm sorry, but it's bad enough I have to see them on the news all day long—I don't want to be running into them in my town. What's next? Citizenship? We barely have enough land to grow enough food for humans, much less Yrdians."

"They're autotrophs," Sarah fired back at him. "They manufacture food within their bodies using sunlight and water. They don't need to eat our food."

"They have mouths, so they do eat," Luna jumped in. "And even if they don't need to eat all the time, they need water all the time. You said so yourself, Sarah. They need water to make their food." Luna turned her attention to Dakota and me. "You guys have been away, so you haven't seen the news, but that's what people are saying. The Yrdians are acting like our best friends, but they're really planning to take our water."

Sarah raised her hands. "Okay, really?" she said. "First of all, the people you're referring to are a small, radical, anti-alien conspiracy group." She turned to look at Dakota and me. "They don't want Earth to have any contact with any alien species. They unsuccessfully tried to detonate a bomb in the new IPPL wing of the Pentagon while you were away. They're nuts. Overwhelming public opinion is pro-Yrdian."

"Says who?" Eddie said, then shifted his gaze to Dakota. "All right, Stone. You lived on another planet. Tell us what the food and water situation was like."

"Dude. There was nothing."

"Seriously?" Luna asked.

"I'm being serious," Dakota said. "The environment was so polluted—you couldn't drink the water even if you wanted to. Everything was flown in from other planets."

Luna slammed her hands on the table. "See? And we're the crazy ones, right? There's no water out there."

"There's no water on Wandelsta," I corrected. "That doesn't mean there's no water anywhere."

"What can I get you guys?" said a gum-smacking, redheaded teenage waitress. Her tone suggested she'd rather be wrestling a porcupine than taking our orders. Still, I was happy for the interruption.

"An apple juice for me," Eddie said, raising his pointer finger. "And one for my friend." He gestured to Dakota. I hadn't taken Eddie for a juice drinker, so his request surprised me.

"I'll take another, too," Luna chimed in, holding up an empty glass.

"Apple juice, huh?" Sarah said, looking as confused by their drink choice as I was.

I nudged Dakota, who'd been abnormally quiet. "Are you okay?" I asked him. He seemed lost in thought. He was back in his element, surrounded by people who shared his anti-alien views, but he seemed detached. Was my brother starting to question his beliefs? Or were his old friends strengthening them?

"Yeah, why?" he said, then changed his order. "I'll take a soda instead." The waitress sighed as she crossed out his original order on her pad.

Eddie changed Dakota's order back to juice. He leaned toward Dakota and said in a low voice, "You can thank me later. This is your first beer, my friend."

"Beer?" I had said the word too loudly, and Luna put a finger to her lips. "Since when do diners serve underage teens beer?"

"Since Dave's dad owns the place," Eddie quipped, tilting his head toward a bearded, heavily tattooed man behind the counter with the same angular jaw and thick bushy brows as his son. "Dave's old man has the right idea," Eddie said. "He knows kids are gonna drink, so he'd rather that we do it where he can watch."

The waitress returned and placed the drinks on the table. She gave me a small shrug as she handed me the large glass of ice water with lemon that I'd ordered.

"A toast to my friend's homecoming," Eddie announced. "Good to have you back, Kote."

"And Resa," Sarah added sternly.

"And Resa," Eddie said, raising his glass to me. Then he and Luna clanged glasses and downed the yellow ale.

Dakota raised his glass with them, but he didn't take a sip.

"It's totally cool. No one's gonna stop you in here, bro," Eddie said. "Trust me."

Luna took a swig and made a face. "It's not the greatest-tasting drink, I'll tell you that much."

"I can't believe you," I said, giving Eddie a glare. "There could be undercover reporters in here, for all we know. We have to watch our public image."

Eddie made a face. "They sealed the island."

"Talk about paranoid," Luna said.

THE SKUNK

"More like responsible," Sarah retorted.

Dakota looked uncertain. He clearly wanted to impress Luna, who was coaxing him to drink. Why was he still interested in her? She looked ridiculous, and she seemed to have changed for the worse while we were gone.

"You'd think the little hippie witch wouldn't be such a prude," Eddie said, winking at me. "Hippies were chill, or so I thought."

I couldn't think of a comeback fast enough.

"I probably lost more brain cells breathing the air on Wandelsta," Dakota said. He took a hard sip. Cheers erupted around the table. I was pissed.

"A prude?" I said, finally responding to Eddie. "Try, 'someone with a spine and a brain.'"

"A crooked spine at that," Eddie said jokingly. Everyone except Sarah laughed. I felt myself imploding.

"Really?" Sarah said, glaring hard at my brother's friend. "You went there?"

I tried to catch Dakota's eye, but he was too busy staring at a strange kid who was sitting alone in a booth on the opposite side of the diner, his eyes glued on our table. Dakota lifted the mug and took another sip as his friends watched. The loner kid snapped a photo.

"Put it down," I ordered him in a harsh whisper, pulling his arm. "Someone over there just took your picture. You're going to be all over the internet tomorrow."

"Welcome back, Stone," Eddie exclaimed proudly, patting his friend on the back. "Let's eat up, here comes the food."

"You're not honestly going to sit here and get drunk with these people?" I said to Dakota in an undertone.

"'These people'?" Luna said, her voice all challenge. "Open your eyes, honey. We're your people. Unless you got green blood running through you now."

Honey? Did she just call me "honey"? She called me honey.

"Don't talk to her that way," Sarah said with just as much attitude.

"Sarah—" I started.

"No. You don't deserve to be spoken to like that."

"It's fine," I said. "We have a bigger problem right now."

Dakota reached for one of the ice-water glasses on the table, avoiding eye contact with me. The loner kid was still staring at us, a creepy expression on his face.

"Don't make it obvious, but does anyone know that kid over there?" I asked, motioning with my head. "He's the one who just snapped a pic of Dakota."

"The freaky albino with the white hair?" Luna said, stretching her neck to get a better view. "No, never seen him before. But he looks like a friggin' skunk." The pale-skinned, white-haired boy had an unnatural tuft of black hair right near the center of his forehead. "Maybe he is with the press," she said, not sounding the least bit concerned. "He just took another picture."

"That kid's no reporter," Dave said.

"You know that for sure?" Sarah said.

"That's it," I said, a growing sense of urgency in my gut. "We have to leave now. Dakota, I mean it. Let's go."

Our waitress nearly took me down from behind as she approached the table, balancing two incredibly large trays of food. I thought for sure that the food was for two tables, but she placed everything in front of us. The smell of deeply fried food and fake cheese sauce was nauseating.

The amount of food was ridiculous. Oversized portions of chicken wings, mozzarella sticks, bacon-and-cheddar potato skins, French fries, hamburgers, pizza, even lobster tails. It didn't seem humanly possible for our table to eat this much junk.

"Let's do this. Dig in," ordered Eddie as he grasped several wings with his bare hands and shoved them into his mouth. Barbecue sauce dripped from his face onto the tablecloth. I felt physically sick to my stomach. I'd forgotten how much of a boisterous, disgusting pig Eddie was. And for some reason, my brother wanted to hang out with him.

"Dakota, we really should get out of here. That kid keeps taking our picture. I'm leaving. Are you coming?"

Luna tried to feed him a French fry but missed his mouth, leaving a trail of ketchup across his cheek. "No, I'm cool," he said. "You go."

THE SKUNK

"We'll take care of him," Luna reassured me. Then she leaned over and cleaned the ketchup off his face with one lick. It was a sickening display.

I stormed out, taking Sarah with me, and we headed back toward my house.

"She's such a bitch now," Sarah said as we cut through the football field of the middle school to make our walk quicker. "Eddie was always a loser, but as soon as Dave and Johnny moved into town, Luna went downhill fast. You shouldn't let her talk to you that way. And I can't believe Dakota stayed. And what was with her licking his face? She's going out with Eddie now. Slightly inappropriate, to say the least."

"Everything about her is 'slightly inappropriate.' I don't know what Dakota's deal is, but he's dead. I'm going to tell my father everything. That he's been smoking and drinking. I don't care. He's acting reckless."

"He might give up the goods on the dreams and the Citrine if you do that."

"They won't make it past the fact that their son is on drugs." I was so angry that he'd ignored me like that back there…and after everything we'd shared.

It was a new moon, and Orion hung low in the black velvet sky. I was in great shape from all my hikes through the decomposition fields, so the trek home was effortless. I vented the whole way about how disappointed I was in my brother. I thought the Citrine and the manual and Gemja would have changed him. I thought we were getting close. How could he have sided with those jerks?

***

I was still smoldering after another hour of talking with Sarah on my front porch. I wished I had thought on my feet faster when Eddie dissed me. His comment about my spine had stung. I wished I had told them all off, but in the moment my voice had left my body, just as it always did when I was taken off guard.

Sarah lived a few houses down from me and insisted she would be fine to walk home alone. We said our goodbyes and I went inside, creeping up the stairs to my room. I shut the door as quietly as possible, since I was in no mood to be asked about why I was home so early or whether I'd enjoyed myself.

I texted Sarah, relieved that she'd made it home safely, and then removed the black spiral-bound sketchbook I had kept on Wandelsta. Flopping onto my bed, I flipped it open to the page where I'd drawn a picture of the Ploompie meeting Dad. Carefully, I tore it out and added it to the collection on my wall, taping it loosely so that it wouldn't be ruined. As I continued to leaf through the book, I tore more pages out and hung them until the new pictures covered nearly all of my original artwork on the wall.

Satisfied, I turned off the light and went to bed.

THE STORM

"Wake up, now."

I stormed in on Dakota, who was cocooned in blankets, snoring like a pig. My insides were still coiled tight at the thought of how he'd treated me the previous night. I was seriously thinking about reporting him to our parents, but before I completely ruined his life, I wanted to have it out with him and give him a chance to explain or apologize or convince me there was some good reason that he'd chosen to act ridiculously moronic with a group of fake friends instead of siding with the person who had shared the greatest secret of his life with him.

"Not now, Rees." Dakota's voice was barely audible from beneath the mountain of bedding.

"Why? Suffering from a hangover? Get up." I tore the covers off him. "What was your problem last night? You're lucky your drunken face isn't plastered all over social media this morning. The last thing this family needs is a scandal."

"What word didn't you understand? Not or now?" He pulled the blankets over his shoulders and rolled onto his side, his back facing me.

"What word didn't you understand? Get or up? What was with you last night? You totally blew me off, and for what? To impress Little Miss Pale Face, Lady of Darkness?"

I heard a faint snicker.

"It didn't bother you that Eddie trashed me? And did you get a good look at Luna? You were fawning all over that—"

"All over that what, Resa?"

My heart sank when I turned and saw Luna standing in the open doorway. Dakota bolted upright.

"Girl," I responded quickly. Again, not the word I had wanted to use. Why did I feel bad about her overhearing me? She deserved whatever I had to say to her after the way she'd treated me.

"Uh-huh," she said, sounding doubtful. "I guess you weren't expecting to see me this morning. Your mom let me in." She tossed her long black overcoat on Dakota's empty guitar stand.

Dakota squinted as Luna pushed his drapes open, letting in the bright rays of sunlight. It was a gorgeous day outside.

"We're having a rare October heat wave, so I decided to play hooky from school. It's like sixty degrees outside. I thought you might want to go to Acadia Park, Dakota? Sands Point Beach?" She was wearing a tight black mini and a crimson T decorated with a pair of feathery white wings, over which was superimposed the word ANGEL. A black slash cut diagonally across the decal. "But I can see you guys are getting into something here."

Dakota looked about as surprised to see her as I was. It was like old times; she had always barged in on him unexpectedly. She was wearing less makeup this morning, which made her seem almost normal. All she had to do was lose the dagger necklace, black fishnets, and fingerless elbow gloves.

"Are you feeling any better, Resa?" she said in a sticky-sweet voice. "After you left last night, Dakota told me how much toxia you breathed in on that planet, how it made you act funny." She lifted Dakota's guitar off the ottoman at the foot of his bed and sat down.

"Oh, he did, did he now?" I looked at him, one eyebrow raised. He was making excuses for me? I wanted to pop him in the face. My gaze shifted to Luna's ears, each of which was studded with at least ten silver mini hoops.

"We didn't really get a chance to talk yesterday," Luna said as she started to strum the guitar. "Tell me. How did you like being on Wanderstal?"

"Wandelsta," I corrected without enthusiasm. I wasn't in the mood for her insincere small talk.

"Dakota said you kept a journal there that you're planning to publish."

This was too much.

"It came out amazing," Dakota said, beaming like a proud parent. "It totally captures the vibe of the place. Rees, show her." He swung his legs off the side of the bed and stuffed his red-checked flannel pajama pants into a pair of black high-top Converse sneakers. He left them unlaced and walked to the mirror, straightening his spikes.

"I'm waiting until it gets published before I show anyone."

"Oh, come on," Luna said. "I want to see it. Where is it? In your room?"

"No, really. I'm not showing anyone yet," I said forcefully. "The publishing house made me sign something about that." They hadn't really; I just wanted her to leave me alone.

"Oh, please. They'll never know." She put down the guitar, and without an invite, she escorted herself into my room. I didn't believe for a second that she was interested in my journal. She just wanted to annoy me. She was succeeding.

"Wow. Look at this place," she said, pointing to one of the drawings of the crimson sand dunes that I'd pinned to the wall.

"Don't touch them. I have to make copies for the publishing house."

"Those are the waste decomposition fields," Dakota explained. "Trash from all over the universe gets buried in the dunes. Resa went out in them every day."

"It must have reeked," Luna retorted, furrowing her nose. "How could you stand being in those fields, Resa?"

As unpleasant as Wandelsta was, the statement offended me. "They were actually quite beautiful, with all the red-garnet sand."

"I can't believe this. And what are these things?" She was pointing to a portrait of Madam Molina. "Is this real?"

"Those people are the Slopees," I said.

"More like humanoid mole rats that live underground," Dakota interjected.

"Dakota!" I snapped at him.

"Ugh, really?" Luna said with a wrinkled nose. "Mole people? For real? That's worse than Yrdians. How could you stand to be around them? I don't think I could deal with that. Mole people? I'll take plant people over mole people any day."

"They're probably some of the most courteous and giving people I've ever met," I defended passionately.

"Resa, they're not people. And I'm not saying that to be mean. Just look at them," she said, gesturing at one of my pictures. "They have tails and claws. They're way weirder than even the Yrdians. Luckily, you're home now, away from all that." She started to click the stud in her tongue against the back of her teeth as she examined the rest of my pictures. The sound was obnoxious.

"Yeah, lucky us," I said.

"So, where's the stone?" she asked, continuing to nose around my room.

"What stone?" I was confused.

"The glowing one."

I felt like I'd been punched in the stomach. She picked up a piece of quartz from my collection and examined it.

"Please don't touch my stuff," I said forcefully, breathing out a sigh when she put the crystal back. I'd have to clean it now to remove her negative energy.

"Was that it?" she pried.

"Was that what?" I played stupid.

"She knows, Rees," Dakota said. "I told her. Just show her the stone."

I wanted to tear every spike out of his head, one at a time, with needle-nose pliers.

"Resa, I'm not going to tell anyone," Luna said. "Come on. Let me see it. Is this the one?" She picked up my favorite cluster of lavender lepidolite and I ripped it out of her hands.

"I honestly don't know what you're talking about."

Luna reached for my prized hot-pink rhodochrosite cluster and I lunged at her.

Suddenly, the room was bathed in soft amber light. Luna squealed like a baby. Dakota was holding my gem, and he was beaming more brightly than the stone itself.

"Let me see it," Luna said, like a child anticipating a gift. "Let me see it!"

"Give that to me, Dakota," I barked at him.

He gave it to Luna instead. My insides sizzled as she stroked my stone's smooth, brilliant faces. It went completely dark in her hands.

"This is awesome. So, this Gemja stuff is really tru—"

Her words were suddenly drowned out by a deafening crash of thunder, followed by the beating sound of thousands of rain pellets cascading against the roof.

"Whoa, where'd that come from?" she said, rising quickly to shut the window. "So much for the beach."

I watched white lightning branch across the sky, and my thoughts started racing. This scene seemed so familiar.

I remembered the freak storm that had struck Wandelsta the day I first found the stone. Then there was our return flight from the red-sands planet and that strange, unexplained storm in space. And now, on a beautiful, sunny October day, a thunderstorm had sprung up out of nowhere.

"It's the storm!" I exclaimed. "The storm is the power of the Citrine!"

I glanced at my alarm clock—10:12.

"Remember 10:12," I cried, slipping on a jacket and bolting down the stairs. Dakota and Luna followed me out the back door and down to the rocky cliffs behind the house. They watched as I climbed onto a jagged piece of pink-and-black-speckled granite and stood in the pouring rain, arms outstretched toward the heavens.

"Look at that!" I cried. "This is amazing!"

THE STORM

The darkened clouds were centered on a small section of the sky covering our house and extended only a short distance down the coast. Beyond the outline of the menacing storm, the clear, sunny sky was visible. Bright rainbow streaks lined the interface between storm cloud and blue sky as the sun's rays were refracted into different, colorful wavelengths of light.

Luna seemed unfazed by the rain on her body as she stood with her head tilted back, mascara running down her cheeks like black ink. "This is so wild," she exclaimed. "Spooky, but wild!"

We all stared in awe at the phenomenon before us. Then, as suddenly as it had begun, it dissipated. The rain stopped abruptly, the rainbows vanished, and the dark, ominous clouds coalesced and appeared to be sucked into an invisible hole in the sky, disappearing into nothingness. The sun returned, restoring the cloudless, crystal-clear blue sky.

"What time is it?" I asked impatiently.

Luna whipped out her phone. "10:27."

I quickly did the math. "Fifteen minutes! It lasted exactly fifteen minutes!"

All three of us jumped like idiots, completely waterlogged, completely exhilarated.

"What were you doing to the stone?" I asked.

"I don't know," Luna said, shrugging. "I was just rubbing it."

I thought for a moment. "Could it be that simple?"

I darted back inside the house, grasped the Citrine, and rubbed its faces. No sooner had I stroked it three times in opposite directions than the room darkened and the storm once again filled the sky above us, thunder crackling and lightning flashing.

"I can control the weather!" I cried, jumping around my room. "I can control the weather!"

I had finally unlocked the secret of the Citrine.

SIGNPOSTS

The following morning, Luna dropped by unannounced on her way to school, wearing a too-tight black dress with a ridiculous purple boa. She wanted to see the stone again. I hated that she knew about the Citrine. Worse, I hated that I had to appease her for fear that she might turn us in if we didn't. I certainly couldn't blame her for wanting to see it again. Now that we had witnessed its power, it was hard not to want to use it.

And Dakota was being reckless.

"This weather sure has been crazy," my mother said, after the second mini-storm in the last hour had exploded over our house. She walked to the kitchen window and gazed out at the dark sky with a furrowed brow. The storm was nearing the end of its fifteen-minute cycle and I feared she would start to ask questions if she saw the clouds getting sucked into the hole. To my relief, she closed the curtain and returned to the stove to flip a batch of buttermilk pancakes on the griddle.

"I have some news," she said. "Your father called. We're going to be hosting the visiting Yrdian family." She dropped a dollop of whipped butter on the griddle, and it sizzled and popped.

Dakota choked on his own saliva. "You're kidding me, right?" he said after clearing his throat and taking his place at the kitchen table. "They're going to stay here, with us? In this house? When, and for how long? It's Halloween next week. We just got back home. Can't we have a little privacy? Can't they stay somewhere else?"

Using a fork, he speared two maple sausages from a platter and added them to his plate. Then he picked a third off the platter with his fingers and stuffed it in his mouth. Luna helped herself to a plate off the counter and sat beside Dakota. I didn't recall anyone having invited her to breakfast.

"No, they can't," my mother said firmly. "It's the Cuticulors, and your father won't have them stay anywhere else. You can still do your Halloween driveway thing for the neighborhood kids. In fact, we won't be here for that. Your father and I are going to meet the Cuticulors in Bangor, and then we're all going to stay over in Portland for interviews." She brought a container of Maine maple syrup to the table, along with a plateful of pancakes sprinkled with cinnamon and fresh apple slices.

"How long will they be here? Not the entire six months that we were supposed to be stationed on Wandelsta, right?" I was with Dakota on this one. Our family was in the spotlight enough as it was, and I didn't want any additional attention, particularly now that I had to figure out what to do with the Citrine.

"Six months is the term, barring any emergencies. They're going to stay with us at first so they can get to know the town. Maybe they'll want their own place after a while, but I don't know. That's up to them."

"Well, we definitely don't want them to stay for that long, so you should encourage them to get their own place once they know how things work around here," Dakota said. "And what exactly is Mr. Cuticulor going to be doing here? Dad had to run a waste management facility. What task does this guy get? Testing the water quality in beautiful Acadia National Park?"

"What is that supposed to mean?" my mother said, the threat clear in her voice.

"Dakota, just drop it, okay?" I urged him. "The food's getting cold. We'll talk about this later. Let's just enjoy our freedom while we still have it."

After breakfast, I helped Mom clean the table and loaded the dishwasher. She went downstairs to rearrange the basement for the upcoming Yrdian visit and I flopped onto the couch in the living room and turned on the TV to make sure that a video of Dakota's drunken face hadn't leaked out.

"Hey, no more messing around with my stone," I said to Dakota as he passed me while escorting Luna to the door. "You need to tone it down. They're going to know something's wrong if you keep brewing up all those storms."

"Who is 'they'?" he said with an attitude, but he handed me the pencil case that concealed the stone.

"You really are paranoid," Luna said as she draped the boa across her shoulder. "People are only going to find out if you keep making such a big deal about it." Then she turned to Dakota. "When are you coming back to school?"

Dakota shrugged. "We're not. We're going to finish out the year with tutors," he explained.

"Lucky you," she said, throwing her arms around him. Then she gave an exaggerated, Miss-America-type wave and slunk down the driveway and out of sight.

"That's the girl of your dreams?" I raised an eyebrow. "I can't believe you told her, Dakota," I said for about the hundredth time. "Really, do you honestly like her? She's not the same. She's so rude now."

"She's not going to tell anybody, Rees."

"Sarah told me that she's dating Eddie now."

"So?" He was trying too hard to sound like he didn't care.

"So. You always wanted to date her. You had to do something to get her attention, right? Is that why you told her?"

His phone vibrated and he pulled it out of his pocket to read a text.

"You better hope she doesn't ruin this. I'm not going to let anyone take my stone."

He didn't look up from his phone. "No one is taking your stone. Relax."

"You shouldn't have said anything," I repeated. Luckily for Dakota, my cell rang, saving him from a longer lecture. It was Meranda. I walked into another room to take the call privately.

"So, I must see this stone Sarah told me about," she said. "Can you come over now, before the shop opens?"

I chatted with her a few more minutes and then packed the stone up in my backpack and headed on foot for Meranda's shop, an eclectic craft-and-antique shop called A Stitch in Time. Her storefront was actually a quaint two-story home with weathered gray barnwood siding and whitewashed shutters, complete with charming window planters and rocking chairs on the porch. She lived on the upper level of the home, taught classes in the basement, and sold merchandise on the main floor. I climbed the creaky front steps and tried the door. It was locked. I gave a knock.

"Resa, darling!" When Meranda opened the door, she was wearing a garish floor-length dress that looked more like a robe due to its shiny floral-print fabric and big kimono sleeves. Several beaded necklaces in varying shades of gold and black hung around her neck. Her shoulder-length, electric-red hair had a dry, overcooked look to it, making her look older than her forty years.

Unexpectedly, a plump black cat shot past her and nuzzled my leg. "Slinky!" I bent down and picked him up, cradling him in my arms. "How's my favorite kitty?" He nuzzled my nose as I brought him inside. "My favorite kitty is packing on the pounds," I said, chuckling. I put him down and took off my backpack, finding it hard to contain my excitement as I unzipped the bag. "So, are you ready for this?"

"I can hardly wait," Meranda said.

I pulled out my pencil case, gave her a devilish smile, and then dramatically opened the cover. Meranda gasped and drew both hands toward her mouth.

"Oh, my...it's absolutely exquisite!" she said, staring at the gem in awe. She gasped as its luminosity increased when I picked it up and held it out for her. She seemed hesitant to touch it.

"Just don't stroke it in opposite directions unless you want a storm," I warned.

She retracted her hand. "You found its power?"

I nodded. "You stroke the stone three times in opposite directions and it storms for fifteen minutes."

She looked at the stone with trepidation and then started to pace. "Oh, Resa. When Sarah mentioned a glowing stone, I knew it would be something interesting. But this…this is…well, impossible, really." She held her breath as she took the crystal from me. In her hands, the glow intensified threefold. We both had to look away.

"Whoa. I've never seen it that bright," I said, shielding my eyes from its glow. "Wow. It's never that bright when I hold it." She returned the stone and its glow diminished in my hands. When she took it back, the light exploded again.

"It must feed off people's energy," Meranda said. She cradled it in her palms like a newborn kitten. "That would account for why my glow is brighter. I've been doing energy work for my entire adult life. You're still learning the ways of the Craft."

"That makes so much sense. My glow was brighter than Dakota's, and Dakota's was brighter than Luna's."

"Oh, my," she said. "So, the story about Gemja in the book Sarah brought me must be accurate…Yes, yes. It only makes sense." She was speaking to herself now. "For centuries, people have known about the powers that lie within crystals and stones, but they could never explain those innate powers. An origin on Gemja could account for it." She stopped speaking and turned to look at me. "Oh, Resa. Resa." She returned the stone to its pencil box and took me by the hand, leading me to a slightly rusted, antique bistro set in the corner. "Sit. Sit."

She didn't release my hand even after I sat.

"Resa," she said. "I don't want to alarm you. But it was by no means an ordinary event for you to find this stone. Nitika was your guide. She came to you for years. Years. Preparing you mentally for when you would find it." She closed her eyes and breathed deeply before continuing. "I believe that we are all here for a purpose. And that there are signposts along the way for each of us—"

"Signposts?"

She shook her head as if my question was unimportant. "Messages from the other side to help us get to where we are going. Most people miss their signposts or pass them off as coincidences. But the point is that very few people have such obvious and undeniable signposts as you did with your dreams."

"So, that's good, right?"

She looked wary. "It means that you are not ordinary. I could be wrong, but it seems as though you are part of a bigger plan, that you are going to play some role in something that's more important than we can imagine. And because of that, I fear"—she hesitated—"I fear it could mean that you yourself are in terrible danger."

My heart sank. "Why would you say that?"

"When I think of many of the progressive people in our past…the great thinkers who were ahead of their times…what has happened to them? Many were killed because they were feared or misunderstood. It was as if their destiny could only be fulfilled by their deaths."

I released Meranda's hand. "First of all, I'm no great thinker. I'm a girl with a crooked spine who collects rocks. I can barely express my own thoughts. I think you're way off base on this one, Meranda."

"Maybe. Maybe not," she said, rising. "But we must be prepared for all outcomes." Then she went to unlock a glass cabinet by her cash register. "Come." She waved for me to join her. "You need some form of protection."

I took my place beside her as she lifted a large ring from the case. It was a blue oval stone set in silver.

"In some native American cultures, it is said that turquoise will protect its owner by lightening in color to warn of impending danger," she said. Grabbing my left hand, she slipped the ring onto my index finger. It was a perfect fit. "Never take off this ring. Notice its color now. Check it often."

I glanced at the ring, which ran nearly the length of my index finger. "Thank you." It was quite a unique piece and very beautiful. I was instantly attracted to it. "So, what's your take on the new arrival? You know, the guy with the purple eyes. Was he trying to harm me? Did Sarah tell you about her demon theory?"

"I think he was a signpost, and that you missed the sign."

I looked at her curiously.

"He was sent to teach you meditation."

"How do you figure? He tried to push me off a dune. He could have just as easily been sent to kill me."

"Was it a drastic approach on his part? Yes. But I think you misinterpreted your meeting with him. His message was a good one: We have no limits. And if we train our minds, anything is indeed possible. He was a signpost, in my opinion—a person you were destined to meet, one who would help you prepare for your fate. And if you had reacted to him differently, you would have spent your time on Wandelsta getting better at meditation and training your mind to be quiet. Then we could have done what needs to be done sooner."

"What needs to be done?" Her thoughts were two steps ahead of her words.

She gazed up at a wind chime hanging from the ceiling, seemingly turning something over in her head. "We need to find out what this Nitika knows about your destiny. It might be our only way to keep you safe."

I was lost. "How? I don't know if Sarah told you, but I performed a spell to banish her from my dreams. I don't think it totally worked, since I saw her when I found the stone, but she hasn't come to me since then."

"That's precisely why you must go to her."

I was puzzled.

"Astral travel, my dear. You need to learn astral travel. And then we're going to send you into your dream to find her."

MATTHEW NUKPANA

That weekend, my mother organized a meeting at our home with Colleen Skipe, the commissioning editor of Brightwater Books, a big New York publishing house with whom she'd made arrangements prior to our departure for Wandelsta. Today would be Colleen's first chance to review my work, but my mind was light-years away from the journal.

I couldn't concentrate during the meeting. Meranda's words hung over my head, and I couldn't stop thinking about how I might be in danger unless I learned to do something that was itself incredibly dangerous. It didn't help that a few hours ago I had seen a blog article with a picture of me emerging from Meranda's store. The headline was: "Witchcraft and dementia: do both run in the Stone family?" The article rehashed my grandmother's life as a practicing witch and her sudden detachment from reality, which had resulted in her hospitalization. Worse, they drew parallels between the two of us, insinuating that I was destined to end up like my grandmother if I kept going to stores like Meranda's.

"Resa, you did a really wonderful job on these illustrations," Colleen said, removing her square, black-framed glasses and placing them on our long, pine plank farmhouse table. With her short blonde bob and gray pencil skirt and jacket, she looked the part of a New York editor. "I feel like I went here with you. The colors and details are phenomenal." She rifled through the illustrations that were scattered on the table.

"Thank you," I said. "It kept me sane while I was there." I wished I'd chosen a different top than the button-down, man-tailored shirt I was wearing. Sure, it looked professional, but with my scoliosis, the cut kept making my right bra strap fall over my shoulder. Every two seconds, I had to fish around through the neckline to pull it up. I tried not to move too much, which probably just made me look uptight.

Colleen smiled. "It certainly didn't have the comforts of home," she said, closely eyeing the picture of the detoxification chamber. "I must say, I do not like that open shower facility."

"It was awful," I agreed.

My heart dropped when Colleen turned toward me a picture of the new arrival sitting on his dune. "I particularly like this one," she said. "It captures the loneliness of the place. Did you know him?"

I glanced at my mother, who was sitting beside me. "No," I replied, with a guilty quiver in my voice. "Just a random dune dweller."

She gathered all the original pictures into a pile and handed them to me. "Well, I think they're magnificent. The only thing I want to see more of are your thoughts and feelings in your journal entries. You do a lot of describing, which I can absolutely understand since the sights were so otherworldly. But I want to see more emotion in your work. Don't just tell the reader that you almost died in the toxia, make them relive it with you. Work on that for me while everything is still fresh in your mind. I'm going to keep the photocopies you made for myself to share with the editorial staff. In the meantime, we'll have our lawyers draw up the paperwork, and if you can sign the contract as soon as possible, I'd be grateful. We want to put a rush on this project. It's going to be fabulous, I promise. If you have any questions, just call me." She slid a card across the table toward me.

"I will, thanks," I replied, lifting the card. The sparse black script on white linen was too bland for my liking.

"Thank you so much," my mother said. She held out her hand to Colleen. "We'll be in touch." She led her to the door.

"Resa," Colleen said and took my hand in hers. "Wonderful, wonderful job."

My mother opened the door for Colleen to leave just as Sarah was walking up the driveway, holding a large paper bag. Of course, her hair was plastered perfection. She had on a cute girly football jersey and sweats. Her oversized black hobo purse hung awkwardly from one shoulder. She gave Colleen a polite hello as the two passed each other on the steps.

"Hey, Pieces," Sarah said, removing her sunglasses. "Hi, Mrs. Stone."

"Hello, Sarah," my mother replied, heading toward the kitchen. "Would you like some lunch or something?"

"No thanks. I ate before I came over."

"I'm so happy to see you," I said with a smile. "Come in."

She raised the paper bag. "You'll be even happier when you see what I have in here." She took a hard look at my man-shirt and slacks and her eyes flew open. "Oh my God. Was that the editor? How did it go?"

"It was good. They want me to sign a book deal with them."

"Oh my God. That's awesome! How rich are you going to be? Why aren't you freaking-out happy?"

I pulled her inside the house and closed the door. "You'd think I'd be all over this, but honestly, I can't even concentrate on it right now. Let's head upstairs."

Once we were in my room, I closed and locked the door and slipped into a comfy T and yoga pants.

"Holy incense," Sarah said, waving her hand through the air. "It's like a sage bomb went off in here." She threw open a window. "I guess you were taking Meranda's advice and trying to meditate?"

"The incense was intended to help shift my awareness."

"I have something that'll help shift your awareness." She pulled a large cup of vanilla frozen yogurt from the bag and I squealed in delight. I squealed even more loudly when she pulled out a separate cup of peanut butter sauce almost as large as the container of yogurt. "Welcome home."

"You're the best." I opened both containers and drowned the yogurt in peanut butter. "You didn't get anything?"

"No, I ate a cone on the way over. And your Gramps is the one you should be thanking. He gave me a freebee at the shop."

"But you didn't have to go into town to get it. You're the best." I scraped the inside of the peanut butter container to get out every last drop.

"Okay. I'm the best," she said, still rummaging through the paper bag. "I really love that ring on you. I know it's not just for style, but at least it looks awesome."

I glanced down at it. "It is cool. I'm not convinced it will change color if I'm in trouble, but it's definitely cool." I took a spoonful of peanut-butter yogurt yumminess.

"Let's hope we never have to find out." She quit rummaging, but her hand was still in the bag. "Okay. Are you ready to take a look at this?"

"What?" I gave her a quizzical look. "You got me something else?"

"Maybe. It could be something insanely huge or it could be absolutely nothing at all."

My interest was piqued. "What is it?"

She pulled out a piece of paper and handed it to me. "Is this your man?"

I nearly gagged on my yogurt. It was a photograph of the new arrival.

"Alrighty, then," she said, raising her eyebrows. "Seems like that's a yes?"

"How did you get this?" I put the yogurt cup down and stared at the headshot of the new arrival. He looked exactly the same, from his black shirt to his slick ponytail. His violet eyes were just as captivating on paper.

"Oganwando's interplanetary missing-beings website. You can access it through the Internet now. They have tons of information on there."

"What? Really?"

She flopped down on my bed. "Well, from everything you told me about this guy, he sounded like someone who didn't want to be known. That left me with three options. I figured he was either a crook, a superhero, or a runaway. I opted for runaway. I registered on the missing persons site and searched for purple eyes. Three names came up. He was the only hot seventeen-year-old, so I assumed he was yours."

"You're a genius."

"Matthew Nukpana from planet Blackiston."

"So he is a real person," I said. "And that's his name?" She nodded. "It's so normal. I was expecting something more mysterious. Where's Blackiston?"

"About seven light years away, which is roughly a week away from Earth in one of the Yrdian ships. It's called that because it receives so little sunlight." She waved her hand in front of his photo. "That's why his eyes look like that. Glowing eyes help them see in the dark."

"You researched all of this?"

"Of course I did," she boasted. "And it gets better. Because there is limited sun, there is also limited plant life, and thus limited oxygen. Matthew is a Hedricon, a species that has a specialized organ system that allows oxygen to be recycled. Basically, these things don't need air—"

"Things?"

"Sorry. People. These people don't need air. Well, they do, but only in the smallest amounts, and they can reuse it for an extended amount of time."

"Unbelievable. That explains everything," I said. "That's why he could stay out longer in the toxia than I could."

"And when he kissed you in the fields after you found the stone, he was probably giving you his oxygen because he knew you were in trouble. He bolted because Coop showed up and our little runaway didn't want to get caught."

"And that's why he covered his tracks. So I guess that means you're dropping your demon theory?"

"I still don't know why he wanted to push you off a dune, but I think he saved your life in the fog that night."

I felt an urgent need to see him, but what could I do? I was here. He was on Wandelsta. How was he getting food and water out in those dunes? Was Willie still there, feeding him?

"I contacted the missing persons bureau and put in a report that he may be on Wandelsta."

My thoughts raced back to that tattoo of his. So, he was a runaway… maybe I had been right about his family situation after all.

"What?" Sarah said with concern.

"I don't know if that was a good idea. I think his parents might be abusive." I wished I'd spent more time getting to know him. I felt a huge responsibility for him all of a sudden.

"Well, someone will be looking for him now. The good news is, he's not a threat to you."

I nodded, still staring at the picture of the new arrival. Matthew. The name just didn't fit him.

PREPARING FOR FLIGHT

My father came back home on a muted gray day without a hint of sunlight. Mom spared no expense on a four-star feast of all his favorites, starting with crocks of creamy lobster bisque as an appetizer, followed by a decadent beef goulash casserole with piping-hot, butter-drenched popovers. Dessert was a classic apple pie with a crispy cinnamon crust topped with Grandpa's homemade Very Vanilla ice cream. She even made a huge Caesar salad.

The table was impeccably set, a Thanksgiving-worthy display, complete with good china, small salad plates, an overabundance of silverware, and a basket of velvety black-eyed Susans in the center of the table. The dreary, rain-laden day was brightened by the flames of the chunky vanilla-scented candles that sat in ornate candleholders on the buffet cabinet.

Grandpa had come over too, and it was one of those rare days that felt like a holiday, when even Dakota stayed at the table for hours, all of us eating seconds and thirds and fourths despite being full, talking about everything and anything. We reminisced about Wandelsta with a curious affection that came from being far away from the wretched place.

Dad tried to describe his experience at the IPPL headquarters on Oganwando and explain the nature of the strife between the Siafu and the Glucosans, but the conflict still didn't seem real to me. I didn't want it to. At this moment, I wanted to be shielded from the darkness, allowed to sit guilt-free in our cozy little house with the candles and the endless food and the joy of our reunion.

"How long will you be home?" I asked, taking what should have been my last scoopful of ice cream.

My dad raised his eyebrows and then smiled widely enough to deepen grooves beneath his dark eyes. "Since the Cuticulors are going to be on the island for half a year, I'm going to be home for a while, barring any emergencies."

My mother looked like a giddy child. Dakota looked like he wanted to say something, probably about the Cuticulors invading our home, but he showed great restraint.

"It's good to have you have home, Dad," I said.

* * *

Later that night, Meranda insisted that I head to the shop to start practicing astral travel. I didn't know what to expect and wasn't looking forward to the whole thing, especially since she had used phrases like separate from your body in every other sentence while trying to explain it to me. Before walking into the store, I camouflaged my hair under a hoodie and wrapped most of my face in a scarf to avoid detection from any potential paparazzi. The last thing I needed was another article questioning my sanity.

"Are you ready to take flight?" Meranda said as she flung open the door before I had the chance to knock. Her dress, which had no discernable waistline, looked like an orange burlap curtain panel. Dangling from a golden chain around her neck was a chunky mahogany bead that could have doubled as a curtain rod filial.

"Come in. Come in," she said. She flexed her wrist like it was a fish out of water.

"You seem awfully excited given that we're about to do something potentially life threatening," I said, unraveling my scarf. I pulled a scarf-fuzzy from my lip and then drew the curtains more tightly on the front bay windows and double-checked that the door was locked.

"No fears," she reassured me, lifting her dress to expose bare feet as she ascended the creaking stairs at the corner of the shop floor. "And don't worry about those windows. We're going up. No one will be able to see us. Come."

I followed her to the attic. I was happy that she had chosen this room for our practice. Meranda's personal sacred space, the sanctuary, already had an air of magic about it. It had dark wood-paneled walls and floors, and the lack of large windows made me feel more comfortable. The room was also high enough that it separated us from the obvious distractions of cars and people out on the road. She had dressed up the daybed in clean white cotton linens.

"Okay," I said, rubbing my hands together. It was a little too cold for my liking. "What do we do?"

Meranda looked displeased. "It's cold up here, isn't it?" She rubbed her hands up and down my arms to help warm me. "I should have started a fire. Let me do that now." She looked like a fire with her blazing red hair and blaring orange dress.

"No, I'm fine. Really," I said. The sooner we started, the sooner we would finish.

"Okay, then. Put your backpack down over here and lie on the bed."

I did as she asked and pushed off my boots before sliding into the center of the bed. Meranda pulled a stool up beside me.

"Tell me more about what we're doing?" My voice actually cracked.

"It's simple, really. We're going to raise energy—"

"Like in spellwork?" I interrupted.

"Exactly. But this will be more concentrated. We need to use the energy to propel your astral self to leave your body." As she spoke, she swirled her hands in the air over my torso like a mystical medicine woman. "Remember that your astral self is a carbon copy of you but made of energy instead of matter. Everyone has an astral double. And everyone's astral double separates from his or her physical body during a deep sleep. The double travels to other realms and dimensions, but the person seldom remembers their double's experiences when they awaken. Our goal is for you to consciously direct your astral body to leave your physical body and enter your dream realm. And it's important for you to remember your experience after your astral body reintegrates. Now you need to breathe. In for four counts through your nose, and then hold your breath for four. Exhale for four counts out of your mouth. Then hold for four." Her voice was calm, and the words were delivered slowly, soothingly.

I did as she asked, and Meranda guided me through several rounds of four-count breathing. I was growing more and more relaxed, but my mind wasn't the blank slate it should have been.

"In for four. Hold for four. Out for four. Hold for four." She was breathing with me as she spoke.

I needed to put a stop to my thinking. I needed to focus. Following her prompts, I tried to redirect my thoughts to the feeling of the air as it tickled the inside of my nose with every inhalation, and then the warm release that came with every exhale.

"You should feel all the tension leaving your body," Meranda said.

I furrowed my nose when she unexpectedly passed a wand of incense over my head, flooding my senses with the sweet scent of lavender.

"When you are completely relaxed, I want you to imagine a bright orb of pure-white light occupying the space between your eyes. Concentrate on that light. Rotate it in your mind. Feel the mounting energy and twist it, stretch it. Make it grow. See the light grow brighter in the space between your eyes."

Meranda was an expert at delivering visual clues, and I could create a perfect mental image of everything she told me. I manipulated the white light in my mind as if it were real.

"Feel the warmth of the light. See its glow. Make the light branch by sending tendrils down your arms and legs. Let the endless white light fill your core. Let it become you. You are the light."

I felt a tickle on my face, and my mind kicked in. Was this a normal tickle? Or was the energy I was imagining turning real? Then the tickle fluttered across my brow and down my arms. Yes. It was real. I was mobilizing energy in my body. A surge of adrenaline amplified the feeling.

"You are pure white light. Endless. Eternal. Limitless."

Limitless.

With that word, a sudden, heavy pressure seized my body, and I lost my breath. I waited for the feeling to pass … but it only intensified. I couldn't breathe. My throat was closing, and it felt like someone was pushing down on my body, hard. It was similar to the experience I had when I found the Citrine.

"You are pure energy."

My chest was caving inward! Couldn't she tell I was in distress? I tried to scream, but I was paralyzed. I couldn't move. I couldn't talk. She was less than a foot away, but I couldn't reach her. Wiggle your fingers. Do something. Get her attention. Still, my body wasn't listening to my mind, no matter what I told it to do. Then, in an instant, I felt a plummeting sensation.

"Allow your astral self to lift from your body. Feel the energy radiating out through the top of your head."

Panic overcame me. I felt a presence. Someone else was in the room. Could it be Nitika? Had she come for me? Was I dying?

And then…pop.

A cool energy radiated through me, from head to toe, like the feeling after a fever breaks. My heart was racing. My breaths were quick and shallow. But I felt in control of my body again, and I could no longer feel a presence in the room.

Meranda was leaning over me with a worried look on her face. "Are you okay?"

It took a moment before I spoke. "No…I don't know. Didn't you see me struggling? I couldn't breathe." I exhaled deeply, trying to relax my body.

"That's quite normal."

"Suffocation is normal?" I said, annoyed. "There was a presence in the room, Meranda. Did you feel it, too?" My hands trembled as if my blood sugar had dropped, and I didn't have enough energy to sit up. I felt cold. Damp.

Meranda smiled. "It was you."

"What?"

"The presence you felt was you. Your energy double left your body. That's what you felt."

"That doesn't make sense. It frightened me… Why would I feel that way about myself?"

"You didn't recognize that it was you. It won't be scary when you and your astral self are connected. That's why I need you to practice this whenever you can. I sent you an audio file on your phone. I recorded myself walking you through the steps. Listen to it. Practice it. Get comfortable with leaving your body. Recognize the sensations when it happens and embrace them. When they no longer frighten you, you won't fear the presence in the room. You will be the presence in the room. You will have full awareness of your astral body and the travels it experiences. Only then can I guide your astral self into your dream."

A HALLOWEEN NIGHTMARE

ABANDON HOPE ALL YE WHO ENTER HERE

I wedged the stake of the store-bought Halloween sign into the soil at the base of our driveway and stepped back to get a better look at the house. "I can't believe how good this looks," I said as I wiped some residual soil from my hands. "We could charge admission."

Sarah stood next to me with crossed arms, admiring our handiwork, too. "And imagine what it's going to look like in the dark," she said. "I wouldn't want to walk up there. This is even better than when your dad used to do it. Brilliance?"

"Five," I stated emphatically. We rated our great ideas on a brilliance scale of one to five, five being reserved for the best of the best.

We had spent the entire morning transforming the long and winding gravel driveway into a haunted walk for any neighborhood trick-or-treaters who dared to come calling at the house later on in the evening. We staggered painted Styrofoam tombstones up and down the driveway, stretched cotton cobwebs over the bushes, and propped human-sized dummies—made of old clothes stuffed with newspaper—into lawn chairs. Some were holding spiders; some, plastic butcher knives. For an added ounce of fun, we'd included folding tables with display bowls of rubber worms and plastic eyeballs coated in vegetable oil. Dakota was perched in the big oak out front, hanging handmade sheet-ghosts from the branches.

"They look awesome," I shouted up to him, just as he finished tying a rope around his fourth and final ghost. He released the rope from the limb of the tree and the ghost swung eerily overhead with his other buddies. Dakota shimmied down the trunk, jumping the last three feet.

"If we have batteries, I'll put the strobe light up there for a lightning vibe," he said, then disappeared inside the garage.

"Lunch?" Sarah suggested.

"Definitely." We headed toward the house and slipped through the sliding doors into the kitchen.

"Dakota seems less jerky today," Sarah said. "Did you guys make peace about him telling Luna?" She sliced open three sesame-seed rolls. "Do you want these toasted?"

"Please. There's nothing worse than a soggy roll." I placed the leftover chicken Parmigiano from last night's dinner in the microwave. "It's weird. I'm still annoyed with him for telling her, but I get why he did it. He just likes the girl, so he wanted to impress her. I mean, I still think about Matthew, even after all the weirdness between us... I dreamt about him last night. When you like someone, you do strange things."

"You're being too nice, as usual. He had no business telling her. I would have disowned him as my brother."

"Of course you would have." I gave her a playful wink. "It's weird. It was like an instant bond formed between us when we witnessed the stone's power."

"I get that. It made you both part of something bigger than yourselves. I don't suppose that feeling carried over between you and Luna?"

I side-eyed her. "I don't trust that girl as far as my scrawny little arms can throw her." My cell beeped. It was Meranda. I didn't pick up.

Sarah raised her eyebrows when she recognized the number. "You don't want to talk to her?"

"She's persistent, I'll give her that," I said. "I'm supposed to be practicing astral travel, but I don't want to... There was something else in the room when she taught me how to do it. She says it was me, but I don't know. I have a bad feeling about the whole thing."

"Then don't even try. Listen to your gut."

"I know. But what if astral travel is the only way for me to find out the meaning of Nitika's message?"

"You do need to find out what it means. That stone is special, and Nitika wanted you to have it."

Dakota entered the kitchen cradling several batteries in one arm, the strobe light in the other.

"Do you have enough?" I asked. "I also want to play some spooky music for when kids walk up the driveway."

"I have plenty," he confirmed. He lined them up on the counter and popped four of them into the strobe light. White pulses filled the room, casting a glow on Dakota's devilish smile. "Heh heh. This is gonna be great."

The microwave beeped and I used potholders to remove the piping-hot dish, which I placed on the counter to cool.

Sarah set the lightly toasted rolls on each plate, and I topped each with a piece of chicken parm. I grabbed ice waters for everyone and we all sat and ate, finalizing our plans for scaring trick-or-treaters.

For the first time in weeks, I was actually having fun. It was a beautiful, cloudless Halloween day. My parents had left to meet the Cuticulors, and we had the whole house to ourselves. It felt amazing to do ordinary things again.

* * *

At about five o'clock, our first visitors arrived—a group of four munchkins who were standing at the base of the drive, deliberating very loudly on whether it was safe to come up. Superman was too frightened. The troll loved the strobe light. The ballerina claimed it wasn't scary at all. And the clown would come up but not if he had to go first.

They debated for several minutes until finally the ballerina led the way. She marched right under the lightning ghosts, announcing to the others that they were nothing more than old, ripped-up sheets. She peered into the bowl of oily eyes, seemingly unimpressed. She inspected the stuffed men in lounge chairs, and just as she declared they were fake and not scary at all… Dakota launched himself from the bushes wearing a ski mask, sending her pink tutu fluttering as she raced back to the base of the hill.

"Brilliant," I said, chuckling from our spot on the front porch. I opened one of the treat bags and searched for a peanut butter cup. Just then someone approached the porch through the grass. I sighed when I recognized Luna.

"Holy identity crisis," Sarah said under her breath with a snicker. It was hard to tell if Luna was a vampire or a pirate. Her face was covered in white powder and there were glow-in-the-dark fangs in her mouth, but she was wearing a shaggy skirt, a white puffy blouse, and knee-high boots.

"Hello, ladies," she said, as if we should thank her for gracing us with her presence. Her fangs glowed neon red when she spoke. "Where's my post?"

"Your post?" I asked, popping a mini peanut-butter cup into my mouth.

"Dakota just called me and said he needed help scaring the kiddies."

"That shouldn't be too hard for you to do with that great costume," Sarah said. It was hard to hold in my laughter. From the way she had said it, it was impossible to tell whether she was being sarcastic. "He's over there." She pointed at Dakota.

Luna forced a fake smile. "Going as yourselves tonight, I see?" Then she turned and headed toward the driveway. She crouched beside my brother in the bushes and gave him a hug.

"I really despise that girl," I said. "I love our capes."

Tonight was the one night when Sarah and I felt comfortable with publicly wearing the beautiful crushed-velvet capes Meranda had given us last year for use in rituals. With their draping hoods and cascading floor-length fabric, they screamed witch. Mine was a deep espresso brown lined with plum-colored silk. Sarah's was midnight black lined with crimson.

"What does Dakota see in her, anyway?" Sarah asked, watching as Luna chased a group of three little monkeys up the driveway.

"Trick or treat!" the kids screamed in unison, breathing heavily. I tossed a goody bag into each of their pails and sent them back down the lawn.

"Your guess is as good as mine. I think he's still trying to find the old Luna in there somewhere."

"He'll have to excavate through a foot of face paint first."

By nine o'clock, the treat cauldron was nearly empty and the foot traffic on the driveway had died down to a trickle. Dakota and Luna had quit and gone inside, so Sarah and I headed into town to grab ice cream at Grandpa's shop.

The line of costumed customers at Sheer Deliciosity extended out the door and halfway down the block. We skirted past them and headed right inside.

"Resa!" my grandpa greeted me from behind the ice cream counter. He looked frazzled. His white apron was streaked with drips of caramel and fudge. What little white hair he had left on his head was jutting in all directions like Einstein's. Sarah and I didn't hesitate. We removed our capes and jumped behind the counter to help with the orders.

"My girls saved me," he said, patting our shoulders. "Lifesavers."

"What happened to Todd?" I asked as I swirled out a scoop of rainbow sherbet from a nearly empty container.

"Called in sick at the last minute."

The three of us scooped cones, sprinkled sundaes, and blended shakes for nearly two nonstop hours before the Halloween crowd died down and we were able to take a break.

* * *

I slid onto a stool and let my head rest on the counter for a moment. Sarah slipped in beside me and gave me a high five. "Nice job, Sitis," I said.

"Back at ya, Pieces."

"You saved me, girls," my grandfather said as he placed two containers of vanilla yogurt with extra peanut-butter sauce in front of us. "You can have all the free ice cream you want."

"Isn't that always true, Mr. Glover?" Sarah said with a wink.

"Always," he said as he took off his apron and went to close out the register.

We helped Gramps clean and close up the shop, and he slipped us each a twenty before Sarah and I headed back to my house. The driveway looked amazing from the road with all the spooky props and candles lining it. I was surprised to hear voices coming from the house. It seemed late for trick-or-treaters. Dakota hadn't turned off the strobe light, which gave the impression that we were still open for business.

"Rees, look!" Sarah pointed to something in the grass. One of our pumpkins had been smashed to bits. Suddenly a teenage genie girl and a lasso-wielding cowboy staggered out of the bushes, laughing and chasing each other across the front lawn. The cowboy roped the genie and the two fell on top of each other in a passionate embrace.

"What the—?" There were dozens of costumed kids milling about. Some were sitting in the grass. Others were on the bluff making out. There was even someone in a tree. I didn't know any of them. The back door was wide open, and people were filtering in and out.

Sarah held out her palms to prevent me from going near the house. "Okay. Don't freak," she said calmly. "Do not freak. Wait here. I'll find Dakota and drag him out here for you. Then you have my permission to do whatever you see fit to him."

My anger mounted exponentially as Sarah disappeared inside the house. She resurfaced alone, shaking her head.

"It's bad in there," she said. "He's coming."

I lost it when I saw him walking toward us, all grungy in his fake-blood-smeared sweatshirt and jeans.

"What is this?" I shouted, like a person possessed. "What is wrong with you? Mom and Dad will be back tomorrow with the Cuticulors! These people are trashing the house, Dakota. Are you insane?"

"I didn't invite them," he said defensively, throwing his hands up.

"It was just supposed to be Luna and Eddie. I don't even know half these people."

"That bitch!" Sarah said. She started to storm toward the house, but Dakota grabbed her arm.

"This isn't your business, Sarah," he said.

"But it's mine," I said angrily. "And it's high time that I told that girl off myself."

Sarah held me back. "Yeah, okay, Spaghetti Arms. The last thing you want is to mess up your hands so that you can't draw. Follow me, but keep your mouth shut."

I loved having a muscular, mouthy friend.

"Neither of you are doing anything. Stay here," Dakota demanded. "I'm going to take care of it."

"Yeah, you've been doing a great job so far. When do you plan on getting rid of them? Tomorrow, when Mom arrives with our guests? I just hope Grandpa doesn't stop by. Or reporters." I jumped at the sound of glass breaking somewhere inside the house. "Out of my way." I pushed Dakota aside and shot through the back door, Sarah at my heels. The air was thick with cigarette smoke and the music blared loudly enough to cause an instant headache. I stormed toward the speaker to lower it and accidentally rammed into Eddie, causing him to spill his…BEER?

"Beer?" I shouted at him in disgust. "You brought beer into my house? Clean that up and when you're done, get the hell out."

"Whoa. Did I hear correctly?" Eddie said, laughing, slurring his words. "Little Miss Hippie Witch is using profane language now? Maybe you aren't too good to have a little fun with us, after all." He was staggering, barely able to stand. "You need a drink."

"You need a life." I pointed a finger at Luna, who was standing next to him. "I can't believe you brought all these people into my house." A crowd started to gather.

Luna raised her eyebrows and took a swig of something from a bright-blue bottle. "The last I checked," she said, "you're not the only one who lives here."

I was stumbling for a reply when Dakota came into the room.

"Looks like that toxia she breathed in did some permanent damage," Luna said to Eddie. Then she winked at me and tipped her bottle in my direction, as if to say she'd only been making a joke.

"That's it," Sarah said, pushing me out of the way.

A cacophony of high-pitched squeals drew our gaze to the door. Dave, Luna's tough-looking friend from the diner, had just barged into the house, wearing a rude costume that poked fun at the Yrdians. He was iced in green paint and covered in long vines of pothos leaves. He had a six-pack of beer in each hand. Luna's eyes met his, and she gave him an air hug to avoid messing up his cakey paint job.

"Welcome to our planet," Luna said and then whispered something in his ear. She shot me a devilish smile. "You love Yrdians, right, Resa?"

My heart dropped when Mr. Swamp Creature started to come toward me, dragging his dirty vines across my mother's cream rug.

"So, this is the lady of the house?" he said, extending his arms toward me.

"It is," I said, backing up, annoyed that he was leaving little specks of soil and paint chips all over the place. "And your costume is making a mess. You can't walk around in here wearing that!"

What happened next was too fast for my mind to process. Dave had passed the beer off to Luna and before I could move or resist, he'd lassoed me from behind with his vines. He pulled me backwards until I was uncomfortably close to him. The vines were deceptively strong, and I couldn't break the tether.

"This is what you like, right? Yrdian-lover?" he said. He yanked me harder into his chest. "You want to get it on with a plant?"

I heard an eruption of laughter as his balmy, alcohol-heavy breath brushed my cheek. I tried to pull away, but he was much too strong. "You like this?" It felt like hours had passed instead of seconds. My arms were pinned, so I tried to slam my heels into his shins, but he shuffled his legs backward to avoid my blows.

"Why do you want to get away from me? I thought you liked plant people?" he said, and then to my utter horror, he started to shift the vines he was using to trap me, increasing his force with each pass. I think he was aiming the vines for my chest—thank God they landed across my stomach instead. "Does that feel good? Huh?"

"Get off her!" Dakota bellowed, charging. Eddie lurched forward to block his path.

"He's just playing, Stone," Eddie said through a laugh, preventing Dakota from passing him. Dakota was no match for his larger friend.

My mind rifled through all the UFC matches I had seen, searching for a move that would help me escape his stronghold.

An even bigger crowd had gathered around us, but no one would meet my eyes besides Luna, whose gaze flickered with wicked delight as she watched us. This could easily turn even uglier. Lord of the Flies kind of ugly.

And then, unexpectedly, I was free.

The vines around me suddenly came loose, and Luna's facial expression turned sour as Dave hit the ground behind me.

I turned in time to see Sarah, fists cocked in the air, delivering what I assumed was her second forceful kick to Dave's knee. She went for a third even though he was coiled like a snail on his side, clutching his leg in agony.

"You nasty bitch!" he cried out. "Someone get her away from me."

My instinct was to grab a weapon, and the closest thing was an iron fireplace poker. I picked it up and held it like a baseball bat so that I'd be prepared if Dave tried to retaliate.

The room fell silent.

"Sarah, what the hell's wrong with you?" Eddie fired at her. "The guy was only playing. Are you insane?" Luna and another girl dressed like a Raggedy Ann doll rushed to Dave's side as if he were a wounded war veteran.

Sarah untied her cape and let it fall to the floor. "Playing, my ass. Try sexual harassment, fool."

"Sarah, it's okay. I'm fine," I said, trying to de-escalate the situation. I was worried about her safety.

"No, it isn't. That guy had no right to put his hands on you." She glared at Eddie. "And you should be protecting Resa, not defending that—"

I had to do something. "I'm calling the cops if everyone doesn't leave now," I said. The trembling in my voice kind of ruined the effect. I repositioned my hands on the poker. "I mean it. Everyone has to go. Now."

"Resa, give that thing to me," Eddie said, walking toward me. "What's the matter with you? The guy was playing. You're so damn uptight."

Dakota blocked the path between Eddie and me. There was fire in his eyes. "You heard her, Eddie. Party's over. It's time to take your friends and leave."

"Give me a break, Stone." Eddie smirked and tried to pass my brother, but Dakota pushed him hard in the chest with both hands. Eddie's face darkened as he fell back against the wall.

"Oh, God," I muttered. I didn't want to use the poker, but if Eddie started to hurt my brother—

"I'm giving you a pass on that one, Stone," Eddie said. Luna had scampered to his side and was helping him up. "Your head must be all messed up from being on that damn planet. Get it together, man. I'm not going to be so forgiving if you lay your hands on me again."

The attention suddenly returned to me when Luna jumped in my face with attitude. "This is all your fault, witch," she hissed. "Stop trying to poison Dakota with all your holier-than-thou, 'Let's welcome the Yrdians with open arms' crap."

My head reeled. She was blaming me for this mess?

"Back away from her," Sarah said as she stepped in front of me.

"Resa doesn't dictate what I think, Luna," Dakota corrected. I lowered the fireplace poker when I realized I was holding it like a sword. "The party is over," he said firmly. "Everyone out. Now."

I put the poker back into its stand on the fireplace and pulled out my cell, poised to make good on my threat to call the cops if things escalated.

Luna's face twisted as she turned to look at Dakota, her mouth agape. Then she started to nod. "Okay, fine," she said, still nodding. "That's what you want? Fine. Be my guest. But don't come crawling back to ask for our help when these plant people take over." The rest of the revelers followed her out like sheep, taunting me as they passed. "Plant Girl" seemed to be their favorite jab.

When the house was finally empty, the three of us stood shell-shocked in the den. Nothing was in its place, the furniture had all been moved, and everything was covered in Dave's soil and paint debris.

"Rees—" Dakota started to say something, but I stopped him.

"I know. Let's just get this cleaned up."

Maybe I could finally have my brother back after this mess was over.

THROUGH YRDIAN EYES

"You must be Resa. Congratulations on your book deal."

I extended my hand to the tall, thin Yrdian who stood at the door.

My father's alien colleague sounded and acted human, but he looked part vegetable, with his nappy white cauliflower hair, long slender neck, and reed-like arms and legs. His wife and teenage daughter shared the same cruciferous features. Red lights flashed at the base of the driveway from the police escorts who would be permanently stationed in front of our home as long as we were hosting the family.

"Thank you," I said. "Nice to meet you." They all bowed in acknowledgment. The Cuticulor family belonged to the Waxilus genus, a species that had evolved biological adaptations over time to better survive on their dry homeland, Yrd. All three had slit eyes, tiny mouths, and smooth, waxy skin the color of broccoli soup.

A chilling gust of wind caught us by surprise. I tottered to maintain my balance, but the Cuticulors bent gracefully with the air. I waved for them to come inside. I could hear my parents' voices in the background, followed by the clunk of luggage being rolled up the driveway.

"Dakota, I presume?" Mr. Cuticulor said, glancing across the foyer to where Dakota was crouching beside the sofa in the living room. A gust rattled the windows and a dozen or so leaves tumbled into the house. I pushed the door shut behind the Cuticulors even though my parents hadn't come in yet.

"Uh, yes," Dakota said. "Hello." He didn't stand or approach our guests, which I thought was rude until I saw the sun reflecting off a stray beer can under the couch.

"You must be exhausted. Let me show you where you'll be staying," I said quickly, whisking the family to the basement so Dakota could remove the can before our parents made it inside. My stomach did a flip at the thought that we might have missed other evidence of the party. As the Yrdians freshened up, I hurried upstairs to help Dakota do one final search, but Mom barreled through the door.

"It's freezing in here!" she barked as she bounded into the house. "Resa? Dakota? Why are all the windows open?" She dropped her overnight bag near the front door and immediately began shutting them. "You're wasting so much heat. I can't believe these are open." Then her eyes shifted to the floor. "Resa, were you painting on the rug?" She'd managed to find a microscopic flake of green paint that I missed during the midnight cleanup.

"Why is this house so cold?" The sound of my father's voice made my heart drop. He looked haggard from too little sleep. He was probably stressed from the Siafu invasion and the long ride home; he would have zero patience for anything not to his liking.

"I tried to make you a cake last night, but it burned, and I didn't want the house to smell like smoke." I breathed a sigh of relief. I had thought of one of the few excuses that was guaranteed not to make my parents angry.

"Help your mother with the windows," my father said briskly, giving me a rushed kiss hello. He removed his overcoat and hung it in the hallway closet. "And Dakota, take up the trash pails from the end of the driveway. They're going to blow away in all this wind."

"Lovely home, Robert," Mr. Cuticulor said as he reappeared in the foyer.

"Thank you, Narvo," my father replied. "We'll get it warmed up in no time."

"Ah, we Yrdians are used to cold desert nights. How about a quick tour of the house?" his guest said. "Resa already showed us the basement."

"A tour it is," my father said. The tension seemed to leak out of his body as he and his friend disappeared into the den.

Dakota looked aggravated. "'Oh, it's so nice to see you, son,'" he said, pretending to be our father.

"Don't let it bother you," I said. "He just wants everything to be perfect for them. Let's get those pails."

"Like he couldn't have done that on his way up the driveway?"

"It's actually better that he didn't," I said. "It'll give us the chance to make sure nothing incriminating fell out when they collected the garbage this morning."

"Tell me about it." He flashed me the inside pocket of his flannel jacket, where he'd stashed the lone beer can.

"Amazing if that's the only one, considering we cleaned the whole place on zero sleep," I said. Dakota winced as he flexed the hand he'd used to punch Eddie. "Are you sure you didn't sprain it?"

"No, I can move it. It just stings like a mother. Hey. I'm sorry about last night."

I hung my head. "It's not your fault."

"You were right about them."

"It's over now."

Just then, Mrs. Cuticulor and her teenage daughter, Sashi, came into the room and formally introduced themselves. Sashi apparently loved matte black, as her ski jacket, headband, and hoop earrings were all the same shade. In fact, her mother was clad in a matte-black wardrobe, too. "Look, Momma," Sashi cried as she raced to the panoramic windows in the dining room, which faced Frenchman's Bay. "They have water, Momma! Water! Can we go see it?"

Her mother was equally impressed by the view. "Do you mind if we step out to take a look?" she asked. I shook my head no, and the two of them practically flew out of the house. I watched through the window as they hiked up the rock bluffs in our backyard. It suddenly hit me why the family wore black. Dark colors were better absorbers of sunlight, which they needed for making food. Sashi was practically jumping in place with excitement as she pointed to two puffins that were being carried by the wind gusts overhead.

"What's up with them?" Dakota asked my mother as she came into the room holding a tray of coffee mugs and condiments. "Not exactly the smartest idea, to stand on a ninety-foot bluff in monsoon-force winds."

"This is nothing compared to the dust storms on their planet. They're just excited. Earth is very different from their planet," she explained. "Speaking of which, they want to go to Bollide Slide Park later. So look good."

"Will the park be closed to the public?" I asked.

"The Yrdians insisted we keep it open. They want the public to get used to seeing them out in society. But the park is only allowing half capacity to better maintain security. This will be our family's first public appearance with the Cuticulors, and I'm sure I don't need to stress how important it is for you to look and act respectful and responsible. Cameras will be everywhere."

* * *

Typically I enjoyed going to Bollide Slide Park, which was a singular experience that was so far and above normal amusement parks, it couldn't be compared. But today's trip felt like a spectacle engineered to make me feel awkward, especially since I quickly realized that I was overdressed in my gauzy black mid-length dress, black moto jacket, and knee-high suede boots. Dakota had played it safe for the trip and was wearing jeans, a black sweater, a jacket, and—of course—his signature blazing-red hair spikes.

A black limo with dark-tinted windows picked us up at the house around 3:00 p.m., and a caravan of police cars with lights flashing escorted us to the park in upstate Maine. When we de-boarded the car at the entrance, at least ten suited officers formed a wall around us. It was suffocating, to say the least, but they shielded us from the reporters. The only thing I had to remember was to smile and to keep my hands in my pockets. Cameras were flashing wildly, and the last thing I needed was for them to catch me rubbing my nose or scratching an itch the wrong way.

As we approached the park, a red-haired woman in a beige peacoat, a camera crew trailing behind her, flagged down my father. She was vocal enough that he stopped to answer some questions.

"Mr. Stone. How does it feel to host an Yrdian family? Many saw it as a logical choice, being that you were the first earthling to ever make contact." She pointed her microphone toward my father as she awaited his response.

"It's an honor and a privilege," my father replied, his voice solid and strong. He rested his arm across Mr. Cuticulor's back. "Narvo and I are not just colleagues in the IPPL, we are friends."

The reporter looked at Sashi. "And I presume this is Sashi, the daughter of Mr. Cuticulor? How do you like Earth so far?"

Sashi eagerly leaned in toward the microphone. "It is beautiful, and you are so lucky to have water everywhere."

"Yes, yes we are. And are you excited about going to Bollide Slide Park tonight?"

"Um, I am quite excited. We do not have amusement parks on Yrd, and I would like to see what they are all about."

My father chimed in. "We thought it would be the perfect place to take the family because we couldn't have put together this particular park without the help of the Yrdian engineers. We did it together—our vision, their technological support."

It had taken a few years to construct the park, which was built under a thick glass dome on a large geostationary meteoroid. The thirty-minute "Stairway to the Stars" transportation service to the meteoroid was actually the coolest part of Bollide Slide Park. Enclosed in a cylindrical, transparent tube was an escalator of moving seats that transported customers to and from the park. The cars would gradually climb, then level, then climb, then level, continuously accelerating until they reached the meteoroid. It was a pure adrenaline rush to watch Earth slip away beneath you.

After we rode the stairway to the top, a park official directed us down a small, narrow corridor, through a set of revolving doors, and into the park.

Sashi was absolutely giddy. "How bright!" she said, barely able to contain her excitement. Her eyes flicked toward every flashing light, every buzzer, every frolicking child. "Your world is so alive!" She jumped backward as a nearby roller coaster took a towering plunge. "We don't have anything quite like this back on Yrd." Her eyes shifted toward two boys who were bouncing fifty feet into the air on the Astro-Blast pogo-stick ride.

"Where to first, Dad?" Dakota asked.

"Not that," I said, gesturing at the pogo-stick extravaganza. Then I nodded at the Ferris wheel. "That's about the easiest thing here."

"Good choice," my mother said. She led the way to the gigantic, sixty-foot wheel, and we followed, surrounded by our armed escorts.

We all fed off the Cuticulors' excitement. The line at the Ferris wheel parted as our caravan came through, allowing us to board instantly. Sashi sat with Dakota and me, and our parents and the Cuticulors shared another cab. The orange and red chaser lights lining the car mesmerized Sashi, and she sat following them with her eyes as I buckled her in.

"I take it this is a big change from Yrd?" I asked her with a smile.

"Oh, yes. Do you know much about Yrd?" I shook my head no, but a short man in a white suit and cap, who was holding a mountain of colorful sticks of cotton candy, diverted her attention. "My, that must be heavy," she said. "How can such a little man hold all of that?"

"That's awesome," Dakota said as he leaned over the seat and waved several dollar bills to get the vendor's attention. "You want one, Rees?"

"No, thanks." Cotton candy was way too sweet for me, but it was fun to see how excited Sashi was.

The man took Dakota's money and handed up two sticky masses of blue cotton candy twirled around large white plastic sticks.

"Yrd is the second-closest planet to our sun, next to Valagaam," Sashi explained as she took her candy from Dakota. "Oh, I see," she said. "It's actually quite light."

"Valagaam's hot and volcanic, correct?" I said, trying to remember the facts I'd picked up from the Gemja manual.

Sashi nodded. "Yes. Yrd is really warm most of the time, but not as geologically active as Valagaam. We don't have any volcanoes like they do. What we do have is lots of salt." She poked the candy with her finger. "What a strange texture. It's so light and airy. What do you do with it?"

Dakota demonstrated by stuffing a gargantuan piece of candy into his mouth. Sashi looked worried.

"He's fine," I reassured her. "There's barely any mass to it. But you should probably try a small piece first." Sashi was hesitant. "So, as you were saying…your planet is made of salt?"

"Yes," she said distractedly as she pulled off a tiny piece of candy and smelled it. "Yrd was once covered by vast oceans. But we are so close to the sun that most of the water evaporated into space, leaving behind huge mounds of sea salt. Our landscape is mostly large, arid salt deserts." She cautiously placed the candy on the tip of her tongue and rolled it around in her mouth. "Ooo, it dissolves into sugar!"

The wheel began to spin, and the car jerked forward. Sashi peered over the side as we ascended and pointed toward the Astro-Blast ride. "There are those jumping boys!"

I was interested in all the little things she found fascinating; it helped me see our world in a new light. "So, after all this, do you still think water is our most impressive feature?"

"Oh, yes. Yrd has very little water," she explained, placing a larger sample of candy in her mouth. "If you haven't noticed already, our skin is quite waxy, and our eyes and mouth are small compared to yours. We developed this way so that more water would stay in our bodies. We don't excrete half as much water as you humans do. Our problem is rainwater. Without rain, what little crops we grow can't develop properly."

"I thought you didn't need food?" Dakota questioned, sounding a tad suspicious.

"Our primary means of nutrition is autotrophic, meaning we can manufacture food in our cells through photosynthesis. However, in times of low sunlight, like during dust storms or nighttime, we can get our energy like you do. Through consumption. Without rain, the crops don't grow. Worse, the Doolie population gets out of control."

"What the heck is a Doolie?" Dakota said, making a face like he'd been sucking on a lemon rind.

"What is a heck?" she replied with an equally sour face.

I laughed. "It's just an expression. It doesn't mean anything, really."

"Oh. Well, Doolies are assembled from salt grains," she explained. "They're hard and sharp, and millions of them can form at a time."

"They're alive?" I asked. "Salt is inorganic. How is that possible?"

"They're not just made of salt. On our planet, extremophiles live dormant in our salt grains."

"What's that?" Dakota said, pulling his neck back.

"Extremophiles are life forms that can live in seemingly impossible locations," I explained. "We have lots of them on Earth, too. Halophiles need a high salt concentration to grow."

Sashi nodded. "Exactly. On our planet, decreased water levels activate these odd life-forms, which prompts the formation of the Doolies. I know it's hard to understand."

"Can't you just step on them?" Dakota asked.

"Um…no." She looked hesitant. "Well, actually, yes. But they're kind of like ants on your planet. You could step on one ant here and there and be fine, correct? But could you step on a million?"

I liked her comparison.

"But unlike ants here on Earth, Doolies don't bite you," she continued. "They scrape you. Imagine being shaved to the bone by millions of pieces of sandpaper that feed off your flesh."

"Ugh." I grimaced and pulled my coat tighter around me.

"The only protection from Doolies is rain. Since salt in soluble in water, they dissolve in rain. But rain on Yrd has been so scarce recently that I'm glad we were able to come here. Many people try to evacuate to other planets until the dry season passes."

"You don't have to worry about the Doolies anymore," I said after a moment. "I think rain is on its way to Yrd."

"I wish I had your confidence Resa. All I can say is, I hope so."

I knew so. I held a beautiful gem that had the power of rain, and I was ready to give it up to save Sashi's people. Dakota's eyes met mine. We'd tell Dad about it as soon as we got home.

"Hey, Plant Girl!"

My heart dropped. Luna was standing at the bottom of the ride with Eddie and his crew.

"You gotta be kidding me," I muttered. I didn't know if Luna's comment had been directed at Sashi or me, but it was unacceptable either way. Had they followed us here?

"What is it?" Sashi asked.

Dakota seemed visibly on edge, but he kept quiet.

"Nothing," I replied. Then I looked at Dakota. "They can't do anything. We have a police entourage waiting for us when we get off this thing. Just ignore them. Don't even look at them. They don't exist."

My heart sped up as I felt the ride slowing. It was hard not to look at Luna's clan when their plant references became louder and more irate. The ride came to a halt, and as soon as we disembarked, the guards surrounded us and led us away from the hecklers.

"So sorry about that," my father said, placing a hand on Sashi's shoulder.

"Not everyone accepts us," Sashi said as soon as we could no longer see or hear the group of thugs. "Do you know them?"

"They used to be my friends," Dakota replied. I could tell how much the whole thing bothered him.

"They just need more time to learn to trust us," Sashi said. "It's okay."

"No, it isn't," Dakota replied. "They shouldn't have treated you that way."

Even with the police escorts, I wondered if we should leave the park so that the Cuticulors wouldn't be subjected to any more potential taunts. The decision to leave the park was made for us when rain began to fall.

"Oh, too bad this wouldn't happen on Yrd," Sashi said, raising her hands to catch the falling water.

I watched as the Yrdian girl started to dance. She was acting like hundred-dollar bills were falling from the sky instead of plain old water. Then I realized just how much we took for granted on Earth. Hundred-dollar bills would mean nothing without water.

Suddenly my heart dropped.

Lightning speared the air and thunder rattled the dome, and we scurried toward the exit. While my family and I were shielding our heads as best we could, the Cuticulors were practically turning their faces up toward the rain.

"It's only water," Sashi said as I pulled her arm, leading her to the homeward-bound part of the staircase. "We're not Doolies. We won't melt."

It wasn't the rain that bothered me; it was the fact that it was happening inside a weather-controlled dome.

The limo ride back to Bar Harbor seemed to take an utter eternity. As soon as we reached home, I bolted from the car and dashed into the house, taking the stairs two at a time until I reached my room.

I held my breath as I lifted the golden pencil box from my artists' table and slowly opened it.

It was empty.

The Citrine was gone.

VALIDATION

My parents didn't respond as I'd expected when I told them about the theft of my magical stone, not even when I told them it might come from a mystical crystalline planet called Gemja or that Dakota and I had personally seen it create rain. They didn't question my sanity or look at me like I had ten heads. They took me seriously instead and demanded to know who else knew about the stone and the legend. I didn't tell them about Meranda, but I gave up Sarah, and Dakota explained that Luna and Eddie were probably the thieves.

My father had called an emergency meeting in his den for everyone except for Luna and Eddie, and we were just waiting for Sarah to arrive. Dakota and I sat on one side of my father's stately, fit-for-the-president mahogany desk, and my parents and Mr. Cuticulor sat staring back at us from the other side. It made me extremely uncomfortable, the way they whispered amongst themselves as we sat there silently. It felt like we were kids in a principal's office, awaiting punishment. It didn't help that we could hear the sound of thunder starting and stopping on a fifteen-minute cycle in the distance. It was a constant reminder of our error in judgment. Luna and Eddie were openly abusing the power of the stone.

Ten minutes later, Sarah arrived at the house and my mother escorted her into the den. We smiled at each other, but then her gaze immediately homed in on Mr. Cuticulor.

"Sarah, have a seat," my father said. He motioned to the empty chair next to Dakota.

"This is very Grand Inquisition–like," she said lightly. She slipped off her colorful pom-pom hat and shoved it into her coat pocket. Not surprisingly, her hair looked perfect. "Is everything okay, Mr. S?" She took her seat, but her eyes kept shifting back to the Yrdian.

"As you can imagine, Resa took us by surprise when she told us that she had found a glowing stone that made rain," my father replied, removing his glasses and laying them on the table. "We wanted to speak to everyone who had seen it."

Sarah held up her hands, palms facing my father. "It's true, Mr. S," she explained. "I know it sounds crazy, but I saw that thing make rain." My father made a face that I couldn't place.

"Dad, just sit and listen to the pattern of the storm for a while," I said. "It's not natural. It's on a fifteen-minute cycle. And if you actually go outside and look, you'll see the clouds get sucked into this hole in the sky."

"And last night it rained in the park," Dakota added. "It doesn't rain in the dome, you know that. Luna and Eddie were making it rain with our stone."

"Our stone?" I said.

"I saw it, too, Mr. S," Sarah chimed it. "If you rub this glowing stone, it makes it rain. It's as real as the hair spray on this head of mine."

My father rubbed his eyes. When he finally spoke, his response startled me. "I know it's true," he finally said. "I just can't believe you know it's true. This changes everything."

"Dad…" I cocked my head.

Sarah's mouth dropped open as she whipped her head around to look at me.

"How do you know it's true?" Dakota said. "We're the ones who found the stone."

"I'm the one who found the stone," I corrected.

"When I first met Mr. Cuticulor," my father said, "he revealed to me the existence of an ancient text that described this place you told me about…Gemja. The legend you've heard is based on that text."

"Written by Kryolite?" I blurted out. Dad gave me surprised look.

"When we were on Wandelsta, we found an IPPL document in the trash that had photocopies of that text in it," Dakota explained.

Mr. Cuticulor shook his head. "I can't believe copies of that original IPPL meeting still exist on Wandelsta," he muttered to himself. "That happened so very long ago."

"Well, according to the text, yes," my father said. "But no one knows who wrote it. No one knows who or what Kryolite is."

"Do you have the text with you?" Mr. Cuticulor asked me.

I nodded. "Yes. I found it down the Slopees' hole. It describes all the planets. The crystals. Everything. It also describes Gemja."

Mr. Cuticulor shook his head and gave my father a hard look. "Remember what we talked about earlier, Robert? It makes sense."

"I agree," my father said.

My mother gave him a concerned look. "Only if they want to."

"Want to what?" I asked.

"Cassandra?" Mr. Cuticulor said to my mother. "Are you sure you're okay with this?"

She hesitated. "Yes. Make them the offer. But it's their decision. I'm fine as long as no one gets forced into anything."

"Forced into what?" Dakota said.

"You see," Mr. Cuticulor said to us, sitting erect, "When the original text was first discovered, an assembly convened, and photocopies were distributed to all senior IPPL representatives for review. After weeks of analysis, they passed it off as a hoax, discarded the paperwork, and abandoned the project. But that changed when an Yrdian reported finding a glowing stone. That's when we started to suspect that the legend might be true, at which point we created a special branch of the IPPL called C-QUEST, dedicated to finding the power stones. That's why we came to your planet—to find Earth's stone. Your father made it easy for us because he had already located it. Well, part of it. Earth's stone was cracked, and only half was recovered."

The words smacked me in the face.

"You found Earth's power stone?" I felt a jolt of energy. "How did you not tell us this? Where did you find it? Where is it? What does it do? Do you have it here?" The words rattled off my tongue so fast that they were barely decipherable to my own ears.

"Your mother and I found it when we were younger," my father said. "We were hiking up Cadillac Mountain in Acadia when we saw a very dull reddish glow in a heap of granite rubble. It was the tiniest little thing. No bigger than a peanut, I would say. Its edges were jagged and broken…we didn't think much of it. Your mother thought it was pretty."

"Honestly, I just thought it was some sort of phosphorescent mineral. It was so small. The glow was so dull. It didn't seem extraordinary. Just pretty," my mother said, her eyes bright. "I kept it in a box with other mementos from when I was dating your father."

"This is unreal." Chills ran up my spine. "Do you still have it? Can we see it?"

"I no longer have it," my father said. "When Mr. Cuticulor came to Bar Harbor and asked me about Earth's geology and glowing stones, I felt compelled to tell him the truth."

"What does it do?" I asked.

"Transportation," my father replied. "It takes you anywhere you want to go."

"Everything makes sense now," Dakota said, looking at the Yrdian. "You invited Dad to join the IPPL because you wanted his stone and you wanted to make sure he kept your secret."

"Confidentiality is a key aspect of our mission," Mr. Cuticulor confirmed.

"So the legend of Gemja is true?" I asked.

"All we can say is that the manual has led us to stones that possess unexplained powers," Mr. Cuticulor said. "As far as the rest of it goes, Kryolite, the planet Gemja…well, we'll have to wait and see until all the stones are found."

"How many have you found in total?" Sarah asked.

"In total, the IPPL has found five additional gems, which are now kept under lock-and-key in a heavily guarded cell back at headquarters in Oganwando," Mr. Cuticulor said. "These were five stones found solely through the written words in that manual. Their powers and mode of activation were exactly as outlined in the manual."

"So only five out of twenty-six?" I said. "Well, six with mine."

"Collecting the stones takes time," Mr. Cuticulor explained. "You can't just waltz in and ravage a planet to look for its stone. If you remember the legend, each species must willingly donate their stone. You first have to make contact. Then develop rapport. Trust. Then there's the challenge of deciphering the clues to locate the gem if it has not yet been found."

"So, why is this so secretive?" I asked. "The more people who knew, the easier it would be to find the stones, no?"

"That's true," my father said. "But the universe isn't ready for that much cooperation yet. Look at how slow our planet is to accept the Yrdians. We're still adjusting. Imagine how people would react to finding out about the magical crystals on top of everything else. And humans aren't the only species that might react badly. Based on Mr. Cuticulor's experiences, most species aren't advanced or educated enough to make informed decisions about Gemja. If it became universal knowledge, we fear that wars would be started by species who wanted the crystals for their personal gain."

I immediately felt guilty. I hadn't even wanted to turn over the stone. The idea of possessing a power that great had been too tantalizing.

"We can't afford to have the power crystals land in the hands of those who might abuse them," Mr. Cuticulor said. "And that's why we've summoned you here. You've seen something that could have a profound impact on all sentient species. Because you are privy to this knowledge, we're offering you an opportunity to enroll in the Academy, an educational program through C-QUEST. The objective is to train the students to take part in the search for the power crystals, with the ultimate goal of reuniting all the stones." He handed each of us a chunky manila envelope. "All the information about the program is in here. These envelopes are confidential, though, and are not to leave this room. Your father will see to that." He rose. "Robert, I'm going to check the progress of the Citrine's retrieval. Stay with the kids while they review the paperwork. I'll need to know as soon as possible, since the semester starts in three weeks for new students."

Mr. Cuticulor left, and each of us reviewed the contents of our envelope under my father's watchful eye.

"I can't believe this. There's a school for this?" I clarified. "For training people to find the power crystals that will reunite Gemja?"

My father gave us a slow nod. "I know this is a lot to digest, but this is a huge privilege for all of you, and I think you should give it real consideration. I don't have to tell you that we are dealing with something bigger than ourselves. You've seen what that one stone can do. It means that Gemja is a real possibility. And you'll be on the forefront of getting us there if you decide to attend the Academy."

"But you don't have to if you don't want to," my mother said quickly. "Sashi declined her invitation. It has to feel right for you."

"Where is the school?" Dakota asked.

"Oganwando," my father replied.

"Oganwando?" Dakota said. "We'd have to move there? For how long?"

We kept firing off questions, one after another. "Can I tell my parents?" Sarah asked.

"We wouldn't finish school here?" Dakota pried.

My father finally shook his head to quiet us. "I know you must have many, many questions. It's intense, the schooling. Five days a week, eight hours a day for two years. You would live in the school building. Each semester is three months long, with two breaks during that time, long enough for you to visit home. Unfortunately, neither break falls on any of our holidays, so you would be away for Christmas. Your second year is hands-on learning in the field on a real stone-collecting mission. The Gemja aspect of your training must be kept purely confidential for your safety and the safety of the stones. The story you would tell everyone is that you were given a scholarship to attend a school whose aim is to spread universal peace. Take a look at the paperwork. There are five potential positions that you can train for within the C-QUEST organization. Read about each of them. I'll be here to answer any questions you might have when you're through."

I riffled through the many leaflets and papers, not knowing where to start. My father walked to the corner of the room to take a phone call, and I heaved a sigh of relief when I heard him confirm that the Citrine had been recovered. From listening to Dad's end of the phone conversation, I assumed that Luna and Eddie were being detained somewhere. They'd probably be debriefed about what they'd seen. But I didn't think it mattered much that they knew the stone's secret. Who would believe a bunch of irresponsible, alcoholic kids who blabbered about a stone that made rain?

"Holy—Resa..." Sarah said. "Find this brochure." She held up a bright-pink pamphlet. "Turn to page two, second paragraph. Hurry."

"What is it?" Dakota asked. He got to the section more quickly than I did. "No way." He glanced up at me with wide eyes.

I rustled through the leaflets and pulled out my copy of the brochure, flipping to the section that had so surprised Sarah and Dakota. There was a list of the five positions: Historian, Persuader, Decoder, Protector, and...

I gasped.

Retriever.

I scanned the summary and read the final sentence out loud. "The ultimate responsibility of the retriever is to collect power stones." I looked up at Sarah with wonder.

"There you go, retriever girl," Sarah said with a shrug. "Destiny-mystery solved."

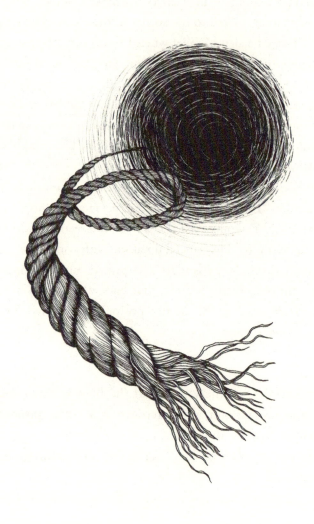

THE BROKEN CORD

I had to get out.

I slipped into my black poncho coat and a slouchy gray wool cap with matching gloves and walked into town to see Meranda. She'd texted me earlier, telling me to practice raising energy in my body to prepare for more astral projection. As much as I didn't want to do that, I decided I'd rather entertain Meranda than spend another moment in my house, pondering the life-changing tsunami that had just washed over me. I'd earned a new nickname from Sarah—RG, short for Retriever Girl. It seemed that the destiny Nitika had warned me about involved moving to Oganwando to become a Retriever, but I didn't want to leave the comforts of Earth, especially not when I had a book deal underway. My reasons seemed selfish, though, especially since everyone else was on board with going. Even Dakota, who was still squeamish about meeting so many new alien species, couldn't stop fantasizing about the four of us on a quest for the universe's magical stones. I had reluctantly committed to being part of the Academy team, but I was confused. Scared. Uncertain. Maybe it was because I knew I had more to lose in the end. Nitika wanted me to find that stone. Not them.

A cold front had swept in, bringing with it a gloomy, misty gray sky that perfectly reflected how I felt. Mom and Dad had gone somewhere with the Cuticulors, so I couldn't ask to use the car. I was the only crazy person out on foot in this weather. Occasionally a car passed, sending leaves scraping down the pavement. Periodic gusts of wind stole my breath, and my eyes started to water from the cold. I shoved my hands in my pockets and kept my head low.

I detoured from my normal route down Jacob Street and turned right onto Apple Drive to avoid a giant black and white Husky that was staring me down from a fenced yard. My nose felt like an icicle. This was the longest walk I could ever remember taking to Meranda's store. I tucked my chin into my chest for greater warmth, which is why I didn't see the person who was walking toward me from an intersecting side road until he'd almost passed me.

I looked up as I heard the quick steps to my right. It was the albino loner kid from the diner—the one who had snapped a photo of Dakota. His eyes met mine, so I gave a wry smile. His milky white skin stood out sharply against his ruby-red blazer, which he wore over a white button-down shirt and white pants. Tan, steel-tipped cowboy boots completed his look. It was an odd combination, but it looked sleek and stylish on him. He must have been freezing without the warmth of a real winter coat. The jet-black stripe that cut through the center of his natural white locks made good on Luna's observation that he resembled a skunk. A hip skunk, though. I hadn't realized I was staring until his eyes locked with mine again.

"I know you," he said, catching me off guard. His voice was deeper than I'd expected. He was still walking a few feet ahead of me. "I know your secret."

What an odd way to start a conversation. I didn't know what he intended, but I was tired of people toying with me.

"Which one?" I called out boldly. He flashed a devilish grin over his shoulder and kept walking for another fifteen feet or so before disappearing into a vegan café. Shaking my head, I walked the final blocks to Meranda's.

When I burst into the store, eager to be out of the cold, I was greeted by the warm smell of an apple-cinnamon candle burning on the front desk. Slinky was curled in a large wicker basket atop an antique curio cabinet for sale. He gave a gigantic yawn when he saw me and then hunched his back before changing his position. Meranda was stoking a fire in the large river-rock fireplace to my right. Her floor-length crocheted sweater blended in with the gray and tan stones of the fireplace. I wouldn't have seen her there at all if it weren't for her fire-red bun.

"You walked?" she said in disbelief. "It's freezing out there. You must be chilled to the bone." She placed the iron poker back in its stand and helped me out of my coat.

"I needed the air. It always helps me think," I said. Then I gave her a quick synopsis of the story of the stolen stone and the Grand Inquisition. She hung my coat and poured me a cup of hot chocolate. "No one can know about that school," I said. "I just figured you already knew about the legend, so I might as well tell you the rest. That and the fact that I can trust you with my life."

"Your secrets are my secrets."

"Thanks," I said as I took the cup, soaking up its warmth through my gloved hands. The velvety drink glided down my throat effortlessly, and my face instantly started to thaw.

"So your father has the Citrine?" she said, wrapping her sweater tighter.

"Uh-huh," I said and took another sip. I savored the rich chocolate flavor and silky-smooth texture.

Meranda looked displeased. "And you're okay with him keeping the stone, even though you don't know how you're connected to it yet?"

"Well, that's just it. I do know that now," I said. "My father told me that the IPPL has a special academy whose goal is the collection of these power stones. I mean, think about it. The Academy has a program that trains its students to retrieve the stones, and Nitika always told me that my purpose is to retrieve something…If I am supposed to play a bigger role, like you suggested—like if I'm Earth's representative for the final reunification ceremony—then it would only make sense for me to give up the stone for the greater good. Everything that's happened since I found the Citrine has taught me that. And the fact that my dreams about Nitika have ended is a sign that I'm on the right track."

"I still think we need to ask her to be sure, don't you?" Meranda's question sounded more like an order than a suggestion.

"I don't agree," I said decisively. "I have a bad feeling about the whole thing, and I don't want to do it. Why do you keep pushing?"

Slinky popped out of his basket and jumped down on the front desk to nuzzle Meranda's hand. She let out a forceful sigh as she halfheartedly stroked the cat. "I just think we need to be completely sure that you're following the right path, Resa. The stakes are higher than ever."

"You always told me to trust the universe," I said. "Come on. It gave me the last name Stone, like that wasn't a big clue about what I'm supposed to do with my life. Not to mention the fact that Dad found a stone. Well, part of one. And then I found one, too."

"What? You didn't tell me that! Your father found a power stone like yours?"

"Yes…I'm sorry. He just told me today. I'm so overwhelmed, I can't keep things straight. That's the whole reason he was invited to join the IPPL."

"The very organization that you must now join to fulfill your destiny. Resa, I implore you. You can't assume you know your destiny. You must, and I mean must, speak to Nitika. We can't assume we're on the right track if you don't." Her eyes had a dark look that worried me. "You said he found part of a stone?"

I nodded.

"Was it red?"

"Yes. How did you know?" I couldn't remember if that part of the Gemja manual was legible.

"I haven't been entirely forthcoming with you. There's something I need to tell you."

As if there hadn't been enough surprises today.

"Your father wasn't the only one in your family who found a stone." It took me a minute to process what she was saying. Her tone implied that she wasn't speaking about me.

"Meranda, please. I can't handle much more today. Who else found a stone?" Her gaze shifted to a photograph in an ornate silver frame. It was of her and my grandmother before my grandmother's illness.

"Meranda? Who else found a stone?" I repeated, this time more anxiously. "Grams? Grams found a stone?"

Meranda tilted her head. "How do you think we met?"

"Grams found a stone," I said again.

"Yes. Well, it was a small, broken stone. Now, in light of what you have told me, the missing piece must have been found by your father."

"Three generations of my family were led to a glowing stone?"

"Indeed. And when your grandmother found hers, she had nowhere to turn except to the crazy lady in the local witch store. Who else would believe that a ghost had led her to a glowing stone?"

I launched myself to my feet. "Grams saw a ghost, too?"

"A young, shrouded girl. You and your grandmother have more in common than you might think."

"And you didn't think I needed this information?" A chill shot through my body in spite of the warm chocolate I'd been drinking. "Where's the stone now?"

"I wish I knew," she said. " 'It's safe' was the only thing your grandmother ever told me about her precious gem. She didn't tell anyone about it, not even your grandfather. She was convinced she needed to do something with it, but she wasn't sure what."

"I cannot believe this," I ranted, pacing now. My situation had been catapulted into a whole new level of weird. To top it off, I felt completely betrayed by Meranda's secrecy. "What am I supposed to do with this information?"

"Find out why your family was chosen. Did you father mention anything about a ghost leading him to the stone?"

"No."

"Can you ask him?"

"Yeah, I'll do it over dinner tonight. Of course not! How could I even bring something like that up?"

"All right, then. The only thing we can do is move forward with my initial plan. You need to ask Nitika flat out what you're supposed to do. Oh, Resa, I'm so sorry. If I had known more back then, this burden would never be on your shoulders. I failed your grandmother, but I won't fail you. I promise you that."

"How did you fail her?"

"I'm the reason that your grandmother is lost."

My heart sank.

"Lost? She got out of the hospital? How do you know?" I pulled out my cell to call home. "Tell me you didn't help her escape from Windamere Hospital?"

"Oh, of course not," Meranda said, motioning for me to put the phone away. "Not that kind of lost. The person in Windamere is not your grandmother."

I stared at her so intently I thought sparks might shoot from my eyes. "Who is it, then?"

"It's just a shell. Your grandmother's life energy, her soul—everything that makes a person who she is…it's floating somewhere out in the ether, and it's all my fault." She was acting spacey, waving her hands in the air.

"You can't blame yourself for what happened to Gram," I said. "She was ill. There's nothing anyone could have done for her."

Meranda cast her eyes down. "But that's just it. She wasn't ill, Resa. She was one of the most insightful people I have ever known. She asked me to send her into her dream—the one with the shrouded ghost—for answers. She had a way about her, your grandmother, and she convinced me to try even though I wasn't experienced enough at the time. It's my fault that your grandmother is lost, and now her role seems to have been passed down to you."

I looked at her, speechless.

Meranda sank into a pale-yellow Victorian wingback chair and rested her head in her hands. "To this day, I don't know what happened that night. We sent her into the dream, and everything was going well. We were communicating just fine…and then…there was some kind of static. I couldn't hear her clearly anymore. All I could make out was the word cord. Something happened to her cord, but I don't know what."

"Stop. Stop!" I said, raising my hands. "You sent her into her dream, and you were talking to her while she was in it?"

Meranda nodded. "It was so easy for your grandmother to slip into a trance and leave her body."

"What is the cord you're talking about?"

"When you sleep, your astral self lifts from the sleeping body. It's attached to the physical body by a silver cord attached to the third eye." She pointed to the space on her forehead between her eyes to show the placement of the third eye. "The cord is the astral self's only connection to the physical body. Somehow your grandmother's cord was damaged or broken, and there was no way for her astral self to reintegrate with her physical body."

As I watched, Meranda stood and flipped the sign on the door from Open to Closed. She drew the shades to give the appearance that no one was in the store.

"So you're telling me that Grams is alive somewhere out there with no way back to us?"

Meranda nodded, looking grim. "Yes. Trapped on another astral plane, dangling a broken silver cord behind her."

FINDING GRAMS

A light snow was falling as Sarah and I drove through the mountains on a desolate tree-lined road to visit my grandmother's hospital, three hours north. Sarah had borrowed her father's tan four-wheel drive, which was excellent in the snow. We had told our parents we were going to Sarah's family's cabin because she wanted to snowboard, and we both wanted a girl's day out before we left for the Academy in three weeks. It was an easier story to sell than trying to explain that I wanted to see if there was any glimmer of Grams left in her body. I doubted they would have understood my concerns about her floating somewhere in another dimension with a broken silver cord.

We had left Bar Harbor at around nine in the morning, but the icy conditions were slowing us down so much that we were barely halfway there come noontime. Sarah pulled off at the only open diner we could find. Situated in a run-down, rusted mobile home, it was a poor excuse for an eatery, but it felt good to get out of the car and stretch. We both ordered grilled chicken-spinach wraps with extra sautéed onions, pico de Gallo, and guacamole. It was a risky choice for a diner in the middle of nowhere. I pulled out a book on astral travel that Meranda had given me after she'd dropped the Grams bombshell and we leafed through it as we waited for the food.

"Look up that silver-cord thing," Sarah said as she squirted some sanitizer on her hands. She had gone casual today in baggy sweats and a tight ponytail. She was still rocking her signature movie-star sunglasses even though there was no sun and it was snowing.

"You know that stuff is toxic," I reminded her as she offered me the bottle. "I'll take my chances with the germs, thanks." I kicked off my boots and folded my legs Indian style on the booth.

"I'll remind you of that when you come down with swine flu again," she said. "So, what does the book say about the cord?" She removed her glasses and squirted some eyedrops into her eyes.

"You're doing a lot of squirting today," I observed.

"I'm going to squirt you in a minute, you squirt. Focus. Cord. What does it say?"

I read its definition in the glossary. "'Silver cord. Also known as a life cord. The cord is comprised of energy and connects a person's physical body and its projected double during an OBE.'"

"OBE?"

"Out-of-body experience," I explained, and then read the definition of that. "'When a person's energy double leaves the physical body and experiences alternate realities in different astral planes. The energy double contains the consciousness of the physical body.'"

"What's an astral plane?"

"'One of many different dimensions or planes of existence with fewer physical laws than our own. For example, in some planes we are able to fly, or travel through walls. Astral planes may or may not be Earth-like. The astral plane is sometimes called the fifth dimension, or the plane of endless possibilities.'"

"So Gemja is an astral dimension?" she suggested.

"Maybe," I replied, reading on. "Oh, this is cool." I read the definition for mind-split effect to her. "'Consciousness can exist simultaneously both in the physical body and in the projected double.'"

"So, you can exist in two different dimensions simultaneously? You could be conscious on Earth and in your dream?"

"Do I look like a rocket scientist here?" I shook my head. "That's what the author makes it sound like. I remember reading about some physics experiments where an electron was in two places at once, so anything's possible, I guess."

I closed the book as a golden-haired waitress in a gray dress and white apron set down our wraps, which looked incredibly dry and unappetizing. I took a bite. The tomatoes tasted sour and the wrap instantly broke apart in my hands.

"So somewhere right now we might be sitting in a diner where this wrap is soft and juicy and fresh?" Sarah said, taking a bite of her own food.

I smiled as the insides of her sandwich slid out the bottom and splattered onto her plate. I opened the book again and started skimming the passages about the cord.

"Listen to this," I said. "It describes the cord as an unbreakable energy filament that allows energy to pass from the physical body to the double to keep it functional and aware. Grams certainly isn't either of those things. Meranda said that her cord was disconnected or broken. This book makes it sound like that's impossible."

"Does it say anything about how to reattach it?"

"No. It implies that it can't be broken."

"Why not?" Sarah gave me a look. "We're not talking about a physical body here. We're talking about energy."

I shrugged. "All I know is that it says it shouldn't be able to be broken." I was getting frustrated, and I wanted to see my grandmother as soon as possible. I convinced Sarah to ditch the rest of her barely edible wrap so we could make it to the hospital sooner.

We pulled through the tall, wrought-iron gates of Windamere Hospital at 3:00 p.m., two hours later than anticipated. The grounds were sprawling and the gravel entry-road swept out in a large circle around the property before bringing us to the four-story, red-brick-faced building. It took a good half hour to make it through the check-in procedure before an expressionless, robotic girl cloaked in standard gray hospital scrubs led us to a corner room on the second floor.

"Do you want me to wait outside?" Sarah asked, removing her sunglasses and placing them in her hobo bag.

"No. Come in with me." My stomach was queasy with nerves when I reached forward to open the door.

Grams was slumped in a chair by the window, her eyes downcast. Her stark white hair shocked me. She'd always dyed it black when I knew her, and the white made her appear very frail. She didn't move as we entered the room. I left the door slightly ajar behind us.

"Hi, Grams," I said in a pitch higher than the one in which I usually spoke. "It's me, Resa." She didn't respond at all. I turned and met my friend's gaze.

"Hi, Mrs. Glover," Sarah said, moving closer to my grandmother. "It's Sarah. How are you?" Nothing. "Try again," she told me. "Get closer to her."

I nodded and squatted in front of my grandmother, resting my hands on the arm rails of her chair. "Hi, Gram," I repeated, forcing my voice to sound cheerful. "Do you remember me? It's Resa." I waited several seconds, but she was completely unresponsive. "I have something for you." I slid my backpack off my shoulders and pulled out a small bouquet of flowers.

"Red daisies?" Sarah said. "You didn't tell me you got her flowers. That was so nice."

I laid the bouquet atop her bedside table. I'd never told Sarah about Gram's theory about red daisies. "Yeah. She always liked these."

"And owls," Sarah said, gesturing toward some of Gram's personal trinkets.

"And owls," I confirmed. Grandpa had brought many items from her owl collection to the hospital. A barn owl statue. A screech owl pendant. A snowy owl photo-frame with a picture of the two of us in it. I picked it up and turned it toward her. "This is me," I said as I pointed to the photograph. "And you. Do you remember?"

Sarah put a hand on my shoulder, which instantly flipped the tear switch, and I felt my eyes welling.

"Grams? It's me, Resa."

No reaction.

"Rees," Sarah said calmly, placing her hand on my shoulder. "Rees, it's time."

I put the photo back and picked up a small quartz crystal from the table. "Meranda says hello," I said, rolling the crystal in my hands. "She told me about your special stone. Do you remember the glowing crystal you found?" I was trying to shock her into action, but she just sat there, lifeless. Sarah tightened her grip on my shoulder as I put the quartz back in its place.

"Gram? Can you hear me?" I was getting frustrated. I clapped my hands together loudly, but Sarah was the only one who jumped.

"She's not in there, Rees," my friend said. "Come on, it's time to go. It's snowing harder, and it's going to take forever to get back."

"Gram?" I lifted her hand in mine, not expecting it to feel like a cool, clammy fish. My fingers fell limp, and her hand dropped like an iron meteorite.

"Rees, it's time to go. She's not in there," Sarah said, this time with more force. "We have the answer. There's nothing more you can do for her here because she's not here." She physically lifted me by my shoulders to get me to stand. I couldn't stop the tears from falling down my face.

She was right—the grandmother I knew was no longer in this body. But she was wrong about one thing. There was something I could do.

I could learn astral projection and find her in another dimension.

AWARENESS

I was angry with Meranda for not telling me the truth about my grandmother's stone, not to mention her failed attempt to return my grandmother safely from her dream. I suspected that she'd withheld the information for fear that I wouldn't trust her to try the whole dream-entry thing again. I wondered if she would have told me anything at all about her previous failure if I hadn't refused to cooperate. I hated being at her mercy, but I needed her help if I wanted to save my grandmother. I had to suck it up, make peace, and work with her on this…praying that she'd learned from her past mistake.

She was thrilled when I told her that I had reconsidered the idea of dream entry, but I deliberately decided not to tell her that I was planning to look for Grams in addition to talking to Nitika. I doubted Meranda would approve, so I kept it quiet. She had kept something important from me, so she owed me one, and I didn't feel a shred of guilt about concealing the truth from her.

Meranda and I practiced every day over the next week, and I managed to leave my body each time. But I still had no awareness of my double other than that fearful feeling of sensing another presence in the room.

* * *

"Are you jeopardizing this deliberately because you really don't want to do it?" Meranda asked, as she sat beside me on the daybed. "Your mind may be subconsciously blocking your ability to connect. You have to want this, Resa. Or we're wasting our time here."

I hadn't even thought of that. Perhaps she was right.

"Do you want to go, Resa, or not?"

"I do, and I don't," I said. I wanted to help my grandmother, but I was afraid of the way my dream about Nitika had always made me feel. "Let me try again. I'll really focus this time."

Meranda nodded and then disappeared. She returned a few moments later with an amber-gray crystal in her hand. "Smokey quartz," she said and tucked it into my hand. "The perfect stone to help you. It collects scattered energy, removes emotional blocks, and provides protection. It's known as the stone of cooperation. Take a moment and feel the energy in this stone, Resa. Connect with it."

I ran my fingers along the smooth, flat surfaces of the crystal. It felt cool at first, but it warmed as I concentrated on the energy within it. I felt a slight vibration.

"Everyone separates when they dream," Meranda reminded me, as I lay there with my eyes closed, palms loosely cradling the stone. "But very few remember what their astral self experienced during the separation. Today you must remember. Say it. 'I must remember.'"

"I must remember," I repeated as I released the tension in my forehead. "I must remember," I repeated after Meranda. "I must remember." The slight vibration I felt in my palms moved into my wrists and then up into my elbows.

Meranda put on hypnotic instrumental music that I liked. Something about the ethereal music helped my mind switch to beta waves—that dreamy state right before sleep—very quickly. I was on the cusp of slumber, but my mind was still processing Meranda's words.

"Energy is rising in your body," she said in a meditative voice.

I felt myself falling.

"Feel the energy growing inside you." She continued to talk but my attention was on the movement of energy in my body. That light vibration in my arms had intensified to prickly pins-and-needles that ran up and over my shoulders and down my back. The cool ripples flooded into my legs and toes and then rushed back to my head. Meranda's words were a ghostly murmur tucked deep down in my consciousness.

"Do not be afraid," I heard her say right as I felt a sudden, heavy drop in the pit of my chest, followed by the now-familiar feeling that I was not alone...that someone was in the room with me. I couldn't move. Or speak. I was paralyzed, once again, by intense fear.

"Let go of your fear," I heard her say. "You will remember."

I tried not to give in to the panic. I am calm and in control, I thought, repeating the phrase over and over in my head. I tried to visualize comforting thoughts, like being wrapped in a pale-pink blanket. A shield. I was safe. Comfortable.

"This time you will remember," Meranda said in a hushed voice. "Connect with your astral self. You are one with your astral self. You will remember."

"I will remember." The mantra repeated in my head as I snuggled safely under my imaginary pink blanket. I was lulling myself deeper into a trance, but I felt light. Airy. Like my body was expanding. Lifting.

I was no longer afraid.

And then I felt the shift.

I can't fully explain the sensation, but it's like I had slipped and fallen in a place with no gravity. My perspective suddenly changed and I was above the bed, floating like a kite, looking down at...me.

My astral body had lifted off, and I had full cognitive awareness of what was happening.

I tried to keep calm as I hovered near the ceiling in the right-hand corner of the attic. Meranda had warned me that the primary reason most people didn't remember their nightly separation from their physical bodies was fear. She had also assured me that I was linked to my body by a cord.

The silver cord. I looked around for it wildly, expecting to see a thick cable.

It was nothing like I'd imagined. Three delicate silver fibers woven around each other extended from the third-eye region of my physical body to the back of my astral head. I touched the cord, relieved to feel that it was stronger than it looked, like a metal spiderweb fiber. This connection comforted me as I gazed down upon my sleeping body, which was the most bizarre experience I'd ever had in my increasingly bizarre life. My hair was bunched up under my head. My arm had a weird kink in it that looked quite uncomfortable. I barely recognized myself.

Meranda was sitting on a stool to the right of the bed, muttering the words, I will remember, I will remember. I wondered if she could feel my presence.

"Meranda," I called down to her. The words traveled as if through water, sounding distorted and echoey. She flinched, as though a goose had walked over her grave. "Meranda," I called again with more force. This time the words were less willowy. Meranda pulled her spine erect.

"Resa," she said. "Can you hear me?"

"Yes," I replied.

"Very good," she said. "Stay calm. Embrace the feeling."

I felt weightless as I hovered in the corner of the room by the ceiling. How was movement achieved in this state? I pushed the air as if I was doing a breaststroke in water and was propelled forward without resistance.

I was heading toward the opposite wall, and fast. To avoid colliding with it, I twisted my body to change direction, but I knew it was too late. My right shoulder was going to hit. I closed my eyes and braced for impact. It never came. All I felt was a cool rush. My eyes jerked open. My shoulder had slipped through the wall. In pure awe, I swam back to the other side of the room with my arm outstretched. I let it cut into the wall like a knife through butter. I thought of Matthew and how he'd described matter as being mostly empty.

"Resa? What's happening? I heard you gasp. Is everything okay?"

A loud creak pulled my gaze downward and I watched Slinky

nudge the attic door open. I smiled when he jumped onto the bed next to my physical body, and just as he put his paw on my sleeping tummy, I felt a hard YANK. My astral self was torn from above and reintegrated into my physical body with a heavy thud.

I popped upright in a stupor, gasping for breath. My body felt heavy under the influence of gravity and I fell backward instantly, clutching my chest.

"Sorry," Meranda said. "I didn't secure the room. Slinky crept in. Any tactile disturbance to the physical body causes instant reintegration of the astral self."

"Fantastic," I said sarcastically, trying to slow my breathing.

Her tone turned jubilant. "You did it, Resa! You really did it. Tell me what you remember. What did you see?"

I paused as I felt the adrenaline subsiding. I exhaled deeply, trying to relax my nerves. "I saw everything," I said as my breathing returned to its normal rhythm. "This entire room. You. Me. Slinky jumping on the bed. But my body felt strange. Airy, not solid. I could even go through the wall."

"Excellent. Excellent! You heard me okay?"

"Yes. Watery at times. But yes."

"I knew you had it. I knew you had the gift!"

* * *

For the next week, Meranda and I spent all day, every day honing our ability to speak with each other while I projected. Sarah and Dakota sat in a couple of times to watch. They both wanted to try projecting, but Meranda wouldn't have it, as she wanted to focus all her attention on me before our departure. I found that sniffing the aromatic oil of frankincense before entering into the trance made it even easier. Meranda was quick with praise and pride, repeatedly telling me that she thought I was even more in touch with the energies of the universe than my grandmother had been. I had to admit that after three days of practice, leaving my body under Meranda's watchful eye felt effortless.

Meranda and I were ready, but she insisted that our real attempt must be done on a specific date: the winter solstice. December 21st, which just so happened to coincide with the full moon and a total lunar eclipse this year.

"A real cosmic triple-play," she had said. "All the energies will work together to make your entry into the dream effortless."

She was shattered when she learned I'd be away at school.

PIXIE DUST

It was impossible to concentrate on anything else except for leaving my body. Only a few short months ago I had dreaded falling asleep each night. Now I couldn't wait for bedtime—it was a chance to try my hand at slipping into the ether with total awareness. Meranda had charged me with the task of directing my projection each night to a specific place in my bedroom. To the right of the bed. Above the bed. In the closet. The previous night, I had successfully projected into the hallway outside my door.

It was addictive.

I was tapping into a new power inside myself. Of the people I knew, only two—Meranda and Sarah—would truly understand what I was accomplishing. Now I knew what Matthew had meant when he told me back on Wandelsta that the witches he had known were head-y. My mind was somewhere else. Worldly things seemed mundane and unimportant, and my family was starting to notice.

***

"What's going on with you?" Dakota asked me. He was sitting on my art stool, which he'd propped in front of the desk in his room. He pulled his guitar onto his lap and checked the tuning while I sat on his desk, holding a workman's light with an exposed bulb over my head. "Should I be worried? You seem detached lately. Is your psycho dream-stalker back or something?"

"No, I'm fine. But my arm hurts, so hurry it up. Just play the song."

He'd been practicing "Surrender" all morning for an amateur video shoot that he wanted to post online. For the backdrop, he'd draped a few black sheets over a rope that he'd stretched from the curtain rod on one side of the room to a nail that he'd hammered into another wall. The sheet was sagging and the whole contraption was seconds away from collapsing. The room was completely dark except for my light, which was beginning to feel like a bowling ball in my hand.

"You look fine," I said. "Come on. I can't hold this anymore. Can't you just set it down somewhere?"

"No. I need the lighting to be right. This video has to be perfect. Now that we're going to the Academy, we'll be all over the news again."

"Don't remind me."

"This video has the potential to go viral. It's got to look good."

Dakota hit the record button on the computer and started singing the song that he had played for me on the night we returned from Wandelsta. It might have been one of the most beautiful love songs I had ever heard. The words were simple, but they were delivered with an emotion that seemed too deep for a seventeen-year-old boy. I started daydreaming about whether my brother's astral self might have experienced things he couldn't remember…perhaps it had visited other times or places that were being channeled in his music.

"What did you think?" Dakota asked when he stopped recording.

I sighed and dropped my arm. I couldn't give him an honest opinion because I'd been too distracted to listen for bad notes.

"Well? Was it good or not?"

"It was good, but let's do it one more time just in case."

He was all too eager to try again. I struggled to raise my arm into position and accidentally stared at the light, creating green spots when

I blinked. This time I was really going to listen. He began strumming, and I focused on the notes he was playing, the words he was singing.

>Lay me down
>Lay me down tonight
>Take my heart
>Take my heart, it's fine
>Use my fire
>Use my fire for your light
>All I want is to be yours tonight
>
>Surrender
>Surrender with me
>
>Use my breath
>For your life
>Take my soul
>To keep you warm at night
>Use my eyes for your sight
>All I want is to be yours tonight
>
>Surrender
>Surrender with me

It was perfect, and we both knew it.

"Where did that song come from?" I asked him, breathing out a sigh of relief as I lowered my arm and rested the light on his desk. "How do the words come to you when you're writing a song?"

He placed his instrument in a standing rack. "You got me. I start humming a melody, and then the words just come."

"It's really that effortless?" I hopped off his desk and pulled down the sleeves of my chunky gray wool sweater.

"The good ones are. Sometimes if I think too hard or try to find the perfect rhyme, it seems fake."

"So you're channeling something?"

He gave me a puzzled look. "What? Like that ghost of yours? I guess it's possible. I wrote this before we went to Wandelsta."

"For Luna?"

"If it was, it wasn't intentional, but I guess she may have inspired it."

"But you were never with her, and that song is so deep. Did you love her?"

Dakota cocked his head and looked at me with a strange quirk to his mouth. "Whatever I felt is gone now, so what does it matter?"

"I was just curious. There are a few songs with that extra something that makes them transcend time and change the way you feel when you hear them. I call them pixie-dust songs. Where do they come from?"

"'Surrender' is a pixie-dust song to you?"

"It is. I can't explain it. It's just a feeling. It takes you somewhere."

"Where?"

I shrugged. Maybe I just related to the song. Matthew's breath had given me life, just like in Dakota's lyrics. Perhaps that's what had drawn me in.

I desperately needed to get my feet back on solid ground before everyone figured out what was going on with me.

***

The following morning, I opened my e-mail to a wonderful surprise. Colleen had sent me a possible storyboard layout for my journal. I had been so preoccupied with Gemja and my grandmother that I hadn't reworked the narrative as Colleen had requested. I was impressed when I saw the pictures. The colors on the computer were vivid, and I could only imagine how good they'd look on high-quality, glossy print paper.

I had given Colleen about forty illustrations from my journal, and she and her team had chosen the twenty that they liked best. She had picked drawings of the dune field, the Molinas' den, the detoxification chamber, the toxia alert system, the Ploompie at the spaceport, and of course, the new arrival. I stared at Matthew and wondered if he was still on Wandelsta, or if Sarah's alert had gotten him caught. I hadn't expected Colleen to include a picture of Willie dune-surfing, but that was in there, too. Colleen's team thought it would be a good idea to include it as a way to convey that there wasn't much to do on the planet and that we had to be creative to entertain ourselves. Willie would be so proud when he saw it in print.

I had so much going on in my life right now with the journal and my attempts at astral travel that I didn't want to go away to school on another planet, but I'd given my word to the others, and in two short weeks, we'd be starting a new semester on another world. I still couldn't believe I'd be away for Meranda's ideal dream-entry date.

Apparently my destiny was school…not saving my grandmother. And somehow I had to be okay with that.

OGANWANDO

The city of Oganwando, the capital of the universe, was sleek and well-designed but it was far too contemporary for my taste. The skyline was geometric perfection—an endless array of cubic, cylindrical, and cone-shaped buildings, all with brushed-metal surfaces in the lightest pastel shades. It was a "pretty" city, located on an island surrounded by aqua water studded with twenty-six lighted flag poles that were evenly spaced around the island. From each pole dangled the flag of a planet in our universe that harbored sentient life. The city was clean and most notable for its multiple glass-enclosed, elevated walkways that connected every building. The raised glass tunnels were an ingenious idea because they kept pedestrians protected from weather and the traffic below. I couldn't wait to see the view from the tunnels.

Sarah, Dakota, and I had flown in on the earliest shuttle with my father and Mr. Cuticulor, as they had a morning meeting about the Siafun invasion, and we touched down just as the sun was peeking over the buildings. It was only 6 a.m. and the temperature was already a balmy 86°F, a temperature that we Maine people would classify as a hot summer's day. Before coming to Oganwando City, I had known it would be warm year-round like the cities on the equator, but I hadn't realized how warm. My summer clothes from home would be too heavy. Luckily, Dad had given Dakota and me some Oganwando currency along with our identification badges, cell phones for use on Oganwando, and dorm-room key cards. The first free second I got, I'd use the money to buy some appropriate clothes.

"Make sure to put in your modulators," my father reminded us. He had pulled his IPPL-issued car up in front of a pyramidal lavender building with a simple sign hanging over the sliding doors that read: THE ACADEMY. I popped in the small earplugs that would translate any spoken word I heard into English.

"Ingenious devices," I said, readjusting the piece in my ear. I watched Sarah make a face as she inserted hers.

"I'm so proud of all of you," my father said, hugging us one at a time.

"Yes, indeed. I am as well," Mr. Cuticulor added, also embracing us. "I don't know if you realize yet how important your role will be in getting us to Gemja one day. And remember, no discussing your schooling with anyone not associated with the school. The Academy is located in the middle of a public building—so as not to draw attention. You must have great self-discipline not to blur the lines. No speaking of your classified studies outside of the Academy's walls."

"We understand," I replied for all of us.

"If you need anything, I'll be just across town at the IPPL headquarters," my father said. "You have the number?"

"Yep," I replied, nodding. "Thanks, Dad."

"No worries. Dakota, you look after the girls, okay?"

"I'm on it," he said, slipping his arm through the strap of an oversized khaki duffle bag.

Sarah made a face. "What? You don't think we can handle ourselves, Mr. S?" she joked, flexing her right bicep, which was rock hard.

"Sure you can. But it makes me feel better to know that Dakota is here with you. Speaking of which, you're going to be bunking in a different place, Dakota. It's the blue building behind this one."

"Thanks, Dad," Dakota said as he pulled the last of his bags from the car. "Rees. Payne. I'll call you later." He gave a wave above his head and headed toward his building.

"I asked them to bring some things from Earth into your room to make you feel more at home."

"Thanks, Dad," I said with a grateful smile.

I was glad he would be staying in Oganwando City for a few weeks while we got adjusted to life here. He and Mr. Cuticulor helped us unload our bags, and we waved from the curb as the car pulled away.

"So, this is it," Sarah said with excitement. "Can you believe we're here? This is like something out of a movie." She looked around. "Look at this place! This is going to be our second home for the next couple of years, can you believe it?"

It sounded like too long, especially since I was wearing a tight, long-sleeved rayon shirt, which was making me overheat. I slung my backpack across my shoulders and pulled up the handle on my rolling suitcase. Sarah looked like a hoarder, with all her bags. She had an entire suitcase just for hair-styling supplies.

"Give me one of those," I ordered on my way toward the door, taking one of her black tote bags to help her keep her balance. I stared up at the massive building that would be our new home. It was at least a hundred stories tall, and it reminded me of the Egyptian pyramids. I felt insignificant in comparison.

The front slid open automatically and Sarah and I entered what felt like a hotel lobby, with its creamy marble floors and mirrored walls. It seemed way too upscale for a school dorm, but everything about this city was upscale. No one was at the front desk; there was just a sign with about ten sentences on it written in different languages. The tenth was written in English. It read, "Will be back in ten minutes." I glanced at the key card my dad had given me. Sarah and I would be living on floor 1, in room 10A. We followed the signs on the wall until we found our dorm and swiped ourselves in.

"This isn't bad," I announced as I set the key card down on the beige laminate countertop to my right. "It's small but really clean. I love the hardwood floors." Behind the counter was a small kitchenette with a student-sized refrigerator and sink. There was no stove, just a small microwave. The three stools at the counter reminded me that we would be sharing this room with a third girl named Planella Facies.

"Speak for yourself," Sarah grunted as she flipped on the bathroom light. "Three girls and one tiny sink? There's no place to put anything. The hairdryer won't even fit on the ledge of the sink."

"There's one already built into the wall," I pointed out. I was more concerned about the cleanliness of the bathtub. I pulled back the generic white plastic shower curtain and was pleased to see that the white grout and white tiles were grime-free. I could live with this despite the overabundance of white.

Sarah rolled her eyes as she examined the preinstalled dryer. "My mouth could blow with more force than this thing."

"Don't I know it." She didn't laugh, but I laughed enough for both of us. Sarah opened the medicine cabinet and immediately began filling it with her toiletries. "You have to save a shelf in there for Planella," I reminded her. "You can't overrun this whole place."

Sarah was visibly distressed about the living quarters. Perhaps I was influenced by my time on Wandelsta, but I didn't think the place was bad. It had nice floors, and a beige futon sat in the living area with a bookcase and a small television.

"Speaking of her, let's figure out the sleeping arrangement," Sarah insisted. She was thrilled to discover that there were two bedrooms.

"This is ours," she said, lugging her stuff into the larger of the two rooms. "Planella can have the one with the single bed."

"I guess you're assuming that I want to room with you?"

"Yes," she said. There wasn't a lick of humor in her voice. I hoped she'd adjust to our new circumstances quickly. I wanted my happy, carefree Sarah back.

I spent the entire morning unpacking, prisoner to Sarah's complaints about the lack of drawer space, flat pillows, stale air, and the safety concerns related to being on the first floor. She was right on all accounts, but it wasn't quite the doomsday scenario she was making it out to be.

***

At about 9:00 a.m., the door flew open and in walked a hazy blue girl dressed in a denim miniskirt and matching vest, which she wore unbuttoned over a white tank. Thin, pastel-striped stockings covered her legs, and pompoms dangled from her furry white boots. She looked blurry, and when she moved, it was as if a second identical but slower image moved behind her, catching up only when she stopped. When she caught Sarah staring, she leered at her and jabbed, "What? Never seen a Hypercoobian before?"

I almost choked. The girl had moxie. But Sarah had moxie and a bad morning going for her.

"Excuse me?" Sarah said with as much attitude as the blue girl had channeled. Her hair seemed to stand on end, a nearly impossible feat, given the way it was plastered to her head. "Give me an Advil, Resa," she ordered, her hand outstretched. "I feel a headache coming on."

I felt a catfight coming on.

Although Dad had told us that we'd be dorming with a blur girl from Hypercoob, a planet of four dimensions, both Sarah and I were taken aback by the girl's appearance. She was pretty and petite, with big almond-shaped eyes that were outlined by wispy gray lashes. Her skin was the color of Alaskan glacial ice, crystal-turquoise with a shimmer of iridescence. Her white hair was drawn into a tight, sleek ponytail that grazed her waistline, and her short bangs looked like needle-thin icicles dangling on her forehead.

Sarah and I had stared at her when she walked into the room, but that didn't warrant her reaction. I tried to diffuse the bomb.

"I'm Resa," I said gently, extending my hand. "And this is Sarah," I added, putting my hand around Sarah's back. "I'm sorry if we offended you by staring. You just have such a great look."

Sarah had an entire conversation with me in a sidelong glance.

"Planella Facies," the newcomer replied curtly. "Happy to meet you, Resa." Then she gave Sarah a sharp glance. "And I'd like to say

I'm happy to make your acquaintance, too, but you seem slightly rude. I'm not the strange one."

"What?" Her words made no sense. Sarah hadn't called her strange.

"But she did, Resa. Ask her." She gave Sarah a hard look. "Tell her how you think my boots and tights are a ridiculous get-up designed to draw attention. And no, I don't shop at Children's Warehouse for my clothes, not that I have any idea what that is."

I stood there, dumbfounded. "Sarah, am I missing something here?"

"No. It's pretty clear to me," she said, leaning in closer to Planella's face. "This girl is a freak."

"No, what's freaky is your ratty, two-toned hair," the girl snapped back.

"Oo-kay," I said. I shimmied between the girls because Sarah's fists were clenched so tightly, Superman would have struggled to unknot them. "What's going on here?" I said delicately. "Knock it off, both of you." I looked at Planella. "I don't know how people act on your planet, but we don't accuse others of things we think they're thinking."

"What about things I know they're thinking?"

I looked at her oddly. "What do you mean?"

Sarah raised both palms in the air and made a face like she'd just spotted a hairy, multi-legged bug shuttling under her bed. "Oh, no," she bellowed. "Oh, no. No way is she staying in this dorm." She pointed sharply at Planella, jabbing her finger as she spoke. "I want her out of here. No way is this blue, mind-reading chick staying with us."

I turned around so quickly, I nearly gave myself whiplash. As soon as I looked into Planella's eyes, I could tell Sarah was right. The blue girl was from a multidimensional planet—it only made sense that her thoughts operated on a different level from ours. Why had my father omitted that piece of information? I immediately shut down my thoughts.

Sarah suddenly keeled over like she'd been hit in the stomach, but she was rubbing her temples, not her midsection. "I can feel her pushing around in my head," she screamed. "This has to be illegal." She looked at me, horrified. "Oh my God, Resa. She's in my brain. I can feel her pushing around in my brain!"

I reached for her but didn't know how to react. "Are you okay? What can I do?"

Sarah lunged for the mind reader. With one hearty tug, she pulled the girl down to the ground by her ponytail. "Get out of my head, you blue freak."

The death grip she had on Planella's hair had to be painful. The blue girl writhed like a snared raccoon, kicking and flailing to break free. All I could hear was a barrage of progressively derogatory curses as Sarah's free arm windmilled through the big blue blur that was our roommate. I hadn't realized that the door was still open until two yellow-coated male security guards who were passing by saw the commotion and barreled in to break up the fight.

"Arrest that freak!" Sarah ordered, trying to break free from the guard who was restraining her. "She can read people's minds. That's an invasion of my privacy. I want her arrested!"

Both guards look stupefied. "Is that true?" Sarah's guard asked Planella.

"She shouldn't think thoughts she wouldn't say out loud in the first place!" Planella screamed back. Her formerly immaculate white hair was a tousled mess. She started hammering her guard's shins with the heel of her foot.

"Planella, stop that," I said. "You're hurting him."

"Not wise," Planella's guard said as he whipped her around and pulled her backward through the door. "I'm taking her to the office. The school should know about this before they let her room with other people."

Sarah's guard kept her restrained until enough time had passed to ensure that Planella was far away. "Are you hurt?" he asked Sarah as he released his hold on her. She pulled away in a huff and smoothed out her clothes.

"My head is pounding," she said, touching her temples. "She better not have done any permanent damage, or I'm going to slap a lawsuit on her and the school for allowing her in here in the first place. Don't you screen people around here?"

"There's a medic on the third floor if you need one," he said. "Do you want me to take you?" Sarah declined by shaking her head no and waving a hand at him.

"Thank you," I said as I raked my fingers through my hair. "We'll be fine. She won't be allowed back down here, will she?"

"I'll tell my supervisor what happened," he said. "We'll give you warning before she comes back."

"Before she comes back?" Sarah growled. "That chick better not be allowed anywhere near me!"

"Thanks again," I said as I helped the guard out. Then I closed and locked the door, purging all my pent-up nervous energy into one sentence. "What was that?"

Sarah flopped onto the futon with her legs flung over the side, her arms stretched straight above her head. "I have never felt so violated in my whole life," she said. "I knew something was up. I knew she was reading my mind based on the things she was saying."

"What else were you thinking that pissed her off?"

"I don't know. I just thought her outfit was ridiculous. She needs anger-management courses…and a good punch to her blue face."

"This is crazy. You can't even have a private thought anymore?" I said, pacing. "I wouldn't be able to exist on her planet if I knew everyone could read my mind."

"And you don't have a mean thing to say about anyone."

"But even good people make judgments sometimes. It doesn't make them bad, does it?" How horrible it would be if people knew everything in my head. Poor Willie. He would have been devastated to know how much he bothered me. Then I felt guilty about ever having mean thoughts about people.

"What did it feel like when she was doing it?" I asked. "Would you be able to tell if someone ever tried to read your mind again?"

"Absolutely. It was like a finger pushing into my brain."

"Sorry, Situs," I said as I plopped down beside her. Then in a more cheerful tone, I added, "But at least it wasn't all bad."

She made a noise that sounded like a sneezing horse. "Said the girl who didn't get probed."

"No, really. The universe gave you exactly what you wanted."

"So I wanted to be prodded by a blue B?"

"No. It gave you your space. And a whole room of it. There's no way they're going to let her back in here with us."

FATE

Shortly after Planella was taken away, a professional-looking, white-haired Yrdian woman in a black pantsuit and heels paid us a visit to take a formal statement about the incident. She retrieved Planella's belongings and assured us that the blue girl wouldn't be coming back. And Planella wouldn't be allowed to room with any other students until a deeper ethical investigation was conducted. As an added perk, the woman escorted us up to the registrar on the fifteenth floor and allowed us to cut the ever-growing line of students so we could get our schedules more quickly, since so much of our morning had been consumed by the incident.

I finished first and stepped aside to read my schedule while Sarah argued with a staff worker who refused to check the rosters to ensure that Planella was not enrolled in any of her classes. I was excited about my course load.

IPL 100: Introduction to C-QUEST
MOR 102: Ethics and Morality
CRY 101: The Power of Persuasion
AST 100: Astrogeography
ART 105: Fundamentals of Planetary Illustration

I heard Sarah huff and then felt her brush up beside me. "At least the blurry blue B came in handy for something," Sarah said, referring to our line-cutting privilege. "We should have almost the same classes, right?" We compared paperwork. "Yep, everything except for your drawing class. I can't wait until we get to MOR 102 so I can bring up the whole Planella incident. Oh my gosh. Look at this"—she pointed to the room numbers and times—"this is crazy. Our first class is in half an hour? Really? We have class today? And it's all the way up on the hundredth floor?"

"We registered late, Situs. Relax. There's an elevator right over there. Let's go."

The elevators in the building were fast, but our cab made so many stops along the way that we reached our floor just as class was beginning. We were ultimately several minutes late, since we hadn't expected to need a security check before class. It was school policy: no entry into any of the classrooms without clearing a thorough security check, which involved an identification-badge scan, a handwritten-signature recognition, and the relinquishing of any recording or photographic devices. I'd have to factor in that lag time when moving from class to class. By the time we actually entered the class, the fifty-seat theater was almost full and a short, elderly man was up front at the podium finishing his introduction. "So, once again, welcome to IPL 100," he said. "My name is Professor Karlson, and I'll be your instructor this term."

The walls were covered in peculiar rugged gray foam, possibly soundproofing material. Sarah pointed to some free seats in the upper balcony, and we quietly made our way to them, taking adjacent seats in the back row. We quickly logged onto the computers on our desks. That was another unusual school policy. Nothing in writing. Nothing came into the classroom with us; nothing left the classroom with us. All classwork was emailed to our accounts in our native language. All our notes had to be entered into the Academy's computers and could only be accessed through the Academy's computers, which were located in the security-protected classrooms. All studying would be done in these rooms.

I scanned the room looking for Dakota and saw him in the second row from the front, off to the left. He didn't see us. Sarah pointed out a stunning boy two rows ahead of us with human features except for his dark skin, which sparkled as if fine, glittery dust had been embedded within it. His long black hair was twisted into dreadlocks that were interwoven with feathers and vines and hung the length of his back. He reminded me of a beautiful show bird.

Mr. Karlson explained the class policies and procedures first, then introduced the five roles in which the Academy trained its students: the Historian, the Decoder, the Protector, the Retriever, and the Persuader.

"Historian," I whispered, nudging Sarah in the arm. "That's you." It was a perfect choice for her since she loved research. The Historian's job was to amass background information on planets and species before any type of stone-collecting missions were begun. She'd done such a great job on finding Matthew. It was right up her alley.

"Let's begin, ladies and gentlemen," Professor Karlson said, clearing his throat. "This is a required course for all first-year Academy students, and it will introduce you to the history and workings of the Interplanetary Peace League, also known as the IPPL. First, I must congratulate all of you for pledging to become the future leaders, peacekeepers, and advocates for change across the cosmos. The future of all sentient species lies in your hands. Now, will everyone please stop typing for a moment?" He glared at a group of students in the front row who were still scrolling through their computers. "Everyone, please." He waited until he had all of his students' undivided attention before continuing.

"Take a moment and close your eyes. I need you to imagine something for me. I need you to imagine what it would be like if there were no war in the universe. Really think about it. What would it be like if there were no hate? No guilt, fear, sadness, or anger?" He paused for several seconds before continuing. "In a universe like the one I've described, only love would exist. Only happiness. Only goodness. Can you imagine such a universe?"

Several students snickered, and many shook their heads no. Sarah raised her eyebrows at me, calling up the entire Planella incident, and I was sure that her answer to Karlson's question was a resounding no.

"Pay close attention now," Mr. Karlson said. "I'm about to give you the most important lesson of your life. The power to change the universe is inside each of you. You are the power. Let me repeat that. You are the power." A few students typed feverishly on their keyboards. "You must open your mind. All things are possible if you believe them to be. A universe such as the one I described earlier can exist. And it will exist, if you command it to."

Mr. Karlson held up a copy of the Gemja manual Dakota and I had found in the Slopees' cavern. A wave of whispers rippled through the crowd.

"There are several shocking revelations in your orientation packet, one of which is the existence of an ancient text that tells of magical crystals hidden throughout the universe. According to this book, which is accessible on all of the school computers, if all the crystals are found and activated, space will warp to reveal Gemja, a glorious crystalline planet where our every wish comes true. The questions we must ask ourselves are, does such a fantastical place really exist? And what must we do to find out?

"This idea of magical crystals may seem impossible to you. Implausible. But I assure you, they do exist. This Friday, I will take you on a field trip to witness the power of the gems that have already been found. You won't believe your eyes. And once you see them, I'm certain that you'll be just as dedicated to our goal as I am. The emphasis in this class will be on the special branch of the IPPL, C-QUEST, that focuses on the collection of these power stones. We hope that by the end of this course, you'll all be longing to join a specific C-QUEST program. The more qualified personnel we have, the brighter our future will be."

Mr. Karlson lectured for nearly an hour longer before class ended and Sarah and I dashed to the elevators to try and beat the rush to the lunchroom on the third floor. We had about an hour before our second class, not including the delay for the security check. Our schedule was grueling, with five classes a day and little time in between. I texted

Dakota to meet us for lunch, but he was heading back to his dorm with an upset stomach. His roommate had dared him to try an Oganwandan vegetable, which wasn't sitting well.

When the elevator opened on the third floor, I was happy to see that the lunchroom wasn't a room at all but a public food court, with separate eateries offering a choice of food and ambience. There was only one Earth eatery, but it featured a wide variety of food. I opted for chicken fajitas and nachos with the works. Sarah went Italian and ordered fettuccine Alfredo, rationalizing that she deserved the decadent dish after her stressful morning.

After we paid for our meals, we brought the food to a glass-enclosed dining hall and sat at a bar-style round table near a corner window that was shaded from the sun by a large potted tree. We sat on stools and inhaled our lunches, partly because we were starving and partly because we didn't have much time before our next class. The view of the city was spectacular from this height. It felt like we were observing a humanoid ant farm as we watched all the people scurrying between buildings in their glass-enclosed tubes.

"We should start heading out," Sarah said after she glanced at her watch. "We have to go ninety-seven floors up and I don't want to be late this time. This is that morality class and I'd like to speak to the professor beforehand about Planella."

Everything seemed so rushed. I stuffed the last cheesy nacho into my mouth as Sarah dashed toward the elevator. I cleared the table and headed for the garbage bin in such a hurry that I practically ran over someone who was walking past me.

"I'm so sorry," I said as I bent to pick up the person's papers, which had been scattered across the floor. "I hope I didn't ruin anything." I was still crouching when I looked up and gasped.

It was him.

"Matthew?" I stared into his violet eyes, which still had the power to turn me to mush. He was dressed in the same black outfit I had seen him wearing on Wandelsta. I quickly wiped my mouth to make sure there wasn't any food on it. What I wouldn't do for a piece of gum.

He looked at me for a long moment, his expression unsure. Then he placed my face and smiled. "Resa?"

I melted. He remembered my name. He remembered me.

"What are you doing here?" We said it at the same time, and both of us started to laugh. He grabbed my hand and pulled me up, still looking into my eyes.

"You go to the Academy?" I said, sounding optimistic. I hoped it was intentional that he hadn't yet dropped my hand. I also prayed that my hand didn't reek of onions.

"No," he said. "I'm waiting to be transferred back home."

"To Blackiston?"

He raised his eyebrows. There was only one way I could know that. I bit my lip and shrugged my shoulders.

"You're the reason I'm here being processed for deportation back home?"

I shrugged again and slid my hands deep into the pockets of my cargo pants. "Actually, that would be Sarah, who is somewhere over—" I glanced toward the elevators and spotted her. "Over there." I pointed. "That's her, the one with the lion's mane who's aggressively waving for me to hurry up. She ratted you out. Sorry about that. I didn't know."

He looked rightfully confused.

"We really need to talk," I said. Sarah was calling my name in the distance, clearly agitated by how long I was taking. She didn't realize I was speaking to Matthew, or she would have come running over. "Can we get together before you leave?" It was a bold question, but I had so much to ask him. I wished I could blow off my next class, but I didn't feel comfortable doing that.

"Yes. I think we should," he replied coolly.

"When are you leaving for Blackiston?"

He raised a lush eyebrow. "Never, if I have anything to say about it."

I crinkled my forehead and he elaborated. "Miss Elsa, my caseworker at the Missing Persons Bureau, is trying to hold up the paperwork to keep me detained here for two weeks until my eighteenth birthday. That way, my father will have no legal right to force me back home." He held up the papers in his hand. "I have to fill out this request for temporary boarding until then. I just came over here for lunch, and then I have to head uptown to drop these off."

I felt a rush of excitement at knowing he'd be local for at least several more days, maybe longer. "Where and when should we meet?" I wasn't leaving without a concrete plan.

"Your dorm? Let's do it tonight."

"Tonight?" I hadn't expected so soon. "I have curfew at ten o'clock and classes practically right up till then. How about this weekend?"

"I still don't see the problem with tonight," he said with a delicious smile. The thought of being alone with him sent sparks through my body. "You're pretty industrious, after all. You managed to get me caught from halfway across the universe. I'm sure you can find a way out of a school dorm. You owe me that, at least." He kissed the back of my hand. "I'll be waiting outside for you. Tonight at 10:15."

It was done. I would be meeting him tonight, which suddenly seemed like it was light-years away. "Just try not to make it obvious that you're waiting for me. I can't get caught."

"No?" he said with a wink. "But you had me caught."

And without waiting for a response, he stole away into the crowd, leaving me breathless, just like he always did.

THE ESCAPE

It was ten-thirty, half an hour after the curfew room-check, fifteen minutes after I was supposed to meet Matthew downstairs, and I wasn't even dressed. I was scrambling and it didn't help that Sarah was still trying to convince me not to sneak out. She stood in the middle of my bedroom with her hands on her hips, getting in my way whenever possible. She had just finished berating me for stuffing heaps of clothing under my blankets to make it look like I was in bed if Newia, the resident advisor, decided to make another round of room checks. It seemed unlikely that she would come counting heads again since this was our first night of school, but I wanted to play it safe. I pulled on a pair of jeans and topped it off with a cream silk cami and a fringed, lightweight linen shawl. I gave my lips a second coat of glimmering gloss.

"You're not a jump-out-of-the-window-after-a-guy-I-barely-know type, Resa," Sarah said, tightening the sash on her short, silky burgundy robe. She had just taken a shower and her kinky locks were dripping on the floor, creating a serious tripping hazard. "This isn't you. You're the goody-goody one in our relationship, the one who follows the rules. And remember, this is the guy who tried to push you off a dune. Where is he taking you?"

THE ESCAPE

She was trying to be a good friend, but I was on a mission and she was slowing me down. "I need one of your hooded sweatshirts, please," I said to her, extending my arm and wiggling my fingers. She stood steadfast with her hands on her hips, a puddle of water growing underneath her. "Please, Sarah. I don't want to miss him. I need a sweatshirt. We'll talk about this later."

"That's assuming you don't end up bound and gagged in a trunk somewhere."

"Stop it. He saved my life when I got caught out in the toxia, remember? Can I just have a sweatshirt?" She didn't budge, so I threw at her a sickly sweet, "Pretty please?"

She huffed, gave me an aggravated look, and then pulled out a bland, manly-looking gray fleece hoodie from her drawer, which she handed to me.

"Thank you, I think," I said, holding the unattractive sweatshirt at arm's length. It was a deliberate choice. She owned cute girlie ones. "I need your sunglasses, too." I zipped the gray sweat jacket and flipped up the hood. It felt tight and uncomfortable over my shawl, but I needed to camouflage myself. Sarah took her time, so I just opened her hobo purse and helped myself to the glasses, slipping them onto my face.

"How do you wear these things?" I said. The dark-tinted glasses covered half my forehead.

"You look like a felon," she said. "I need to know where you're going with him, Resa. I'm being serious."

"I'll text you when I know." Then I held up two pairs of shoes. "Flip-flops or combat boots?"

"Combats," Sarah replied. "You might have to flee for your life again."

I rolled my eyes as I slipped my feet into the boots and tightened the laces. I slung my backpack over my shoulders. "Shut the light, I'm leaving."

I slid the sunglasses lower on the bridge of my nose because I couldn't see a thing once the room went dark. I opened the largest window in the living room and removed the screen, setting it on the floor. Still grumbling unhappily, Sarah helped me through the opening. Luckily, our window faced a line of storefronts that were all closed at this hour, so there weren't any pedestrians to witness my first-ever escape attempt. Dakota's building was well to the left and out of view.

"See what I mean about the security issues of being on the first floor?" Sarah said. "Anyone, and I mean anyone, could climb in here."

"Close it up. I'll text you when I know where I'm going and when I'll be back."

"Keep checking the ring Meranda gave you," she reminded me. "If it gets lighter, don't even question it. Just run."

Guilty adrenaline flowed through me as I stole briskly to the opposite side of the road, my combat boots echoing loudly on the pavement. I assumed he would be waiting in the front, which was the worst possible place since there were video cameras in the lobby. I circled the building, resisting the urge to slip behind every bush and tree.

I traveled in the shadows and crossed the road so that I was opposite the Academy. Traffic was heavier here, and I felt vulnerable. I saw him sitting on a bench at the front of the building, directly to the right of the sliding doors. He was hunched slightly forward, looking down, his forearms draped across his thighs. A large black messenger bag sat beside him. His lack of forethought aggravated me. He seemed painfully out of place, and it was obvious he was waiting for someone.

I waved to get his attention, but his attention was on the road, and he didn't seem to notice me. Like a wild animal's, his eyes shone in the headlights as two vibrant violet dots. I thought about aborting the plan, but when I waved my hands again, he finally caught sight of me. He stood and draped his bag over his shoulder and then walked, far too slowly for my liking, across the road.

"Really? You waited in the front of my building?" I shoved my hands into the pockets of my sweatshirt and turned in the opposite direction from the Academy, walking briskly away from the school, my head down.

"Says the girl wearing a hooded sweatshirt and sunglasses on a balmy eighty-degree night." He sounded too relaxed. I was too high-strung. "Where's your sense of adventure?"

"I'm here, aren't I?" I said hastily, picking up my pace. "I must be nuts. You tried to push me off a dune and yet here I am, sneaking out in the middle of the night to talk to you."

He stopped short and grabbed my arm, unintentionally yanking me to a halt. "Resa, you know I wouldn't have let you fall," he said, his face painfully serious.

"I hope that's true." I blocked his wrist to prevent him from lowering my hood.

"It is." He turned me around so I was facing him. I didn't resist when he gently removed my glasses and placed them in my pocket. He held both of my shoulders and looked into my eyes with uncomfortable intensity. "I never meant you any harm. I'm sorry if I scared you," he said softly. "I was trying to prove a point, and I clearly went too far. It's just…there was something about you. I'm sorry if I scared you."

I wanted so desperately to understand him. I suddenly felt foolish. "I must have looked completely ridiculous, running away from you like that."

"I found it charming," he said with a delicate smile. "Let's just say, I hope your school's track team makes valuable use of your talent."

His teasing took some of my tension away, and I slapped the back of my hand gently against his chest. "Oh, and how did you manage to fall backwards off the dune without killing yourself?" A car seemed to slow as it passed us, and I motioned for him to resume walking. I hated being out in the open.

He crinkled his eyebrows. "What do you mean, I fell?" I pulled his arm and he started to walk with me.

"When I ran away from you. I looked back and saw you fall off the dune."

His face smoothed as he realized what I was talking about. Then he smiled and reached a hand over his head to hit an approaching storefront sign that was a good two feet above him. As we passed beneath it, his torso extended several inches, allowing him to slap the sign without reaching. Without any apparent effort on his part, his body compressed back to its normal height.

I nearly toppled over. "What was that?" I growled. "Did you just make yourself taller?" He answered the question by instantly growing three inches in height. My jaw gaped open. "How did you do that?"

"The Hedriconian extendable spine." He made it sound like I should know what he was talking about.

"Well, stop it!" I ordered. He returned to his normal height. "Your spine stretches? By how much?"

"Two feet, so far."

"'So far'?" I twisted my face.

"Why? Did it bother you to see that?" he asked, extending ever so slightly before compressing.

"I don't know. No. I just wasn't expecting it." He extended higher with a wicked grin. "Come on, seriously, stop it. It's freaking me out a little. I could never handle watching people with double joints do strange body tricks."

"So I repulse you? That's nice to know." He'd said it casually, though, so I knew he wasn't offended.

"No, you hardly repulse me…Disgust? Maybe. Repulse? No." I gave him a wicked smile. "I'm just not used to seeing things like that. Believe me, I'm sure there's some human quality that you'll find odd when you first see it."

"Such as?"

I shrugged. "I'm sure you'll let me know when the time comes."

"I doubt there's anything about you that I would find odd." He flashed me a grin. He was flirting. I suddenly wished I hadn't said anything mean about his spine.

"So, are you going to tell me how you fell off the dune like that without getting hurt?" I should have flirted back, but I couldn't think of anything to say that wouldn't sound cheesy.

"It would be easiest to show you, but I don't want to repulse you."

"Come on. Don't make me feel bad." I tilted my head to the side. He squeezed my shoulder as a sign that he was only playing.

"Sitting in one position all day strained my back," he explained, slipping his hands into his pockets. "After you ran away from me, I did a backwards stretch. From a distance, it probably looked like I was falling. You weren't exactly in your right mind, you know." He winked.

"No, not after you tried to kill me," I said, looking up at him through squinted eyes. "Now, I don't suppose you have any other deep, dark Hedriconian secrets that you'd like to share with me before they show up in unexpected ways in unexpected places and make me think that I'm going crazy?"

"I hardly classify Hedriconian anatomy as a secret." There was an ease to his gait that I envied. I felt like a sandpiper in comparison.

"You know what I mean." I slapped my arm into him again. He didn't seem to mind my playful hits, which was good, because I was pretty sure I couldn't stop myself.

As we moved into the city, we hit a crossroad where the traffic was more intense. There were buildings everywhere, many with obnoxious neon signs that glowed like Matthew's eyes. "Is the IPPL headquarters anywhere nearby, do you know?" I asked.

He shook his head. "Why?"

"I don't want to run into my father." Headlights were ripping past us faster now. I wanted to get off the main road as soon as we could.

"Your father works for the IPPL?"

I nodded. "He's the newest member."

"Robert Stone?" he said, looking impressed. "That explains why you were on Wandelsta."

I wondered if he'd treat me differently now that he knew I was the daughter of an IPPL delegate. Then I felt bad for not asking about his family situation. "Speaking of fathers," I said, "did yours have anything to do with you running away? And to Wandelsta, of all places."

"Wandelsta wasn't by choice," he said quickly. "It was just easy to get there. Security on garbage shuttles is practically nonexistent."

I furrowed my nose but said nothing.

"Yes," he said, as if responding to a direct question. "I sat in garbage for days."

I wished I hadn't made the face. "Now, that's repulsive," I said in jest, hoping to brighten the mood.

"No, what was repulsive is the way my father treated me," he said. Instant uneasiness. He could obviously tell I was uncomfortable, because he lightened his tone. "Sitting in garbage was a step-up."

I found myself wishing, for about the millionth time in my life, that I was better at making conversation. Maybe he wanted to talk about what his father had done to him, but I didn't feel right about asking. "You weren't scared to leave everything you knew behind?" I asked, leaving an opening for him to return to the subject of his family if that was what he wanted.

He furrowed his brow as if my question was illogical. "Why be scared when it was my choice to leave? Once you make a decision about anything, you have to surrender to it or it's not worth making the decision in the first place. I looked at it as an adventure."

I felt my face contort—I couldn't imagine doing something like that without being scared. "You weren't worried about where you'd sleep?"

"There's always the outdoors."

"Trust me, I'm a nature girl. I love being outdoors. But I couldn't do that long-term. Not with bugs. I hate bugs."

"You'd be surprised at what you could do if the situation called for it."

"Maybe. But I don't know." I crinkled my nose at the thought of sleeping out in the open with the night crawlers. Then for the first time it dawned on me that the Siafu had insect-like qualities. Those poor Glucosans. I would die if a bug-like species invaded Earth. I quickly diverted my thoughts back to Matthew's situation. "You had to be worried about food and water, though, right? And what if you got hurt?"

"If you believe the universe will take care of things, it will. I never had any wants on Wandelsta. I befriended a Slopee family, who were helping me. And Willie found me on my first day there, and he was all too eager to bring me food."

"But what if he didn't?"

"What's the point of what-ifs? You can't be too much of a worrier if you risked your life every day in that decomposition field." He placed one hand on the small of my back as he motioned for me to cross the intersection. "No more talk of fathers or fears. I want to show you something that will blow your mind. Can you handle a good walk?"

I tilted my head. "Can I handle a good walk? Come on. I did marathon hikes through decomp fields with toxic air. Let's go." I was secretly doing a happy dance that I'd opted for the combat boots. "So, what is this thing you want to show me?"

"It can't be described. Only experienced."

He had an uncanny way of driving me absolutely mad. Despite my continued pleas for more information, he wouldn't tell me where we were going, but he had no qualms about increasing the suspense to a painful level as he led me a couple of miles north to an area of the city where the trees outnumbered the buildings. Under any normal circumstances, I would have never wandered off so far with a virtual stranger, especially in a foreign place where not a soul, not even me, knew where we were going. But here I was, allowing…no, welcoming him to take me away. Everything about him was a mystery. A mystery that I so desperately wanted to unravel.

SUNQUIN KISSES

A city park?
It was a bit of a letdown after the way he'd carried on. The huge limestone-cobble arch at the entryway was quite impressive, but overall, the surprise was far from mind-blowing.

"Hmm," I said, standing with my hands on my hips, gazing at the archway. "A park, huh?"

"You're doubting its ability to impress?"

"I just wasn't expecting a park. Although Earth does have some mind-blowing ones."

"So tell me. What makes your Earthly parks so special?"

The enormity of the Grand Canyon came to mind. "I can't put it into words. Like you said, you need to experience it."

"Try me."

"I went to the Grand Canyon with my parents a few years back. It's this incredibly enormous gorge, and you feel so small next to it. And then there's Niagara Falls, an enormous waterfall that doesn't seem real, there's so much water flowing over it."

"So your mind is blown by a big hole and lots of water?"

"Wiseguy...No. I'm amazed by the power of nature to create those special places. Forget about my Earth. Let's use Wandelsta as our common frame of reference. The dune fields there were magnificently beautiful. How does this park compare to the dunes?"

"What I have to show you is far more magical than the dunes."

"Really?" I said, sounding deliberately skeptical. I felt like a criminal as we passed a huge sign displaying in bold red letters, "No entry after sunset. Violators will be prosecuted." All the lamps lining the paths were dark and I tripped on a loose cobble, stumbling into Matthew. I nearly ripped off his shirt while trying to stabilize myself.

"Careful," he said, grabbing my wrists.

"Sorry." I felt his arm slip under mine. "I can't see very well in the dark."

"Luckily, you don't need to. You have my eyes." He allowed his eyes to cast a mellow lilac glow on the pathway.

"That's an amazing gift you have," I said. "Does the light hinder your ability to see?"

"Actually, quite the opposite. It amplifies everything. Objects seem to jump out at me."

"Wow. Compared to you, humans are boring. We don't have anything quite like that."

"We all have our own unique gifts," he said as we resumed walking at a slower pace. I was pleased that he kept his arm joined with mine, well past the point when I needed his help. My fall had given him a reason to get closer to me.

"So, how did you find out about this place?" I asked, tightening my grip on his arm to let him know I was interested in being close to him, too. "Is this where you take all the girls whom you lure out late at night?"

"Hardly. Miss Elsa told me about this place."

"You and Miss Elsa," I said, pretending to be jealous. "Tell me about her."

"She's my fifty-year old caseworker." He smiled. "She says I remind her of her son. She took a liking to me."

I raised one eyebrow. "Of course she did. I bet all the ladies take a liking to you."

He playfully grabbed my waist, and I flinched. "Ah, you're a ticklish one," he said, a mischievous glint in his still-glowing eyes.

"No, you just startled me, that's all," I lied.

"Is that so?" He dug his fingers into my side, and I squealed, lunging out of his reach.

"Quit it," I said, swatting him. "You're gonna get us caught. My dad would flip if he knew I was out here with you." I made an impressive ninja-style maneuver to avoid another attack and he gave up, slinging an arm over my shoulder instead.

"You told me on Wandelsta that you felt safest in nature," he said, pulling me closer. "I can't wait to see your reaction to my great surprise in the morning."

"Who said anything about staying 'til morning?" Now he was pushing it. I couldn't let Sarah stay up all night, waiting and worrying about me. Then I gasped.

"What?" he said.

I'd forgotten to text Sarah. I fumbled for my phone, which apparently I had accidentally left on silent mode, in my backpack. She had already left dozens of texts, each one sounding progressively more urgent. I dialed her number and held the phone to my ear. "I hope she didn't freak and tell someone I snuck out with you," I said. "I was supposed to check in with her. She was convinced you were a serial killer."

"And yet she let you come?" he said, appalled.

It went straight to voice mail.

"Damn," I muttered. I shot her a quick text assuring her that I was alive and well.

"Will she have the IPPL cavalry searching for you?" he joked. I didn't smile. This was bad. For all I knew, Sarah had panicked and alerted the school and my parents that I might be out with a murderer.

"We have to go back," I said. My entire body felt like an entwined thorn bush. "How could I have been so stupid?"

"I'd hate to see how you'd react in a real crisis," Matthew said lightly. His composure wasn't contagious. I felt like I was teetering on a tightrope.

"You don't understand," I said, squeezing my palms together. "It's not like me to sneak away like this."

"But you did. Some part of you wanted to be with me tonight despite the risk. That's what I call being alive."

"That's what I call, I'm freaking out inside," I said. I wanted to be with him but worry and guilt were suffocating me like toxia. "I'm the responsible kid in my family. I don't do things like this. See what you do to me? You—"

"I'm sorry. If that's how you feel, we don't have to see each other again."

"No. I—I want to see you. That's not what I mean. It's just—"

"Resa, you're creating this drama, do you realize that? For all we know, Sarah fell asleep and couldn't hear her phone."

"You don't know Sarah."

"No, but I'm getting to know you. And you say you're a witch. A witch creates her own reality. No?"

"Yes."

"Then stop resisting where the universe wants you to be. Make your own reality right now. You and me in nature with no worries. Remember what I told you before about surrendering once you've made a decision? Release all the worry. You have power over your own world."

I envied him his outlook. "You just sounded like my first lesson in IPL 100."

"Then maybe there's some truth to what I'm saying."

Just then, my phone beeped. I held my breath as I read the text.

> If he doesn't kill you, I will. You owe me big time. Tonight better be worth it.

My worried guilt instantly vaporized. I held up the phone for him to read the message.

"What did I tell you?" He opened his arms to me. I couldn't resist him. I fell into his embrace like a droopy rubber band. "We can still head back if you want," he said.

I exhaled deeply, safe inside his arms. "No. This is exactly where I want to be."

"Are you sure? I don't want you to feel uncomfortable."

"I'm surrendering to the moment," I said, mimicking him.

"I'm being serious," he said in his slow, calming way. "I can show you this place another time if you want."

I pulled back from him. "Didn't you hear me say, 'I surrender'? Look." I held my palms up and facing him. "I'm surrendering."

He shook his head, smiling, and took one of my hands in his. "Okay, then trust me when I say that you'll be able to waltz right back into your dorm through the front door tomorrow if you want."

"Just to be safe…" I texted Sarah to confirm I would be out till dawn and to ask that she leave the window open.

"Ye of little faith," he said as we resumed walking, hand in hand. "This Sarah of yours sounds interesting. When will I have the pleasure of meeting her?"

I pulled my head back. "You want to meet her?"

"Why, you don't want me to?"

I shrugged. "No, it's just that Sarah likes things her way. She wasn't exactly thrilled about our evening tonight. I don't want her to give you a hard time."

"That's precisely why we should meet. Unless you want her worrying every time we're together. I plan on spending as much time as possible with you while I'm here."

I playfully nudged him with my shoulder. "And you just assume that I want to spend time with you?"

"You don't?"

I felt my face flush. "Did I not jump out a window for you? Did I not follow you into a poisonous fog, nearly killing myself in the process? In fact, I have no idea how you get me to do all these things for you."

"You like me." His voice had a playful tenderness to it.

I put on a tough front. "I suppose I do. And more than I should, I might add." I didn't want him to know that my insides were melting faster than an ice cream cone under the Oganwando sun.

He squeezed my hand and guided me left at a fork in the pathway. I felt alive and tingly, just like when I'd found the stone. Straight ahead through a vast clearing of trees, the stars looked like crystalline jewels studding the ebony sky. I searched for the Big Dipper before remembering that this was a foreign sky. I wondered which of the stars was our Sun.

He led me to the edge of the path, which is when I realized we were on a fifty-foot-high cliff, looking down at the water surrounding the island with the perfect, jeweled sky as our backdrop. It was the fairy-tale romantic setting. It wouldn't have surprised me if shooting stars began to magically trace out love notes across the sky.

My heart danced as Matthew unzipped his messenger bag and pulled out a thin blanket, which he spread open on the ground. He assumed his Wandelsta pose, only this time he was facing the water instead of the incinerators. His eyes were dark now, and it took a moment for my eyes to adjust to the duskiness of a starlit night.

"Come sit with me," he said, holding out his arm.

My senses heightened as I grabbed his hand and he pulled me toward him. This was new territory. I'd never had a serious boyfriend before, and I'd never been alone like this with a guy. Part of me wanted him to know how inexperienced I was. Part of me was embarrassed. What did he expect? What did I want to happen?

"I think it's safe to take this off now," he said gently, drawing down the zipper of my jacket. "You must be boiling in this thing. This utterly horrific thing."

"I know. It's atrocious. You can thank Sarah for that." He helped me take off the sweatshirt, and I shuddered as his fingertips grazed my skin. My shawl had come off with the jacket, and I crossed my arms, feeling underdressed in the silk cami, which suddenly seemed awfully low-cut.

"Now isn't that better?" He stroked my arm with the back of his hand.

"Indeed," I replied, trying to keep my composure as his touch triggered a landslide of chills down my arm. I froze when he slipped one finger under my spaghetti strap.

"I like this," he said, caressing the fabric "Silk?"

"Yes," I nodded, feeling about ready to lift off into orbit.

He withdrew his hand and I felt simultaneous disappointment and relief. He tucked one arm behind his head and lay back, gazing up at the stars. His shirt was splayed opened and I saw the darkened outline of his tattoo. I wanted so desperately to know about his father and the conditions that had brought him to Wandelsta, but he had set the ground rules earlier—no more father talk.

"Come lie with me and look at the stars." He put his hand on the small of my back.

I grabbed my sweatshirt and wadded it to make a pillow, slipping the cloth beneath his head.

He gave a breathy, "Thank you," and patted the blanket. "Come down here. The view is magnificent."

He was older than me. He probably expected more from me than I was ready to give… Still, I couldn't say no. I lay down on my side, my head in my hand, propped up on one elbow. He pulled me lower, and I curled into him, resting my head on his chest. He draped his arm around me. I nervously stroked the contours of his chest muscles, but then stopped abruptly when I realized it might be sending the wrong message. He rolled toward me and grazed my cheek with the back of his palm.

"You are very beautiful, Resa Stone." He brushed his hand ever so lightly against my cheek. "What do you make of this? It's so unlikely that we would find each other again here, and yet we have."

My heart pounded with nervous delight. "It doesn't seem like a coincidence," I whispered. "When I first saw you on that dune, I felt this intense attraction, it was like—" I stopped myself. I had almost said, love at first sight.

"Like what?"

"Like I was destined to meet you. Like there was some greater force drawing us together." I couldn't bring myself to tell him about Nitika.

Suddenly I felt embarrassed about what I'd said. "That didn't come off as too clingy, creepy, or stalker-like, did it? I didn't mean it to sound like—"

He placed one finger on my lips to stop my sentence. "Not at all. I appreciate your honesty."

"You're not just saying that?"

"No," he said, taking my hand in his. "I felt that same energy."

"You did?" I said with excitement. "It was real, right?" It was hard to ignore the way he was studying the contours of my hand within his own.

"So real, it scared me," he said as he ran his fingertips along my palm, then over my knuckles.

"It didn't scare me, but I couldn't stop thinking about it," I said. "I kept wondering if I had imagined it. What do you think it was?"

"At first, I thought you might have cast a spell on me."

"You didn't, really?" I smiled and squeezed his hand. "I am pretty powerful," I teased. "It was almost like the sparks you feel when you touch a Van de Graaff machine."

He cocked his head. "Not a machine I've heard of before."

"It felt like lightening arced between us," I clarified.

"Yes, that's exactly it," he said. He finished his examination of my hand and started moving higher, allowing his palms to stroke my wrist, then my forearm. "Do you know how hard it was for me to stay away from the dunes after feeling such an intense connection with you?"

"Why did you?"

"I was frightened of you."

"Of me?"

"No. Of you and me together. Of us getting too close. Energy literally moved between us, and we barely knew each other. From that moment onward, I couldn't stop thinking about you...and I didn't even know you. It was a scary thing. A powerful, scary thing."

"I wasn't so much scared by our connection, as I was obsessed with it," I confessed. "I looked for you every day afterward. I couldn't help myself."

He traced his forefinger along the edge of my chin and my lips parted. "I'm sorry I stayed away," he said softly. "And sorrier still that you almost died because of me."

"I would have died if not for you," I corrected. My mind flashed back to that moment and I yearned for him to kiss me. He didn't try. He just caressed me, every touch triggering a waterfall of pure energy inside me. I wanted to pull him toward me. I wanted to...

"We were supposed to meet, you and I." He swept a lock of hair behind my ear. "The energy was a sign. Do you believe in signs?"

"If only you knew."

"Tell me."

"Yes. I wholeheartedly believe in signs. They come to me all the time. And in very obvious ways."

"As obvious as this?" He slipped his hand behind my neck and pulled me to him, slanting his lips to mine, the kiss setting my entire being ablaze. His lips sent waves of bliss through my body. I hoped this moment would never end.

"Promise me something," he said, giving me small kisses between the words.

"Anything," I managed to say.

"That we never hurt each other."

I paused, holding a kiss, and then pulled back from him, my hands on his chest. His comment had broken the mood. "Why would you say something like that?"

He became serious. "That energy between us is raw. Primeval. Untamed. Just promise me."

"I would never intentionally hurt you."

"You say that now."

"I would say that always."

He kissed me again, with a fierce intensity that left me weak. I couldn't get enough of him. The sounds he made. The feel of his hands on my face, my neck. His fingers in my hair.

And then, painfully and without warning, he pulled back, leaving me an electrified ball of goo. My moist lips throbbed, and the skin around my mouth was raw from abrasion with his. My heartbeat was audible in my ears. I was sitting in an awkward position—my left hip on the ground, my legs bent sideways, my torso propped up by one arm. I was trembling all over.

"Are you okay?" I managed to stammer. I wondered if I'd done something wrong to make him want to stop.

"I'm more than okay," he murmured, much to my relief. But he was too far from me, sitting Indian style three feet to my right.

"Why did you stop?" I asked, inching closer to him.

"We have to."

"Why?" I don't know what came over me, but before I could think better of it, I slipped into his lap, facing him with my arms around his neck. I wanted him to kiss me again. I couldn't believe how bold I was being.

"Be careful," he ordered as I nuzzled my nose against his.

"Why?"

"I may never let you go." He leaned in as if he was going to kiss me again, but then he dropped his hands around my waist and threw me playfully to the side.

"Hey!" I squealed. As soon as I landed on my back, he started to tickle me. "Don't tease me like that!"

"You need to get some rest," he said through gritted teeth, still continuing his tickle torture.

"Quit it!" I swatted at him.

"You have classes in the morning. I fear Sarah's wrath if you fail school because of me."

His comment hit me harder than astral body reintegration. "Yes, she's a tough cookie, for sure," I admitted, breaking free from his grasp. I felt like an overinflated tire decompressing. But I couldn't even imagine getting any sleep.

His remark provided a nice segue to the story about the whole Sarah-Planella ordeal, and we spent hours in each other's arms, just talking. I didn't tell him about Nitika, but I did tell him about my family. My grandmother. My witchcraft. My journal. I was hoping he'd shed some light on the situation with his father, but he always directed the conversation back to me when I asked about his background.

I don't remember when I fell asleep, but I awoke in his arms just before sunrise, my head safely cradled in the nook of his armpit. He was looking down at me.

"You're even more beautiful when you sleep," he said, massaging my shoulders. I wiped the sleep from my eyes. "I hope I didn't drool on you," I said groggily.

"That would have been repulsive," he kidded.

Suddenly, I heard voices and popped upright.

"It's all right," he assured me. "Lots of people will be arriving soon." He helped me stand and packed up the blanket. "Come with me. I want to find a good spot for us."

I slipped into my sweatshirt and followed him to the wooden fence that bordered the cliff. To the far right was an informational board.

The glow of the sun beneath the horizon illuminated a cluster of cumulous clouds in such a way that they looked like mountains lining the water. As the sun ascended, the cloud mountains turned light pink, then hot pink. It was absolutely beautiful.

I rested my hands on the fence and Matthew shimmied behind me, standing as close to me as a person could. My heart skipped when I felt his head slip into the crook of my neck and his arms wrap around me. I felt like I'd been with him forever. People were arriving in masses and the fence was quickly filling up with gawkers. I saw a few kids wearing Academy sweatshirts, and Matthew smiled.

"I told you not to worry. You can walk right back into your dorm. If anyone asks, just tell them you went to see Sunquin Kisses."

"Sunquin Kisses?" I said, giving him a searching look. Just then, I heard an excited flurry of oohs and ahhs from the crowd.

"It's starting," a young child squealed giddily from his perch atop his father's shoulders. My eyes followed the boy's pointed finger to the bottom of the cliff. I hadn't noticed the darkened outline of what appeared to be a square field. Suddenly a yellow sparkle in the field caught my eye. Then a red one. Then a blue. Something was happening down below. Suddenly, a wave of colorful sparkles rippled through the field until the entire square burst into a twinkling rainbow under the glorious golden sun. Electric rainbow sparkles.

I thought of Gemja.

"What is that?" I asked in awe. The crowd continued to murmur throughout the display, but I couldn't look away until a spurting sound drew my eyes to thin metal pipes surrounding the field, which ejected the finest mist of water above it. Actual rainbows took form, dancing above the field of sparkles. It was the most beautiful sight I had ever seen.

When the sprinklers were extinguished, I pulled Matthew by the hand to the informational board. I read the sign out loud while Matthew stood behind me, his hands on my waist. "'When nearly three thousand mechanical sequin flowers tilt their heads to be kissed by the morning sun, their reflective surfaces return its light in a magical display of colorful, glittery sparkles.' What an incredible idea," I said.

"I knew you'd like it."

I didn't want to waste another moment reading. I pulled Matthew back to the fence, disappointed that we'd lost our place in front. Matthew saw a couple leaving to our right and quickly rushed me into the spot.

"It's amazing," I said. "I wonder how tall they are."

"About three meters high," an elderly man to my right offered. "Each covered with thousands of sequins. The flowers are motorized to twist their heads around. That's what causes the sparkles."

"It's absolutely beautiful," I said in a hushed whisper.

I felt Matthew's warm breath caressing my neck. "But not nearly as beautiful as you," he purred in my ear.

I melted seamlessly into him, beaming brighter than three thousand sequin flowers being kissed by the morning sun.

A WHITE WARNING

I had never been in love before, but I was pretty sure I was falling hard, and I didn't know what to do about it. Me and a spine-stretching, glowing-eyed, gorgeous Hedricon? What would people think? My father would be thrilled. What better PR for universal peace than the daughter of an IPPL official getting involved in an interspecies relationship? My mother would be neurotic about me getting pregnant, although I wasn't even sure if Matthew's DNA was a close enough match to mine for that to be possible. And considering that we had only spent one night together talking, I certainly should not have been having thoughts like that…But oh, what a night it had been.

"So he didn't try anything with you?" Sarah asked. We were in a small, bohemian-flair boutique in town called Hippy Chic. It was the only Earth-inspired store in town, but it carried hip clothes, costume jewelry, scarves, and sunglasses, along with dorm-room staples like lava lamps, candles, colorful sand hourglasses, and glow-in-the dark artwork.

"No, we just kissed," I said. "And then he held me, and we talked all night. It was amazing. Everything about it. The setting. The conversation. It was completely magical."

"Mmm…hmm."

"Seriously. We just kissed. I was actually being the forward one, if you can believe that."

"Um, no. I don't believe that."

I rolled my eyes. "Think what you want. I'm telling you, he's a really great guy." Just the thought of him made me tingle.

"Or he knows the law," Sarah clarified. "He's eighteen, right? He probably didn't want to get arrested."

"Technically, he's not eighteen until two weeks from now. And that's a stupid law if there's barely a one-year age difference."

"Maybe he's lying about his age."

We were both here to find outfits for the Academy social, a dinner-and-dance event that was being held later in the evening for Academy students to unwind after their first week of school. Guests were allowed, and I thought it would be the perfect opportunity for my best friend and my new guy to meet, although Sarah's attitude left something to be desired.

"Guess who I had breakfast with this morning while you were out getting sun-kissed?" Sarah said, pausing to examine a sheer, off-the-shoulder black tunic. "Bird Boy."

"Who?"

"That gorgeous male creature with the sparkling skin and feathers in his hair who we spotted in class on the first day of school."

"That's nice," I said as I lifted a hanger off the rack to get a better look at a cute, kimono-style minidress that wrapped around and tied at the waist. I held it up. "What do you think?"

"Too short. And the colors are too washed out." I put the dress back. "So, anyway," she continued. "I ran into him at the food court and introduced myself. His name is Tico Micah, and he's from a planet called Gargon. We got to talking, and well, I think you'd like him. He's a nature guy. His people actually live in these nest-like huts up in trees. He seems really cool."

"Nice. So are you two going to hang out?"

She contorted her face. "No. I don't want him, but I think he'd be good for you. I told him I had a nature-girl friend who was checking him out in class, and that I could introduce you two at the social."

"You didn't?" I said, aggravated. "Sarah. Why would you do that? You know I'm going out with Matthew. What is it about him that you don't like, besides the fact that I like him? I think you're jealous of him."

"Please. No. And I don't dislike him," she said. "I dislike the power he already seems to have over you. You're doing things you normally wouldn't do, Resa. You almost died chasing after him on Wandelsta. You stayed out all night. You have a starry-eyed look when you've only been in this guy's company, what? Four times, total? It reminds me of how Dakota fawned all over Luna. I'm just worried, that's all."

"Well, stop worrying. You'll keep me in check, I'm sure." I winked at her.

"You're right about that," she said. "And it starts with you talking to Tico tonight. I'm not saying you have to date him. Just talk to him. Options, Pieces. It's good to know what your options are." Her eyes lit up and she lifted a hanger. "Now these have your name written all over them. You're the only one who could pull this color off."

The flapped pockets staggered down the leg made them look like cargo pants, but they had feminine flair—the fabric was gathered at the ankles, and the color was an incredible deep persimmon with a slightly iridescent shimmer. They could be worn with a casual outfit or a dressy one. I whistled when Sarah handed them to me. "Try them on," she ordered.

She didn't have to say it twice. I grabbed the silky pants and a black tank and headed for the dressing area. I slipped into the furthest dressing stall and got changed. Sarah nodded in approval when I stepped out and did a runway walk for her.

"It's perfect," she said.

I agreed wholeheartedly. The outfit looked, and fit, amazing. Back at the dorm I had a carnelian pendent necklace that perfectly matched the peachy-red pants, which would dress the look up even more. I bought the outfit and then fiddled in a basket of assorted crystals on the counter while Sarah finalized her selections: flared jeans, wedges, and a layered, leopard-print blouse.

Both outfits looked even better in the evening, after we had showered and primped. Pleased with our appearance, we got into the elevator and punched the button for the twenty-fifth floor. Dakota's stomach still wasn't right after eating that strange vegetable, so he opted to skip the social and stay close to the bathroom. Matthew was going to meet us in front of the ballroom where the event was being held.

"You look good," Sarah said as I fiddled with the feathered clip in my hair, which I had left long except for a couple of strands that were pulled back in braids. "It's like belly dancer meets Native American meets safari girl. He's gonna love it."

"I'm surprised you want him to love it. Be nice, okay? I really like him."

"I'll behave."

The elevator doors opened, and we stepped out. Directly in front of us, wide-open double doors led into an enormous room with gleaming hardwood floors, crystalline chandeliers, and dozens of round tables draped with white linen. The tables were decorated with votive candles and clear bud vases filled with white roses and green ferns. A mammoth disco ball hung over an empty dance floor. The DJ—DJ Sammy Sam, according to the flyer on the wall—was wearing a white suit, a baseball cap, and sneakers. He wasn't having much success in getting the party started, apparently, since only twenty people or so were in the room, none of them on the dance floor. Most of the kids were milling around in the hallway.

Sarah hit my arm and pointed to Matthew, who was sitting on a bench to the right of the entryway. He was being ogled by a trio of giggling blonde girls who looked relatively human except for their skin, which had no pores and resembled shiny plastic. They reminded me of life-sized Barbies.

When Matthew saw me, his eyes glowed…literally. I'd never seen his eyes radiate that way during the day. He smiled and approached me, sweeping my hands up in his. It was hard not to throw my arms around his neck and kiss him. Looking visibly disappointed, the blonde trio headed into the ballroom, whispering amongst themselves.

"I didn't think it was possible for you to get more beautiful," he said, kissing the backs of both of my hands. He had on his standard outfit. His standard hairstyle. And everything about him was as gorgeous as it always was.

I could hear Sarah's thoughts, so I grabbed her hand and pulled her to my side before he could become more affectionate with me. "This is Sarah Payne." I waved my hand at her as if she were his prize.

He bowed and took one of her hands in his, his manners as good as royalty's. "Pleased to finally meet you, Ms. Payne," he said and planted a soft kiss on the back of her hand.

"Oh, this one's gonna be trouble," she said, her tone both playful and suspicious. "I'm watching you, Hedricon. You better be good to my friend, here."

"I'll be better than good," he corrected as he pulled me closer to him. "Resa is a very special person."

"I'm glad to hear it," Sarah said firmly.

The meeting hadn't gone exactly as I'd hoped, but as the night progressed, Matthew chiseled away at Sarah's butternut-squash skin, so much so that by the time dinner was served, the two of them felt comfortable enough to unite against me in an all-out tease-fest. They playfully tormented me about everything from my Wandelsta freak-out over Matthew falling off the dune to how nervous I was about sneaking out.

I had fun dishing it back. "At least my hair doesn't need its own suitcase," I said to Sarah, barely able to get the words out through my laughter. "And you…" I pointed at Matthew. "Maybe I should call you Rubber Boy?"

"That's not fair," Sarah said, waving her finger at me. "You can't target someone's body with a nickname. That would be like him calling you Crooky."

Matthew looked perplexed. "Crooky?" My heart dropped. Sarah immediately understood her error.

"She has scoliosis," Sarah said nonchalantly. "But it's nothing. She makes such a big deal about it, but you can't even tell. What I wouldn't do for her bod."

I went quiet, feeling as if all my flaws had been stripped bare. Matthew, who was sitting to my right, put his arm around me and traced his fingers along my spine, from the nape of my neck to my waist. I would have preferred to undergo a root canal than for him to discover my deformity.

"I guess we really are a perfect match," he said after a thorough investigation of my back. "My spine stretches. Yours bends." He squeezed my shoulder.

Sarah gave me a look as if she'd just witnessed a parade of fuzzy, floppy-eared puppies marching by.

I loved his answer.

"Sarah?"

The male voice took me by surprise. When I looked up, Tico the bird boy was standing there, wearing pants and a matching vest that looked like they were woven from moss. Bright aqua and emerald feathers laced his dark locks.

"Hi," Sarah said, her voice playful. She jumped up and put her hand on his shoulder. "Let me introduce you to my friend." She extended her hand to me. "Resa. This is Tico. Tico, Resa."

"Hi," I said, standing to shake his hand. His exquisite looks had caught the attention of the Barbie triplet, who migrated to the edge of the dance floor closest to our table, making moves that were dangerously revealing in their barely-there miniskirts.

"You look fantastic," Tico said, much too emphatically for my liking. It was painfully awkward, the way he was openly checking me out. Perhaps that was acceptable behavior in his culture, but I certainly wasn't used to it. "I love your outfit. The feather in your hair. And that ring." He lifted my hand to gaze at it. Matthew kept a straight face but tilted his head as he watched Tico studying my ring. I was ready to kill Sarah for creating this unbearable situation.

"Thanks," I said, pulling away from him. I put my hand on

Matthew's shoulder. "Tico, I'd like you to meet my friend Matthew." Matthew stood and extended his hand to Tico.

"Nice to meet you," Tico said. He shook Matthew's hand while giving him a weighing look. "So you two met at the Academy?"

"Oh, no," I chimed in, not allowing Matthew to respond. "We met on another planet. But that's a long story."

One of the Barbie girls did a calculated twirl and deliberately careened off Tico and landed in Matthew's lap.

"I'm so clumsy," she said in a bubbly voice, batting her lashes, which seemed too thick and long to be real. Tico and Matthew helped her to her feet, and the other two Barbie girls conveniently ran to her rescue.

"Oh, please," Sarah said, loudly enough for them to hear. "Can you say, pathetic?" The girls didn't react to the comment, but when they realized that the guys were more interested in each other than they were in them, they left, all three of them pouting.

Tico pulled a chair up to mine, sitting so close that his knees grazed mine. I shot Sarah a look and she innocently raised her eyebrows.

"So, how was your first week of school?" Sarah said, trying to divert Tico's attention from me. "Any thoughts on what program you'd like to join?"

"Protector," he replied.

"Ah," Sarah said. "Protectors look after Retrievers on stone-collecting missions. Resa wants to be a Retriever."

I turned my head, slowly and deliberately, toward her. My face said all that needed to be said.

Tico looked at Matthew. "What about you? Do you know what program you're planning to choose yet?"

"I'm not enrolled," Matthew said coolly, holding up his hand. He offered no further information.

"Really? I know it's our first week here," he said. "But school policy prohibits any Academy students from discussing Academy business around non-Academy students." He shrugged at Matthew. "Sorry. It's policy."

"We're hardly talking business," Sarah said.

"There should be no talk about the programs. They made that clear in IPL 100 on day one," he continued firmly. "I still don't understand why they allow civilians in here to begin with."

"Civilians?" Sarah said. "So we're in the army now?"

"What's your name again?" Matthew said, looking at Tico.

"Tico Micah."

"Mr. Micah, I'm not interested in whatever secrets lie behind your Academy's closed doors," Matthew said coolly. "I'm interested in only one thing your Academy has to offer." He gave me an intense glance and then leaned over and slid his palm across my wrist.

Sarah's gaze shifted between the guys. Matthew's eyes were fixed on me. Tico's eyes were fixed on Matthew.

"Perhaps I'll apply to the school," Matthew said. "I want to be as close as possible to my girl here."

He called me his girl?

"You have a parent in the IPPL?" Tico asked.

"I have no parents."

"No parent, no entry. No exceptions." Tico exuded a sense of smug satisfaction.

"You gotta be kidding me," Sarah snarled, breaking the tension. Staring at something across the dance floor, she ripped off a piece of what looked like some sort of bread item at the table and chomped into it as if it had gravely insulted her. "That girl had better stay far away from me."

I turned and gasped when I saw the blue dust devil on the dance floor. Let's just say that Planella's mind-reading ability wasn't the only thing about her that should have been illegal. Her gyrations put the Barbie trio's moves to shame. I welcomed the distraction. This Tico-and-Matthew thing was too painful to bear.

"I'm surprised they let her come to the social," I said. Turning toward Sarah, I added, "No trouble tonight, okay?"

"We'll be fine if she keeps her snotty blue self away from me," Sarah huffed, tearing into the bread loaf for Round Two.

Matthew turned to look. "So that's the mind reader?"

"Mind reader?" Tico said.

I nodded. "Another long story."

Sarah was still staring at our former roommate. I stood and grabbed my purse off the back of the chair. "Come with me to the bathroom?"

"Yeah," she said. "I'm suddenly feeling sick."

"From that bread thing, or Planella?"

"Do I really need to answer that?"

I didn't want to leave Matthew with Tico, but I could tell that Sarah was getting ready to pounce.

"We'll be back in a few," I said, grabbing my friend's bicep. Then I turned to look at Tico. "It was nice meeting you," I said. "If I don't see you later, have a great night." I hoped he wouldn't be there when I got back. I looked at Sarah. "You ready?"

"Ready to pop that girl if she comes anywhere near me."

"Alrighty then. Let's get you to the bathroom before that happens." To avoid Planella, I took the long way to the restrooms, leading Sarah around the perimeter of the room instead of cutting across the dance floor.

"You need to ignore her," I said as we entered the lounge area of the spacious bathroom, which had two giant floor-length mirrors edged in thick, gilded wood. To the right of the mirrors was a vanity with four sinks and a basket of complimentary toiletries. I applied a second coating of shimmering gloss to my lips as Sarah tousled her mane. "You'll know if she tries to get into your brain," I reminded her. "And if she does, we'll make a bigger stink about it this time. It wouldn't be worth it to start anything with her...for one thing, you can't get thrown out of school. I can't make it here without you."

"I'm not going anywhere," she said with attitude. Still, I had the sinking suspicion she didn't agree with me on how to handle the whole Planella situation. "Speaking of starting something," she continued. "What was up with Tico? He got all territorial back there. I'm so sorry. I had no idea he would act that way."

"Well, that's what you get when you tell guys from different planets that your friends are interested in them." I smacked my lips to even the color and then used a brush to fluff my bangs. "It was very awkward. He was rude to Matthew."

"Oh, really, now? You thought Mr. Micah was being rude?" She said it in a pompous, British accent.

I smiled. So she'd noticed Matthew's formal address to Tico, too.

"Trust me," Sarah said in her normal voice. "Your little Hedricon can handle himself. I must say, I loved his passive-aggressive jab about you being his girl."

"You would. You like to start trouble," I chided. Sarah's eyes suddenly turned to ice.

"What?"

"Your ring."

When I twisted my hand toward my face, I felt the ground fall out from under me. The formerly turquoise stone was practically white. Sarah and I looked at each other, aghast.

"When's the last time you checked it?" Sarah said. "How long has it been that way?"

I shook my head. "I don't know. I wasn't paying attention." I felt unsafe. I wanted to get away from all these people and get back to the dorm. "Let's get Matthew and get out of here."

I threw my hairbrush into my purse and dashed for the door, but Sarah pulled me to a hard stop before I could make it.

"That's the last thing we're doing," she warned, her fingers digging more deeply into my wrist. "Did you check the stone last night when you were out with him?"

"What? No. It was dark. This has nothing to do with him. He's no threat to me."

"I told you to check it, Resa. You knew I didn't have a good feeling about him. My hunches are usually spot-on."

"That's not how you felt about him ten minutes ago, when the two of you were ganging up on me, thick as thieves."

"That's before I knew your ring had turned the color of milk."

The bathroom door opened, and my heart dropped when two short, stocky girls entered. I watched them intently, wondering if they posed a threat. I relaxed when I realized they were too busy gossiping about the blurry blue dancer to be any threat.

"Maybe this has something to do with the Barbie girls," I suggested in a low voice when the girls disappeared into toilet stalls. "I thought I heard them make a comment about my pants. Clearly they're interested in Matthew and I'm an obstacle for them. Or maybe Tico's the threat? He seemed weirdly possessive back there."

"Oh God, I hope not," Sarah said. "I would never forgive myself if I introduced you to a psycho. All the more reason for you to stay here. I'll be back in a minute."

I made a face. "I'm not staying in here alone." I grabbed her arm and followed her back to the table. My senses were all on high alert as I scanned the room, looking for anything or anyone that seemed out of place. Matthew was sitting alone, sipping an iced tea with a garnish of mint. He immediately picked up on my anxiety.

"What happened?" He set down his drink. "You look like you've seen a ghost."

"I have." I lifted my ring to show him. "This used to be blue."

"I don't understand."

"We'll explain later," Sarah interrupted. "She's in danger. Can I trust you to help me get her back to the dorm?"

Matthew didn't hesitate. He tucked me away under one arm and whisked me to the door, Sarah forming a tight shield on my other side. I felt like a celebrity being protected from rabid paparazzi.

Just as we tried to exit, a suited Yrdian man with a thin, wiry mustache and a walkie-talkie pulled the doors shut.

"No one is leaving," he ordered, holding his hands up in the universal "stop" gesture as he barricaded the exit. "I need everyone to go back to their tables and sit."

"But you don't understand," Sarah pleaded. "This is an emergency. We have to go."

"No one is leaving. Go back to your seats on your own or we'll help you get back to them." Just then, a handful of other suited men with walkie-talkies came barreling through the door. The music stopped, and the amber mood-lighting morphed into full-on, blinding white. Silence descended on the crowd.

This must have been what the ring was trying to warn me about. Something was happening, something big. Matthew pulled me more tightly to him. I wanted to stay close to the exit, but the suited men herded all the stray students back to the dinner tables.

"This is an emergency situation," said a different suited man who forced his way onto the DJ's microphone. "Everyone needs to remain calm and take a seat."

There was a loud shuffling as dozens of students sat down in unison, whispering urgently amongst themselves. The mind-splitting feedback from the microphone caused me to wince and grab my ears.

"What's happening?" Sarah said as she shimmied her chair as close as possible to mine.

"I don't know," I whispered in panic. The snow-white stone in my ring made me feel like a black rabbit in the Arctic.

"There's been an attack," the man on the microphone announced staunchly. "The Warner-Crivice Intergalactic Banking building experienced a terrorist attack, resulting in significant damage and potential casualties. We are under lockdown while we await further instructions."

"My friend just texted me," a student at a nearby table announced. "It's the Siafu. It was an aerial bombing. The building is literally melting from the corrosive venom."

My heart dropped. "The city's under attack," I whispered to Matthew and Sarah. "Did you hear what they said?" I immediately pulled out my cell to call my father, but I no longer had reception. I heard many people around us complaining about the lack of service, too. I hoped that the IPPL headquarters was safe.

Sarah touched the screen on her phone. "I don't have a signal either."

"The most important thing is to stay calm," Matthew said, stroking my arm. "I'm sure your father is fine."

"But what if he was in the bank?" I scoped the room for any potential weapons we could use against the Siafu if they should barge through the doors. Oh God! I wasn't sure I could handle seeing the human-sized bug-like creatures. I noticed that the walkie-talkie men were now all holding aggressive, military arms.

Suddenly, what sounded like an enormous thundercloud of fireworks exploded overhead. Chandeliers shook. Water glasses toppled. People began to scream. A second explosion set a human tsunami heading for the doors, and I was knocked out of my chair by a clumsy, heavyset, furry creature as it lumbered toward the exit. I looked to the side and saw that Matthew was on the ground too.

"Matthew," I called out. I lost sight of him through the forest of legs and skirts. I heard Sarah shouting my name, but her voice was getting steadily fainter. I felt a cool chill on my cheek, and when I touched my face, my fingers came away with red liquid on them. Instant panic. I was not a blood person, but if I passed out now, I'd be trampled for sure.

A third explosion shook the ground and the four-inch stiletto of one of the Barbie trio cut my left calf as she barreled over me.

Then I heard something even more alarming.

A clattering, like broken glass, getting steadily louder. There was a high-pitched scream. Then I saw it. The chandelier above me was gyrating. Its crystal pendants rattled as the ceiling buckled under its weight and finally gave way.

I was suddenly alone, directly in the path of the massive chandelier, which was accelerating under the pull of gravity. Time stopped. My thoughts flew in a million directions. Then an arc of black shot toward me, and I felt a hard pull. Somehow Matthew's body engulfed mine, shielding me from ricocheting glass bullets as the chandelier came crashing down just inches away.

TO FEEL ALIVE

It's amazing how in crisis situations you can deal with pain that would normally cripple you in daily life. Matthew had about thirty lacerations on his body, ranging from a three-inch gash on his neck to paper-cut sized incisions on his cheek. His clothes looked like they'd been shredded on a cheese grater, yet all his attention was on me. We were both covered in a dusty film, thanks to the partial roof collapse.

Sarah, who had escaped without major injuries, was playing Florence Nightingale, armed only with a tube of Neosporin and a handful of adhesive strips retrieved from the abyss of her hobo bag. She used all the strips on Matthew except for one, which I earned for a nick on my forehead.

My leg, however, was a disaster. I should have already passed out from the gash in my calf that was courtesy of the heel stampede. Sarah did an excellent job of concealing the wound in a fabric tablecloth so I couldn't see the spigot of blood.

"Here, take these," she ordered, forcing two Tylenol into my mouth. She made Matthew do the same.

"We need to go," he said. "They're moving everyone to emergency shelters in the basement of the building. Sarah, hold her leg." I winced in pain as he scooped me up in his arms, Sarah hovering over us, holding the tablecloth firmly to my wound. A duo of Yrdian armed guards saw us and pointed. I felt light-headed from blood loss.

"This is Robert Stone's daughter," Matthew informed them as they approached us. "She's injured." The guards immediately radioed that they had found me, which reassured me that my father was okay. Three more armed men converged on us. The elevators weren't working, so the men carried me down the twenty-six flights of steps to the basement, where a large, gymnasium-sized room was quickly filling up with students. The guards bypassed the room and took me into a smaller one where there was only one other student, a white-haired Yrdian boy with a badly injured right arm, who was sitting on the floor in the corner. The room had no furniture except for a metal examination table and a few cabinets of medicines and other medical devices. The lighting reminded me of the inside of my fridge, a mellow blue LED.

The guard lay me on the table and unwrapped the cloth from my leg. Matthew grabbed my hand and positioned himself so I couldn't see the wound. Even though I couldn't see it, I could feel it, and it was pulsating as if alive. It didn't help that the guard audibly gasped. He called for assistance on his walkie-talkie, and a few minutes later a tiny, black-haired woman came into the room. Her white skin was as smooth as porcelain, and she reminded me of a beautiful china doll.

"Resa," she said in a thick accent that sounded almost Russian. "You need some stitches. I'm going to apply a local anesthetic. You may feel a little pain."

Local anesthetic? I clenched Matthew's hand as I felt her insert the needle. Sarah had her hands on my shoulder.

"You won't feel pain," Matthew said calmly. "Believe it. Say it. 'I won't feel pain.'"

"I won't feel pain," I repeated. My face hurt from the tension I held in it.

"You can create your reality," he reminded me. "You won't feel pain."

I felt something, but it wasn't pain. She was pushing on my skin, or at least that was the sensation I registered.

"Okay," the china doll said after several minutes. "You're all done. But it will be sore when the anesthetic wears off."

"I'm done?"

"You're done," Sarah confirmed.

I hadn't felt any pain at all. I looked down at my leg, which was now covered in thick white gauze. I exhaled heavily as my friends lifted me to a sitting position.

"Take this for the pain," the china doll said, handing me a blue pill from a jar she had taken out of the cabinet, along with a small cone of water from the water dispenser. Then she left in a hurry, leaving us alone with the injured Yrdian boy.

"I'd rather be on the floor," I said. "I don't want to fall off this thing. I feel woozy."

"Okay. Hold on to me." Matthew lifted me off the table and helped me position myself on the ground, allowing me to use his body as a backrest. "Better?"

"Yes. Thank you. I can't believe this is happening." I rested my head back on his warm chest. "I'm sorry I'm so much trouble."

"It's amazing how quickly things can get done in an emergency," said the Yrdian boy, speaking for the first time since I'd been brought into the room. "That just took ten minutes. They set my broken arm in record time, too."

"I hope I wasn't whining too much," I said as I readjusted my leg. "I'm Resa. This is Matthew behind me."

Sarah held her hand out to the boy. "Sarah."

The boy nodded. "I'm Nini. And no worries. I'm glad for the company."

"I guess that's the one good thing about us being injured," I said. "We don't have to be packed into that gym with all the rest." My stomach was queasy, and I felt uncomfortably hot. "Can I have another water?" I asked.

Sarah nodded and started to fill another paper cone. The medicines in the cabinets rattled to the muffled sound of another explosion on the surface, and Matthew tightened his grip on me. It was strange. The situation was dire, but I felt calm down here, tucked away in the small medical room.

"Whoa," Sarah muttered as a second, more forceful explosion caused her to stagger. She lost half of the water in the cup.

"I heard them talking," Nini said, holding his shoulder as he straightened into an upright sitting position. "It's the Siafu up there attacking us. They're retaliating because we intervened with their plan to occupy Glucosa. They were aiming for the school. Not the bank."

"The school?" Sarah said as she refilled the cone and handed it to me. Then she started to snoop through the medical cabinets, which the china doll had forgotten to relock. "That doesn't make sense. The kids here didn't do anything to them. Why would they attack us?"

"That's exactly why the school," Nini responded. "They knew it would be the most devastating attack they could make. They'll do anything to make us stop the Glucosa intervention."

"We just don't want them attacking an innocent civilization," Sarah said. "What is wrong with these things that they can't understand that?" Sarah slipped something into her pocket.

"What did you just take?" I asked in disbelief.

"More of those pills she gave you. Who knows how long we're going to be down here. They may move us, for all we know, and you'll need them. You might need these, too." She leaned a pair of crutches against the wall next to me. "You won't want to put pressure on that leg for a while."

"Excellent suggestion," Matthew said, readjusting the crutches to make them more stable.

"See. I told you she comes in handy sometimes," I joked. I didn't feel bad about taking them in case she was right about us having to move to a new location. I didn't want anyone to have to carry me anymore.

"Are you guys all Academy?" Nini asked.

"Yes," I said for simplicity's sake, nudging Matthew with my elbow. I trusted him with my life and didn't want Nini to treat him the way Tico had.

"Well, maybe you can give me your opinion on something, then. Don't get mad at me, or report me, or anything. For all I know, those big blue horse pills they fed me might be messing with my mind."

Sarah stopped rummaging, a look of interest on her face. "Did you kill someone?" she asked. It hadn't even occurred to me to suspect something so gruesome. "If so, Resa will definitely report you."

I gave her a look. "Like you wouldn't?"

"Of course I didn't kill anyone," Nini said. "This attack is just making me question the Academy's goal. What if universal peace is not possible? What if Gemja is unattainable? Do I really want to devote my life to a goal that can't be reached?"

"Gemja?" Matthew asked. "What's Gemja?" My heart dropped. He was about to be exposed as non-Academy.

Nini thought it was a rhetorical question.

"My point, exactly," Nini said to Matthew. "What is it? Is it Heaven? Nirvana? Nobody knows. But clearly the universe is not interested in peace. Who are we to try and force it? I mean, think about it. The Academy is essentially going to teach us how to persuade the rest of the universe into donating their crystals because we think going to Gemja is a good idea. What if others don't want to donate their stones? What if they don't want to go? Then what? Do we steal them? Start a war for them? That's completely opposite of the goal of reuniting Gemja. I'm sorry, I'm just confused right now."

He reminded me of Dakota. Dakota! I felt guilty that I hadn't thought of him until now. I prayed that he was safe in his dorm.

"It's not like we're brainwashing anyone," Sarah said. "It's common sense." Then in a sarcastic tone, she added, "Okay, everyone who likes war, pain, and sadness stand in this corner of the room. Everyone who wants happiness, peace, and harmony stand in the other. Come on. No one in their right mind would willingly head into the sadness corner. You're telling me that you like war? You're happy we're being bombed?"

"No, of course not," Nini said. "I'm just questioning the possibility of real peace. I truly think there are people who are too interested in personal power to care about anyone other than themselves. Look at the Siafu. They have no interest in peace or in living harmoniously with others, and it seems impossible to convince them otherwise."

"But it would make the universe a better place if we did," I said. "A little less sadness and hurt is always better, no?"

Matthew put his hand atop mine. "Yes and no," he said.

"How do you figure?" I couldn't wait to see how Mr. Philosopher could defend that position.

"I understand where Nini is coming from," Matthew said. "And I'll take it one step further. Let's just say that we did go to this place, that we all went to live in peace and harmony on this—" He looked to me for help.

"Gemja," I replied.

"On this Gemja," he said. "Then what?"

I shrugged. "We'd live in peace and harmony, that's what. Not to mention, on Gemja, anything is possible. All your wishes and dreams could come true." It seemed obvious that this was a desirable outcome.

"Okay. Imagine yourself on a world like that. What would your day be like?"

"Eating troughs of fettuccine alfredo with extra parmesan without gaining a pound," Sarah said. "Having whatever we want, whenever we want. It would be awesome."

Matthew looked at me. "It would be boring."

Nini's eyes lit with new interest and he started nodding vigorously. He looked at Matthew in admiration. "You are so right," he said emphatically. "After you had and did everything, you'd be bored to tears."

"And then what would people do?" Matthew said. "Perhaps they would start to do things they shouldn't be doing, just to feel something. Breaking rules. Acting out…And the cycle continues."

Matthew could tell I was conflicted about what he was saying. "Think about it," he said to me. "If you never had to work for anything, if you never had any wants, you would have no emotions. You would feel empty."

"Speak for yourself. I'd be happy enough," Sarah said crisply.

"Happiness is relative," Matthew reminded her. "You can't know happy if you don't know sad."

"I couldn't have said it better," Nini said. "Very deep stuff, my friend. Very impressive." He pointed at him with his good arm. "Where are you from?"

"Blackiston."

"My brain hurts again," I said, making a cute face at Matthew. He smiled and patted my arm. "I think your species are more advanced in your way of thinking about things."

"I'm just saying that maybe the universe is perfect as it is," Matthew said. "Maybe peace will be achieved when we stop fighting the way we are. Or maybe we aren't meant to achieve peace at all."

"You like things as they are?" Sarah said, unable to let it go. "You like seeing Resa in pain?"

"Without pain, you wouldn't be able to appreciate feeling good," Matthew said. "No, I don't want Resa to be in pain; but I do want her to feel alive," he said. "To be alive means to experience. To want. To feel."

"Trust me, I'm alive," I said, clenching Matthew's arm. The local anesthetic had worn off. I felt pain. Lots of it.

***

We were stuck in the medic for about six hours before a group of IPPL men evacuated us to a van waiting out front. They had orders to return me to headquarters. At my request, the men agreed to bring Sarah and Matthew, but Nini had to stay behind in the medical room since there was no more room in the van. I could have kissed Sarah for finding the big blue pills and crutches when we were first tucked into the room. I was able to move myself to the stairs, at which point I had to be carried one flight up to the emergency door that led outside.

The night air had a peculiar odor, a mixture of burning rubber and sourness. I flinched as I heard what sounded like a truckload of silverware crashing to the floor in the distance. Several of the city's elevated glass walkways had been shattered, leaving deadly daggers of glass dangling in midair, falling at random intervals. Billowing spires of smoke ascended from multiple spots throughout the city. Sirens screamed everywhere. Many of the beautiful pastel buildings were discolored, worn from reactions to the Siafus' corrosive venom.

The Warner-Crivice Bank was in the worst shape.

The once-pointed peak of the triangular skyscraper looked as if it had melted and re-hardened into an uneven globular mess. It reminded me of a Salvador Dali print, since the windows on the top twenty floors were runny and distorted.

The van was equipped with a red light and a siren, which helped us pass the traffic until we pulled into an indoor parking lot in the IPPL building. We cleared security and met my dad in a large room filled with computers and oversized hanging screens that displayed the destruction in various parts of the city.

"Resa," my father said, his voice heavy with relief. He gave me a huge bear hug, nearly knocking me off the crutches. He gave Sarah a big hug, too. I felt instantly safer in his presence.

"Dakota wasn't with us," I said quickly. "Have you heard from him?"

"He's fine. He's already here."

"Oh, thank goodness. Dad, this is Matthew," I said, pulling him closer. "Matthew, this is my father. Dad, he saved my life. I wouldn't be here without him."

My father stared into Matthew's eyes as he listened to me recount the Cliffs Notes version of the chandelier story.

"I owe you, son." My father shook Matthew's hand.

"You owe me nothing," Matthew said. "Having Resa alive is payment enough."

But I wasn't willing to let this opportunity pass. "Actually, Dad, he could use your help. Is there any way you can help him into the Academy?"

"We'll talk about it later," he said as another agent approached and whispered something in his ear. I overheard something about the shuttle being ready and the need to hurry before the airspace closed. Before I knew what was happening, someone was strapping me into a wheelchair.

"Go with them," my father said, kissing the top of my head. "I'm sending you home. Dakota's already on the shuttle."

"But Dad, Matthew needs to come with us. He saved my life. We need to help him. He has no one. Please."

"You have to go, now," my father said. "We'll take care of your friend." He nodded to a suited man who began pushing my wheelchair down a corridor leading to the air-shuttle terminal. Sarah was jogging to keep up with me. I looked back at Matthew, who was trotting after me but slipping behind. I wanted to push the IPPL man aside, flip the wheelchair, and run to him. I wanted to scream, I love you. I didn't care that Oganwando was dangerous. I didn't want to leave him. My heart dropped when Matthew ended his pursuit. I hadn't kissed him goodbye.

He waved and smiled wryly as I was wheeled into the terminal.

I read his lips. "No resistance."

People crossed between us as the guards whisked me down a small corridor that led to the shuttle. I deciphered only one last word from his lips before a heavy door closed behind me.

Surrender.

A NOTE OF INSPIRATION

I sat on the rocky peaks in my backyard, listening to the sound of the waves crashing against the granite bluffs below. I was perched dangerously close to the edge with my legs dangling over the side of the cliff. The stinging December night air had stolen the feeling in my feet and hands and nose. I welcomed the numbness. It dulled the ache in my calf. It dulled the ache in my heart for Matthew.

I don't know how long I'd been out there staring at the orange dot in the lower right-hand corner of Cassiopeia, the W-shaped constellation that could be seen year-round here in Maine. The dot was Oganwando's sun, and seeing it made me feel closer to Matthew. Maybe he was looking back at my sun and thinking of me, too.

I kept replaying what Matthew had said about bad things being necessary to appreciate good things, as if that would somehow ease the overwhelming sadness I felt about being so far away from him. School had been postponed until a better assessment of the threat to Oganwando could be determined, which meant I wasn't going to see him anytime soon. And I didn't have a number or an address for him. For all I knew, he'd been deported back to Blackiston.

Matthew would need to find me. Hopefully, he'd paid attention to what I'd told him about my home life. Hopefully, he'd remember I was in Bar Harbor. Maybe he would run away to Earth on some new adventure.

I jumped when I heard someone walking on the rocks behind me. I wished it could have been Matthew. It was only Dakota.

"No, it isn't abnormal for people with leg injuries to be climbing on icy rocks in subarctic weather on the edge of a fifty-foot cliff."

"Hey," I said dryly.

He threw a blanket at me.

"Mom wanted me to give you that," he said.

"Thanks."

"I'm just going to be straight with you. She sent me out here because she thinks the attack messed with your head. She's afraid you're going to jump. She's looking up psychologists for you."

I pulled the blanket off my head and repositioned it around my shoulders. "She's the very reason I'm out here. I needed my time alone. I'm not about to jump."

Dakota dropped down beside me, visible only as a dark silhouette wearing a baseball cap underneath a hooded jacket with the pull strings untied. Mom was standing inside the back door with her arms crossed, looking in our direction. Her breath was fogging up the glass, so I doubted she could see us clearly.

"That's good," Dakota said. "Because we all know Mom and Dad won't be the ones cleaning your guts off the rocks down below."

I huffed out a laugh. "I wouldn't do that to you."

We sat silently. Eventually, Dakota said, "You were pretty quiet on the ride back. When you fell asleep, Sarah told me about some Matthew dude. Who's this guy who has you sitting on a ledge?"

"The wolf," I replied.

"The wolf was in Oganwando?"

"Yes. What did Sarah say about him?"

"That she had some reservations about him."

"Matthew saved my life. Twice. First on Wandelsta. Then on Oganwando." I told him the chandelier story, including the part about the ring.

"How did he end up on Oganwando?"

"He was a runaway. Sarah found him. Long story."

"Sarah found him where?"

I didn't want to get into the whole thing. "It doesn't matter." Thankfully he decided not to press the Matthew issue.

"So, any news on the ghost front?"

I'd been away at school for only a week, but it felt like ages since I'd last thought of Nitika. Matthew's hold on me was far greater than any she'd ever had. "No. I'm just an ordinary girl again. Doing ordinary things." Like falling in love. Like having my heart torn to shreds.

Dakota blew on his hands as he rubbed them together. "Okay. I hate to break up the party, but it's hypothermia-cold out here. I'm going in. I suggest you come with me, or she'll have that therapist make an emergency house call."

It was my first unforced smile in hours. Dakota helped me with my crutches, and we headed inside for a cup of cocoa.

* * *

Dad came back home the following week, bringing unexpected news about Matthew. My father had taken my request to help Matthew seriously. Grateful that Matthew had saved my life, he'd conducted a background check on him—a necessary step for any prospective Academy student.

The disturbing news he uncovered made me sick.

Matthew had been tossed from foster home to foster home throughout his life, since his mother had died young and his father was always in and out of jail for repeated bouts of drunkenness and disorderly conduct. There were many filed reports of physical abuse inflicted by his father and the foster parents. It was torture to learn this without being able to hold him. To tell him that I would never hurt him.

"So, what's going to happen to him?" I asked. "He's not going to be sent back home, is he?"

My father shook his head. "His family life makes him a risky choice for the Academy, but he has a nice caseworker who's looking out for him. He'll be fine. He's very mature for his age, which isn't uncommon for kids who've had a tough start in life. And he couldn't ask enough about you and how you were healing. He wanted me to give this to you."

My father pulled a folded envelope from his pocket and handed it to me.

"He wrote to me?" I tried hard not to make it seem like my heart was doing tumbles in my chest. "That was nice of him," I said, downplaying the gesture. "What does it say?"

"I didn't read it. It's for you."

I tilted my head and shrugged, not wanting to open it in front of my dad. "Well, that was nice of him. But I should be thanking him. Any news on when school is going to reopen?" The note felt like an open flame in my hand. I wanted to sprint away and tear it open somewhere private. Matthew was right here in the palm of my hand. He was with me. I could barely comprehend my father's words.

"Nothing decisive until we see what we're dealing with here. I would say no earlier than the spring semester, if even at all."

"Spring?" That was three months away. "Or never?"

"The Siafu were targeting the school, Resa. We're not taking any risks. We're letting the offensive in Glucosa play out for a while in the hopes that everything will settle down. The parts of the city surrounding the school need to be rebuilt. We're hoping for the spring."

"Robert, Narvo is on the phone," my mother said, popping her head into the living room. My father rose and went to talk to Mr. Cuticulor.

I stole away into my room, locked the door, and dove onto my bed. I flipped the envelope over. A delicate copper scrollwork embellished the flap. My hands trembled as I tugged to break the glue seal.

The note was written in blue ink on pale yellow paper that matched the envelope. His penmanship was edgy, and the sharp edges and long strokes showed an artistic flair.

Dear Resa,

I saw you resist leaving Oganwando and wanted to remind you that the universe always has a perfect plan. The airspace closed after you left, so I had no choice but to stay here. I'm eighteen now and living with Miss Elsa. Please don't be jealous of that. ;)

They say the school will reopen in a few months. I'll be waiting to see you when you come back...well, that's if Sarah will let you. Remind her that I saved your life, twice to be exact. Ms. Elsa was kind enough to arrange a job at a bookstore for me. I hope to see your Wandelsta journal on the shelves soon. I keep thinking about our night together, and that energy between us. You are very beautiful, Resa Stone.

Until we meet again...

Matthew

A NOTE OF INSPIRATION

The sadness inside me dissipated. The three months until school began again seemed bearable now that I knew he would be waiting for me. I read the note at least twenty more times before hiding it between the pages of an old sketchbook in my closet. I immediately felt inspired to finish the revision of my journal, motivated by the daydream that if I could work quickly enough, Matthew might see my completed journal in one of the boxes at the bookstore before he saw me again in person.

For the next three hours, I hit the computer, perfecting my writing. I took a break only when Mom surprised me with a bowl of hearty chicken stew with popovers swimming in melted butter. She was thrilled to learn that I was almost done. She'd already added Colleen's number to speed dial for when I was ready to submit my final version.

I was so proud of my work when it was finally finished a couple of days later. It was everything I'd imagined it would be while sitting in the red sand on those dunes.

And Matthew was right about the universe having a plan. The journal had kept me so engaged that December crept up on me without warning. I realized that the next day was December 21st.

The attack had brought me home in time to rescue my grandmother.

ON A WINTER'S SOLSTICE NIGHT

Downtown Bar Harbor at Christmastime was like a picture in a dreamy storybook, with snowcapped roofs, dripping icicles, and twinkling colored lights.

Despite all the bulky velvet ribbons and metallic bulbs dangling about, it felt more like Halloween to me. The full moon hung overhead, and the smell of magic permeated the air. It was December 21st — the night of the winter solstice and the lunar eclipse.

The night I would enter a dream from which I might never return.

I wrote a letter to my family and one to Matthew, explaining everything in the event that something bad happened. I gave the notes to Sarah with the specific instructions not to deliver them unless I ended up like Grams. Sarah was livid that I had sent such a negative message out to the universe in writing, which made me nervous that I might have jinxed myself.

"Thanks for the ride," I said to Sarah, who sat gripping the steering wheel, trying to wear a positive face, even though I knew she was just as worried as I was. I had told my mother I was spending the night at her house. Instead, she had driven me to Meranda's.

"Good luck tonight," she said as she turned down the heat in the car.

The heat didn't need to be readjusted; she just had lots of restless energy. I did too. On the ride over here, I had twisted my ring around my finger so much that my skin hurt. The stone's color had not yet fully returned from the Oganwando nightmare, which made me wonder if I was still in danger, or if there was just a waiting period before the turquoise fully restored itself.

"Are you sure you don't want me to come up with you?" Sarah asked again.

I shook my head. "No. I don't want my mind to wander. The fewer distractions, the better. Not that you're a distraction."

"I get it," she said. After several silent seconds, she raised her eyebrows and tapped both hands on the wheel. "Well, I guess this is it. You're about to find out your destiny, RG."

"Yep." I nodded. I knew I should just get out of the car—prolonging the inevitable was only going to make things worse. I put my hand on the door latch.

"Call me immediately after it's over," Sarah fired, as if I were going on a date instead of into another dimension. "I want to know everything. I'm going to wait up, so it doesn't matter what time you call."

"That's if I come back," I said with a nervous smile.

"Stop putting negative energy out into the universe," she said angrily. "If you really feel that way, you shouldn't go."

"I have to."

"Then knock it off. Put on a happy smile and go do this thing." She leaned over and gave me a hug. "Seriously. You're coming back. We're not going to act like we're never going to see each other again, okay? I'll talk to you later."

"Okay."

"I mean it. Call me."

"I will." I opened the car door, but Sarah grabbed my wrist.

"Here"—she reached into the back seat—"you almost forgot this." She had trouble lugging my backpack over the center armrest. "What do you have in here? How can your spaghetti arms hold this if I can barely lift it?" The overstuffed bag slid open and out came a bottle of glue, a roll of tape, and a spool of thread. Sarah looked at me like I was insane. "You're planning to craft in between saving your grandma and finding your destiny?"

I couldn't help but smile as I gathered the fallen supplies and shoved them back into the bag. "I'd rather be over-prepared," I said.

"With a spool of thread?" She handed it to me. Then she reached into the back seat again and grabbed my ceremonial witch cape. "Now, this is something you'll need."

"Thank you," I said. I took the cape from her and draped it across my shoulders.

"Are you sure you don't want me to come? You're acting weird. I won't get in the way. At least let me carry the bag to the door. You don't want all this weight to put excess pressure on your leg. Does it still hurt?"

"It's fine, really. I'll call you later." If she kept insisting, I knew I'd probably say yes, so I just waved and walked away. She idled in the car for a moment before pulling onto the street.

As her red taillights faded, I felt terribly vulnerable. The full moon cast an eerie blue haze on Meranda's shop, which looked vacant except for the faint amber glow emanating from the small round attic window. Chills rolled down my neck as I climbed the creaky front steps and rapped my knuckles lightly on the door. I heard Slinky meow and then the sound of Meranda's brusque footsteps on the stairs. The door unlatched and she pulled me inside.

"Come, come," she said, bolting the door behind me. "We haven't time to waste."

"It's only 7:00." I suddenly worried that I had gotten the time wrong. "I thought the eclipse was at 11:11?"

"It is," she replied quickly. "Follow me."

The house was dark except for a small votive candle burning inside the cast-iron lantern Meranda held as she waved me up the stairs toward the attic. The urgency in her voice and her short, quick steps made my muscles clench even more tightly. She unlocked the attic door with a large ornamental key she wore on a black cord around her neck. I gasped when I caught sight of what was inside.

The daybed, which now stood in the dead center of the room, was dressed in crimson satin linens, its headboard adorned by ropes of winterberries and white, flowering ivy. On the floor surrounding the bed stood a circle of twelve-inch-high pillar candles that were already burning. In fact, the room looked like a candle store—waxy pillars glowed from atop every wall shelf and flat-surfaced piece of furniture. Dozens of all sizes and thicknesses flickered in the fireplace. They must have been burning a while, since they all had an uneven, drippy look. To the left of the bed was an altar, immaculately adorned with crystals, stones, and candles.

"You performed a spell?" I asked. Her altar was a four-foot-long rectangular chest that looked like something a pirate would own. I could see smoke rising from a small black cauldron in the top left corner of the chest, and the whole space smelled of the familiar musk of frankincense.

"Yes. I charged mugwort for protection and safe astral travel."

Meranda was wearing full ceremonial garb—a long black gown under a stately black robe. On her head rested a silver tiara headdress with a single blue gem centered on her forehead. A prominent blue spinel ring adorned her middle finger, and her crystal-tipped willow wand was secured by black fabric ties to a homemade fabric belt she wore knotted around her waist.

I slid my backpack off my shoulders, and it landed with a thud on the wooden floor.

"You brought the sketches that you made of your dream?" she asked me, eyeing the bag.

"Yes." I opened the bag and handed her my sketchbook. "I brought some other things, too."

"Like?"

"Just stuff I thought I may need."

She looked hesitant. "I don't know if they'll cross with you, but I don't suppose it would interfere with our process. Put the bag by the bed."

I carefully sidestepped the candles on the floor and did as she asked.

"Stay in the circle," Meranda ordered me. "You must feel completely at ease. Lie down and get comfortable. Step one—relax. I'll take care of everything else."

The bed looked so beautiful that I didn't want to mess it up. I sat atop it and drew my legs up over the side, pulling my bag up with me. The satin sheets were slippery and felt cool to the touch. The ivy and berries had a fresh, dewy odor that I liked. "You did a great job in here," I said, adjusting my cape. "It looks amazing."

"Thank you. Now, no more talking. Relax. Clear your mind."

I rested my head back and sank into the cool, fluffy pillows. I closed my eyes and folded my hands across my stomach. Meranda was fiddling about with things, providing white background noise. I tried to free my mind of worry, but I couldn't escape the reality that this could be my last night in this dimension. I suddenly wished that I had never found the stone, that I had never experienced the dream. The striking crimson bed sheets reminded me of my grandmother's saying about red daisies. If only I could be the normal, average, white daisy, whose biggest worry was falling hard for a guy.

As I took several deep breaths and tried to relax, Meranda turned on the meditation music. I focused on my breathing, inhaling for four counts, holding for four counts, then exhaling for four counts, just like we'd practiced.

It took a while, but I eventually fell asleep. I awoke just before eleven with Meranda standing over me, passing the smoke of mugwort over my head.

My stomach clenched when I saw the time on Meranda's watch, and I popped upright.

"It's time," Meranda informed me, handing me my sketchbook. "Find a picture of the place where Nitika comes to you."

"The channel," I replied, flipping to the picture of a clearing in the woods where the tree branches arched to form a natural roof overhead.

"Listen to me carefully," she instructed. "Keep the picture next to you. You must visualize the channel while summoning the energy in your body. Otherwise, your astral self will not know where to go."

"What if another thought sneaks in?"

She shook her head. "It can't. You must focus on the channel. Now breathe. Start to relax."

I didn't feel relaxed despite having napped. My body was trembling. I repositioned myself to get more comfortable and rested my arms at my sides, palms facing upward. Meranda placed several stones on the bed around me and then looked deeply into my eyes.

"I'm okay," I reassured her, seeing the concern in her eyes.

"You'll be fine," she said, placing a gentle hand on my shoulder. Then she slipped a pocket watch into my hand. "Watch the clock. I'm going to pull you back in thirty minutes."

My chest tightened. "What? No. Why? That's not enough time. You never said anything about a time limit. Don't pull me back unless something goes wrong." It aggravated me that she hadn't bothered to tell me that until now.

"If I lose communication with you, I won't know if something has gone wrong. I lost contact with your grandmother at the forty-five-minute mark. I'm not going to leave you in for that long."

She was increasing my stress level, which couldn't be good for the projection. "I don't want to feel rushed, Meranda. There has to be another way. What if I pull on the cord? Will you be able to see that on my body somehow?"

She rubbed her chin in thought. "I don't know if that would work." She walked to the window and gazed upward. "But we don't have enough time to test it now. The moon is almost in complete shadow. Come, we need to put you in trance. Remember. You have thirty minutes over there."

I could have easily exploded, but I knew it would be counterproductive.

"It happens in five minutes," Meranda warned me. "You need to start raising energy."

I closed my eyes and took a deep breath, but my muscles were all bunched and tense. I had five minutes to slip into trance, but I couldn't let go of the new thirty-minute rule. It just didn't seem like enough time to find Grams and speak to Nitika. Meranda passed an open vial of frankincense oil under my nose to help me relax, but I was wound tight.

"Breathe," she said rigidly. "Breathe. You are light and airy. Breathe." I could hear the urgency underlying her words, which only made me tenser.

This wasn't working. I ignored Meranda and thought of Matthew instead. I remembered his cool calmness. Surrender, he would tell me at this moment. Don't resist. I let his messages play on a loop in my head and slowly let go of my fear, allowing the frankincense to work on my brain. I felt my shoulders droop as I released the tension in them. Matthew was the one lulling me into trance, not Meranda. I felt the cool ripples of energy begin to course through my body.

"Three minutes," Meranda announced.

I focused harder on his message. You have the power, he would tell me. Surrender. I held the image of the channel firmly in my mind as I repeated his mantra again and again in my thoughts. Surrender. Surrender to the channel. Surrender to the dream. Take me there, now. To the channel. Take me to the channel.

"Two minutes."

My thoughts became watery. I felt something change in the air around me, as if the very molecules of air were shifting. My eyes were closed, but I started to feel a seasick vertigo, like the room was spinning. The room was spinning. It was difficult to hold the image of the channel because I felt like I was falling.

"One minute."

No, I was spiraling downward. My body felt runny, like the windows in the bank building on Oganwando. I was dripping like a fluid, flowing outward from my core. My thoughts became runny, so much so that I could barely understand them.

"Time."

I felt a tear. Then a cold, hard rush of air.

My eyes popped open. Everything was black.

I was no longer in the attic.

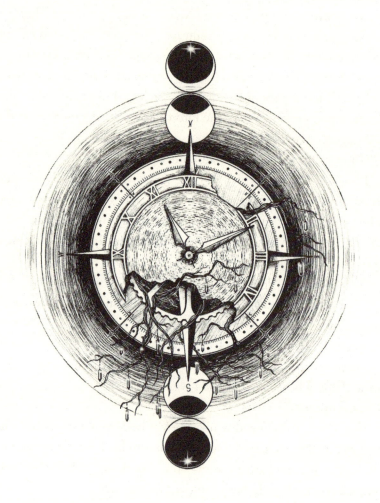

TOO LITTLE TIME

Strangely, I felt solid.

My bones. My hair. The cord coming from the back of my head. There was no difference between my projected self and my physical self, which lay in Meranda's bed back on Earth. I'd expected to be airy, like when I had practiced with Meranda. Maybe it was because I'd slipped into a completely new dimension. Maybe you only felt airy when you projected into your own dimension.

I felt something graze my back and my body jerked, though the movement was softer than I'd expected. It was as if I were in water but without the water. I reached over my shoulder and felt…my bag. It had crossed over with me! My heavy, barely-could-lift-it-on-Earth bag hung weightlessly over my right shoulder. And best of all, the soreness in my calf was gone. It was as if I had never been injured.

"Resa? Can you hear me?"

"Meranda!" Any residual anger I had felt toward her vanished.

"Resa?" It sounded like she was speaking to me from inside my ear; her voice was as tinny as if it were being projected through an old-time radio.

"Meranda, I'm here. Can you hear me?"

"Are you all right?" she asked, her voice anxious.

"Yes, I'm okay," I assured her. "I'm okay, but… I really can't see anything. I don't know where I am." My heart was racing. I took a deep, slow breath to try and calm myself.

"Just breathe," Meranda said calmly. "I'm right here. You're not alone. Keep talking to me. Tell me what you're feeling."

"I feel solid. I thought I would feel airy, like when I projected in the attic. But this is very different. I feel like I have a normal body. Only I can't feel temperature. It's not hot, or cold, or warm. There's nothing." My eyes hadn't yet adjusted to the intense dark either. I grabbed the cord at the nape of my neck and tugged it hard, three times. "I just pulled the cord. Did you see anything?"

There was about a ten-second delay before I heard her respond, "Oh my. Yes, yes. Your forehead moved ever so slightly. Three twitches."

"Okay," I mumbled to myself, my heart still pounding. Then, addressing Meranda, I said, "You're okay with me staying longer, then?"

"Pull again," she ordered. I tugged three times. "Yes. There they are. Three twitches again. You were right about that."

"Okay, then. Don't pull me out early," I ordered. "I'll tug three times when I'm done or if I get into trouble."

"What time does your watch read?" Meranda asked.

"It's too dark, I can't see the watch," I said. "Meranda, I'm perfectly fine. Really. I'm okay now. I'll pull if I'm in trouble. You have to promise me you won't pull me back before I'm ready. I didn't come all this way not to find answers."

My surroundings brightened under the glow of the full moons and I started to see shapes around me. My heart dropped when I recognized the opening of a clearing in the woods less than fifty feet ahead. A familiar corridor through the trees—the channel. Nitika always appeared to me at the end of it. Behind me, a meandering trail of glittery sediment disappeared into the woods.

"I won't wake you," Meranda said. "Just keep talking to me if you can."

"I will, but even if we lose each other, don't pull me back."

"I won't unless there's another reason for me to worry."

When my eyes fully adjusted to the darkness, I noticed two parallel lines about a foot apart, running the length of the trail into the woods. It was as if someone had carved the marks by dragging sticks in the sediment, though there weren't any footprints beside them. Then I remembered something.

I was always able to float in my dream.

My eyes shot down to my feet, which hovered several inches above the ground. Then it clicked. The lines in the sediment. Perhaps someone had traced them with their feet while floating.

Maybe my grandmother.

"Meranda, I didn't cross in the right place," I fibbed, eager to start my search for her. I would look for Grams, and then I would try to find Nitika. "I can see the channel, but I need some time to get there. Remember, don't wake me up unless I pull three times."

"Three times and I wake you," she said. "Be careful. Keep talking to me if you can," she added again.

"I will, I promise." Being able to communicate with her was comforting.

The air was eerily still. No wind. No rustling leaves.

Just dead silence.

I turned away from the channel and entered the forest, gliding three inches above the glittery sand pathway, which had a subtle lavender glow to it. Everything around me, from the sky to the trees, was somewhere on the spectrum between purple and black. I still couldn't get over the fact that I could float even though my body felt solid. Floating was an odd thing, controlled solely by thought in this dimension. Up, down, left, right, stop, start. All I had to do was think about the movement and it happened.

"Everything all right?" Meranda asked. "Can you describe what you're seeing?"

"I'm floating," I said, breathing hard. "This is crazy. I'm floating, yet my body is solid."

"Stay calm. Tell me what you see. What's around you?"

"Uh…I'm in a forest, but it feels all wrong. There's no sound at all. Oh my God. This is creepy."

"Have no fear," she said firmly. "I can pull you back in a second if anything happens. Just give me the word and you'll awaken."

"No, I'm okay," I assured her. "I just have to get used to this silence."

The deeper I went into the woods, the darker it became. The overhead vines and hairy fronds that clung to the tree branches created a thick mat, which blocked out most of the light from the two full moons. I stopped hearing Meranda after a while, and I suspected that the dense overgrowth was the explanation. I hoped she would keep her word about not pulling me back.

The air was uncomfortably still and I missed having Meranda's company as I forged forward, following the tracks. I wanted to call out for my grandmother, but I feared that the vibrations might shatter the lifeless world around me.

I stopped gliding and gently lowered myself, allowing my feet to touch down in the soft sediment. The air was so quiet that I actually heard them make contact with the delicate, powdery sand. I pulled a flashlight from my backpack. Much to my relief, it worked, and under the bright beam I saw the true color of the sediment—a light, glittery cream, not lavender.

I continued on foot, following the parallel tracks in the sand until the sediment became disturbed. It seemed like there were more lines here, crossing in multiple directions in a puzzling pattern. Then I heard something rustling to my right. I quickly extinguished the flashlight and poised my hand to pull my cord. I was shaking from an adrenaline rush.

"Who's there?" I heard a female voice ask from the dark.

It wasn't my grandmother's voice. This woman sounded much younger. I didn't know what to do, but I stood erect, keeping as quiet as possible.

"Who's there?" the woman repeated. "Please. I need help. I can't move. I'm stuck over here. If someone is there, can you help me, please?"

This just didn't feel right. Who would need help in a dream realm? Still, what if she was in trouble, and I was the only one who could do something about it? With one hand firmly grasping the cord, I shone my light in the direction of the voice.

A woman with a long dark braid was sitting on the ground in front of a spiny bush, her legs bent into her chest. She wore knee-high, caramel-colored boots and a chocolate-colored suede dress with beaded fringe at the neck and hemline. Her hand was blocking the light from her eyes.

"Ooh, sorry," I said, redirecting the beam.

She lowered her arm, revealing her thick, jet-black hair and dark, soulful eyes. Something about her was so familiar that my fear immediately lifted.

"Resa?" she said, her eyes filled with joy.

"Yes?" I said, stunned. I couldn't place her.

"Honey, it's me," the woman said.

I studied her thin nose and olive-toned skin. She had my mother's features. She had my eyes.

And then it hit me.

This was my grandmother, only younger.

"Grams?"

The woman smiled and motioned me forward. "Yes! I didn't think you'd recognize me. You didn't know me when I looked this way. Come here, darling. Come."

I didn't hesitate. I dropped on my knees beside her, unable to tear my eyes from her smooth, youthful skin and silken black hair. I could see my grandmother in her face, but this woman didn't seem like my grandmother. She was so young and thin and beautiful.

She fell forward and pulled me into a tight embrace. "Oh, Resa," she said. "My dear, why have you come here?"

"Grams! Look at you! How is this possible? You're so young!" My fingers brushed against something sharp on her back and I quickly withdrew my hand. "Oooo! What was that?"

Her face turned solemn and she shifted to show me her back. My light glinted off a garbled silver mess behind her.

"Grams. No!" I cried. It was her cord, but it looked like an overstretched Slinky that had wrapped around itself at least a hundred times. The three filaments of her cord had unraveled and become entwined with each other and with the thorny bush behind her. A single filament was all that remained connected to her head. "Grams, no! How did this happen?" I dropped my light and tried to detangle the knotted ball.

"It's all right, my darling," she said, grabbing my hand. "It's no use. Even if you could get all the knots out, the cord is too damaged for me to become reintegrated with my body. Just sit with me for a moment."

"But I thought the cord couldn't be broken?"

"That's what I thought, too," she said. "Please, come sit. I need to tell you something very important."

I kept pulling at the filaments, but it was impossible to detangle them.

"Please, Resa," she said. "We don't have much time."

"Grams, there has to be some way to untangle this mess. Maybe I can work backwards. How did you do this?"

Her eyes widened and she raised her forefinger to her lips. "I didn't. But you have to speak quietly. I don't want it to know you're here."

"It?"

"Honey, we don't have much time to waste," she urged. "Please, stop. It did this to me, and it can do the same to you. I need to tell you what happened, so you're prepared. It could come for you."

"The person who tangled your cord?"

"The thing that tangled my cord."

She had my attention. I sank onto the ground next to her, grabbing the light. "Is it still here? Should we shut the light?"

"I don't know where it is, but you're right. Turn it off. We don't want to draw attention."

I extinguished the light, immediately feeling vulnerable.

My grandmother grabbed my hand. "I don't want to scare you, honey," she whispered, "but something came after me here. I don't know what it was, but it had white, glowing eyes and a guttural voice. It kept asking me, 'Where is the kreyliss, witch?'"

"What is that?"

"I haven't a clue," she said, patting the back of my hand. "It thought I was lying, but I wasn't. 'Where is it, witch?,' it kept saying over and over."

"You must have been so scared."

"I was," she admitted, much to my dismay. "But it never hurt me. It just left me here like this."

"Oh, Grams," I said, tears in my eyes. "You don't know why it did this to you?"

"It thinks I know something about this kreyliss," she said, shaking her head in defeat. "It appears every now and then to ask me about its whereabouts."

"You haven't any idea?"

"None. I don't know what it is, much less where it is. I had a vision that led me to a stone, which led me here. The white creature found me before I could ask my guide what I was supposed to do."

"I found a stone, too, just like you did," I said. "Your guide. Was her name Nitika?"

My grandmother's eyes widened. "Why, yes. She came to you, too?"

"I've dreamt about her on and off ever since you were admitted to the hospital. And she actually appeared to me in a vision when I found the stone. Why is this happening to us? Why is this ghost haunting us?"

My grandmother sighed and pushed a dangling strand of hair behind my ear. "I don't know why she's haunting this family, but I feel it's my fault that she has come to you. I couldn't figure out what she wanted from me. Now she's looking to you to help her."

"Help her do what?"

"If only I knew."

"Well, let's find out together. Let me get you out of this mess, and then we'll ask her together."

She grabbed my hand to prevent me from touching her cord. "There's only one way to get me out of this mess, Resa." She clutched my hand in hers. "Help me detach this." She pointed to the single unbroken filament.

"What? No! You'll die! You can't ask me to do that!"

She delicately patted the back of my hand again. "Resa, honey. I'm not dead. I'm right here with you. That person back on Earth isn't me. This is me." She pointed to herself. "This is who my soul yearns to be. Young and beautiful and full of life. But I'm still connected to that old, crumbling body. And my true self is trapped in this realm by a tangled cord. You must help me cut the cord."

"You're asking me to kill you?"

"I'm asking you to set me free. Being stuck here alone, unable to move, isn't much of a life, is it? As long as I'm attached to this bush by a tangled cord, this is what my existence will be."

"But what about Mom and Grandpa? I can't take you from them. It's not my place."

"Honey, they already think I'm gone," she said. "That person in the hospital isn't me. They'll be relieved and happy that I went to a better place. You can tell them you spoke to me, if you'd like. That will help bring them peace."

"That'll bring me a one-way ticket into Windamere, right alongside your shell," I said. "Mom would have me committed."

My grandmother gave a hearty laugh, which made me happy inside despite the circumstances. "Yes, I suppose you're right," she said. "I don't know where your mother got her paranoia, but it certainly wasn't from me. Okay, then. Maybe you should keep our meeting here a secret from your mom. But you can tell your grandfather. He knew everything about the stone. He knew I was going to try and enter my dream. He'll understand."

"Grandpa knew? He never said anything. Meranda said you didn't tell anyone."

"Meranda was my dearest friend," Grams said, "but she could be intense at times—"

I snickered. "Tell me about it."

"Let's just say, your grandfather didn't share my affection for her. I didn't want her burdening him with questions and concerns, so I thought it best to leave him out of the equation. He didn't want me to come here. He was angry at Meranda for even suggesting it. I can only imagine how he feels now."

"I'm sorry, Grams. When I go back, I'll tell him I saw you."

She smiled. "Yes, he'll be so happy to hear that."

"Either that or he'll think I've lost my mind."

"Oh, no. He wouldn't. But if you're worried that he won't believe you, you can give him our code word as proof. Can you remember it?"

"You have a code word?" I pulled out a piece of paper and a pen from my backpack. "What's that?"

"A word or phrase that you share with someone in case of an emergency. Something that only you and the other person know."

"What was it?" My pen was poised, ready to write it down.

She laughed. "I'll never forget it. Banana buttons."

"Banana buttons?" I don't know what I had expected, but it certainly wasn't that. I wrote it down the best I could in the dark, smiling widely. "I'm almost afraid to ask, but how did that come about?" I put the paper and pen back in my bag.

"After I started having recurrent dreams about Nitika, I thought it was a good idea for us to have some secret code-word in case something terrible happened. When I told your grandfather, he was eating a banana sundae at the shop and I was sewing a button on his work shirt. Banana buttons. Once he hears that…"

I could hear the joy in her voice. If only she could return to him. It wasn't fair. She was right here, in front of me. Talking to me. There had to be a way to get her back home.

"What will happen to you if I cut the cord, Grams?"

"When you cut the cord," she corrected with calm confidence. "Something wonderful, I imagine," she said, sounding starry-eyed. "And even if it's not so wonderful, it can't be worse than being stuck on a thorny bush in the dark."

Grams always focused on the positive. And she was right. This was no way to live.

"Grams, have you heard of Gemja?"

She shook her head. "No, what is that?" She pulled me toward her so that my back was leaning against her.

"A magical crystal planet where only peace and love exist," I said, not doing the legend justice. "Maybe it's where we'll all meet again one day." I didn't want to leave her. I rested my head on her shoulder.

"Ah, then it must be a wonderful place," she said, stroking my hair. "If I can go to this Gemja, I will," she reassured me. "I'll wait for you there."

"Promise?"

"Of course," she said, "but you had better make me wait a very long time. There is so much for you to do in your realm. Come now. It's time." She patted my arm as a signal for me to stand. "You have to go meet Nitika before it's too late. I fear the white creature will come for you unless we stay one step ahead of it." She held out the single filament. "It's time. Help me sever it."

I dug into my bag, feeling for something that could snap the filament. I pulled out a pair of wire cutters.

"That's my girl," she said. "Always prepared." She held out the filament for me to cut, but I hesitated. "It's all right now," she said, laughing. "You're giving me life. What better gift could there be?"

I had to see her one last time, so I turned on the flashlight. When I looked into her eyes, there was no fear in them. No uncertainty. They were shining brightly with hope.

I opened the cutters around the filament and paused. I wished that she could have closed them herself, but the angle was all wrong. "Still want to be the lone red daisy?" I asked, trying to lighten the mood.

Her answer startled me. "I would have it no other way," she said. "And I'm hardly alone. I have you. Both of us were chosen…to do something wonderful, I imagine. The universe doesn't give you more than you can handle, so you must embrace being red." She put her hand to my face. "No tears. This is not the end. You're giving me life. Remember to tell your grandfather."

"I will, I promise." I didn't want to leave her. I had so much to ask her. So much to tell her. I had just said hello, and now it was already time for goodbye?

"Hurry, you must turn off the flashlight," she said. "Do it now. Both our lives depend on it."

"I love you, Grams," I said.

"And I you, my darling. It's time. I'm ready to go."

I wasn't ready. Still, I forced my hand shut. The cord snapped. And my grandmother floated upward, transforming into a beautiful barn owl before flying out of sight, leaving one lone feather and a sparkling trail of violet stardust in her wake.

THE MEANING

The sight of my grandmother ascending in the form of a majestic barn owl, her longtime favorite animal, left me with a feeling of absolute peace. I had set her free and she was soaring now. I wasn't at all sad because I knew, without a doubt, that we would be reunited one day. And she had left me a gift—a lone feather—a piece of her that I would forever carry with me.

The only gift I had left to give her was to fulfill her—our—destiny.

I returned to the channel and stood just outside it, awed by its haunting beauty. The trees here had stiff, jagged branches that arched overhead to form a natural cathedral ceiling. Gems of every size and color, sparkling more brilliantly than the moons' light, hung from every branch, creating a jeweled sky above me. In my dreams, I had never noticed the ground in the channel, but it too was mesmerizing—a carpet of woven pine needles coated with glimmering, champagne-colored crystalline frost.

Suddenly, an icy breeze rustled the leaves, and the gems began to flicker wildly as they swayed on their tethers. It was the first motion in this otherwise-dead world.

She was coming.

THE MEANING

A hazy glow pulled my eyes to the end of the channel, where a fuzzy mass of soft amber light hovered above the ground. It approached slowly, pulsating, twisting, and growing larger as it neared me.

I couldn't move.

The luminescent orb transformed into Nitika's familiar shrouded silhouette. The barefoot girl held her salmon cloak shut, clutching the fabric tightly from underneath. Her skin was fair and her hair was a delicate honey-brown color. She looked as solid as a real person. Nitika stopped about five feet before me, rigid as a stone statue.

I didn't know what to do. Part of me thought I should bow or kneel, but I stood paralyzed.

"You are the one," she said in a breathy whisper, slowly enunciating each word.

I had no voice.

"You are the one."

I was empty. Hollow. Frozen in place.

"You are the one."

She repeated the words but their meaning eluded me. I hadn't come all this way to simply hear the message again. I had to ask for clarity. I had to find my voice. I inhaled deeply, visualizing that cool pink blanket washing over me again, taking my fears with it. Somehow I forced the words. "What does that mean?"

"It is you. You are the one," she repeated, as if that clarified anything.

"I don't know what that means. I'm the one who has to do what?"

She stood motionless and silent.

"What is my destiny?" I was almost as still as she was, filled with painful anticipation as I awaited her answer.

Suddenly I felt something. An unnerving heaviness had crept into the air. It was the same uneasy feeling I always had when Nitika visited me in my sleep. It was a feeling of being watched.

We weren't alone.

I wheeled around, my eyes spotlights searching for the source of the heaviness. Something was there. I could feel it.

And then I saw it.

Two white eyes peered through the night sky, all but five feet behind me.

My body froze. The white thing that had hurt my grandmother had indeed come for me.

"Where is the kreyliss, witch?" it hissed. I saw nothing of its body, just two evil white beacons in the moonlight.

Nitika stood motionless, saying nothing. Doing nothing. Why wasn't she helping? I threw my backpack down and pulled out a sorry pair of scissors to use as a weapon. I backed up toward Nitika, the scissors poised over my shoulder like a javelin.

"The kreyliss, witch!" it hissed again. "Where is it?" The being came into focus. It was a person. Someone I recognized. My heart sank.

It was the skunk.

It was the albino boy who had snapped the photo of us in the diner, only his eyes had changed. They exuded shards of demonic white light.

"You have a choice," he hissed. "Tell me where it is, and you live. Or hold your tongue, and, well, *not*."

My instinct was to run. No. Pull the cord. Pull the cord! It was suspended several inches from his reach. I had to get in three fast tugs or I would be trapped here forever. I couldn't show fear or tip him off about what I was planning to do.

"I know your secret," he said. "You can't hide from me. I know your secret."

"Which one?" I asked boldly, hoping to distract him.

My question infuriated him. "Wrong choice." He lunged toward me, his human face morphing into that of a bony white beast with hollow eye sockets and the horns of an elk. Two incisor teeth dropped from its mouth, elongating into shiny steel daggers—daggers that were millimeters from splicing my only connection to my physical body.

I fumbled for the cord, yanked it three times, and fell backward into Nitika just as I felt a hard SNAP!

Before I knew it, I was back in the attic, back in my body, heaving for air. I heard Meranda gasp, partly because I was back, and partly because all the candles in the room had changed. The flames were stretching needle-thin, climbing to the ceiling.

"What's that noise?" Meranda asked, looking at me with icy eyes.

Then I heard it, too—a freight train whistle, getting steadily louder. Could it be a tornado?

"Meranda? What's happening?" I pulled myself erect on the bed as the whistle grew louder and the floor began to tremble. I rolled onto my knees, sitting back on my heels. "Meranda?" The train sounded as if it were in the room with us.

I followed Meranda's petrified stare to the air above her altar, which was shimmering, bordering on iridescent. A shock wave of cold, windy energy blasted us backward as the air above the altar rippled and Nitika was pulled through the rift.

She hovered above the altar, awash in a pale-blue light, wrapped from head to toe in that same salmon-colored cloak, her head down, her eyes closed. She looked like a hologram, transparent and ghostly. She was thin, barefoot, and beautiful.

Meranda collapsed into a heap on the floor, her hand on her chest, her eyes fixed on Nitika's image, which was flickering in and out of focus. I had to act fast before she disappeared. "Nitika! Tell me my destiny!" I had mouthed the words, but there was no sound. Fear and panic had stolen my voice. Without warning, a chilling wind swept across the attic, taking with it anything lightweight. The pages of Meranda's spell book fluttered, and feathers and incense-dust took flight. My hair rippled to the left, covering my face, and Nitika's image disappeared.

I leapt off the bed and knelt on the ground before the altar, struggling to keep my hair from my eyes as the wind blew with more force through the room. She had to come back! I was in danger. I needed her. I looked at Meranda, panic taking hold.

"Nitika!" Meranda bellowed, pointing her wand at the altar. "I command thee. Show yourself to us, that we may see."

The wind howled and swirled upward, taking the candles on the altar with it. An end table skittered across the floor, and a picture fell from its hook, the wooden frame splintering on the floor. The vortex seemed to be sucking all the air from my lungs.

"Call for her, Resa!" Meranda ordered me, her cape flapping in the wind. "Command her to come back. Make her listen to you. You're the one who must make her come to you!"

The wind was too powerful. I clutched the headboard to stabilize myself.

"Call for her! With force!" Meranda demanded as she staggered to keep her balance in the whirlwind. She was cowering in a corner now, her arms latched onto the leg of a heavy wooden armoire. "Resa, now! She's fading. Now, before you lose her forever!" Meranda's voice disappeared beneath the howling of the wind.

I had to succeed; I couldn't fail my grandmother.

I braced myself against the headboard and pulled myself upright, digging deep beneath my fear and dread to the place where I was the powerful one. To that place from which I had conjured the wind that night long ago.

I no longer fought the wind's force. I didn't resist it. I let it take me. I became the wind.

"I am limitless," I said in my mind. I released my grip on the bed and welcomed the air with outstretched arms. I tilted my head backwards, mouth open, and drank in the endless air, allowing it to fill my lungs. To fill my body with power. I was the air. Endless and powerful.

And that was when I found my voice. Five mighty, commanding words.

"NITIKA! TELL ME MY DESTINY!"

All fell silent and still. The wind abruptly ceased, and objects that had been aloft settled to the ground. Nitika came back into focus, more tangible than ever. The sound of her voice cut through my fear.

The time had come. She was about to reveal my destiny.

"A Retriever collects the stones," she said slowly, sounding as light and airy as the wind itself. "And it is not until all of the stones are found and brought together that reunification can occur."

"So my task is to bring all the stones together once they've been collected? Is that what I'm supposed to do?"

Her image flickered. Her words sounded watery. "The most vital element for the reunification is the keystone—the object through which all the energy must be channeled for space and time to warp and reveal Gemja. The keystone must be protected, for without it, Matchewa will rule forever."

"Is my destiny to find the keystone and to keep it safe?"

Suddenly all the air around us went cold, and a biting chill swept through my body. The shadows on the walls became still as the candle flames froze into tiny crystals of ice.

Nitika raised her head and opened her eyes. I couldn't breathe. She had jewels for eyes—bright, sparkling, iridescent jewels. My body turned electric, tingling with warm energy.

"You are the keystone," she said as she stared at me with her crystalline eyes. "You are the object through which all energy must pass. You are the one."

And in that instant Nitika's image shattered into hundreds of tiny sparkling stones that bounced onto the wooden floor of Meranda's attic.

ACCEPTANCE

"So, tell us, Ms. Stone. What was it like to be a teenager on another world?"

My mind raced with possible responses as I readjusted the microphone, which sat on the podium before me. A flurry of white lights snapped in the background. I couldn't place the reporter who had asked me the question, so I directed my attention to an abstract picture of a watercolor oak tree on the far wall of the newsroom. Staring at it was less nerve-racking than looking into the eager eyes of dozens of nameless faces.

"It changed me," I said, my voice cracking slightly. The lights flickered wildly as I spoke. I cleared my throat, embarrassed by the sound it made. My hands trembled as I reached for the cup of water in front of me and took a sip. "It made me realize how special Earth is," I said, sounding more like myself. "We take so much for granted here. Like water. Air. Food."

"Is that why you accepted the IPPL's invitation to join the C-QUEST Academy?" said a male voice to my left.

I returned the cup to the table. "Uh. I think so," I said. I couldn't tell who had asked the question, so I addressed the oak tree again. "The

ACCEPTANCE

Academy's goal is a good one—to try and unite different species and spread universal peace."

The sound of camera clicks was deafening.

"And you think that's a plausible goal?" asked a stern male voice to my left. "It sounds very idealistic. It shows your youth."

His statement offended me. "Anything is possible if we command it to be."

A woman's voice pulled my attention away from him. "Your choice to attend school on a different planet is a bold one. Are you scared to go?"

"Uh. No," I replied, still staring at that tree. My eyes followed its swirling brown branches and droopy, greenish-orange apples. "I made a decision to go. And once you make a decision about anything, you should surrender to it."

I heard the stern male voice again. "Do you think you're fit for representing Earth in the IPPL?" he asked. "We know that mental health issues run in your family. Your grandmother, the witch, was committed for it." There was a lull in the photo flashes, and I placed his face. A dark-haired man from WNBC, channel 6.

The audience reacted to his comment with astonished gasps and disgusted huffs.

"Resa, I apologize for my colleague's behavior," a familiar voice interjected. It was the red-haired reporter who had stopped my father for questions when we had taken the Cuticulors to Bollide Slide Park. She was close enough up-front that I could read her name badge—Bea Smith of Channel 5 News. "Perhaps Mr. Haughton was unaware that your grandmother passed away last night. I was so sorry to hear that. And we recognize your courage and bravery for keeping this scheduled interview in spite of what happened."

"My grandmother was a wonderful woman," I said, giving Haughton a hard stare. "Sir, the word witch doesn't mean crazy. Witches direct their energy to make things happen, which is more than I can say for most. Witches don't just talk about things. They do things. My grandmother is looking down at me now and smiling, happy that I'm willing to try and spread peace, as unrealistic as you think that might be. And I'm going to make her proud by making a difference. A real difference. You'll see."

For perhaps the first time in his life, Mr. Haughton was rendered speechless.

I was fighting hard to hold back tears. Luckily someone announced that the Q&A period was over and escorted me into a back room. Against the wall were two folding tables draped in rustic burnt-orange linens, piled high with a dessert spread the likes of which I had never seen. I wanted to disappear and cry my eyes out, but I had to stay strong. Trying to shake off the feeling, I went straight for the dark-chocolate-covered pineapple slices, but a hand on my shoulder stopped me in my tracks.

"You did a great job, Resa." It was Bea, the red-haired reporter who had saved me from the piranha. "Loving the flower, by the way."

"Oh. That. Thanks." I had forgotten about the small red-daisy stem I'd tucked behind my ear. I readjusted the flower.

"You look like a little modern-day hippie with the flower, that bright-red peasant dress, and those knee-high brown suede boots. Only, this hippie will be spreading peace on different worlds. A brilliant fashion choice, if you ask me." She squeezed my shoulder.

"It wasn't planned. My grandmother just loved red daisies, and I wanted some part of her to be with me tonight."

"She was, and I'll tell you this: I'm sure she's so proud of you and the way you handled Haughton. I am completely confident that you will soar at C-QUEST. If you ever need anything, please call me." She handed me a card and gave my shoulder a final squeeze before crossing the room to talk to another reporter.

I spotted my parents being questioned by a mob of reporters near the doorway, but I deliberately turned to avoid their attention. I studied the treats on the dessert tables and grabbed the largest pineapple wedge I could find. The acidy, cool sweetness made my tongue tingle when I took a big bite.

"Nice job," said a lady in a gray trench coat as she passed the table. I couldn't answer because my mouth was full of juicy goodness.

"You're a natural," another woman said as she slid in next to me to dunk a chunk of pound cake in a caramel fountain.

The compliments kept coming, but I felt anything but confident. I had told the reporter the truth earlier when I said that I wasn't scared. I wasn't.

I was petrified.

Petrified by Nitika's haunting message that I was the keystone; that the energy of the twenty-six power stones must first pass through me before the portal to Gemja would open. It didn't seem possible that I would have been chosen for this role. Who had made the decision? Was it the diamond dude, as Dakota called him? Would I survive the unification? Was I even meant to?

Whatever the case, I knew that I couldn't let my grandmother's death be in vain. She had been tortured by an evil white beast, a beast that now hunted me as I stood here with my chocolate-covered pineapple, in a roomful of people who had no idea what role I was intended to play in our universe.

I found a secluded bench in a far corner of the room near a coatrack and slipped onto it, hoping to fade from sight. I felt so desperately alone, even though there were people everywhere. The desire to see Matthew, to be cuddled securely against the contours of his chest, hidden from the world, was almost painful. But if he were here now, I knew he would tell me to be strong. He would convince me that I wasn't alone. That I had gotten to this place with help from friends, family, and even complete strangers. The universe had spoken through them, sending its messages to me through the words and actions of others. All I had to do was listen.

"Resa!" I heard my mother call, waving for me to join her and my father with a reporter.

I reluctantly stood and made my way toward them. Like it or not, this was part of my life now. People watching me. Wanting to know about me. Wanting to talk with me.

"Resa, this is Mr. Tuttle from Channel 2 News in Bangor," my mother said excitedly, pointing to the handsome, polished-looking man beside her. "He's interested in doing a news piece on your schooling experience at the Academy."

I extended my hand to the reporter, who seemed like a doll with his perfect hair, perfect face, and perfectly straight tie. The Barbie trio would have loved him. "Hello."

"Hello, Resa," he said. His smile exposed perfect white teeth. "I was just speaking with your mom. I was interested in doing a piece about your experiences at the Academy."

"Sure, I guess," I said, looking at my parents with raised eyebrows.

"Maybe I could get clearance to come to Oganwando, and we could meet weekly."

"Oh. Oh, no. I don't know about that," my mother interjected quickly. "Resa needs to concentrate on her schooling. And I don't know if C-QUEST would allow it."

"Out of the question. All interviews will have to wait until she returns to Earth," my father said bluntly. I smiled up at him, appreciative that he cared so much about my privacy.

The man nodded in agreement. "Okay, okay. Understood. Resa, maybe you can keep a journal while you're away, like when you were on Wandelsta? A log of your thoughts and experiences. Then we can get together when you come back. I'm excited to get to know you better."

I nodded and smiled but said nothing. No matter what I told the man, he'd never know the true me. I had a secret to protect—a secret that not even my parents could know. Part of me wanted them to discover it so they could rescue me from my fate. Selfish, I know. But that wouldn't solve a thing. My role would then be passed on to someone I loved. Maybe Dakota. Maybe my own child, one day. No. I couldn't do that.

I didn't know why my family had been chosen. I didn't know why this burden had fallen into my lap. I didn't know much of anything right now, except that the universe had a plan for me. And wherever it tried to take me, in this world or the next, in this realm or the next, there was only one thing I could do about it.

Surrender.

ACKNOWLEDGMENTS

A very special thanks to:

For channeling your wise, intuitive, and knowledgeable inner owl.
You don't miss a thing.

CHRISTINA HANLEY AND KATIE WEHMANN: for playing games that inspired me to write this story. Although you were too young to remember, you helped me name the book. You're also cool sisters.

NATALIIA PAVLIUK: for your uncanny talent to effortlessly create art that surpasses all expectations…and for being one of the nicest people on the planet!

RAVVEN: for your stunningly beautiful digital cover art. I could stare at it forever.

MICHELE PAGE: for insisting that I shouldn't have teenagers running around in toxic air unprotected.

CASSANDRA ZAWOJEK: for offering a teenager's opinion of an early draft when you were my student. It's come a long way since Dakota was the lead!

ANGELA POLIDORO: for lending an unattached set of eyes.

MARIA DICOSTANZO: For being the "Lades of all Lades." Or should I call you Sarah?

STEVEN AND LUNA MESSINA: for making every moment of every day magical.

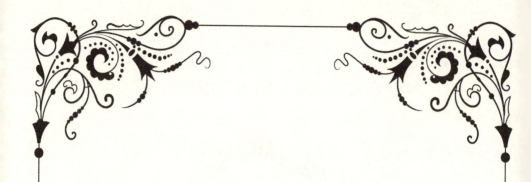

A creative spirit needs only ink
and canvas to work her magic.

NATALIIA PAVLIUK
ABOUT THE ILLUSTRATOR

Nataliia is the founder and creative force behind **ArtPavo,** a design agency that specializes in handcrafted watercolor and digital arts. A lifelong artist and illustrator from Ukraine, Nataliia has turned her passion into a thriving career, creating countless pieces of art for clients worldwide.

You can learn more about her endeavors by visiting:

www.behance.net/artpavo
www.instagram.com/inspiring_artlife

Perseverance and belief
make all things possible.

K.M. MESSINA
ABOUT THE AUTHOR

Kim is an earth and space science teacher, a dog mom, and a lover of all things mystical. Her black German shepherd Luna inspired her adorable picture book, *IF YOU COULD ASK YOUR DOG ONE QUESTION*, which won the Best Independent Book Award (BIBA) and the Moonbeam Children's Book Award for best picture book for all ages. She lives on the rocky coast of Long Island, New York, where she enjoys bird watching, moon gazing, and adding to her ever-growing collection of stones and crystals.

You can learn more about her endeavors by visiting:

www.kmessina.com
www.instagram.com/k.m.messina
www.myhumannme.com
www.happylovesprinkles.com

Made in the USA
Las Vegas, NV
21 February 2024